'Each to his own,' said Tiny pompously. 'We're here to kill, so I do it the way I like best. Everyone's got their favourite way of doing it.' It was true, I suppose. We each had our own preferred methods. The Legionnaire was a devotee of the knife, while Porta was a crack shot with a rifle. Heide liked playing about with flame throwers, while for myself I was accounted pretty hot stuff with a hand grenade. Tiny just happened to enjoy strangling people . . .

Also by Sven Hassel

WHEELS OF TERROR
THE LEGION OF THE DAMNED
COMRADES OF WAR
MONTE CASSINO
MARCH BATTALION
LIQUIDATE PARIS
SS GENERAL
REIGN OF HELL
BLITZFREEZE
BLOODY ROAD TO DEATH
COURT MARTIAL

and published by Corgi Books

Sven Hassel

Assignment Gestapo

Translated by Jean Ure

CORGI BOOKS

A DIVISION OF TRANSWORLD PUBLISHERS LTD

ASSIGNMENT GESTAPO
A CORGI BOOK 0 552 08779 3

First publication in Great Britain

PRINTING HISTORY
Corgi edition published 1971
Corgi edition reprinted 1971
Corgi edition reprinted 1972 (twice)
Corgi edition reprinted 1973
Corgi edition reprinted 1974 (twice)
Corgi edition reprinted 1975
Corgi edition reprinted 1976
Corgi edition reprinted 1978
Corgi edition reprinted 1980 (twice)
Corgi edition reprinted 1981

This book is set in 10/11pt Intertype Plantin

Corgi Books are published by Transworld Publishers Ltd,
Century House, 61-63 Uxbridge Road,
Ealing, London W5 5SA

Printed and bound in Great Britain by
Collins, Glasgow

Assignment Gestapo

From somewhere behind us came the sounds of men shouting and of a general uproar. Tiny and the Legionnaire had stayed to guard the rear, while the rest of us pressed on. They were lying in wait amongst the thick undergrowth of the copse.

Four Russian soldiers appeared, hurrying through the trees. They wore the green insignia of the NKVD. They were still very young, very keen; still eager to chase and to kill.

They came charging round the bend in the path. The Legionnaire silently turned down a thumb, and Tiny grinned in anticipation. Their sub-machine guns cracked into the silence almost simultaneously.

Tiny had jumped to his feet and was firing from a standing position, the gun jammed hard against his hip. The whole of his massive frame shook under the recoil.

The Legionnaire, calm and collected as always in moments of action, was gently singing one of his interminable songs of death.

The Russians plunged forward, head first, on the damp earth. Only two of them still showed signs of life by the time the bombardment had ceased, and Tiny stepped forward to put the finishing touches to their handiwork. It was a necessary precaution, in these days of war: never mind about not hitting a man when he was down, even the mortally wounded are capable of picking up a gun and firing it.

'Sorry, chum!' Tiny looked down dispassionately at the dead soldiers. 'We just can't take any chances, however much we love you!'

'Too bloody right,' muttered the Legionnaire. 'They'd put a bullet through our backsides as soon as look at us.'

The platoon had been taken by surprise when in the midst of a drunken debauch – celebrating Porta's birthday in the only way we knew how. We had been in no fit state to welcome the Russian patrol which had burst so unexpectedly upon us. The first we knew about them was when the windows blew in upon our faces and we found ourselves staring into the gaping black mouths of four powerful PMs. Our instinctive reaction was to hurl ourselves to the floor and cover our heads. The Legionnaire and Porta had retained sufficient presence of mind to lob a series of hand grenades through the shattered windows, but how we escaped with our lives was nobody's business. We were still reeling and weak-kneed from the shock.

We met up again at the far end of the wood. Eight men were missing.

'I saw two of 'em go down,' volunteered Porta.

We wondered, briefly, what had happened to the others.

When Tiny reappeared, he was dragging with him an unwilling Russian lieutenant. The Old Man said firmly that we should have to take him along as a prisoner.

Shortly before we reached the mine field, we heard the lieutenant give a cry. We heard Tiny laugh, and the Old Man swore violently. Seconds later, Tiny emerged from the bushes . . . alone.

'Shit tried to get away from me,' he explained, cheerfully. 'He asked for it, didn't he?'

We remained silent. We could see, hanging from Tiny's pocket, the length of steel wire that had come in so useful on so many occasions; whenever a quick, silent death was required . . .

'Did you strangle the poor bastard?' asked the Old Man, disbelievingly.

Tiny shrugged.

'I told you,' he muttered, 'he tried to get away . . .'

'In other words, you murdered him,' said Stege.

CHAPTER ONE

The Informer

ALL of us that remained of the Fifth Company were stretched out on our bellies beneath the apple trees, watching dispassionately as the reserve troops came up. We had been waiting for those troops for the last four days, and by now we were past caring whether they sent them or not. They arrived in trucks, moving slowly up the road in a double column. Their uniforms and their arms were still brand new, smart and shining and almost unbelievably virginal.

We watched them come with jaded eyes. No comments had been passed, and none was necessary: the approaching troops spoke for themselves. It was obvious to us that we could have nothing in common. We were soldiers, while they were only dilettantes. It showed in the careful way they carried their equipment; it showed in their stiff and shining boots. So beautifully polished and so utterly useless! No one could march very far in boots of such uncompromising newness. They had yet to be rubbed with their baptismal urine, which was the best treatment we knew for softening up and at the same time preserving the leather. Take Porta's boots, for an ideal example of a soldier's footwear: so supple that you could see every movement of his toes inside them. And if they gave off an almost overpowering stench of urine, that seemed a small price to pay for comfort.

'You stink like a thousand pisshouses!' Porta was once told, rather sharply, during the course of a parade.

That was our Colonel, sometimes irreverently known as Wall Eye, on account of the black patch he wore over one empty socket. It seemed to me significant that in spite of his testy observation on the subject of urine, he never put a stop to our habit of pissing on our boots. He'd been in the Army long enough to know that it's the feet that make the soldier. You got bad feet and you're worse than useless.

Tiny, still watching the arrival of the reserve force, suddenly nudged the Légionnaire in the ribs.

'Where d'you reckon they dug that lot up from? Jesus Christ, it's enough to make a cat laugh! The Ruskies'll mop them up before they've even found out what they're supposed to be doing here . . .' He nodded importantly at the Legionnaire. 'If it weren't for people like you and me, mate, we'd have lost this perishing war years ago.'

The Old Man laughed. He was trying to shelter from the pouring rain beneath a rather pathetic bush.

'High time they gave you the Knight's Cross . . . a hero like you!'

Tiny turned and spat.

'Knight's Cross! You know where they can stick that, don't you? Right up their bleeding arses . . . I wouldn't give you tuppence for it!'

There were sounds of cries and curses from the officers at the front of the approaching column. One of the privates, a little frail creature who looked older than God, had lost his tin helmet. It had rolled to the side of the road with a noise like a hundred tin cans collapsing, and the old chap had instinctively scrambled off the truck and gone toddling after it.

'Get back into line!' roared an Oberfeldwebel, outraged. 'What the bleeding hell do you think you're bleeding playing at?'

The old boy hesitated, looking from his precious helmet to the apoplectic Oberfeldwebel. He scuttled back into the ranks and marched on, and the Oberfeldwebel nodded grimly and remained where he was, blowing his whistle and every so often shouting his lungs out, intent on hustling these raw amateurs on their way to certain death.

As I watched the column advancing, I could see that the little old man was already near to breaking point; both physically and mentally, I guessed. The loss of his tin helmet had probably been the final straw.

Lt. Ohlsen, our Company Commander, was standing to one side chatting to his counterpart, the lieutenant who had led the reserve troops up here. Neither of them had noticed the incident, neither of them had noticed that one of their men was on the point of cracking. And even if they did, what could they do about it? At this stage of the war, it was a commonplace occurrence.

The old chap suddenly fell to his knees, began crawling down the hill on all fours. His fellow soldiers looked at him nervously. The Oberfeldwebel came running up, bellowing.

'Stand up, that man there! What do you think this is, a bleeding tea party?'

But the old man never moved. Just lay on the ground, sobbing fit to break your heart. He wouldn't have moved if he'd been threatened with a court martial; he couldn't have. He didn't have the strength left, and he didn't have the will any more, either. The Oberfeldwebel walked up to him, stood over him chewing at his lower lip.

'All right ... all right, if that's the way you want to play it, I'll go along with you ... You've got to learn a thing or two, I can see that ... You think you're exhausted, eh? Well, just you wait till you've got a load of screaming Ruskies coming at you, you'll move fast enough!' He suddenly stepped back and rapped out an order. 'Pick up that spade and get digging! At the double, if you don't want to get mown down!'

Obediently, the little old chap groped for his spade, which had fallen from his pack. He began trying to dig. It was comical and pathetic. The rate he was going, it would take him the next thousand years to dig a hole for himself. According to regulations, it should take a man no more than 11½ minutes from the time he got the spade in his hand. And God help anyone who took a second longer! Of course, when you'd been in the front line as long as we had you learnt to do it in even less time – you had to, if you wanted to survive. And we'd had enough practice to put us in the champions' class. The holes we'd dug stretched in a practically unbroken line from the Spanish frontier to the summit of Elbroux in the Caucasus. And we'd dug them in every conceivable sort of terrain. Sand, snow, clay, mud, ice – you name it, we'd dug holes in it. Tiny was particularly gifted in that direction. He could provide himself with a dug-out in 6 minutes 15 seconds flat, and he boasted that he could do it even quicker if he really put himself out. He probably could have, only he was never put to the test because no one ever set up a new record for him to aim at.

The Oberfeldwebel stretched out a foot and pushed at his victim.

'Come on, grandfather, you're not building sandcastles! At this rate we'll all be dead and buried before you've even scraped away the first layer!'

Grandfather suddenly expired. Just lay down and died, just like that, without even asking permission. The Oberfeldwebel seemed genuinely astonished. It was a good few seconds before he turned round and bellowed to the two nearest men to come and pick up the body.

'Call themselves bloody soldiers,' he muttered. 'God help Germany if this is what's being used to protect her . . . but just you wait, you innocent load of bastards! I'll get you licked into shape before you're very much older!'

Oberfeldwebel Huhn, the terror of Bielefeldt, rubbed his hands together in anticipation. There weren't many men he couldn't lick into shape, once he'd set his mind to it.

And perhaps, after all, his treatment of the old man had had its effect: certainly none of the others dared to collapse.

'What a callous bastard,' said Porta, carelessly; and he stuffed his mouth with a mutton sausage rifled from a dead Russian artilleryman.

We were all eating mutton sausages. They were stale and salty and hard as stone, yet they tasted pretty good for all that. I looked at my half-eaten sausage, and I remembered the occasion when we had acquired them: only five days ago, and it seemed five months.

It was on our way back through a vast tract of thickly wooded land that we had stumbled upon the Russian field battery. As usual, it was the Legionnaire who had first spotted them. We attacked with more speed and stealth than even Fenimore Cooper's Indian braves, cutting them down silently with our kandras.* By the time we'd finished it looked as if a

* Siberian knives with a double-edged blade

heavy shell had exploded in their midst. We had come upon them quite out of the blue. They had been lying in a clearing, sleeping, sunbathing, relaxing, totally unprepared for any sort of attack. Their chief had been drawn out of his hut by the sounds of the struggle. We heard him calling out to a lieutenant, his second-in-command, just before he appeared.

'Drunken bloody swine! They've been at the vodka again!'

Those were his last words. As he appeared at the entrance of the hut, his head was severed from his shoulders by one well-aimed blow, and two spouts of hot blood burst from his body like geysers. The lieutenant, who was behind him, didn't stop to inquire what was going on. He turned and plunged into the undergrowth, but Heide was on him almost immediately with his kandra. The lieutenant fell like a stone.

We were horrible to look upon by the time the massacre was over. And the scene of the carnage was like some nightmare from a butcher's shop. Several of us vomited as we surveyed it. The spilt blood and the trailing intestines smelt disgusting, and there were thick black knots of flies already settled on every juicy morsel. I don't think any of us really liked the kandra, it was too primitive, too messy – but, on the other hand, it was an excellent weapon in certain circumstances. The Legionnaire and Barcelona had taught us how to use it.

We sat down on the ammunition boxes and the shells, with our backs to the corpses. We were not so squeamish that we denied ourselves the pleasure of eating Russian sausages and drinking Russian vodka. Only Hugo Stege seemed to have no appetite. We all used to make fun of Stege on account of he'd had a good education and was reputed to be brainy. Something of an intellectual. And also because no one had ever heard him swear. That in itself seemed to us totally abnormal, but even more incredible behaviour came to light when Tiny discovered that Stege always, and assiduously, washed his hands before eating!

The Old Man regarded the store of sausages and the crate of vodka.

'Might as well take them with us,' he decided. 'Those poor devils won't be needing them any more.'

'They had an easier death than many,' remarked the Legionnaire. 'They never really knew a thing about it.' He ran a finger down the razor-sharp edges of his kandra. 'Nothing brings death as quickly as one of these.'

'I find them disgusting,' said Stege, and vomited for about the third time.

'Look, they asked for it,' argued Porta, fiercely. 'Lazing about with their thumbs up their bums and their brains in neutral . . . there is a war on, you know! It could just as easy be us lying down there with our heads hacked off.'

'That doesn't make it any better,' muttered Stege.

'So what are we supposed to do about it?' Porta turned on him, furious. 'You think I enjoy ripping people's guts out? You think I *like* this sort of life? Did anyone ever bother to ask you, when they dragged you into the flaming Army – they ever bother to ask you if you *wanted* to go round killing people?'

Stege shook his head, wearily.

'Spare us your home spun philosophies,' he begged.

'Why?' said the Legionnaire, rolling his cigarette from one side of his mouth to the other. 'It may be simple, but it's none the less true . . . we're here to kill, whether we like it or not. It's the job we've been given and it's the job we're expected to do.'

'Besides,' added Porta, beating wildly at a cloud of flies that was trying to get up his nose, 'I don't remember you being particularly backward when it came to clobbering people . . . and what about when you took the thing in the first place?' He jerked a thumb at Stege's kandra. 'What about when you nicked it off that dead Rusky? What was the point of taking it if you didn't intend to use it? You didn't want it for cleaning your nails, did you? You took it in case you needed it to stick in somebody, just like the rest of us.'

At this point, the Old Man dragged himself to his feet and jerked his head impatiently.

'Come on. Time we were moving.'

Unwilling and protesting, we nevertheless picked ourselves up and formed a column, single file, behind the Old Man. We moved off through the trees, to be joined shortly afterwards by Tiny and Porta, who, following their usual practice, had stayed behind to do a bit of looting. From the state of their faces, there seemed to have been some disagreement between them, and it looked as if Porta had been the victor: he was proudly displaying two gold teeth, while Tiny had only one.

As always, the Old Man raved at them without it having the least effect.

'One of these days I'm going to shoot the pair of you. It makes me sick! Yanking the teeth out of the mouths of dead men!'

'Don't see why, if they're already dead,' retorted Porta, in cocky tones. 'You wouldn't leave a gold ring to rot, would you? Or set fire to a bank note? So what's the difference between them and teeth?'

The Old Man continued silently to simmer. He knew, as well as the rest of us, that in every company you always had your actual 'dentists', who went round the corpses with a pair of pincers. There was little, if anything, that could be done about it.

And now, five days later, we were sitting beneath the fruit trees, watching the reserves come up and stuffing ourselves with mutton sausages. The rain was slashing down, and we pulled our waterproofs higher over our shoulders. These waterproofs served a variety of purposes, being used, according as circumstances demanded, as capes, tents, camouflage, bedding, hammocks, shrouds, or simple sacks for carrying equipment. A waterproof was the first item to be handed to us when we went to collect our kit, and it was the one we valued above all others.

Porta screwed his head round and squinted up into the wet sky.

'Bloody awful rain,' he muttered. 'Sodding awful mountains ... worst bleeding sort of country you can get ...' He screwed his head back again and glanced at his neighbour. 'Remember France?' he said, longingly. 'Jesus, that was something! Just sitting on your arse in the sun, drinking wine till the cows came home ... that was something, eh? That was quite something!'

Heide was still staring moodily down at the approaching column of men. He pointed with his mutton sausage towards

Huhn, who had tortured the little old fellow with the tin helmet.

'Going to have trouble with that one,' he said, sagely. 'Feel it in my bones.'

'No bastard gives us any trouble and gets away with it!' declared Tiny. He glared in the direction of Heide's pointing finger. 'Let him just try and he'll get what's coming to him ... One thing I am good at, that's exterminating rats like him.'

'That's all any of us are likely to be good at, by the time the war comes to an end,' said Stege, bitterly. 'Killing people ... that's all it's taught us.'

'At least it's something useful,' jeered Tiny. 'Even in peace-time, I reckon, there's always a need for professional killers ... ain't that so?'

He jabbed at the Legionnaire for confirmation. The Legion-naire solemnly nodded. Stege merely turned away in disgust.

The lieutenant who had brought up the reserve troops now began to assemble them in ranks preparatory to his own de-parture. He had delivered them as ordered and was now sud-denly anxious to be gone, prompted perhaps by some instinct warning him that it would not be wise to hang about too long. The area was not a healthy one.

With the men ranged before him, he delivered his parting speech. They heard him out with an air of total indifference.

'Well, men, you're at the Front now, and pretty soon you'll be called upon to fight against the enemies of the Reich. Re-member that this is your chance to win back your good names, to become honourable citizens of the Fatherland and earn the right to live amongst us once again as free men. If you acquit yourselves well, all marks against you will be expunged from the records. It's entirely up to you.' He scraped his throat self-consciously and fixed a stern eye upon them. 'Comrades, the Führer is a great man!'

There was total and uncompromising silence following this observation. And then Porta's evil laugh rang out, and I'm pretty sure I caught the muttered comment, 'Balls!' In all the circumstances, it seemed a likely enough sort of comment. The lieutenant swung round and let his glance range over us. The blood poured up his neck and into his cheeks. He stiffened, and his hand went automatically to his holster. He turned back to his own band of villains.

'Let there be no doubt in your minds! All your actions will be noted and recorded!' He paused, significantly, to let this sink in. 'Do not disappoint the Führer! It is up to you to take this opportunity of making amends for the crimes you have committed against Adolf Hitler and against the Reich.' He breathed deeply and glanced once more towards the twelve of us, sheltering beneath the apple trees. He met the defiant stares of Tiny and Porta, the one looking a complete half wit, the other with a face as low and cunning as that of a fox. He blenched slightly, but nevertheless pressed on. 'You will find yourselves fighting side by side with some of the bravest and best of Germany's sons . . . and woe betide any one of you who shows himself a coward!'

His voice went droning on. The Old Man nodded, appreciatively.

'I like that,' he said. 'The bravest and best of Germany's sons . . . Tiny and Porta! That's a laugh!'

Tiny sat up indignantly.

'What's so funny about it? I'm certainly the bravest and best of *my* mother's sons—'

'God help us!' said Heide, shuddering. 'I presume she hasn't got any others?'

'She did have,' said Tiny.

'What's happened to 'em then?' Porta looked at him challengingly. 'They get killed or something?'

'I'll tell you. The first one, bleeding idiot that he was, went off voluntarily to the Gestapo – *voluntarily*, I ask you! Bloody fool . . . Stadthausbrücke, number eight,' recited Tiny, as if it were engraved for ever on his memory. 'They wanted him for questioning about something or other – I forget what exactly. Something to do with painting slogans on a wall. He was a great lad for painting slogans on walls . . . Anyway, he went off one fine day and wasn't never seen again . . . And as for the next one – as for Gert—' He shook his head, contemptuously. 'You know what he went and done?'

We all wonderingly assured him that we didn't. Tiny made a gesture of disgust.

'Only went and volunteered for the bleeding Navy, didn't he? Ended up in a U-boat, didn't he?'

'What happened to him?' I asked.

Tiny spat. Heroes were evidently not in his line.

'Went down with the bleeding boat, beginning of '40 ... We had a post-card from Admiral Doenitz about it. Lovely, it was. It said, Der Führer dankt Ihnen.* And it had a lovely black border and all.' He suddenly gave a short bark of laughter. 'Bet you can't guess how that ended up!'

We could, knowing Tiny, but we didn't want to ruin his story.

'My old lady used it to wipe her arse on ... Went to the shit house one day, discovered she didn't have no bog paper in there, so she calls out to me to bring her some what's nice and soft. Well, I couldn't see no newspaper nor nothing, so I grabbed up the Admiral's post-card and shoved that through the door to her ... She was calling him all the silly buggers under the sun, afterwards. Scraped her bum to pieces, it did. Hard and rough, she said it was. Hard and bleeding rough ...'

We roared our appreciation, and Tiny roared louder than any of us.

'So now you're the only one left?' I said, when the laughter had died down.

'That's it,' agreed Tiny, proudly. 'Eleven down, one to go ... The Gestapo nabbed some of 'em. Three got drowned at sea. The two youngest kids, they was burnt alive in an RAF raid. Their own stupid fault, mind you. Refused to go into the shelter, didn't they? Wanted to stay up top and see the bleeding planes go by ... well, they saw 'em all right!' He nodded, owlishly. 'So anyway, there's only me and the old lady left now. And that's some doing.' He looked round at the rest of us, studying each in turn. 'I bet there ain't many of us have, sacrificed what we have. Eleven at a blow, and all for Adolf ...' He gnawed hungrily at his sausage and took a turn at the vodka bottle. 'Sod the lot of 'em!' he decided, defiantly. 'So long as I get out of it alive, I don't care no more ... and something tells me that I'm still going to be here at the end.'

* The Führer thanks you

18

'That wouldn't surprise me in the least,' murmured the Old Man.

The Legionnaire was crouched over a cooking pot, absorbed in stirring the contents. Porta craned over his shoulder, stuffed one or two fairly dry logs into the fire. The thick, globulous mass in the pot heaved itself up in a series of miniature geysers, which exploded and left craters behind them. It smelt rather strong, but that was hardly surprising: we had carted that mess everywhere with us for days past, each of us transporting a share in his water bottle.

'It has to ferment,' explained Barcelona, when some of us began to show signs of rebelling.

It had now, it appeared, duly fermented and was ready for distilling. The Legionnaire fixed a tight lid over the cooking pot and Porta set up the distilling apparatus. We sat round in a circle, waiting breathlessly for something to happen.

Our meditations were interrupted by some half-hearted cries of 'Sieg heil!' coming from the assembled ranks of the reserve troops.

The visiting lieutenant drove away in an amphibious VW, and Lt. Ohlsen, losing no time, took the newcomers in hand and delivered one of his special pep talks. When at last they were told to fall out they did so almost literally, collapsing to the ground, huddling together beneath the trees in wet, miserable groups. They threw down their equipment and some of them even stretched full length on the soaking grass. I noticed they kept a respectful distance from the rest of us. It was plain that we intimidated them in some way.

Oberfeldwebel Huhn walked across to us and straight through our midst, his step heavy and confident. As he passed by the cooking pot, he caught it with the side of his boot and the whole thing rocked. The Legionnaire managed to set it upright, but not before a few precious drops of liquid had spilled over the side. Huhn glanced down and went on his way without a word of apology. We smelt the newness of his equipment, heard the creaking of his unbroken leather boots as he passed.

The Legionnaire pursed his lips together. He gazed thoughtfully after the retreating Huhn for a few seconds, then turned towards Tiny. Not a word passed between them. But the Legionnaire turned down a thumb, and Tiny nodded.

With his sausage still in his hand, he heaved himself to his feet and marched purposefully after the Oberfeldwebel. His waterproof billowed out behind him, so that he looked rather like a walking barrage balloon.

'Hey, you!' he called. 'You spilt some of our schnaps!'

At the first cry of 'Hey, you!', Huhn had gone on walking – evidently never dreaming that anyone of lower rank could dare to address an Oberfeldwebel as 'Hey you'. But at the mention of the word schnaps he must have realized that it was, indeed, himself that Tiny was accusing. He turned, slowly and incredulously. At the sight of Tiny his jaw sagged and his eyeballs strained at their sockets.

'What's got into you?' he roared. 'Didn't anyone ever teach you the right way to address your superiors?'

'Yes, yes,' said Tiny, impatiently. 'I know all that crap. But that's not what I wanted to talk to you about.'

Huhn's cheeks grew slowly mottled.

'Have you gone stark starving raving bloody mad?' he demanded. 'Do you want me to put you under arrest? Because if not, I advise you to watch your bleeding language! And just try to remember, in future, what it says about it in the HDV.'*

'I know what it says in the HDV,' retorted Tiny, imperturbably. 'I told you once, that's not what I want to talk about. We can discuss it afterwards if it really interests you. But right now I want to talk about our schnaps what you knocked over.'

Huhn breathed deeply and carefully, right down to the bottom of his lungs. And then he breathed out again, with a prolonged whistling sound. Doubtless, in all his seven years of Army service, he had never had a parallel experience. We knew that he had just come from the harsh military camp of Heuberg. Certainly if anyone there had dared to address him as Tiny had just done, he would have shot them out of hand. From the way he kept twitching at his holster, I guessed that he had half a mind to shoot Tiny out of hand. But it was not so easy to

---

* Heeresdienstvorschrift – Army Service Regulations

get away with it, in front of so many witnesses. A silence had come upon us, and we were all leaning forward, craning our necks for a first-hand view of the affair.

Tiny stood his ground, the sausage still absurdly clenched in his huge paw.

'You knocked over our schnaps,' he repeated, obstinately. 'The least you could have done was apologize, I should've thought.'

Huhn opened his mouth. It remained open for several seconds. Then his Adam's apple bobbed up and down a few times and he closed it again without a word. In its way, the whole scene was quite ludicrous. Even if he hauled Tiny before a court martial, they would almost certainly never believe a word of the indictment. Yet something had to be done. An Oberfeldwebel couldn't allow a cretinous great oaf of a Stabs-gefreiter to stand there insulting him and get away with it.

Tiny jabbed his sausage into Huhn's chest.

'Look at it this way,' he suggested. 'We've been carting that stuff around with us for days now. It's been everywhere with us. And not a drop wasted, until you came along with your clumsy bleeding boots and went bashing into it. And not so much as a by your leave or a word of apology!' He shook his head. 'I don't know what *you're* complaining about, I'm sure. Seems to me it's us what ought to be complaining, not you. Here we are, minding our own business, brewing up our schnaps—'

Huhn brushed the sausage to one side and took a step towards Tiny, his hand clutching the butt of his automatic.

'All right, that'll do! That's quite enough of that! I'm a patient man, but I've had as much as I can take . . . What's your name? You've asked for trouble, and believe me I'm going to see that you get it!'

He pulled out a notebook and pencil and waited expectantly. Tiny just raised two fingers in an unmistakable sign.

'Get knotted! Your threats don't mean a damn thing out here. You're at the front now, remember? And we're the boys that have survived . . . And you know why we've survived? Because we know how to look after ourselves, that's why . . . And I'm not at all sure that I can say the same for you. In fact, I got a very funny feeling that you ain't going to see out this particular spell of duty ... You need a very strong head to survive out here, and I just don't think you got it ...'

God knows what would have happened next if Lt. Ohlsen hadn't intervened and spoilt the fun. It was just getting to the really interesting part when he walked up to Tiny and jerked his thumb over his shoulder.

'Get lost, Creutzfeldt. At the double, if you don't want to end up under arrest.'

'Yes, sir!'

Tiny gave a quick salute, smacked his heels sharply together and left the scene of combat. He came slowly back to the rest of us.

'I'm going to get that bastard one of these days!'

'I told you,' said Heide. 'I told you we'd have trouble with him.'

'Don't you worry.' Tiny nodded significantly and closed one eye. 'I got his number. It's only a matter of time—'

'For God's sake!' burst out the Old Man. 'You're going to find yourself in real trouble one of these days if you keep bumping off every NCO you take a dislike to.'

Tiny opened his mouth to reply, but before he could do so there was a wild cry of triumph from the Legionnaire.

'She blows! Quick, give me the connection! Get a bottle!'

We were at once thrown into a hectic activity. I thrust the rubber tube into the Legionnaire's outstretched hand, Porta shoved a bottle next to the cooking pot. The apparatus was connected and we watched breathlessly, like children, for the first miraculous signs of distillation. The vapour was already turning into precious drops of liquid.

'She's coming!' yelled Porta.

The excitement was almost unbearable. I felt the saliva collect in my mouth; I suddenly knew a thirst such as I had never known before. Heide ran his tongue round his lips. Tiny swallowed convulsively. Slowly, the bottle began to fill.

All night long we maintained our watch. Bottle after bottle was taken away full of home-brewed schnaps. We forgot all desire for sleep. Lt. Ohlsen watched us for a bit, his expression decidedly sceptical.

'You must be nuts,' he declared, at last. 'You're surely never going to try drinking the vile looking muck?'

'Why not?' demanded Tiny, belligerently.

The Lieutenant just looked at him and shook his head.

Lt. Spät also took a fatherly interest in our brewing activities.

'Aren't you going to filter it?' he asked, anxiously.

'Not worth the trouble,' said the Legionnaire.

'But my God, you drink it in that state and you'll be bowling about the ground in hoops!'

'So long as it's alcoholic,' said the Legionnaire, calmly. 'That's all that matters.'

Lt. Ohlsen shook his head again and retired with Spät. Clearly they did not give much for our chances.

The following day found us still at peace beneath the apple trees. For the moment, the war seemed to have passed us by. We continued our brewing, only by now we had outworn our first mad rapture and had split ourselves up into groups to spread the work load.

All day long and well into the evening we tended our schnaps. Shortly after midnight we heard the sound of a vehicle screaming down the mountain road towards us. It came to a halt nearby and an NCO jumped out, covered in mud and in a fearful lather.

'Where's your commanding officer?' he shouted.

Lt. Ohlsen was woken up. He took the message and the man went chasing off again at full speed. We watched with foreboding.

'Hell and damnation,' muttered the Legionnaire. 'That's put the cat among the flaming pigeons.'

He went off to see how the brewing operation was progressing.

'Step it up,' he ordered. 'If we're quick about it we'll manage to get another bottle or so before we're moved on.'

'We already got thirty-one,' announced Porta, triumphantly. 'I been counting them!'

Tiny seemed agitated about something.

'What I want to know is, when are we going to get stuck into it?'

'When I say so, and not before.' The Legionnaire glared at him. 'I find anyone dipping his fingers in before I give the O.K. and there's going to be trouble!'

Tiny shrugged a sullen shoulder and walked off, muttering to himself. At that moment, Lt. Ohlsen's whistle blasted shrilly through the darkness. It was a most unwelcome sound.

'Fifth Company, get ready to move! And don't take all night about it!'

Reluctantly, we set about dismantling our still. While we were at work, Oberfeldwebel Huhn came busying up to us, shouting as usual at the top of his voice.

'Come on, you lazy bastards! Get a move on! What's the matter with you? You deaf or something?'

'You'll be deaf in a minute,' muttered the Legionnaire, threateningly.

Huhn swung round on him, but at that point the Old Man rather surprisingly stepped into the fray. He walked up to Huhn, standing so close to him that their steel helmets were almost touching.

'Oberfeldwebel Huhn,' he began, calmly, respectfully, but with menacing overtones, 'there is something I have to say to you. Something I feel you ought to know . . . I am in command of this section, these are my men and it's up to me to see that they carry out orders. I don't quite remember what the procedure is back home in the barracks, but I do know what it is at the front . . . which apparently you have yet to learn. And all I'm saying is, either you keep your nose out of my territory or I shall give my men full permission to go ahead and teach you a thing or two . . . and they could, believe you me!'

Porta gave a loud, annoying bray of laughter.

'Might as well talk to the cows in the field for all the good that'll have done!'

Huhn took a step towards him, then stopped sharp at the look from the Old Man. He contented himself with a tight-throated cry of, 'You needn't think you'll get away with this!' flung over his shoulder as he went running off to complain.

We saw him buttonhole Lt. Spät, who listened with half an ear for the first few minutes and then walked off leaving him in full flood. Lt. Ohlsen called impatiently from the road. Porta and Tiny picked up the heavy cooking pot between them and took their place in the column a short way ahead of the Lieutenant, who pretended not to have seen their extra item of equipment.

The new troops came up at a panic-stricken run, disorganized and uncertain. One of them banged into Porta and sprang back, terrified.

'You do that again and you'll get your teeth rammed right down the back of your flaming throat!'

The man grew pale, but sensibly kept quiet.

'Bleeding amateurs,' growled Tiny.

Lt. Ohlsen shouted a command and we came smartly to attention. Section leaders relayed his orders as we did a half turn to the right.

'Porta, where's your flaming helmet, for God's sake?' The Lieutenant's voice came ringing irritably towards us. 'What the devil is that monstrosity you've got on your head?'

Porta reached up a hand to his old yellow hat.

'I haven't got one to wear, sir. The Ruskies swiped it.'

Lt. Ohlsen exchanged a despairing glance with Lt. Spät. They always gave up when it came to dealing with Porta.

'All right,' said Ohlsen, wearily. 'Put it back on again – whatever it is! You can't march bareheaded.'

'Yes, sir.'

The deplorable yellow hat was once more crammed on to Porta's head. The column moved off in the inevitable rain, which was blowing straight at us and stinging our faces. A moment of excitement was caused by a hare suddenly running across our path, almost upsetting the precious cooking pot as Porta, in his usual eagerness for food, made an involuntarily swipe as the creature shot by.

'What the bloody hell are you doing?' shouted Tiny.

'We could have skinned it and ate it,' said Porta, regretfully. 'We could have put it in the pot along with the booze.'

Tiny looked at him.

'Who'd want to ruin good booze with a lousy hare?'

'They do in high-class restaurants,' said Heide, who always

25

knew everything. 'They're regarded as a great delicacy, hare done in wine . . . jugged, they call it.'

'Sod the hare,' said Tiny, suddenly. 'I'd sooner have a bird . . .'

And with one hand, he demonstrated the kind of bird he meant.

'I've almost forgotten what they look like, to tell you the honest truth . . . remember that Russian what had it away with a goose? Got hard up for a bit of the other, so he had to make do with a goose. Not sure I couldn't do with a goose myself, come to think about it . . .'

'Crap,' said Heide. 'You couldn't do anything if it was handed to you on a plate. Not in this weather, you couldn't.'

'Who are you kidding?' jeered Tiny. 'The way I feel right now, I could do it stark bollock naked at the North Pole . . . what about that time at the Turkish frontier? You forgotten that, have you? Snow was inches deep on the ground—'

'That's different. You could do it in snow, but you certainly couldn't do it stark naked at the North Pole,' objected Steiner, very seriously.

Steiner was a driver, who had been sent to us as a punishment for having sold an army wagon to an Italian in Milan. He tended to have a very literal mind.

'Nobody could do it at that temperature,' he insisted. 'It'd be a physical impossibility.'

'Speak for yourself!' retorted Tiny, very much insulted. 'It's the temperature inside you what counts . . . just depends how much you want it, don't it?'

'That's just not true,' said Steiner, obstinately. 'I mean, for a start, you couldn't even get the thing *in* . . . not in that weather you couldn't.'

'Who says?' Tiny swung round on him so violently that the contents of the cooking pot rose up and slopped over the edge. 'You might not be able to, but I'm bloody sure I could! Why, I can still remember—'

'Keep your voices down!' snapped Lt. Ohlsen, a few paces behind us. 'We're not far from the enemy, we don't want to advertise ourselves.'

We turned off the main road and began toiling up towards

26

the mountains. We were walking on grass, now; thick springy stuff that muffled the sounds of our footsteps. Somewhere nearby, in the shadows, a cow blew contentedly through its nostrils and we smelt the warm milky smell of the beast. All orders were given in a low voice.

'Single file from this point on—'

Oberfeldwebel Huhn lit a cigarette. Lt. Spät caught the flicker of the match and strode up in a fury.

'What the hell do you think you're playing at? You ought to have more sense than that, for Christ's sake! Put the bloody thing out and get down to the rear of the column and stay there!'

Huhn disappeared, his tail between his legs.

Suddenly, through the misty gloom, we were able to make out the shape of a building. It was a farmhouse, with a faint light coming from one of its windows. Lt. Ohlsen held up a warning hand, and we shuffled to a halt. We had had experiences with farmhouses before. They sometimes contained innocent farmers and their families; but on the other hand, they had been known to hide a platoon of enemy troops and a nest of machine guns.

Ohlsen turned and beckoned to us.

'Heide – Sven – Barcelona – Porta . . .' He picked us out one by one and we crept forward. 'Go and get the place cleaned up. And watch your step: if the Ruskies are there they'll have set up a guard for sure . . . don't shoot unless you have to. Use your kandras.'

We pulled them out and slipped silently forward through the shadows. As always on these occasions, my whole body was taut and trembling.

We had covered only a few yards when I became aware that Tiny had joined us. He had a knife clenched between his teeth and his length of steel wire in one hand. He laughed delightedly at our expressions and put his mouth close to Porta's ear.

'Any gold teeth going, I claim half of 'em!'

Porta shook his head and said nothing. He was the first of us to reach the objective. Silent and supple as a cat, he hauled himself up to the window ledge and was inside the farm before the rest of us had even arrived. We followed him in and stood shivering in the dark. Somewhere in the house, a door creaked. Heide jumped several feet in the air and pulled out a hand grenade. Barcelona closed his fingers over his wrist.

'Don't be a bloody fool!'

Tiny, the knife still between his teeth, flexed his length of wire. Porta turned and spat over his left shoulder: he said it brought him luck.

We waited a moment, listening, and then Tiny suddenly plunged off into the blackness. After a bit we heard a faint sound; a faint gurgle, a faint choke. Then silence again.

Tiny returned, with a dead cat in the wire noose.

'Poor pussy!'

He dangled it before Heide's face, and we breathed again.

'It could have been the Reds,' muttered Heide, defensively, but he put the hand grenade away again.

Tiny laughed and tossed the dead cat into a corner.

Having disposed of the enemy, we began to make free with the place, opening all the drawers and cupboards to see what took our fancy. Tiny found a pot of jam. He took it away to a corner, sat down cross-legged on the floor and happily dug into it with his fingers. Porta picked up a bottle, looked at the label in the dim light and came to the conclusion that it was cognac. He took a large swig, then shook his head and held out the bottle to Heide.

'Funny sort of cognac,' he remarked, plainly very puzzled.

Heide sniffed at it, cautiously took a mouthful, swilled it round a bit, then spat it out in disgust. He kicked the bottle angrily across the room.

'Some bleeding cognac! That was more like tetrachloride, you stupid sod!'

Tiny cackled contentedly.

'Ought to stick to jam . . . know where you are with jam!'

'Piss off!' said Porta, furiously.

And now, again, we heard a door creak. Instantly we froze to the spot. A moment's silence, then Tiny and Barcelona dived behind a cupboard. The pot of jam rolled across the room and the contents spilt out over the carpet. Porta charged across to the door and kicked it open.

'Whoever you are, we've got you covered!'

Silence.

I stood nervously fingering the hand grenade that I had pulled out. There certainly had been someone there. We could all feel it, and we crouched like wild beasts waiting to spring. We were in the mood where killing would be partly a necessity, as an act of self-preservation, and partly a positive animalistic pleasure, a release of tension and a source of deep satisfaction.

We listened.

'We ought to call up the Company,' muttered Barcelona.

'Sooner set fire to the place,' suggested Tiny. 'Then we could pick 'em off like flies as they come out . . . Nothing like a nice bit of fire for flushing a place out.'

'Oh, give your flaming arse a chance!' snapped Porta. 'They'd only see the perishing flames for miles around, wouldn't they?'

Again there came that creaking, as of a door or floorboards. Unable to bear the tension any longer, Porta switched on his torch and went charging out through the door at the far end of the room. We saw him, with scant regard for the possible consequences, flashing the beam into the shadows. He struck lucky. Pressed against a wall, seemingly trying to merge into the darkness, was a young girl. She had a large club gripped in one hand, and she was plainly terrified.

We stared at her, disbelievingly. Heide was the first to recover. He turned to Tiny with a suggestive smile.

'There's your bird,' he said, simply.

Tiny walked across to her, chucked her somewhat brutally under the chin and tickled her behind the ear with the tip of his lethal steel wire.

'You speak German, do you?'

She stared up at him out of wide open eyes.

'I'm afraid I had to strangle your cat,' said Tiny, gracelessly. 'But I can always get you another, if you're nice to me . . .'

The girl licked her lips with the tip of her tongue.

'I – I not partisan,' she stammered. 'Nix, nix! I not Communist bastard – I like very much soldiers germanski . . . panjemajo*?'

* Understand

29

'Sure we understand,' said Porta, with a leering laugh. 'You not partisan, you not Commie bastard, you love German soldier . . . so what's the idea of putting tetrableedingchloride in a cognac bottle, eh?'

She shook her head.

'Njet understand, Pan* soldier.'

'No one ever does understand when they're being accused of something nasty,' sneered Heide.

Tiny waved a hand towards the girl's club.

'What's that great lump of wood for? Bit heavy for you to lug about, ain't it? Here, give it me. I'll look after it for you.'

He snatched the club away from the terrified girl, who shrank further back into the angle of the wall.

'I not beat soldier germanski,' she said, imploringly. 'I beat only Russki . . . Russki wicked men. Germanski good, good men!'

'More than that, darling, we're bleeding angels!'

Heide laughed, sarcastically Barcelona moved closer to the door.

'Are you alone?' he asked, in Russian.

The girl looked up at him, wonderingly.

'Are you an officer?'

'Of course,' lied Barcelona, with his usual aplomb. 'I'm a general.'

'Well . . .' She hesitated a moment, then seemed abruptly to make up her mind. 'The others are down in the cellar. There's a trap door beneath the carpet.'

She waved a hand towards a corner of the room, and on closer inspection, and rolling back the rug, we discovered that there was indeed a trap door sunk into the floor. It was well camouflaged and I doubt if we should ever have noticed it by ourselves.

'Russian soldiers?' asked Barcelona.

'Njet, njet!' The girl shook her head, vehemently. 'Only family and friends. Not Communists. All Fascists. Good Fascists.'

Heide laughed and rubbed his hands together.

'That'll be the day!'

* Mr.

30

There were sudden movements in the room next door. We sprang round, gripping our kandras. The girl whimpered and made a sudden dash for the door, but Barcelona grabbed her by the arm and dragged her back.

'You stay where you are. We like you here with us.'

A pause, and then Lt. Ohlsen appeared, followed by the rest of the section.

'What's going on?' he demanded. His gaze swept round the room, taking in the empty jampot, the bottle of apparent cognac, and the girl. He glared at us. 'Have you taken leave of your senses? There's a whole Company waiting out there, while you sit on your arses and stuff yourselves with jam and cognac!'

Porta put a finger to his lips.

'Not so loud, sir.' He nodded towards the trap door. 'There's a whole battalion of Russian Fascists stashed away down there ... And as for the cognac—' He kicked disdainfully at the bottle – 'that was a filthy trick, if you like. It's full of tetrachloride. Could have poisoned ourselves.'

Lt. Ohlsen frowned, walked across to the trap door and squatted down to examine it. The Legionnaire and the Old Man came into the room after him, both of them preparing Molotov cocktails.

'They're down there?' said Ohlsen. 'In the cellars?' He turned to Tiny. 'All right, get it opened up.'

'What, me?' Tiny gasped, indignantly, and took a step backwards. 'No, thank you very much! I may look simple, but I'm not such a fool as all that! Anyone opens that lid gets a bundle of fireworks in his face, seems to me.'

'Oh, for Christ's sake!' snapped the Legionnaire. He joined Ohlsen, bent down and seized the ring that opened the trap door. 'O.K., here goes! Watch out for squalls!'

Before he had a chance to do anything, the girl had hurled herself towards him, screaming and knocking him off balance.

'Nix, nix! Small child in there!'

The Legionnaire threw her impatiently away from him. Porta picked her up and pushed her to the far side of the room.

31

'Come off it,' he said to the Legionnaire. 'You ain't going to kill a kid, are you? I thought the bleeding Froggies was meant to be gentlemen, not child murderers?'

'Have you finished?' asked the Legionnaire, coldly.

'No, I haven't,' said Porta. 'Not by a long chalk, I haven't. I—'

Lt. Ohlsen, got to his feet, white with anger.

'Look, we haven't got all day to wait while you sit down and argue about the ethics of the thing! It's either them or us, and it's my job to make damned sure that it's not us!'

Tiny, seating himself on the edge of the table and swinging his legs to and fro, began thoughtfully to rub his length of steel wire up and down his leg.

'Sir,' he said, hopefully, 'I ought to report that I strangled a Russian cat just before you came . . . I could strangle the rest of 'em easy as pie if they'd only come up here and let me—'

'I'm not interested in cats, Russian or otherwise!' Ohlsen turned and jerked his head at the rest of the section. 'Get the trap covered with light machine guns and PMs. The first man to come out with any sort of firearm and he gets what's coming to him. And any funny business from any of 'em and they'll find themselves blown out of existence.'

With a quick, determined gesture he whipped open the trap and called down into the cellars.

'All right, you can come out of there. One at a time with your hands above your heads . . . I'll give you five minutes, and then you can expect trouble . . .'

We stood round, waiting. The first to emerge was a little old hag, her sticklike arms held trembling above her skull-like head. After her came five other women. One was carrying a small baby in her arms. A pause, and then the men arrived. There were several of them, most of them young. Heide and Barcelona searched each and every one of them, and Tiny demanded plaintively that he be allowed to search the women, which only provoked a fresh outburst of rage from Lt. Ohlsen, whose temper was never at its sweetest when Tiny was around.

'You lay so much as a finger on any one of them and I'll

32

shoot you, you great oaf, so help me God I will . . . Are there any more of 'em down there?'

The Russians all solemnly shook their heads. We gazed at them, not sure whether to believe them. Porta jabbed Tiny in the ribs.

'Why don't you try your strangling trick on one of 'em? We can at least be sure of getting at the truth that way.'

Tiny, of course, was only too happy to oblige. He stepped up to the nearest Russian and adroitly twisted the wire round his neck. He tightened his grip a moment, then relaxed it. Porta smiled.

'All right, tovaritch*' Now you know what's coming to you if you're telling whoppers, don't you? . . . Have you left anyone else down there or haven't you?'

The man shook his head, eyes bulging and Adam's apple working frenziedly.

'Let him go!' snapped Lt. Ohlsen. 'How many more times do I have to tell you two that I will not stand for this sort of thing? We're supposed to be soldiers, for God's sake, not Gestapo gangsters! He turned back to the prisoners. 'All right, now let's have the truth out of you. Is there, or is there not, anyone else left in the cellars?'

A row of heads silently replied in the negative.

'O.K. . . . Kalb, toss a couple of Molotovs down there!'

The Legionnaire shrugged a shoulder and prepared to do so. Immediately, one of the women gave a harsh cry.

'Njet, njet!'

The Legionnaire cocked an eyebrow at her.

'What's up with you, old woman? Any objections to our blowing up an empty cellar?'

Lt. Ohlsen walked forward to the trap.

'All right, we know you're down there . . . you might just as well come up in one piece as be blown to smithereens.'

Two young men came slowly up the steps. The Legionnaire looked at them and nodded.

'Another three seconds,' he said, grimly. 'That's all it needed.'

Heide and Barcelona ran their hands over the two men,

* Comrade

33

searching for weapons, and Lt. Ohlsen looked sternly at the Russians.

'I hope that really is the lot, this time?'

It was the Legionnaire and I who went down into the cellar. We crouched for a moment behind some barrels, and hearing no sound we crept forward. We explored the cellar thoroughly. It was a vast place, running the whole width of the house, and there were many places where a man could hide, but we found no one. As we were about to turn back, a sudden noise made us spin round, our fingers twitching neurotically on the trigger.

It was Tiny, beaming all over his large moronic face.

'Come to see if there was any more birds down here,' he explained, when the Legionnaire and I had run out of abuse. 'Thought I'd help you look for 'em.'

'Well, we don't need your flaming help,' hissed the Legionnaire. 'And in any case, you've missed your chance, the place is empty.'

Pushing Tiny before us up the steps, we rejoined the others. Porta had uncovered a fresh cache of bottles, and he was cautiously tasting the contents of each one in turn.

'Vodka?' he asked the Russians. 'Nix Vodka?'

They stared at him, silent and unsmiling.

'You search the whole place?' asked the Lieutenant. 'O.K., let's get going.'

He went outside with the rest of the section, leaving us behind with the Russians. I noticed that Heide was staring at the two young men, the last to emerge from the cellar, with narrowed eyes. Barcelona and Porta, too, seemed to be fascinated by them.

'What's up?' I said.

'That couple there ...' Barcelona looked at them and nodded. 'They're not babes in arms. They're professionals, or I'll eat my hat.'

I looked at them in my turn.

'Deserters?' I queried.

'Deserters, my arse!' Barcelona spat contemptuously. 'I know their type. I've seen too many of 'em before ... Only two places you find rats like that: the NKVD or the SS. And people don't desert from either of them.'

'So what would they be doing here?'

'That, of course, is the question . . .'

Tiny bustled up with his steel wire.

'Shall I finish 'em off?' he asked, with all his usual eagerness.

Lt. Ohlsen came back at this point. He eyed Tiny sourly.

'What's going on here?'

Barcelona turned to Porta.

'Try them in Russian,' he suggested. 'You speak the lingo better than I do.'

'Feldwebel Blom!' The Lieutenant strode over to us. 'Who is in command here? You or I? If there's any interrogating to be done, *I* shall give the orders for it. Until that time, perhaps you'll be good enough to leave these men alone.'

'Yes, sir,' said Barcelona, between his teeth.

Porta shrugged his shoulders in disgust, picked up his tommy gun and followed us from the room. At the door he turned to look threateningly at the two boys.

'You've got away with it this time, mate, but don't try chancing your arm again . . . at any rate, not when I'm around, see?' They stared at him, unblinking. Porta suddenly laughed. 'I'll tell you what,' he said. 'You can thank your lucky stars we'd got an officer with us. I don't reckon he understands too well what this here war's all about . . . but we understand, you and me . . . Panjemajo, tovaritch?'

Outside, we fell into line, single file, behind Lt. Ohlsen.

'Where the devil's Tiny got to?' demanded the Old Man, as we moved off. 'And the Legionnaire? Where the hell are they?'

No one knew. The last time we had seen them, they had still been in the farmhouse. With foreboding, the Old Man made his report to Ohlsen, who swore long and loud in language totally unbecoming to an officer.

'For Christ's sake! Don't you have any control at all over your section, Beier? Take some men and go back and find them. And don't take all day about it, we've wasted quite enough time as it is. I don't intend to wait for you, so you'll just have to try and catch us up.'

The Old Man led us back to the farmhouse.

'They'll be down in the cellar, pissed to the eyeballs,' said Heide, bitterly.

'If they've discovered a secret horde of schnaps and haven't told me about it, they'll get the rough edge of my tongue!' declared Porta.

Just before we reached the farmhouse, we were brought to a halt by a low, warning whistle. The Legionnaire rose out of the shadows before us.

'Where the blazes have you been?' snapped the Old Man. 'Where's the other stupid sod got to?'

'Out hunting,' said the Legionnaire, with a grin. 'Our two comrades back there thought they'd play a few tricks on us. Only we had other ideas, and we've been keeping an eye on them.'

'Out hunting?' repeated the Old Man, testily. 'Hunting what? And by God,' he added, 'if he lays a hand on any of those women he'll be in hot water!'

He pushed past the Legionnaire towards the farmhouse, but the Legionnaire hauled him back.

'I shouldn't, if I were you. It's liable to get pretty hot round here in a minute.'

The words were scarcely out of his mouth before an object came flying through the air towards us. Barcelona acted promptly, caught it as it fell and hurled it back whence it had come.

There was the sound of an explosion, then a flash of light.

'Amateurs,' said Barcelona, coolly. 'Can't even throw a hand grenade properly.'

The unmistakable, trumpeting voice of Tiny came to our ears. From somewhere nearby, in the darkness of the under-growth, there were the sounds of a violent struggle. Loud oaths in German and Russian. The noise of snapping twigs, and of steel clashing against steel. Someone choked and gurgled. Then silence. We stood waiting, wondering what the outcome had been.

'That's the first one dealt with,' said Tiny, making a brief appearance before joyously plunging off again.

There came the sound of running footsteps, and then a shot.

'What's going on round here?' demanded Heide, furiously.

'Better go and take a look ... spread out and watch your step,' commanded the Old Man.

In the bushes, we tripped over a corpse. Porta knelt down to inspect it.

'Strangled,' he said, briefly.

It was one of the two young Russians. By his side we found a pouch of grenades. Enough to wipe out an entire company.

'Meant for us, presumably ... just as well you did stay behind,' conceded the Old Man. 'Though, mind you,' he added, 'that still doesn't in any way excuse your behaviour. The Lieutenant's hopping mad, and I don't blame him.'

The Legionnaire gave a superior smile.

'Lieutenants don't know everything. If I'd relied on lieutenants all my life, I doubt if I should still be here to tell the tale.'

'Anyway,' I said to Barcelona, 'it looks as if you were right about those kids being NKVD.'

'Course I was right,' he rejoined, scornfully. 'I've been around a bit. I know a thing or two.'

'And like he said,' added Porta, jerking a thumb at the Legionnaire, 'lieutenants don't know everything. Not by a long bleeding chalk they don't.'

We stood in silence a while, straining our ears in the darkness but hearing no further sound from the direction in which Tiny had disappeared, and then the Old Man turned to the Legionnaire with a question which had obviously been troubling him for some time.

'How did you find out what they had in mind?'

'Who? The NKVD lads?' The Legionnaire shrugged. 'The girl told us. Just before we left.'

The Old Man narrowed his eyes.

'She told you?'

'That's what I said ... she told us.'

'Why? What she do that for? Why'd she want to go and shop her own countrymen?'

The Legionnaire raised a cold eyebrow in the face of the Old Man's obvious suspicions.

'Do you know, I didn't stop to ask her ... I can only assume she didn't like the look of them. They weren't all that pretty.'

Porta laughed, cynically.

'More likely you held a pistol at her head!'

'Such things have been known,' agreed the Legionnaire, smoothly. 'Only as it happened, in this case it wasn't necessary. She volunteered the information.'

'She must be nuts,' I said. 'Any of her mates find out and she'll be for the chopper.'

'That's her problem,' said the Legionnaire, indifferently.

There was the sound of heavy footsteps and of deep breathing somewhere behind us, and we instantly held our rifles at the ready, peering through the darkness and expecting God knows what to burst upon us, a herd of wild animals or an enemy platoon at the very least, but it was only Tiny.

'Shit got away from me! These flaming fir trees could hide a whole bleeding regiment and you'd never be able to find 'em ... Anyway, I got his gun off of him. I'm pretty sure I hit him, but he still managed to give me the slip.'

The Old Man took the heavy pistol from Tiny and weighed it thoughtfully in his hand.

'A Nagan, eh? Well, that smacks of the NKVD if anything does.'

'What we said right at the start,' said Porta, in disgust. 'I tell you, if people only listened to us a bit more than what they do, I reckon this flaming war might be over by now.'

The Old Man handed the Nagan back to Tiny and we set off warily through the night to rejoin the rest of the Company. Barcelona was nagging on about the girl again. She obviously worried him, and I don't think, at that stage, that any of us were inclined to believe the Legionnaire's story of her having volunteered the information. It sounded totally unlikely, and for my own part I was pretty certain that Tiny had been at her with his lethal steel wire.

'Why didn't you bring her along with you?' demanded Barcelona. 'You know bloody well what those bastards are likely to do when they find out. You've seen the way they treat people—'

'That's no concern of ours,' said the Old Man. 'We're just here to fight the war, not play nursemaid to traitors.'

38

'I disagree,' said Barcelona, hotly. 'Paid traitors are one thing. People who are forced to be traitors are quite a different matter. You put a pistol to someone's head and—'

'Look,' said the Legionnaire, 'for the last time, nobody forced that bitch to be a traitor. She chose to. Of her own free will. That howling brat they had back there – that was hers. And you know who the father was? A Scharführer in the bloody SS! That's the sort of whore *she* was!'

'He probably raped her,' said Barcelona.

'I don't give a sod what he did to her,' said the Legionnaire, coldly. 'All I know is that on her own admission she's been busy betraying her own people right, left and bloody centre whenever the opportunity's arisen. She told us so herself. Seems to think it's her mission in life. And in my book that's treachery, and any traitor can go and get stuffed for all I care, whichever side he's on.'

'She,' said Barcelona.

'She, he, or flaming it,' retorted the Legionnaire, 'it's all one to me.'

'She probably thinks she's in love with the bloke—'

'Christ almighty, a second ago you were saying he raped her!'

'Anyway, she was a bitch,' said Tiny, in conclusive tones, 'and I don't give a monkey's crutch piece what happens to her. She shopped her own mother, she told us so. Got her sent off to Siberia, all for nicking a leg of pork . . . I'd have done her in on the spot, except we had more important things to think about.'

It seemed obvious, now, that the girl had indeed volunteered the information. Tiny would have been the last to conceal another victory for his steel wire, and the Legionnaire would have seen no reason to conceal it if the truth had been dragged from her by force. He was never wantonly vicious, but he could be ruthless when the need arose and he never made any secret of the fact. On the whole, therefore, I was now inclined to believe his story, and I accordingly felt little concern for the girl's probable fate. Barcelona continued to harp on it purely, I think, as a matter of principle.

'She doesn't stand a chance,' he said. 'They'll polish her off in no time. You ever seen what they do to traitors in this part of the world? They're only half civilized, these people. They're—'

'Spare us the details,' said the Old Man. 'Do you mind?'

Stege suddenly laughed; bitter and reflective.

'The enemy values treachery yet scorns the traitor . . . Schiller was quite right, apparently.'

'Schiller?' said Porta, blankly. 'What the hell's he got to do with anything? He's dead, ain't he?'

'Oh, long since,' said Stege. 'Before you were born . . .'

'You should have seen the way his tongue came out of his mouth,' said Tiny, boastfully.

We turned to stare at him, thinking, naturally enough, that he was referring to Schiller. Not a bit of it, however: he was merely reliving his latest moment of glory with the steel wire, when he had strangled the NKVD man.

'He had his hands round my neck, but I was too strong for him. He never said a word. Just choked and gurgled and made odd noises. They do that, when you really put the pressure on. They—'

'Jesus Christ!' said Heide. 'That's all you seem to live for . . . sex and strangulation!'

'Each to his own,' said Tiny, pompously. 'We're here to kill, so I do it the way I like best. Let's face it,' he said, in eminently reasonable tones that forestalled all attempts at argument, 'everyone's got their favourite way of doing it.'

It was true, I suppose. We each had our own preferred methods. The Legionnaire was a devotee of the knife, while Porta was a crack shot with a rifle. Heide liked playing about with flame throwers, while for myself I was accounted pretty hot stuff with a hand grenade. Tiny just happened to enjoy strangling people . . .

The crows objected most strongly when we came along and disturbed their feast. They had settled in a great black cloud on the corpses, and as Porta fired into their midst they rose up in annoyance, circled round our heads in a brief moment of panic and then flew off to the nearest trees, where they set up a harsh chatter of protest. Only one remained behind: it was entangled in a mess of intestines and was unable to free itself. Heide promptly shot it. We dragged the bodies inside and piled them up in heaps. Lt. Ohlsen came to look at our handiwork and began swearing at us. He insisted that we laid them out decently, in neat lines, one next to another.

'Some people,' observed Heide to Barcelona, 'are a bit funny about these things.'

Grumbling, we nevertheless rearranged the bodies as the Lieutenant wished. But as for the officers who had been murdered in their beds, sprawled over the side in their silk pyjamas, with their throats cut, we left them to rot where they were. Dark patches of blood stained the floor, and the flies were already thick on the ground. In one room a radio was still turned on. A persuasive voice was crooning:

'Liebling, sollen wir traurig oder glücklich sein?'
(Darling, shall we be sad or gay?)

We sprinkled petrol over the entire garrison and retreated. Once outside at a safe distance, Barcelona and I tossed half a dozen grenades through the windows.

From the other side of the hills, we heard the drunken singing of jubilant Russian troops:

'Jesli sawtra wouna,
jesli sawtra pochod,
jesli wrasrhaja syla nahrima,
jak odyn tscholowek.'
(When, tomorrow, the war arrives . . .)

The Old Man looked in their direction, away across the hills in the misty distance; and then back at the burning garrison with its murdered men.

'Well, there it is,' he said. 'That's their war, that they seem so happy about . . .'

CHAPTER TWO

Special Mission

WE caught up with the rest of the Company in a pine wood.
Lt. Ohlsen was not, on the whole, very pleasant about our prolonged absence, and it was some considerable time before he
was able to express himself in language that did not bring a
blush of modest shame to our cheeks.

Over the next few days we had several skirmishes with
parties of marauding Russians, and lost perhaps a dozen men in
all. By now we were becoming fairly expert in the art of
guerilla warfare.

We had with us six prisoners, a lieutenant and five infantrymen. The lieutenant spoke fluent German, and he marched
with Lt. Ohlsen at the head of the company, all differences
temporarily forgotten.

To compensate ourselves for having to drag prisoners along
with us, we made two of the infantrymen carry the stewpot
containing our fermented alcohol.

It was early in the morning – with the sun shining, by way of
a change – that we spotted the chalet, a mountain hut with a
balcony running round it, two German infantry men standing
guard at the entrance. As we approached it, two officers came
out and stood waiting for us. One of them, the more senior, was
a lieutenant colonel, wearing a ridiculous monocle that kept
flashing in the sun. He raised a hand in patronizing salute to Lt.
Ohlsen, and as we moved up he looked us over with a con-
descending stare.

'So you've arrived at last . . . I expected you some time ago I
don't ask for reinforcements unless I have need of them – and
when I do have need of them, expect them straight away.' His
monocle moved up and down our ranks, glinting con-

temptuously. 'Well, your men look to be quite an experienced band . . . one hopes that one's confidence does not turn out to be misplaced?' He removed his monocle, breathed, on it, polished it, screwed it back again and addressed himself to us over Lt. Ohlsen's shoulder. 'Just for the record, should like to make it clear from the start that we're rather hot on discipline in this neck of the woods. I don't know what you chaps have been up to out there, but now that you're here you can start pulling your fingers out. Hm!' He nodded, apparently satisfied that he had made some kind of point, and turned back to Ohlsen. 'Allow me to introduce myself: Lt. Colonel von Vergil. I'm in command here.' Lt. Ohlsen saluted. 'I sent for reinforcements some days ago. I expected you long before this. However, now that you've arrived, I can certainly use you. Over that way, on the edge of the woods. Hill 738. Enemy's been rather busy there just lately. You'll find the left flank of my battalion nearby. Make sure you maintain good lines of communication.'

'Sir.'

Lt. Ohlsen saluted again, with two fingers to his helmet. The Colonel opened his eye and dropped his monocle.

'Do you call that a regulation salute, Lieutenant?'

Ohlsen stood to attention. He clicked his heels together and brought one hand up very smartly. The Colonel nodded a grudging approval.

'That's better. We don't tolerate slapdash ways here, you know. This is a Prussian infantry battalion. We know what's what, and we maintain the highest standards. So long as you are under my command, I shall expect that you do the same.' The Colonel placed his hands behind his back and leaned forward slightly, frowning. 'What's this foreign scum you've brought along with you?'

'Russian prisoners, sir. One lieutenant and five privates.'

'Hang them. We don't keep that sort of trash round here.'

There was a moment's pause. I could see Lt. Ohlsen swallowing rather hard.

'Did you say – hang them, sir?'

'Of course I said hang them! What's the matter with you, man? Are you slow-witted or something?'

The Colonel turned on his heel and stalked back inside the

chalet. Lt. Ohlsen followed him with his eyes, his expression grim. We all knew the Colonel's type: an Iron Cross maniac, with not a thought in his head beyond that of personal glory and gratification.

The Russian lieutenant raised an eyebrow at Ohlsen.

'So what happens?' he murmured. 'Do we hang?'

'Not if I can help it!' snapped Ohlsen. 'I'd sooner stand by and watch that buffoon strung up!'

A window on the first floor was flung violently open by an NCO, and the buffoon himself looked out.

'By the way, Lieutenant, one word of warning before you take up your positions: when I give an order, I expect it to be carried out immediately ... I trust I make myself clear?'

'Bloody hell,' muttered Porta. 'That's all we needed. A bleeding Prussian nut ...'

Lt. Ohlsen turned sharply on him.

'Do you mind? There's no need to make the situation worse than it already is.'

The Colonel's Adjutant, a young pink-faced lieutenant, appeared at the door with orders from the Colonel that we were to take up our positions immediately ... and to do so strictly according to the rule book. Whatever that may have meant. After years of fighting at the front, you pretty well make up your own rule book.

We reached Hill 738 and set about digging ourselves in. The earth was hard, but we'd come across harder, and it was better than endless footslogging across enemy-infested countryside. Tiny and Porta sang as they worked. They seemed exaggeratedly happy. 'They've been at that bloody schnaps,' said Heide, suspiciously.

Lieutenants Ohlsen and Spät were sitting in a dug-out with the Russian officer, talking together in low, urgent voices. Barcelona laughed.

'I bet they're giving Ivan the times of the local trains!'

'So what?' demanded Stege, fiercely. 'Ohlsen's not the type to go round hanging prisoners just because some pathological Prussian tells him to do so. He'll see they get out all right.'

'Surely to God,' said Heide, incredulously, 'he's never going to let the bastards go?'

'Go?'

'What else can he do?' said Barcelona. 'If they're still here this time tomorrow, old Barmy Bill's likely to string them up himself – and the Lieutenant along with them.'

'Serve him right,' decreed Heide, self-importantly. 'He ought to obey the orders of a superior officer. That's what he's here for ... In any case, I don't go along with all this balls of taking prisoners. What's the point of it, unless you want something out of 'em? And when you've got it, shoot the buggers ... Prisoners are nothing but a sodding nuisance. You may have noticed,' he added, smugly, 'that *I* never take any.'

'Sounds fine when you're sitting here in your own trenches,' allowed Barcelona, 'but you can bet your sweet life you'd sing another tune if you were in the hands of the Russians.'

'If ever I were,' said Heide, with dignity, 'I should take what was coming to me. And if they kept me prisoner instead of shooting me, I should think they were a load of damn fools ... Only thing is, I don't ever aim to be in the hands of the Russians.'

'Big talk!' jeered Barcelona.

'Look—' Heide turned on him, angrily. 'How long have I been in the perishing Army? Nine years! And in all that time I've never been captured ... and you know why? Because I'm a bloody good soldier, in a way the rest of you could never be in a million years!' He faced them, challengingly. 'I go according to regulations; right? I got a crease in my trousers, just like the book says – right? I got a proper knot in my tie, I got a parting in my hair – God help us,' he even snatched off his helmet to display it! – 'there's not one little thing about me or my uniform that doesn't go along with the rule book. You can laugh if you like, but it's a starting point. You don't start right, you'll never make a good soldier. And when I decided to join the Army, I decided to do the thing properly. And I have, right from the very beginning. And I don't give a tinker's cuss what the blue blazes we're supposed to be fighting for, I just do what I'm told ... I'd kill my own perishing grandmother if I was ordered to. I'm a soldier because I *like* being a soldier, and what I like doing I like to be good at.'

There was a moment's pause.

45

'I don't really see what all that has to do with taking prisoners,' objected Stege.

'Jesus, how thick can you get?' demanded Heide, in disgust. 'And you a student! Listen—' He leaned forward towards them – 'I never went on to secondary school. Nothing like that, see? But take it from me, I know what I'm doing and I know where I'm going. And one thing I know for sure is, never take prisoners ... How do you think I've managed to survive for so long? Why is it that I was made an N.C.O. after only five months, while you're still only a Gefreiter after four years? Why is it that hardly any students end up as officers – whereas I'm going to become an officer in record time just as soon as the war's over and I can get to start training? Why is it—'

'Oh, I don't know,' said Stege, growing bored. 'I daresay you're quite right.'

'Of course I'm bleeding right! I don't need a kid like you to tell me I'm right.' Heide sat back, satisfied. 'I'm not letting those Russian bastards get out of here alive, don't you worry.'

Stege jerked his head up again.

'You touch them and I'll go straight to Lt. Ohlsen!'

'Try it! Try it, and see what he does!' jeered Heide. 'He can't afford to lay a finger on me!'

Stege looked at him contemptuously.

'I can only say thank God *I'm* not a model soldier,' he remarked.

'Ah, get stuffed!' retorted Heide.

We had just finished digging when the first shell came over. We heard the familiar whistling sound as it went to earth somewhere nearby, then the shrill screams of a man in agony, and one of the new recruits leapt out of his hole and fell sprawling on the ground.

'I've been hit!' he yelled, at the top of his voice.

Two of his comrades came after him. They took him up between them and ran off with him, back behind the lines, away from danger. Barcelona pulled a face as he watched them.

'Don't you worry, mate ... they'll get you out of here just as fast as their legs can carry 'em ... perishing miles away, to the farthest hospital they can find ...'

'Beginners' luck,' muttered Heide, sourly. 'Not an earthly of what to do with a machine gun, but give 'em a wounded man to carry and they're off like greased lightning. Didn't take 'em long to learn that, did it?'

At the bottom of a dug-out we had installed our stewpot, well covered with the lid held tight by a pile of stones, so that nothing short of a direct hit could possibly upset our precious liquid.

By now it was almost night. The moon was hidden by a carpet of cloud and the sky was a thick velvety black.

'God, it's so quiet,' murmured the Old Man. 'If I hadn't been at the game so long I'd almost feel tempted to go for a stroll up top and see what's happening.'

In the distance, we heard a dog bark.

'Where the hell *are* the Russians, anyway?' demanded Barcelona.

The Old Man pointed towards the pine trees, standing stiff and straight like sentinels.

'Out there in their dug-outs ... wondering why it's so quiet and what the hell we're up to.'

'Well, wish they'd bloody come out and fight,' grumbled Heide. 'There's nothing like silence for driving you crazy.'

A spine-chilling laugh suddenly cut through the night, but it was only Porta, cheating at dice with Tiny a few dug-outs away. Somewhere on the other side a machine gun began barking. One of ours replied with a few melancholy salvos. As we watched, over beyond the pine trees, an ocean of flames rolled forward, leaping skywards wave upon wave, and each wave preceded by a gigantic explosion. It seemed as if the very mountains were trembling with fear.

'Rocket batteries,' observed the Old Man. 'So long as they don't come any closer ...'

Again, we heard the guard-dog barking at the machine guns. In the dark night, somewhere to the north, a series of luminous flashes tore open the sky.

In the midst of it all, a messenger arrived from the Colonel. He was going at top speed, red in the face and screaming aloud like a madman.

'Message for the Fifth Company! Message for the Fifth Company!'

Lt. Ohlsen strode up to him in a fury.

'Keep your voice, down, you lunatic! The whole front's liable to go up in a sheet of flame if you carry on like that!'

'Yes, sir. Sorry, sir. But it's a very important message, sir. The Colonel wants to see you immediately to have your report and give you some new orders.'

'For crying out loud . . .!'

The Lieutenant turned away, muttering. The messenger stood a moment, bewildered. He had a smooth, scrubbed face, a spotless uniform and an air of curious innocence. Porta looked him up and down a few times.

'Where do you lot come from, then?'

'Breslau,' was the proud reply. 'Forty-Ninth Infantry.'

And the pink face looked down wonderingly at Porta in his dug-out. Porta gave one of his satanic laughs.

'You're another of the medal boys, eh? Well, run off and get your Iron Cross, you're welcome to it . . . you'll find it lying in a pile of shit somewhere!' Startled—as well he might be, not knowing Porta – the messenger turned and ran back to the Colonel.

The mountains trembled again, as if shaken by some deep internal agony. Streaks of red and blue fire shot across the sky. The countryside for miles around seemed bathed in a sea of perpetual fire, and we screwed up our eyes against the glare and cowered deep into our dug-outs. For the moment it was the Russians who were bearing the brunt of it, but we ourselves were in no very happy position.

'Jesus Christ!' whined Heide, wiping the back of a trembling hand across his brow. 'I don't know what those flaming Do batteries do to the Russians, but they put the shits up me all right. Half the time the silly sods don't seem to know which way they're aiming the pissing things—'

'Watch out!' yelled Steiner. 'The Ruskies are joining in!'

Almost before he had finished speaking the ground began to heave and shake as the heavy Russian guns joined in the bombardment. We curled up in our holes, nose to tail like dogs left out on a winter's night, our hands clasped protectively over our helmets. Through half-open eyes I saw the wall of fire rise up behind us as the 12 cm. shells landed from the Russian lines, and I felt the hot blast of air wash over me.

Then suddenly so suddenly that I knew a sense of shock, there came a lull. The barrage stopped and not a sound could be heard.

Those of us who had been through it all before stayed crouched in our holes, but several of the newcomers incautiously raised their heads to see what was going on. Lt. Spät shouted from his dug-out.

'Keep your heads down, you damn fools!'

It was too late for some of them, for as suddenly as the silence had fallen there now rained down upon us a new series of explosions. Disconcertingly closer than the previous lot – right outside our front door, as you might say.

'Third time lucky,' I heard Barcelona mutter. 'It'll be smack on the button next time.'

I felt he was probably right. They couldn't go on just missing us for ever. The luck was bound to change.

'They've got a sniper up in those pine trees somewhere,' said Steiner.

During a second lull, he risked sticking his head out a few inches and yelling to Porta.

'Hey, Porta! Pick that chap off, can't you, and then perhaps we'll get a bit of peace.'

'I'll have a bash,' said Porta. 'Anything for a quiet life . . . if only I can spot the bastard.'

He crawled out of his hole and wriggled forward, lying full length on the ground and scanning the pine forest with the infra-red sights on his rifle.

'I could have a go at him,' suggested Tiny, pulling his length of steel wire from his pocket and starting out of his dug-out. 'I could reach him, I bet. Just let me get this round his neck and we'll—'

'Get back!' hissed Lt. Spät, waving an angry hand.

Just in time. As Tiny dropped back into his hole a new salvo was fired. It landed amongst the trenches, and from farther along the line we heard the usual cacophony of shrieks and screams coming from hideously injured men.

'That's it,' said Barcelona. 'Some poor sods have copped a packet . . . maybe now they'll leave us alone for a bit.'

'Sure, until we start up again with that flaming Do!' rejoined Heide, bitterly.

The Legionnaire had wriggled out to join Porta. With his sharp eyes he had spotted a movement amongst the pine trees, and he reached across and jabbed Porta in the ribs.

'There he is – just on his way down ... do you see him? To the right of that bloody great tree over there ... Look sharp or you'll miss him!'

Porta settled his rifle into his shoulder and glared despairingly through the sights.

'Where, for Christ's sake? I can't see him—'

'Look – you got that big tree over there? Head and shoulders above all the other trees? Three fingers away to the right ...'

'Got him!' Porta jubilantly stuck up a thumb. 'Yeah, I can see the bastard all right now ... just working his way down ... not suspecting a thing ... the poor sod's got the Order of Stalin pinned on his chest! Would you believe that? The Order of bleeding Stalin ...'

'For fuck's sake, stop babbling and get on with the job!' hissed the Legionnaire, between his teeth.

'All right, all right, don't panic,' said Porta, equably. 'Plenty of time yet. No need to get your knickers twisted ...'

As he spoke, he curled his finger round the trigger. There was one short, sharp crack and the unsuspecting sniper crashed down into the forest with half his head blown away. The Legionnaire nodded.

'Good. Let's have your book and I'll mark it up.'

Porta handed over one of the little yellow notebooks that were carried by all the crack shots in the Army for the purpose of recording their scores. The Legionnaire marked up his latest success and flipped back through the preceding pages.

'Not doing so badly,' he commented.

'I've got just as many with my steel wire,' said Tiny, jealously. 'And that takes a helluva sight more guts, let me tell you ... no sitting about on your arse with your eye glued to field glasses – you got to be right out there in the thick of it, right up close ...' He nodded aggressively at the Legionnaire, and then, struck by a sudden thought, turned back to Porta. 'Hey, what about his choppers?'

'Never saw 'em,' said Porta, regretfully. 'The bastard never smiled . . . Why don't we go take a look at him? Fifty-fifty?'

Tiny needed no second invitation. They went crawling off into the pine woods, risking their necks for the chance of some gold fillings.

Lieutenant Ohlsen was also taking the opportunity to stretch his legs.

'Take over for a bit, will you?' he said to Spät. 'I'd better go and see what that old woman of a Colonel wants. Shan't be away long.'

He leapt out of his hole and set off at a run away from the trenches, making for the comparative safety of the wooded area where the Colonel had set up his headquarters. A machine gun began spitting out a steady stream of luminous projectiles, but the man was obviously no expert and they fell short, landing harmlessly some way off.

Lt. Ohlsen arrived panting at the chalet and asked to see Colonel von Vergil. The Colonel showed some reluctance to be disturbed, but eventually, and with an air of indifferent boredom, condescended to hear Ohlsen's report – which he himself had been demanding as a matter of urgency only a short time since. The seven officers with him listened with an equal lack of interest.

They were seated round a table, laid with a thick cloth and supporting a rich spread of food and wine. Ohlsen, feeling himself to be in some kind of wonderland, took in all the details as he talked: cut glass vases full of flowers; a shining crystal chandelier; blue porcelain crockery; batmen in white coats hovering respectfully at every elbow . . . For a moment his voice faltered, as he felt he must surely be talking in his sleep. It seemed hardly possible that vicious slaughter and luxurious dinner party could be taking place simultaneously, only yards away from each other.

As he faltered, Colonel von Vergil screwed in his monocle and took stock of this insolent lieutenant who had come hot foot from the fighting to interrupt his meal. He looked first at the thick crust of mud on his boots, then let his gaze move slowly up the filthy black uniform, creased and torn, and stiff with the accumulated dirt of several months' hard wear in the front line.

51

The death's head insignia of the Hussars, yellowing and rusted, grinned mockingly at him; proclaiming without shame that it was a long, long time since it had been polished to the looking-glass shine laid down in Regulations. The soiled red ribbon of the Iron Cross ended not in a medal but in a fraying tattered fringe. The Iron Cross itself had been lost some time back when the Lieutenant's tank had gone up in a sheet of flame. The left sleeve of his greatcoat was hanging by a few threads. The leather flap on his holster had been wrenched off. In place of an officer's belt, he was wearing one that should have belonged to an ordinary common soldier. His right hand was black with congealed blood.

The Colonel let fall his monocle and turned away with his top lip curling in distaste. It was as he had always suspected: these officers one found at the front had no sense of style, no sense of rank. They were not the type of people one would care to know socially – obviously, or they would not have been at the front in the first place. The Colonel himself was there only through the grossest of mistakes and the most ludicrous bungling by some cretin in the Bendlerstrasse.

His regiment, the 49th Infantry, was both rich and aristocratic, and until now it had seen no front line action except for the occupation of Denmark and two days in France before the armistice. Life was easy, and life was opulent.

And then came the fatal day when the blundering idiot in the Bendlerstrasse had chosen to promote the Regiment's commanding officer, Colonel von der Graz, to the rank of brigade general, and had sent him off with an infantry division to the Balkans. That was only the start of it. The full tragedy of the situation had not at once come home to the bereaved 49th, then happily installed at Breslau. For some time they had lived in the belief and hope that the Colonel's successor would be chosen from amongst their own élite. They had two lieutenant colonels who were due for promotion to full colonel, and the more venerable of these, whose connections were unimpeachable, had even gone so far as to announce in advance the changes he intended to make when he was in charge of the Regiment.

The dream had been shattered one unforgettable Friday

morning, at twenty minutes to nine – a time and date that were imprinted on the memory of every officer in the Regiment, for at twenty minutes to nine their new Colonel had arrived to take over. A Colonel whom nobody knew and whom nobody wanted. He had come straight from active service in Demjamsk. There was none of the dilettante about him: he was tall and craggy, and tough and outspoken, and he wore a patch over one eye.

Throughout that fateful Friday he roamed about the barracks with a black frown of displeasure gathered on his lined forehead, and his nose to the ground like a dog on the scent of trouble. One of the orderly room officers, seeking to ingratiate himself, struck on the bright idea of introducing the new Colonel to the Regiment's wine cellar, which was famed for miles around, and which was stocked with sufficient delights to gladden the heart of any connoisseur. Perhaps the Colonel was not a connoisseur. At any rate, he merely picked up one or two of the dusty bottles, read the labels, raised a cold eyebrow at the officer and marched out without a word. It was that eyebrow, together with the total lack of comment, which really rattled the officer. An hour later he packed his bags and departed, anticipating what he felt to be a certainty.

It was late in the day before the Colonel ceased his wanderings and seated himself in his predecessor's chair, behind the large acajou desk. The majority of the officers were already in the Casino, bravely attempting to carry on as usual, but the champagne tasted somehow different and the charms of gambling seemed suddenly to have vanished. The stormclouds were gathering about their heads, and they felt menace in the air.

And then the blow fell: the Colonel called his officers back to barracks. Most of them, in fact, had gone off for the weekend on a forty-eight hour pass extending from Thursday evening to any time on Monday. It was, perhaps, stretching things a bit, but it had long since been accepted as normal procedure in the 49th.

Having recalled as many of his officers as could be found, the Colonel then demanded to be told the exact total strength of the Regiment. This should have been kept daily up to date by reports from company commanders, but through some oversight – ascribed by the officers concerned to slackness on the part of the Hauptfeldwebels – it was many weeks since anyone had taken the trouble.

The Adjutant rang languidly round the various companies to see what the position was. His interest in the result was purely academic: he had an uncle who was a high-ranking staff officer in that part of the Army which still remained on German soil, and as far as he was concerned the new Colonel was of no more real inconvenience than a wasp in a jam jar. Noisy perhaps, but easily brushed aside.

With a slight smile on his lips, he reported back to the Colonel with the results of his telephone calls.

'I regret to say, sir, that the exact strength of the Regiment cannot at this moment be ascertained . . . The Hauptfeldwebels are all on 48-hour leave.'

The Colonel ran a thoughtful finger beneath the rim of his black eye patch.

'Where is the Ordnance Officer?' he asked.

The youngest lieutenant in the Regiment came up at a gallop. He saluted, breathlessly.

'Lt. Hanns, Baron von Krupp, Ordnance Officer, sir.'

The Colonel looked at him a moment, then nodded slowly; and the way he nodded was rather sad and rather contemptuous.

'So that exists here, too, does it?' He grunted. 'Well, Baron von Krupp, perhaps you wouldn't mind checking that at least we have mounted a guard – or are all the sentries also on leave, I wonder?'

Lt. Hanns saluted again and turned to go, but as he opened the door the Colonel called him back and dropped another bombshell.

'I want an accurate figure for the number of men at present in the barracks – and I'll give you quarter of an hour to get it.'

The Adjutant smiled again, in his superior manner. He was pretty certain that the figure would prove to be only thirty per cent of that laid down by Regulations. It was many months since anyone had troubled about matters of such trifling importance. Breslau, after all, was not Berlin: no one ever came to Breslau.

Left with his officers, the new Colonel commented – politely enough, but not concealing his astonishment – on the fact that not one of them had a decoration from the front.

'Oh, no, sir!' said Captain Dose, rather shocked. 'We've never been sent to the *front*, sir.'

'Have you not, indeed?' The Colonel slowly smiled, and it was a smile which chilled the hearts of his assembled officers. 'Well, rest assured that that shall be remedied. You shall have your chance the same as everyone else. The war is not yet over . . . Before the night is out, I shall expect to receive from each one of you a request for transfer to active service at the front.' He turned to the Adjutant, who was still suavely smiling. 'I want you to send telegrams to every man on a 48-hour pass. All leave is cancelled forthwith. They are to report back to barracks immediately. And you can sign it in my name . . . I imagine you do know where these men can be found?'

The Adjutant just perceptibly hunched a shoulder. In point of fact, he had no idea where any of them were likely to be. The best he could do would be to send out men in search of them, which meant combing every bar and every brothel in the town. And that was likely to be a long and unrewarding task. He looked across at Captain Dose and decided to indulge in some buck-passing. Dose was known to be something of an idiot.

'I think that's your pigeon?' he said pleasantly, and he picked up a sheaf of telegram forms and thrust them at the astonished captain. 'Here. Send one to every man on leave. I presume you have their names and addresses?'

Too stunned to speak, Dose staggered from the room. He spent the rest of the night alternately looking up non-existent or out-of-date addresses in an address book and praying feverishly for a passing aeroplane to drop a bomb on top of the Colonel's quarters.

Despite all his efforts, he succeeded in rounding up only nine of the 1,800 men who had left the barracks.

On Monday, according to their habit, the remaining 1,791 rolled up at various different times of the day, according as fancy took them, looking forward to a few hours of peace and quiet in which to recover from the debauches of the weekend. And for each man, a shock was in store: the entire barracks had been changed overnight from a free and easy and relatively luxurious hotel to a disciplined military establishment. On every officer's desk was a terse note to the effect that the Colonel wished to see him straight away.

The youngest and least experienced dropped everything and ran. The more prudent put in a few telephone calls to see the lie of the land, and several of them at once fell gravely ill and were taken away by ambulance.

Amongst the former was Captain (Baron) von Vergil. Three hours after reporting back to barracks he found himself with orders to proceed to the Russian front. Promoted, it is true, to the rank of lieutenant colonel, but that was small comfort when he considered the probable horrors of front line warfare. Not only the danger, but more than that, the discomfort. He thought of lice and mud and stinking bodies and rotting feet, and it was almost too much for a white man to bear. He could have cried very effectively, had there been anyone likely to sympathize with him.

Eight days after the arrival of Colonel Bahnwitz, the 49th Infantry Regiment had disappeared, along with its famous wine cellar. Each officer had carried away his share of the booty. No one had left with less than two trucks full of wine, and the Baron had taken three.

And now here he was on the Eastern front, experiencing the harsh facts of warfare. In what must almost certainly have been record time he had succeeded in getting himself and his men hemmed in by the Russians. He had at once sent out furious appeals for help in all directions, and had been soothed and reassured: help was on its way. And now help had arrived, and what help it was! A tank company without a tank to its name; band of ruffians and scoundrels wearing filthy rags and stinking to high heaven. It was little better than an insult. Colonel von Vergil, after all, could not be expected to know that this band of ruffians, led by two tough and experienced officers, was a gift from the gods and probably his one chance of getting out alive. This one company, in fact, was worth an entire regiment of sweetly smelling, freshly laundered troops from a barracks at Breslau.

Colonel von Vergil sipped his wine and stared over his glass at the white ribbon fixed to Lt. Ohlsen's left sleeve. On the ribbon were the words, 'Disciplinary Regiment', ringed with two mutilated death's heads. The Colonel twitched his nostrils: the Lieutenant smelt of blood and sweat and looked as if he had not seen a bar of soap since the start of the war. The Colonel put down his wine and took out a cigarette to drown the stench of unwashed body.

'Thank you for your report, Lieutenant.'

He paused a moment, lit the cigarette with a gold lighter and leaned back in his chair.

'You are aware, of course, that according to Regulations each soldier—' and here he leaned rather heavily and meaningfully on the word 'soldier'—'each soldier is obliged to clean his equipment and see to his uniform immediately after combat. In this way it will not deteriorate and should remain in much the same condition – allowing, naturally, for normal wear and tear – as when it was first issued. Now, Lieutenant, I think you'll agree with me that one quick glance at your uniform is all that is required to convince anyone but a blind man that you have been almost criminally negligent in this respect. I am not at all sure that it could not even be classed as active sabotage ... However—' He smiled and blew out a cloud of smoke. 'In your case, I am prepared for the moment to be lenient and to take the view that it is more a question of fear and of personal cowardice that has led to this negligence on your part, rather than any deliberate attempt at sabotage. When a man's nerve is gone, so I am told, he may well act in curious ways.'

Lt. Ohlsen's face grew slowly scarlet – with rage, not shame. His fists clenched at his sides and his eyes glittered with a moment of fury. But he was too experienced a soldier not to have learnt self control. One word from this clown Vergil and Lt. Ohlsen could well find himself a dead man, and while dying for your country might still have a certain tatty glory clinging to it, dying for a fool like Vergil was just plain idiocy.

'I'm sorry about my uniform, sir.' The Lieutenant spoke stiffly, through half-closed lips. 'The Company was sent out on a special mission three and a half months ago. We've been in continuous action ever since. Only twelve men survived from the original company, so I think you'll appreciate, sir, that in the circumstances none of us has so far had much of a chance to sit down and polish our equipment or mend our uniform.'

The Colonel took another sip of wine and patted his lips with his white starched napkin.

'Excuses are totally irrelevant, Lieutenant. Furthermore, I should wish to remind you that when being interrogated you do not speak unless a question is put to you. I did not put a question to you ... Should you wish to make any sort of observation, you should request permission to speak in the usual way.'

'Very well, sir. In that case I wish to request permission to speak.'

'Certainly not!' snapped the Colonel. 'Nothing you say can possibly alter the facts. Get back to your Company and never let me see either you or your men in that deplorable state again.' He paused, looked across at Ohlsen with a triumphant gleam in his eye. 'I shall give you until 10 a.m. tomorrow, Lieutenant, by which time I shall expect the matter to have been attended to. I shall come round personally to inspect you at that hour ... And, incidentally, that reminds me of another matter that should have had your attention by now. Those Russian prisoners you had with you – have you got rid of them yet?'

Lt. Ohlsen swallowed, hard. He looked the Colonel straight in the eye.

'Not yet, sir. No.'

The Colonel raised an eyebrow. He sat for a moment, tapping the ash from his cigarette and gravely staring into the ashtray.

'Sabotage,' he said at last, in a low, intense voice. 'Sabotage and insubordination ... But after all, we are human, Lieutenant. We give you once more the benefit of the doubt. Possibly we did not make ourselves sufficiently clear in the first instance ... ten o'clock tomorrow morning, Lieutenant. That is an order. I shall expect the prisoners to have been hanged by then. I look forward to receiving your report in confirmation.'

Lt. Ohlsen licked his lips.

'Excuse me, sir, but – I can't just hang them – not just like that, in cold blood. They're prisoners of war—'

'Is that so?' The Colonel seemed amused. 'Whatever they are, Lieutenant, I believe that your first duty is to carry out the orders of your superior officers ... not to question either the validity or the wisdom of those orders. I trust, for your own sake, that all is as it should be tomorrow morning.' He waved his napkin as a sign of dismissal, turned back to the dinner table and picked up his glass. 'Your health, gentlemen.'

The seven elegant officers raised their glasses. Lt. Ohlsen turned abruptly and left the room. As he made his way back to the Company through the dangerous darkness, he prayed aloud to the Russians to drop a few shells in a few selected places.

'Just a few ... just a few very little ones ... just enough to blow that load of po-faced nincompoops sky-high off their great fat arses ... dear Ivan, that's all I ask!'

But the night remained dark and the silence unbroken. Ivan was evidently not listening to his prayers.

Lt. Ohlsen regained the Fifth Company and jumped down into the trenches, where he sat a moment with clenched fists, trembling with rage against the Colonel.

'What's up?' asked Spät, looking sagely at his brother officer over the empty pipe he was sucking.

'That bloody man ... that bloody man!'

For a moment it seemed that this was all he could say. He spat it out viciously between his teeth, while we watched him sympathetically and at the same time waited hopefully for more. And at last it came, in language that we could understand and appreciate. The invective rolled out of him in a fine unbroken flow of obscenity, and the Old Man shook his head and regarded the Lieutenant with an air of grave paternal anxiety.

'What's he done now?' he said, when at last he could get a word in.

Lt. Ohlsen looked at him wildly.

'I'll tell you what he's done! He's arranged an inspection for 10 o'clock tomorrow morning! Make sure we're all neat and clean and polished in accordance with Regulations! Take time off to polish our rifles and sew on our buttons!'

'You what?' said Porta, startled.

The lieutenant turned on him.

59

'You heard!' he snapped irritably.

Porta gave a great cackle of delighted laughter. He turned and shouted into the darkness.

'Hey, Tiny! You catch that? We got to change our ways, you and me. Got to wash our faces and brush our uniforms. Got to get our holes swept out by ten o'clock tomorrow morning, make sure we're living nice and clean and tidy, like, without no crumbs on the floor!'

The answer came roaring back down the trench.

'What holes you on about? Arseholes?'

Our laughter must have been heard for miles around.

'For Christ's sake,' implored Lt. Ohlsen, who had had a trying enough time already, poor man, 'don't make so much bloody noise.'

'Sh!' hissed Porta, laying a great grimy finger on his lips. 'We'll wake the Ruskies up!'

'Yes, and that won't be as damned funny as it sounds!' snarled Ohlsen.

We subsided into silence. The tops of the mountains were lost in swirling cloud, and the moon had disappeared behind a thick blanket. The night was black but peaceful.

Lt. Ohlsen settled down in the trench between Spät and the Old Man and beckoned them to come closer to him. He began speaking in low, urgent tones.

'Look, I'm in a bit of a jam,' he said, frankly. 'If you've any suggestions, I shall be only too glad to hear them ... That stupid cunt of a colonel up there insists that we dispose of our prisoners by ten o'clock tomorrow morning. He's coming round for a personal inspection to make sure the job's been done properly ... So what I want to know is, what the hell are we going to do about it? How do we arrange it so that they keep their heads on their shoulders and that blimp's satisfied we've done the job?'

There was a silence, while Spät frowned into the darkness and the Old Man pulled deeply on his pipe.

'That's a pretty tall order,' he said, at length. 'Means hiding the six prisoners and finding six dead bodies to show the Colonel ... not so easy.'

'Suppose,' suggested Spät, 'we just closed our eyes and let them escape?'

'You heared what Boris said,' objected Ohlsen. 'They'd be shot the minute they got back to their own lines.'

'What – just for having been taken prisoner?' Spät shook his head. 'He must be exaggerating. I find that very difficult to believe.'

'Well, all right, let's ask him. See if he's got any ideas. Damn it all, it's his head I'm trying to save.'

Spät sent off for the prisoner, and a few moments later the young Russian lieutenant jumped down into the trench. Ohlsen briefly explained the position to him.

'So that's how things stand,' he ended up. 'And frankly there's not a damn thing I can do about it unless you've got any bright ideas.'

The Russian smiled rather grimly and shook his head.

'I only wish I had . . . Unfortunately, they're no more civilized on our side of the line than yours. We've only got to show our faces back there and we'd be shot immediately as traitors.' He caught the sceptical expression on Spät's face and nodded sadly at him. 'Oh, yes. It's quite true, my friend, I can assure you of that. A soldier in the Red Army is supposed to die for his country sooner than let himself be taken prisoner . . . words of Uncle Joe!'

'How about the partisans on our side of the line?' the Old Man wanted to know. 'Couldn't they be any help?'

'It is a possibility,' allowed the Russian, but he didn't sound too enthusiastic. 'Only trouble is, each group of partisans is in direct communication with headquarters, and while a local group might not see any discrepancy in our story, you can bet your sweet life that the boys at H.Q. would know bloody well that our detachment is nowhere near this section of the front. Obviously we can't tell them we're escaped prisoners, they wouldn't take at all kindly to it . . . All we could hope to do is string them a line about having been cut off during an attack and say we've been in hiding every since, and frankly I doubt if they'd wear it. Probably wouldn't even bother to hear us out. Shoot first and see who you've shot afterwards, that's their motto . . . and believe you me, they stick to it. I've never known such a trigger-happy mob.'

Lt. Spät lit a cigarette, crouching over it and shielding the glow with a cupped hand.

'If the worst comes to the worst,' he suggested, 'I suppose we could always organize a sort of perpetual hide and seek . . . Get hold of some German uniforms for you and push you in amongst the men. Sooner or later you'd presumably get your chance to push off somewhere—'

'If we hadn't already been shot as spies first!' retorted the Russian. 'My men can't speak German, remember? I know you're doing your best to be helpful, and don't for God's sake think I'm not grateful, but frankly I don't fancy the idea of dressing up in enemy uniform and sitting back to wait for the axe to fall.'

Spät shrugged his shoulders.

'I can't say I blame you.'

There was a long, troubled silence, broken eventually by Lt. Ohlsen.

'We don't seem to be getting anywhere, do we?' He turned to the Russian. 'Have you no ideas at all?'

'Not so much as a single germ,' confessed the prisoner, with a faint, fatalistic smile. 'And considering you're putting your own lives in danger, I'm only surprised that you're bothering your heads over us . . . it's really only a question, when it comes down to it, of which side hangs us, yours or ours.'

'Why don't we try asking Porta?' said the Old Man, suddenly.

Lt. Ohlsen looked at him a moment, then laughed.

'Three officers and a Feldwebel and we can't produce a single sound idea amongst us! We have to turn round and ask a semi-literate rogue of an Obergefreiter!'

Spät smiled, and the Old Man hunched a shoulder.

'It's a totally ludicrous suggestion, and well you know it – but it's certainly far and away the best we've had yet,' conceded Ohlsen, with a grin. 'Call the bugger over here and let's see what he's got to say. Knowing Porta, it wouldn't surprise me in the slightest if he came up with something!'

Porta wriggled into the trench on his stomach, heaved himself into a comfortable position and leered round at the assembled company.

'What's up, then?' he demanded, cheerfully. 'Dirty work at the crossroads, I know, or you wouldn't want me here!' Spät offered him a cigarette, and he clawed one out of the packet and stuck it behind his ear. 'Ta. Don't mind if I do. Never refuse a fag, that's the only motto worth having round this dump.'

He glanced expectantly at Lt. Ohlsen, who came straight to the point.

'Porta, we need your help. We've got to do something to keep our prisoners' heads on their shoulders, and we've got to do it pretty fast. Any smart ideas?'

'Ah, now you're asking,' said Porta, maddeningly. 'The boys have all been discussing it, ever since you come back from seeing the Colonel.'

'How did they know about it?' demanded Lt. Ohlsen, indignantly.

Porta laid a finger along the side of his nose.

'We got ways of knowing these things, don't you worry.'

'So what conclusions have you come to?'

'Well, Heide, for a start: he don't want nothing to do with any of it. Letting 'em go, I mean. He swears blind that you let 'em go and he'll shoot the lot of 'em as they're crossing the line. Could be that's probably the best idea. Save you a lot of trouble, any rate.'

The Old Man took his pipe from his mouth and clicked his tongue impatiently.

'Come on, Porta, wake your ideas up! You can do better than that, don't let me down . . . If that was the way the Lieutenant felt about it, he'd go ahead and shoot the prisoners himself. We're trying to find a way of saving them, not of murdering them . . . and we haven't got all night to do it in, either!'

'O.K., O.K., keep your wig on and have a bit of patience . . . as the spinster remarked when she tried it out on herself with an overripe banana . . .'

'Christ almighty!' said Spät, swallowing a burst of laughter and half choking himself as a result.

'Never mind the funny business, people's lives are at stake!' snapped the Old Man.

'Get you!' said Porta, scornfully.

Lt. Ohlsen reached across and tapped him on the shoulder.

'Porta, please ... I've told you, we desperately need your help. I know you're a resourceful chap, so if you've any useful ideas don't hesitate to trot them out.'

Porta looked at him reflectively.

'Well, I did have a sort of idea ... dunno whether you'll go for it, though.'

'Let's hear it.'

'It's kind of complicated to explain, but what I thought was, if we could get hold of six bodies – well, we've got three already, we picked off some of their snipers, and we can easy get another three from somewhere, that's no problem—'

'So?'

'So, well, then – me and Tiny and one of the lad's, the Legionnaire, perhaps, we go up and we have a butcher's at the enemy, right? Make sure they're all kipped down for the night, then a few quick bursts of the old machine gun fire up and down the trenches—' Porta demonstrated what he meant, spraying the three officers with imaginary bullets – 'They'll soon get the wind up. Make 'em think a whole bloody battalion's about to burst in on 'em. Soon as we've woken 'em up, we get the hell out of it and head back home again. Like this ... right?'

With the point of his bayonet, Porta sketched out the proposed movements. The Old Man and the three officers nodded, doubtful but vaguely beginning to follow the tortuous drift of his thoughts.

'So then, of course, everything starts up for real,' continued Porta. 'We get Barcelona standing by with a flame thrower, and as soon as I give the go ahead he lets 'em have it good and proper in the outposts. Then you come in with the big shells. And by that time, nobody but us knows what the hell's going on – but it's a safe bet those silly buggers over there on the rocket battery'll start shitting themselves. Only a matter of seconds before they join in the fun, and once that happens the enemy's bound to think that a whole flaming Army's attacking them, and they'll throw in everything they've got. And that'll wake up the Colonel and his glory boys over there—' He jerked a contemptuous thumb in the direction of Colonel von Vergil's troops on our flank. 'Soon as they know what's going on, you can bet your sweet life they'll do a bunk. They won't stick around to see what's going to happen next, not that load of queens. I reckon we'll be shot of the whole damn lot of them before you can say knife.'

Lt. Ohlsen made a faint noise of approval.

'And how about our Russian friends here?'

'Yeah, well – soon as the balloon goes up, they hop it, don't they? They scarper back to their own lines ... Mind you—' Porta turned to the Russian officer. 'I'm afraid we'll have to rough you up a bit,' he said, none too regretfully. 'Make it look like you've been in the wars and all that ... still, Tiny can see to that side of things. I've got it all worked out, see? Your story is, you was cut off in your own sector and fell in with some partisans, what took you off to a farm with 'em – same one we flushed out farther back, right? Tell you about it later. So anyway, one of the partisans got killed, the other escaped. Just like actually happened. You and your men managed to get out, didn't know where you were, but in the end you arrived here, at this particular spot, see? Behind the enemy lines, couldn't think how to get back to your own side, so you do the only thing possible and open fire on us – you with me?'

The Russian officer grinned.

'You mean, it's us that's supposed to have started the whole thing off and forced your troops over there to abandon their trenches?'

'Well, why not?' said Porta, reasonably. 'Wouldn't take more than one man with a couple of hand grenades to send that lot running off.'

'But what about your own Company?' asked the Russian. 'The minute we get back to our own side and tell them the position, they'll be well aware of the fact that some of your troops have pulled out. They're not going to sit around twiddling their thumbs. They'll start moving in to occupy the abandoned trenches.'

'Tell you something.' Porta leaned forward. 'That lot over there—' He nodded his head contemptuously towards the Russian lines – 'are just about as bleeding useless as that lot over

65

there—' again, contemptuously, his thumb jerked in the direction of the Colonel's troops. 'You think Tiny and me could've gone out and picked up three corpses just like that? Not on your nelly! Not if they'd been soldiers worth their salt, we couldn't. I tell you, the way they carry on over there you'd think they was out for a Sunday afternoon walk in Moscow, not fighting a bleeding war!'

'May I ask,' said Lt. Ohlsen, 'when you and Tiny were thinking of seting the ball rolling?'

'Say, three o'clock?' suggested Porta. 'Seems like a good sort of time. What I pictured was, me and Tiny and the Legionnaire, say, we'd set off about two-thirty, and at three o'clock sharp the balloon would go up.'

'Why three o'clock?' Spät wanted to know.

'Well, for one thing, nobody expects an attack to come at three o'clock in the morning. I mean, you wouldn't yourself, would you? Because it's a bleeding stupid sort of time to get into a fight, if you know what I mean . . . Most of the silly sods'll be asleep, anyway. Theirs and ours. Won't even know what hit 'em. Even so—' He turned to the Russian – 'you'll have to move pretty fast when the time comes. I'll show you the best way to go.'

The Russian nodded, gravely.

'Thank you. I must say—'

'One other thing,' interrupted Porta. 'Keep out of Tiny's way. He's a big chap with a bit of steel wire what he's sort of got into the habit of knotting round people's necks when they're not looking. He's kind of over-enthusiastic about it just at the moment. You bump into him and I won't answer for the consequences. He tends to get a bit excited, if you know what I mean . . . Then there's Heide. He's just a murdering bastard, pure and simple. If he can pick you off, he will, but there's nothing I can do about that. As for the new boys, I dunno what they're like but I don't reckon they're much cop. Anyway—' He jerked his head at the Russian – 'you come with me and I'll show you the way you'll have to go. And keep your head down if you don't want it to get blown off. Your little red brothers have a lot of snipers in this part of the world.'

They pulled themselves out of the trench and crept towards

66

the barbed wire, on the other side of which lay no-man's land. They were soon swallowed up in the darkness.

They returned fifteen minutes later. Judging from the continued silence of the night, they had not been spotted.

'O.K.,' said Porta. 'That's settled, then.'

'It would seem so,' murmured Lt. Ohlsen, with a somewhat rueful smile.

They synchronized their watches. The time was then 22.05. Porta crept back to his own dug-out, which he shared with Tiny. We heard a muffled conversation between them, then a great shout of laughter from Tiny. The Legionnaire swore at them, a stray bullet passed overhead, and then all was silent again.

Shortly after midnight, the two officers left the trenches for a tour of inspection.

'I wonder why silence is always so damned unnerving?' muttered Lt. Spät, staring up at the dark, cloud-covered sky.

They moved slowly up the hill, placing their feet with care, making as much use as possible of trees and bushes, melting from one shadow to another. They had gone only a few yards when a disturbing sound came softly to their ears. It was deep and regular, like a cross between the growling of a dog and the grunting of a pig. They stood still and listened, guns at the ready.

'What the devil is it?' hissed Ohlsen.

They went on listening, then an incredulous grin spread over Spät's face.

'It's some silly bugger snoring!'

Cautiously they moved forward, walking across the wet spongy grass, and almost fell into a deep hole, at the bottom of which, curled up nose to tail, was an N.C.O. His sub machine gun was lying carelessly by his side and he was snoring fit to wake the dead.

Lt Spät bent down, closed his fingers over the gun and brought it slowly out into the open. He then pointed it into the man's chest and woke him with a smart tap on the side of his head.

'What's going on?'

The man instinctively moved to sit up, but found himself thrust down again by the mouth of his own gun.

'That's what I should like to know,' said Ohlsen, grimly. 'Just what the devil *is* going on? You'd have looked pretty sick if we'd been a couple of Russians, wouldn't you?'

'I've set all the guards—'

'I'm sure you have! And the chances are they're all taking the opportunity to have a kip ... a fine example YOU set them, don't you? You deserve to be shot on the spot.'

The man sank back, cowering. Ohlsen regarded him contemptuously a moment, then jerked his head at Spät and they continued on their way. A little farther on they heard Tiny's jubilant laugh ring out. Dimly they discerned Porta's grotesque yellow hat in the darkness and heard the rattle of dice.

'Christ almighty!' said Spät, with a certain grudging admiration. 'Don't they ever give up? How can they even see the spots in this light?'

Ohlsen shrugged.

'They probably can't. They probably prefer it that way ... gives them more scope for cheating each other!'

The two officers completed their tour of inspection and returned to their trench as the field telephone was ringing.

'Emil 27,' said Heide, in a low voice. He listened a moment, then passed the headset to Lt. Ohlsen. 'It's the Colonel for you, sir.'

Ohlsen pulled a hideous face.

'If I must ...' He took the headset and raised an ironical eyebrow at Spät, who smiled and turned away. 'Lt. Ohlsen here, sir ... Yes ... Yes, I see ... Of course, sir. Whatever you say.' He thrust the headset back at Heide and turned to the Old Man. 'That was the Colonel. You may have gathered ... He wants the First Section up there at 10 a.m. sharp tomorrow, all nicely brushed and polished and ready for inspection. The Second Section to follow at 11, the next at 12, and so on.'

'Charming,' murmured Spät.

'I don't know about charming,' said Ohlsen, dryly. 'He also wants to see six corpses produced along with the First Section.'

68

They looked at each other, shrugged their shoulders and retired into their blankets for a couple of hours' sleep.

As for the rest of us, now we knew what was to happen we found it quite impossible to do more than cat nap. At half-past two we watched Porta, Tiny and the Legionnaire move out of the trenches. We watched them crawl under the barbed wire, and we saw them swallowed up in the darkness. The Old Man and Barcelona alerted us for action. Three groups of mortar batteries were already standing by.

Barcelona was hugging the heavy flame thrower against himself. For the umpteenth time, he was checking the mechanism.

'If I could only change this blasted valve,' he muttered. 'I know the damn thing's going to give way sooner or later. I had to mend it with chewing gum last time, and I haven't been able to get hold of a new one yet.'

'No good worrying about it now,' said Ohlsen. 'We've only got four minutes to go.'

Heide turned threateningly from his position behind the heavy machine gun and addressed a group of the new arrivals.

'Any one of you lot doesn't move when I move and he gets a personal bullet from me right up his backside ... panjamajo?'

The youngest of the recruits, a boy who could not have been more than seventeen at the very most, promptly burst into loud sobs of panic. Heide moved away from the gun and slapped him sharply two or three times across the face.

'Stop that flaming racket! Nothing's liable to happen to you that won't happen to anyone else. We all stand to get our perishing heads blown off, you're not the only one.'

The boy seemed transfixed by terror. He opened his mouth and screamed; a long, tearing, uncontrollable scream of fear. The other recruits looked at him nervously, rolling the whites of their eyes and shying away like frightened horses. Heide took hold of him and shook him, slapping him back and forth across the face as he did so.

'Stop bleeding whining, for God's sake! You want me to finish you off before the enemy have a chance to get at you?'

Lt. Ohlsen and the Russian Officer stood side by side, watching the scene in grave silence. Heide's actions were brutal but necessary. The new recruits were already unsettled and uncertain, and if the boy's fears had been allowed to run their course his panic might well have spread like wild fire throughout the entire Company. But from now on, Heide's section would at least be kept at their posts through a common fear of Heide himself, probably transcending even their fear of the enemy.

'That's a good man you've got there,' remarked the Russian.

'He's all right,' agreed Ohlsen, shortly. 'So long as we're at war, I suppose we have to have men like him.'

Seconds after he had finished speaking, an explosion shook the ground beneath us and the reverberations echoed through the night, rolling and crashing like a gigantic thunderclap. It was followed by the long, harsh cry of someone in agony. And then, silhouetted against the dark sky, lit up by the sudden burst of flames, Tiny's familiar shape surged into view near the enemy trenches. His sub machine gun was jammed into his hip, and we saw the endless stream of bullets ploughing up the earth, a flashing series of brilliant red dots moving through the night as he sprayed the gun along the front line of trenches. At the same moment we saw the fugitive figures of men, hurling themselves panic-stricken away from this unexpected attack and flying in all directions.

As he watched, the Russian lieutenant pursed his lips and gave an admiring whistle.

'Some troops you got there!'

Lt. Ohlsen turned and shouted to Barcelona, who came up at a run with the flame thrower. The chewing gum held, the valve did its work, and now the scene was lighted by a sea of fire. Black smoke curled upwards, and across the stage ran screaming human torches, men demented by pain and terror.

Ohlsen held up a hand . . . and dropped it. It was our signal to join in. Heide howled like a demon as he sent across salvo after salvo from the heavy guns. His men worked with him, hardly aware of what they were doing but too scared to stop.

'Mortars, fire!'

As Lt. Spät gave the command, the mortars went into action. Shells were sent across to add to the general confusion, curving across the sky and landing on the far side of the Russian trenches.

I folded up the tripod of the heavy M.G., ran forward and installed myself in a shell hole in the middle of no-man's land, my loader following with the ammunition. From the trench in front of me a whole group of men surged up, running blindly towards me. I lay flat on my belly, hugging the butt against my shoulder, taking my time, taking aim, just as if I were back on the practice range in camp.

As I fired the noise of the gun was lost in a new series of explosions. The Russians had had time to collect their scattered wits and had opened up with their rocket batteries. The shells were whizzing over and exploding behind us, and the whole sky was alight with screaming missiles.

I scuttled back from my exposed position, throwing myself down near Lt. Ohlsen, gripping the machine gun and waiting for the storm to subside. The Russian lieutenant took his opportunity and struck out towards his own lines, followed by his men. I was too concerned at that moment for my own safety to care very much what happened to any of them.

The Colonel's battalion reacted exactly as Porta had foretold: they took to their heels and ran. That was not so very surprising. What was more surprising was that the Russians did not at once move forward into the attack, but we subsequently discovered the reason for this: most of their troops, also, had departed rather abruptly from the scene of battle!

It was seven hours before the sector calmed down and settled back into its normal routine. Even then there was a continuous and half-hearted exchange of gunfire.

Towards the end of the afternoon we were able to re-establish contact with the battalion. It seemed that the Colonel had temporarily lost interest in our forthcoming inspection and had cancelled it in favour of more pressing business.

There was a great scurrying to and fro of men, frantic exchanges of messages and urgent repairs carried out to severed telephone wires. And amidst all the hectic activity, no one really knew just what had happened. Lt. Ohlsen was able to report that a surprise infantry attack had taken place and a detachment had been sent over to try to capture our trenches. Fortunately the neighbouring company gave roughly the same garbled explanation and it was never queried.

As soon as the lull came, we went on a scavenging expedition and returned with the bodies of six Russian soldiers, which we solemnly hung up in the trees for the benefit of Colonel von Vergil. Lt. Ohlsen sent in a written report confirming that he had carried out his orders.

The following day, the Colonel sent along his Adjutant to verify the truth of this statement. Having gone to all that trouble we were pretty anxious to show off our handiwork, but the adjutant must have had a weak stomach or something: he didn't want to see the dead bodies hanging in the trees.

'I'll take your word for it, old boy . . . just a matter of form, you know.'

And nothing would persuade him otherwise. Lt. Ohlsen watched him walk off with a handkerchief to his nose and shook his head in disgust.

'All that killing to no purpose whatsoever . . .'

Later that evening, we received an order to send out a reconnaisance patrol behind the Russian lines, with the object of seeing the strength of their artillery and whether they had any tanks.

Of course, it was our section that was sent. It had to be. None of the new recruits would ever have lived to tell the tale.

One after another we left the trenches and stole across towards the Russian lines. Tiny was actually running, gripping his steel wire in one hand.

'Half and half!' he hissed as he shot past Porta.

We knew what he meant, of course: in theory, if not in practice, he and Porta always went halves in any gold teeth they discovered.

'Don't blame me,' grumbled the Old Man. 'Don't blame me when they have you up before the firing squad . . . God almighty, the times I've warned you about it! It's not only the moral issue, it's the fact that you're breaking regulations. Two regulations, actually.'

'Go on!' said Porta, wonderingly. 'You don't say!'

'I do say, and I'll tell you what they are and then you'll know what you're in for. First of all, you're nicking things off corpses – and that's against the law the whole world over. Second, you're not passing on the stuff you pinch. Gold teeth, gold rings, gold watches, anything like that, as you very well know, belongs to the State and should be handed over to the nearest SS bureau. And that's law in Germany, if it isn't anywhere else. And the penalty for breaking it is death, so don't say I haven't warned you.'

'Old Man, you're nothing but a bleeding pessimist!' declared Porta.

'I'm not handing mine over,' said Tiny, who had slowed down to a walk and had been listening to the conversation. 'I'm keeping mine till the end of the war . . . Know what I'm going to do, then? I'm going to buy me a pork butcher's shop and a brothel.'

'With other people's gold teeth,' muttered the Old Man, who never would be reconciled to the idea.

'Well, and why not?' demanded Tiny, hotly. 'I've heard that in the concentration camps they yank 'em out while people are still alive and kicking and might need 'em . . . we at least have the decency to wait until they're dead.'

'Decency!' said Stege. 'You must be joking!'

Porta at once rounded on him.

'You keep out of it, pansy face! Get back to your books and mind your own bleeding business!'

Stege merely shrugged an indifferent shoulder and turned away. He was accustomed to a constant stream of abuse from people such as Porta.

We were some considerable way behind the Russian lines when the Old Man suddenly brought us to a halt and stood pointing into a ravine at the side of the road.

'Something down there,' he said, tersely.

Tiny and the Legionnaire pushed their way through the bushes and lay flat on their bellies, staring down over the edge of the ravine. The Legionnaire turned and waved.

'It's O.K. . . . . they're pals of ours! Come and take a look!'

We all moved forward through the bushes, staring over in our turn.

'Pals?' queried the Old Man, gravely looking down at the five corpses.

'Yeah, and they didn't fall and they weren't pushed,' said Porta. 'Shot in the back of the neck, that's what they were, poor sods.'

'What's that pinned on 'em?' demanded Tiny. 'There's a bit of paper stuck on their chests.'

Porta scrambled down the side of the ravine and came back clutching one of the pieces of paper. On it was written in Russian: 'Traitor to his Country'.

'All that hard work for nothing,' muttered Barcelona, regretfully. 'Makes you wonder if it was worth it, doesn't it?'

The lieutenant's not there,' said the Old Man. 'I suppose he might have got away—'

'They're more likely reserving V.I.P. treatment for him, seeing he's an officer.'

'Poor bastard . . .'

'Jesus Christ!' said Heide. 'Why waste your tears on that lousy load of scum? If I'd known what was going on I'd have shot 'em all myself, I've said that ever since the start.'

Barcelona looked at him through narrowed eyes.

'People like you,' he said, contemptuously, 'always lose out in the end. You know that? They always do. I've known others of your type. When I was in Spain there were several of 'em. Great loud-mouthed cunts that never knew when to stop.' He shook his head. 'They're all under ground now. Where they belong. They asked for it and they got it. And so will you, in the end.'

'Only you won't be here to see it!' hissed Heide.

It was almost daylight when we arrived back at our own lines. Everything was quiet, and we settled down comfortably in the trenches and prepared for a rest. We kept an eye open for surprise attacks by the Russians, who were fond of that sort of thing, but they showed no signs of aggression.

'If you're all sitting comfortably,' said Lt. Ohlsen, in a friendly 'once-upon-a-time' sort of voice, 'I'll tell you a story.' We looked at him suspiciously. 'I've kept it until now as a nice

surprise for you . . . You'll be pleased to hear that the Colonel
has overcome his stagefright and has renewed his invitation to
the Company to present itself for inspection tomorrow morning
. . .' Our faces fell. We looked down at our black hands and our
filthy uniforms, and Lt. Ohlsen beamed round upon us. 'There.
I knew you'd be over-joyed. I said to Lt. Spät at the time, I
can hardly wait to tell them. I can hardly wait to see their little
faces light up and the tears of gratitude come into their
eyes—'

'Like fuck!' said Porta. He spat out a mouthful of sunflower
seeds that he was chewing. 'Jesus Christ almighty, where do
they dig up these cretins, for God's sake?'

Lt. Ohlsen shook his head, looking suddenly weary. He
pursed his lips together and there was a hard streak in his eyes
and bitter lines round his mouth. Despite the bantering tone he
had used to break the news to us, you could tell that the Colonel
and his autocratic stupidity had brought him almost to breaking point.

Porta, meanwhile, went raving on. He was a great talker
when once he got started, and although his choice of adjectives
tended to be limited he delivered them with such vehemence
that we never tired of hearing them. Having told us all very
forcibly exactly what he thought of the Colonel, and of the
Colonel's parents and the Colonel's grandparents, and having
gone on to suggest in graphic detail several alternative courses
of action open to the Colonel (suggestions which ranged from
the mildly indecent to the grossly obscene) he then switched
abruptly to a better humour and fell to hectoring Tiny, always
the butt of Porta's heavy-handed wit.

'Look at you!' he roared. 'Call yourself a soldier! You're
nothing but a bleeding disgrace! Look at that uniform – that
was in good nick when you first had it. Look at it now – knackered! Completely bloody knackered! Half the buttons off of it,
covered in shit, all tattered and torn – how the hell have you got
it in that state, anyway? You been fighting again, have you?
You ought to be ashamed of yourself, getting into that horrible
state . . . And what about your tin hat, eh? Where's that gone?
And what about that nice gas mask they give you? You've gone
and lost it, haven't you?' He made a gesture of disgust. 'What's

75

the use, eh? I ask you, what IS the use of giving people like him lovely new uniforms, when all they do is go and mess 'em up? Is it any wonder the poor bleeding Colonel has to go and disturb himself giving us the once-over when we got people like you stinking the place out?'

He leaned forward to the startled Tiny.

'When did you last wash your bum, that's what I'd like to know . . . it's bleeding horrible! I bet if you took your knickers down and had a look you'd find it full of bloody great clinkers . . . and we have to live with it! Us, what's managed to keep ourselves clean and decent and not ponging like a million arseholes!'

He stared round at the rest of us; stinking, louse-ridden and dirt-encrusted.

'We're decent enough blokes,' he said, virtuously. 'We're used to certain standards of hygiene. Like the Colonel. That's why he has to call inspections in the middle of the war and make sure we've not got ingrowing toenails nor fungus in our belly buttons.' He stared very hard at Tiny. 'These things are important, you know. You might think it's more important to stay down here in the trenches and keep an eye on them Russkies over there. In case they take advantage of our absence, like. But that's where you'd be wrong, see. 'Cos unless you're a nice clean soldier what brushes out his pubic hairs now and again and stops to polish up his perishing buttons before he goes into an attack, you won't be FIT to fight the bleeding Russkies! How do you think a Russian's going to feel if he sees a scarecrow like you coming at him with a bayonet? He won't be able to take you serious, will he? I mean, he can't be expected to, can he? I mean, let's be reasonable about it. A perishing dirty great lout like you, what can be smelt stinking for bleeding miles around . . . he'd laugh his bleeding bollocks off!'

'No, he wouldn't,' objected Tiny, who as usual had followed the whole of Porta's argument with the utmost seriousness.

'What you mean, he wouldn't? Course he would! Anyone would!'

'Well, they bloody wouldn't, so that's just where you're wrong!' Tiny pointed triumphantly at Porta. ' 'Cos I'd have stuck the bayonet in 'em before they had a chance, wouldn't I?'

Porta turned to the rest of us with a wide gesture of despair, and we looked at Tiny's face, puckered with bewilderment, even now not too sure whether he had scored a point, and we fell about laughing. Even Lt. Spät was grinning. Lt. Ohlsen was the only one to keep a straight face. I was not even sure that he had been listening. He was staring along the lines, watching men who were dog tired, who had been under constant pressure and without sleep for days on end, painfully scrubbing themselves with icy water. There were no towels for drying. There was no soap, there were no razors. Uniforms that were beyond all hope of cleaning or repair were being sponged down in pathetic attempts to make them fit for the Colonel's inspection. Equipment was being polished on pieces of filthy rag.

As our laughter died away, we followed Lt. Ohlsen's gaze, reflecting in sombre bitterness that soon we ourselves should have to put our protesting bodies to work and begin on our own spit and polish. I looked across at the Lieutenant and saw a muscle twitch in his face.

'Great screaming queen,' he suddenly muttered, through clenched teeth. 'Stupid sodding pig-headed bird-brained bastard!'

A sudden shocked silence came upon us. We stared at the Lieutenant, stunned by the vehemence in his voice. It was not so much what he said that startled us – God knows, compared with Porta's more choice expressions his language was mild indeed – but more the way he said it. We had known the Lieutenant in his moments of anger and exasperation, we had known him impatient, we had known him sarcastic, but this was the cold, grim, almost desperate bitterness of a man who has taken just about as much as he can stand, and even Porta was moved to silence.

Ohlsen turned slowly to look at us. He shrugged his shoulders apologetically and rubbed a hand across his brow.

'Sorry,' he said, abruptly. 'It gets you down at times.'

'What can one do?' muttered Spät. 'They treat you like machines, only you're not machines, you're human beings, and now and again something happens that reminds you of it, and then you feel so damned sick at the things you have to do . . .'

The inspection took place the following morning as planned. We lined up like a load of renovated scarecrows. Any officer who had been at the front as long as we had would have been agreeably surprised by our appearance. We had indeed wrought miracles. At the risk of catching pneumonia, we had bathed in pools of icy water. A certain amount of dirt was still engrimed, but the top layer at least had been removed. Our uniforms were still damp and creased, but the few buttons that remained were highly polished and gleamed quite indecently bright in the pale morning sunshine. Altogether it was a brave show, and we felt that we deserved commendation.

Unfortunately, Colonel von Vergil, being fresh out from a home billet, set far higher standards than any fighting officer. He raged over torn uniforms, he fumed over missing buttons, and he became almost apoplectic over the state of our boots. His own were shining like any looking glass, but when Lt. Ohlsen asked him whether we were supposed to carry tins of polish into the trenches with us, in preference to boxes of ammunition, he dismissed the question as being both irrelevant and insubordinate.

Another inspection was called for the following day, and when that also failed to satisfy him we were hauled back the next day, and the next day, and the next. It was a wearisome farce that exhausted everyone to no purpose and cost the life of at least one man, who collapsed with a haemorrhage as his section was being forced to crawl five miles on their stomachs, dragging gas masks and full equipment with them. Lt. Ohlsen was almost out of his mind, but the Colonel had the immovable obsession of the insane and there was nothing to be done. We tried on several occasions to contact our Regiment, but without success: the entire front was in a state of confusion and most of the lines of communication had been cut.

When the idea of constant inspections began to lose its appeal, the Colonel hit on the fresh notion of sending us out on endless and increasingly pointless patrols. And never a day passed but Lt. Ohlsen had to make the hazardous journey from the trenches to the Colonel's headquarters to answer a string of meaningless questions.

It was fortunate, during this period, that the Russians were apathetic and for the most part left us alone. We had regular exchanges of sniper fire, but these, I think, were conducted on both sides more for show than anything else. Further away towards the north we knew that there must be very heavy fighting. We heard the sounds of gunfire and explosions both by day and night, and the sky was almost always a blaze of fire on the horizon.

'It's got to come our way soon,' muttered Heide, pessimistically. 'We've had it easy long enough.'

'Easy?' Porta gave a derisive laugh. 'You call it easy, living with that nut breathing down your neck the whole time? I'd rather have a skirmish with the Russians and be done with it!'

'Don't worry,' said Tiny, confidently. 'I reckon the war'll be over pretty soon. You and me'll be back home within a couple of months.'

The little Legionnaire opened one eye and raised a sardonic eyebrow.

'Don't you kid yourself . . . this war's going on a lot longer than a couple of months.'

There was a wild shout, as Barcelona came running up.

'They've broken through on the left flank! It's started up again!'

The Old Man sighed. He calmly knocked out his pipe and stood up.

'Ah, well, we knew it had to happen. Silence is only made to be broken.'

Already Lt. Ohlsen was shouting orders. Already the scene was breaking up into that confusion which leads eventually to a strict order where every man has his place and knows what he must do. We picked up our weapons, began checking them, cramming our helmets on our heads, preparing once more for action. Those sections which had been resting were brutally woken and came up at a run, stumbling and yawning and still not too sure what was about to happen. Behind us, we could hear the crack of rifles and the explosions of mines and hand grenades. Lt. Ohlsen turned to Spät.

'Stay here with the first section and keep the road clear.

We'll need you to cover us on the way back. The rest of the Company, come with me.'

We fell in behind him, single file. As we moved forward, we stumbled on two men of the Colonel's battalion, hiding behind some rocks and half dead with terror.

'Come on, come on, buck your ideas up!' Lt. Ohlsen nagged them to their feet and pushed impatiently at them with the butt of his PM as they stood shivering and incoherent before him. 'What happened? Where are the rest of your section?'

'Gone—'

They shook their heads, still dumb with fright.

'Gone where? You mean they're dead or they've run off or what?'

'The Russians came at us – suddenly – out of nowhere . . .'

They babbled to a halt. Only by dint of much coaxing and bullying did Lieutenant Ohlsen prise the story out of them.

It appeared that despite persistent warnings from one or two front line veterans, Colonel von Vergil had seen no necessity for having more than a couple of men on guard. The experienced soldiers had been contemptuously dismissed as cowards and old women, and the Colonel had given it as his opinion that the Russians were on the point of packing up and going home after their last abortive attack and the comparative silence of the past few days. Only yesterday he had been overheard telling the Adjutant that in fact there was far more danger back home in Germany, from R.A.F. bombing raids, than he had yet to meet at the front. The result was that when the Russians ultimately launched the attack that we (but not the Colonel) had been expecting, they met with virtually no resistance. The two men on guard had apparently been taken by surprise, since they had not sounded the alarm, and according to the two babbling survivors – who frankly confessed they were still alive only because they had taken to their heels – the whole attack had been incredibly rapid and incredibly silent. No guns or grenades had been used, only bayonets and kandras.

'So in other words, it was a massacre?' demanded Lt. Ohlsen, grimly.

'Yes, yes!' they cried, eager to impress upon us the ghastliness of the experience.

And one, perhaps wishing to show that they had not given in without a struggle, however, did add that Lt. Kalb had managed to throw one hand grenade before being run through with a bayonet.

'I see.' Lt. Ohlsen stared up the path that led to the Colonel's chalet. He turned back to the survivors. 'And – ah – how about the Colonel?' he asked, casually.

They didn't know: they hadn't seen the Colonel.

'Let's hope they stuck a bayonet up his backside,' muttered Porta.

'Perhaps,' suggested Tiny, 'we ought to hang about down here until they've finished the job? Make bleeding sure of it?'

'Creutzfeldt, keep your voice down!' snapped the Lieutenant. He waved his arm at the column of men and pointed up towards the chalet. 'Follow me, we're going up there.'

We heard the Russians long before we reached the chalet. The sounds they made were familiar to us. They were the joyous sounds of men carousing.

'Pissed to the eyeballs,' murmured Barcelona, with a smile. 'They'll have found the Colonel's wine store.'

'Jesus Christ!' said Tiny, nervously. 'Let's get up there quick before the bastards drink it all!'

As we came in sight of the chalet we could see, as well as hear, evidence of Russian occupation. The windows were open, and through them came snatches of drunken song and a continuous hail of paper, boxes, crockery and German uniforms.

'Look at 'em,' said Porta, half jealous, half contemptuous. 'Call that war? Looks more like a bleeding debauch to me.'

Heide ran a hand caressingly along his rifle.

'You wait till we get stuck in there amongst 'em . . . won't know what's hit 'em till it's all over!'

'Particularly,' added the little Legionnaire, with a grin, 'when they discover we're not the same papier-mâché soldiers as the last lot they had to deal with . . .'

Lt. Ohlsen gave the order to fix bayonets, and we charged. I found myself hurtling up the hill towards the chalet with the Old Man and the Legionnaire by my side, the Lieutenant just ahead of us, Porta and Tiny screaming like savages just behind.

I saw one or two round Russian faces staring open-mouthed in horror as we launched ourselves upon them. They didn't stand a chance, that first lot. We cut straight through them and surged onwards to engage in a vicious hand-to-hand combat which soon became a tangled nightmare of interlocked men, slashing and cutting amongst the corpses of their companions, slipping and squelching in pools of spilt blood, crushing underfoot the writhing bodies of the wounded.

I looked up suddenly to find an enormous Russian lieutenant bearing down upon me. He was wielding his machine gun like a club, and I was able to sidestep the lethal blow just in time. As a purely reflex action, I brought up my bayonet and thrust it blindly at my enemy. There was a moment of resistance, then the blade slid smoothly into the soft flesh of his groin. He fell backwards with a scream, taking my rifle with him. In my terror and my haste to retrieve the weapon, I leaped forward with both feet planted squarely in the face of a wounded man. Whether he was one of ours or one of theirs, I didn't stop to see. I snatched up my rifle and plunged onwards, with his agonized shrieks ringing in my ears.

Now and again, in the hideous confusion, I caught a brief glimpse of one of my own companions. At one point I was dimly aware that Porta was by my side, but then he was swallowed up in the vicious scrum of bodies and disappeared. I fought my way out into the courtyard and saw Tiny. He had lost his gun and a couple of Russians were heading straight for him. I gave a loud yell, but Tiny had already swung round to meet them. With two enormous fists he caught them each by the throat and their heads went crashing together. As they fell, he snatched up one of their guns and began spraying bullets in all directions. We had reached that stage of desperation where it was every man for himself and if you mowed down some of your own side then it was just their hard luck.

I saw a Russian crouching behind a pillar, taking aim with a pistol. Before he had time to fire it, I had blown off half his head, and I watched dispassionately as he crumpled up in a bloody heap.

I turned and saw Porta charging with his bayonet, plunging

it deep into the back of a young Russian who was attempting to run away.

I saw Heide trampling savagely upon the face of a dying man, who even in his last moments of agony was still clutching his gun to his chest.

How many men had been killed, and how long the slaughter had continued, I had no idea. Was it minutes or was it hours before we reassembled, victorious, in the courtyard behind the chalet? At that point we neither knew nor cared. For the moment, it was enough that we had survived.

We threw ourselves to the ground, panting, exhausted, covered in mud and blood, our uniforms torn, our helmets and our weapons tossed wearily to one side. Some of the youngest of the new recruits had tears rolling down their cheeks and making channels in the grime. For the rest of us, once the first shock of being still alive had worn off, we began searching with blood-shot eyes for our companions. Were they still with us? Or were they lying inside in the charnel house with their guts ripped out or their heads blown off?

I saw Barcelona a few yards away, stretched out full length, his uniform in ribbons. The Old Man was leaning against a tree trunk, smoking his inevitable pipe. Tiny and Heide were still there, Heide with his eyes closed, Tiny in a quite indescribable mess, looking as if he had dipped his head in a bucket of blood. My gaze roamed further afield and I saw Stege, lying on his back and staring bleakly up at the clouds overhead. And there was the Legionnaire, sitting on some steps smoking a cigarette and already hard at work stripping down his gun ready for the next action. The Legionnaire was a professional soldier. He had been fighting for fifteen years and his first thought was always for his weapons. Further off were Porta and Steiner, sharing a bottle of spirits they had found somewhere. Steiner looked to be already half drunk.

They were all there. All the old hands, the ones who had lived through it before and were still here to tell the tale. But over a third of the new recruits had gone. Their bodies lay where they had fallen, sad islands of death amongst the survivors. Someone hesitantly suggested that we might bury them,

83

but we took no notice. Why tax our strength any further, digging holes for corpses? We were alive and exhausted, while they were dead and could feel no more.

Lt. Ohlsen came out of the chalet. He had lost his helmet and had a deep gash running from the corner of his eye to his mouth. He sank to the ground, and we looked at him expectantly. He hunched a shoulder.

'They were all dead before we got here.'

Porta gave him a cigarette.

'How about the Colonel, Sir?'

'Him as well . . . his throat was slit from ear to ear.'

There was a silence, then a malicious grin spread itself across Porta's lips.

'Maybe there is a God after all,' he muttered.

The Lieutenant frowned and turned to Heide.

'Take two or three men and go and collect all the identification discs.'

'What, Russians as well?' demanded Heide.

'Of course. You ought to know that without being told.'

As soon as Heide had completed his task, we set fire to the chalet and made our way back to the road, losing more men as we did so, thanks to the Russians waking up again and pounding us with mortars.

'Always us,' grumbled Porta, running for cover. 'Anything goes wrong, and it's always us that gets caught up in it.'

Tiny and the Legionnaire were already setting up the heavy machine gun. Lieutenant Ohlsen turned back to wave an impatient hand at the new recruits, who were lagging behind, uncertain whether to follow the rest of us up the road or dive into the nearest shell hole.

'Stop dithering and get a move on, for God's sake! This is no time to hang about admiring the bloody scenery!'

They shambled forward like a load of terrified sheep. One suddenly gave a shrill howl of pain and began running in circles, both hands pressed to his abdomen. Sanitätsgefreiter Berg at once turned back for him. He dragged the boy to the side of the road and tore open his uniform, but he was too late, he was already dead.

We watched as Berg slung his Red Cross bag over his shoulder and ran forward to rejoin us. Shells landed before and behind him. His helmet was blown off his head and he staggered from the blast, but somehow he made it. A loud cheer went up. Berg was deservedly popular. We had watched on many occasions as he risked his life to help an injured man, caught in enemy fire as he lay wounded in the middle of a mine field or tangled on the barbed wire. I remembered at Sebastopol, when Berg had deliberately gone back into a burning building and staggered through the inferno with an unconscious Lieutenant Hinka slung over his shoulders. He had been offered the Iron Cross for that particular exploit, but had politely refused it, saying that he had no interest in collecting scrap iron. Two years later, his uniform was still bare of any form of decoration save his Red Cross medal.

The Company eventually staggered to relative safety in a thickly forested area which projected beyond the mountains like a wooded fjord. We were on our own once again: the battalion from Breslau had been completely wiped out.

We had been on the same train for several days, ever since leaving the front, and we had stopped at many stations. Frequently we had been shunted into sidings and left there for hours on end, to make way for trains carrying more important cargoes – arms or ammunitions, perhaps. We were only soldiers returning home, and therefore fairly far down on the list of priorities.

Now, on the seventh day of our journey, we had come to yet another stop. The train shuddered to a halt and for several minutes we stayed where we were, sitting on the straw in our cattle truck, too lethargic even to open our eyes. After a while, Porta stirred himself sufficiently to pull open the sliding door and have a look outside.

'Hamburg!' He turned back to the rest of us. 'We're in Hamburg!'

'Hamburg?'

We cheered up slightly. The Legionnaire stretched luxuriously and the Old Man was moved to pull out his pipe and stick it in his mouth.

'It's Whitsun,' he told us, suddenly.

We all looked at him.

'So what?' said Heide. 'What's Whitsun got to do with anything?'

The Old Man shrugged his shoulders.

'I don't know . . . it just occurred to me . . .'

'This time last year,' said Porta, 'we were at Demnanks.'

'And the year before that,' added Tiny, 'it was Brest-Litovsk. Do you remember Brest-Litovsk? Do you remember—'

'Put a sock in it!' said the Legionnaire, irritably. 'I wish you wouldn't keep looking backwards all the time, it's morbid and unnecessary. Why can't you try looking forward for a change?'

'All right, if that's what you want . . .' Porta closed his eyes a moment, and a smile of beatific lechery appeared on his lips. 'First thing I do tonight, when they let us out of here, is find me a brothel . . . How about that? That appeal to you?'

From the cheers that went up from the assembled company, it seemed that it did!

86

CHAPTER THREE

Hamburg

WE were sitting in the canteen, waiting for Barcelona. We had been sitting in there for some time, and one or two of us – notably Porta and Tiny – were well on the way to becoming exceedingly, gloriously drunk.

The place smelt of stale beer and frying, and the air was thick and heavy with cigarette smoke. The serving women, rushed off their feet and in no very good mood, were deliberately making as much noise as possible, throwing piles of knives and forks into the sink and clattering the crockery on the draining board. They grumbled incessantly as they worked.

Porta, prompted by God knows what drunken whim, suddenly leaned across the table and pointed an accusing finger at a Dutch SS man, who had been sitting in a peaceful coma, minding his own business, ever since we had been there.

'Look at the ugly great swine,' he said, his voice slightly blurred by drink. He turned to the rest of us, and with a gesture invited us to inspect the unfortunate man. 'Look at his sodding great ears! If there's one thing I can't stand, it's ears that look as if they're about to take off.'

I stared with interest at the man's ears. They certainly had a tendency to stand out at right angles from his head, but perhaps I hadn't yet drunk enough to see this as sufficient reason for pitching into him.

A girl came up with a tray of beer mugs. She slapped them down before us, and the beer frothed over the edge and made a great stinking lake over the table. Porta planted both elbows in it and turned his attentions to more likely prey, a young soldier wearing the silver insignia of the SD* on his collar. The Dutch SS man had remained totally unmoved by the reference to his ears, and was probably even more drunk than Porta, but the young soldier was already looking nervous.

'Listen, you bastard—' Porta blew his nose loudly between finger and thumb and wiped it across his sleeve – 'I got a knife here. We all got knives. Me and my friends, we all got knives . . . You know what for? You know what we use 'em for?'

The SD man turned away and wisely kept his mouth shut, but Porta was out to annoy someone and he dragged the man round to face him again.

'You want me to show you?' he asked, with a revolting leer. 'We use 'em for cutting things off . . . You want me to show you what it is we cut off?'

He made an obscene gesture in the air, and Tiny obligingly guffawed.

'Really, I'm not in the least interested in your wretched knives,' said the man, and he yawned and turned away again.

His attempt to assume an air of lofty disdain merely provoked Porta into a drunken fury. He brought his fist crashing down on to the table. All the beer mugs jumped and rattled and a fresh wave of beer came slopping over the edge.

'Why don't you bugger off and leave us alone?' shouted Porta. 'What right have you got to sit here at our table, you filthy swine? Get out of it before I throw you out!'

I picked up my half empty beer mug and watched the scene unfold with a fuddled, and consequently somewhat dispassionate, interest. The Legionnaire leaned back and crossed his legs at the ankle, sliding half out of his chair. The Old Man was staring mournfully into his beer mug. Tiny seemed the only other person to be really very much interested.

The SD man voiced what seemed to me, in the circumstances, a mild and reasonable objection to Porta's rude hectoring.

'I was here first, you know . . . And I really don't think it's up to you to give the orders.'

Porta snorted and spat.

* Sicherheitsdienst – Security Service

'So what if you've been here since the beginning of the bleeding war? I'm telling you, now, to get the hell out of it!'

'And I'm telling you,' retorted the SD man, growing pardonably exasperated, 'that I shall do no such thing!'

Porta looked round wildly at Tiny for support.

'Insubordination! You heard that, did you? Refusing to obey the orders of a Stabsgefreiter!' He staggered to his feet, thrust out an arm and pushed it under the man's nose. 'You see that?' He jabbed a finger at his stripes. 'You know what they mean, I suppose?'

The SD merely took hold of the arm between finger and thumb and delicately swung it back towards Porta, screwing up his nose as if he could smell a bad smell – which he most likely could.

'Well, bugger me!' cried Porta, growing ever more excited. 'If that don't beat all! You see that, did you?' He turned again to Tiny, who nodded eagerly and pushed back his chair. 'Make a note of it! Take his name and number! He used violence on a Stabsgefreiter . . . Go on, get it wrote down!'

'Fuck off,' said Tiny, sullenly. 'You know I can't bleeding write.'

'Then take him outside and beat the living daylights out of him!'

'Look here, you uncouth bastard—'

The SD man rose to his feet, and Tiny rose with him. They faced each other across the table. Tiny scratched his enormous chest, hitched up his trousers, reached out a hand and closed it over the man's collar.

'Come on, little one . . . let's go talk outside.'

The SD man opened his mouth to shout, but such was the pressure of Tiny's vast paw that only a strangulated squawk came out. Tiny frogmarched him to the door and Porta sat down again, red in the face and still angry.

The Dutch SS man was now lying across the table with his head in a pool of beer.

'Look at that,' I said, to the Legionnaire. 'He's passed out.'

And I laughed hilariously, as if it were the funniest thing in the whole world. The Legionnaire, who rarely if ever lost control, merely smiled pityingly at me.

A few moments later, Tiny reappeared – alone.

'Where's he gone?' I said.

'Lying in the gutter,' said Tiny. He sent his fist crashing into the palm of his hand and winked at me. 'Out like a light first go ... Hey!' He looked round at the Legionnaire. 'You remember the day you and me first met?'

'I remember,' said the Legionnaire.

'What happened?' I asked, just sufficiently drunk to be obliging and give Tiny the chance to show off.

By way of reply, he grabbed my hand as if to shake it in normal greeting and slowly began crushing it until I gave a loud yell of pain.

'That's what happened,' said Tiny, proudly.

'Very amusing,' I said, shaking my hand up and down. 'What's the point of it?'

'Ah,' said Tiny, winking. 'That'd be telling, wouldn't it?'

The Legionnaire gave one of his patronizing smiles and shook his head at me.

'Allow him his little moment of glory,' he murmured.

'Well, that's what happened!' protested Tiny.

'Of course it is,' agreed the Legionnaire, smoothly. 'But never again, my friend! I don't get caught twice the same way!'

'Nor me,' I grumbled, tucking my injured hand beneath my armpit.

Porta was banging on the table again, calling loudly and lewdly for more beer. The girls just sniffed and turned their backs on him, but Big Helga, the superintendent, left her place behind the counter and came storming over to our table. She placed herself before Porta, legs apart and arms akimbo, her vast body a mass of indignant ripples.

'How dare you call my girls by such names? What do you think this is, a brothel?'

'Brothel, my anus!' retorted Porta. 'With a scabby crew like that? Times might be hard, darling, but nobody's that desperate!'

'I shall report you,' said Big Helga, as she said many times a day to many different soldiers. 'We do a good job here, and I'd like to know where you lot would be without us.'

'I could tell you,' said Porta.

Big Helga took a step away from him.

'They're all good girls here, and Gertrude, let me tell you, has a boyfriend in the SD. If there's any more lip from you people I shall have her report you.'

'Ah, stop bellyaching!' said Tiny. 'You know you love us, really.'

'All we want is some more beer,' I added. 'Anyone'd think we'd asked for six whores, the way she's carrying on.'

Big Helga just sniffed and went back to the counter. She picked out Gerda, the least attractive of a rather poor bunch, and grudgingly sent her over to us with the order. Gerda wasn't a bad girl, but they didn't call her 'Beanstick' for nothing. She was the nearest thing to an animated telegraph pole I ever saw.

'If you only had a bit more bum on you, I'd be almost tempted to take you to bed with me,' murmured Tiny, regretfully sliding a hand up Gerda's skirt and trying to feel her non-existent bottom.

Gerda showed what she thought of this invitation by slamming the tray hard on to Tiny's head and stalking away again.

At this point we were rejoined by Barcelona, who brought the unwelcome news that we were on guard duty as from that evening.

Barcelona was wearing an enormous bandage round his neck, which obliged him to hold his head stiff and straight. During our last days in the mountains he had been wounded in the throat by a stray hand grenade, and he had now been temporarily exempted from active service. He could, and should, have stayed in hospital, but thanks to Lt. Ohlsen pulling a few strings he had been allowed to come back to the Company and take up duty in the orderly room – not that he was very often to be found in the orderly room. He was more frequently in the canteen or the armoury.

There were people who thought he was a fool for not having taken advantage of a few months' rest in hospital, but Barcelona had been in the Army long enough to know that once in hospital and separated from your comrades almost anything was liable to happen to you on your discharge. The chances of being sent back to your own company were remote, and in these days of the war it was almost certain death to be the newcomer in an established group of people. All the worst and most dangerous tasks would automatically come your way, and death seemed to be a foregone conclusion.

'Jesus!' said Barcelona, looking at the table with its array of beer mugs. 'You've been packing it away, haven't you?'

'Never mind that,' said Porta. 'What I want to know is, where we're supposed to be on guard duty . . . I wouldn't mind the local brothel—'

'No such luck.' Barcelona shook his head and picked up someone's beer mug. 'It's the perishing Gestapo.'

'What fool thought that one up?' demanded the Legionnaire.

Barcelona hunched a shoulder and threw a sheet of paper on to the table. The Old Man prised it up from a pool of beer and looked at it indifferently.

'Nineteen hundred hours . . . Place Karl Muck, Hamburg . . .'

Gloomily he folded the paper and put it in his top pocket. Steiner came suddenly to life and glared at Barcelona as if he personally had made the arrangements.

'Bloody Gestapo!'

'Don't look at me,' said Barcelona. 'I'm not the clown who thought it up . . . Anyway, just thank your lucky stars it's nothing worse. The Fourth Section's on duty at Fuhlsbüttel . . . execution squad for the Wehrmacht.'

'I wouldn't mind swopping,' said Tiny, perverse as ever. 'There's always the chance of picking up a bit of extra lolly on executions. We've done it before now, let's face it . . .'

'How?' demanded Stege, suspiciously. 'How have you done it?'

'Easy. You promise some guy his life and he's willing to give you anything you ask for.'

'You mean you'd take money from a condemned man?' said Stege, sounding as if he could hardly believe his ears.

'Well, and why not?' said Tiny, aggressively. 'You'd be willing to pay someone for getting you off the hook, I bet.'

'Any case,' added Porta, 'it ain't that easy. They find out what you're up to and you'd be for the high jump yourself.'

Stege opened his mouth to protest, but before he could speak Heide had woken from a deep sleep and found himself confronted by a solid wall of empty beer mugs. He swept them away, angrily.

'We've drunk too much!' He belched and reached out for the nearest full mug. 'How did we get through all that lot?'

'Beside the point,' said Tiny. 'We did, and that's all that matters . . . apart from the fact that it's you what's going to pay for them. You're the only one with money.'

'Me? I'm broke!' said Heide, at once.

'Like hell! You've got a whole wad stuck down the inside of your boot!'

Heide looked at him incredulously.

'How do you know that?'

Tiny shrugged his shoulders.

'I had a look, didn't I? I wanted some money the other day, so I went through your cupboard. It's the only one with a faulty lock, you ought to get it looked at. Doesn't close right, you see.'

'You mean you deliberately went through my things?'

'Yeah. I suppose you could put it that way.'

'So it was you nicked that 100 marks?'

'Now, look,' said Tiny, 'just watch it, mate. I never said I took nothing, did I?'

'But it's bloody obvious you did!'

Tiny sneered.

'Try and prove it!'

'I don't have to prove it! You've as good as admitted it . . . By God, you're not going to get away with this!' warned Heide, his face sheet white with rage. 'I'll see you in Torgau if it's the last thing I ever do. I'll see you hang for this. I'll see you—'

'For Christ's sake,' said the Legionnaire, languidly, 'does it really matter?'

'It does to me!' snarled Heide.

'Look here,' said Porta, as if suddenly possessed of an idea that would solve the entire problem, 'why don't we take a few bottles of booze on duty with us? Old Beanstick wouldn't mind slipping them to us under the counter.'

'Yeah? And what do we do with 'em when we get to Karl Muck?'

'Stash 'em away somewhere safe. It's O.K. I know one of the boys that's been on guard duty there just recently, he says it's a real doddle of a place. Right down in the cellars, like. Nobody ever bothers to come and take a look at what you're doing.'

'What about the cells?' Steiner wanted to know.

'What about them? None of the prisoners ain't never there for more than one night. Most of 'em are got rid of the following morning. The ones the Gestapo want to pull about a bit, they take up top with 'em. More convenient. Saves 'em running up and down the stairs every time they feel like yanking a few finger nails out ... You don't want to worry about the cells. The prisoners won't bother us none.'

'How about that statue of the Emperor on his horse?' suggested Heide suddenly forgetting his hundred marks and taking an interest in Porta's idea. 'The legs are hollow. I bet you could stuff quite a few bottles up there and no one'd notice.'

'I already thought of that,' claimed Tiny. 'I was just about to say it myself. I always think of good places for hiding things in ... That's why I looked in your boots that time,' he confided to Heide, who at once relapsed into fierce sulks.

'We'll get half a dozen large bottles,' decided Porta. 'We'll have a mixture.' He beckoned to Gerda, who peeled herself away from the side of the counter and suspiciously approached us. 'Six bottles,' he told her. 'Dortmunder up to there—' He showed her with fingers and thumb held apart – 'and the rest, Slibowitz. That O.K.?'

She shrugged.

'If you say so. I shouldn't fancy it myself, but there's no accounting for some people's tastes, is there?'

She turned away with a sniff, and Porta rubbed his hands together and looked towards the Legionnaire for confirmation.

'That's right, ain't it? Put the beer in first, then the Slibowitz?'

The Legionnaire inclined his head, an expression of faint amusement on his face, as if he were watching a crowd of children.

Gerda came back with the first bottle, shaking it vigorously to mix the two liquids. Porta snatched it from her, horrified.

'What the bleeding hell are you trying to do? Blow us all up?'

'With any luck,' she said, sourly.

She brought the rest of the bottles, banged them noisily on to the table and silently held out her hand for the money. She stood there counting it and checking every bank note to make sure it was not a forgery. While she was doing so, Steiner came out of the bog. He stood by the table, belching and doing up his flies, regardless of Gerda still counting her money.

'Nothing more satisfying than a good slash,' he informed us, with a sigh of contentment. 'Specially when you've held on to it a bit . . .'

He picked up his beer mug and emptied it in a few quick gulps, his Adam's apple bouncing vigorously up and down his throat. He then belched again and wiped his lips along the back of his sleeve. Gerda gave him a long, slow look of contempt, placed the money in a bag she wore beneath her apron and marched away from us, her back held very straight.

'What's satisfying about it?' demanded Porta, who was in a mood to quarrel with anyone over anything, no matter how banal.

Steiner looked at him.

'What d'you mean, what's satisfying? You've pissed often enough, haven't you? You bloody well ought to know what's satisfying about it.'

'Well, I don't,' said Porta. 'What's the matter with you, anyway? You kinky or something? You some kind of a pervert? You—'

'Ah, fuck off!' said Steiner, trying to sit down and discovering that Porta had spread himself out over half the bench.

Porta banged his beer mug on to the table and staggered to his feet.

'Nobody tells me to eff off and gets away with it!' he roared.

He swung an arm wildly in Steiner's direction. Steiner ducked and promptly retaliated, catching Porta a blow on the side of the head. Porta stepped backwards, knocking over the bench, and Steiner followed him, his arms going like piston rods. For a few moments they fought each other in dedicated silence, merely tossing off the occasional oath to encourage themselves, and then Steiner, growing suddenly adventurous, picked up a beer mug and hurled it at Porta's head. Porta bent sideways and the missile flew past him and smashed into the far wall.

Immediately, Gerda was upon us, a large wooden truncheon clasped in her hand.

'Who threw that beer mug?'

Enthusiastically, we pointed to Steiner. Gerda, without a second's hesitation, brought her truncheon crashing down upon his shoulder, and while Steiner was reeling from the blow she followed it up with a quick chop to the head.

Steiner promptly forgot his quarrel with Porta. Howling with pain and indignation, he turned upon Gerda, who took to her heels and fled for the comparative safety of the counter. Steiner plunged after her, turning over tables and chairs as he galloped after her across the room. He caught up with her just before she reached the counter, and pushing her hard against the wall he began thumping her head backwards and forwards against it. Gerda fought like a tigress, biting, scratching and kicking, using her teeth, her nails, her knees, anything that was handy, and all the while howling at the top of her voice.

Suddenly, the door behind the counter opened and Big Helga appeared. She took in the situation at a glance, calmly picked up a champagne bottle and sallied forth to join in the action.

Steiner was far too preoccupied to notice this new and highly dangerous attack on his right flank. Helga took careful aim and the champagne bottle caught Steiner neatly in the nape of the neck. He crumpled instantly into a sawdust heap, blood and champagne mingling together.

'Murderer!' screamed Helga, kicking him ruthlessly where he lay.

'Sex maniac!' screeched Gerda, snatching up the broken neck of the champagne bottle and attempting to carve open Steiner's face.

With surprising agility for one so enormous, Big Helga prised the broken glass away from her – not that she had any sympathy with Steiner, only that a murder on the premises might not go down too well with the authorities. Gerda had to content herself with a stream of obscenities, the like of which I swear I had never heard before, accompanied by a furious kicking of Steiner's bloody and unconscious body.

The girl named Gertrude, who had a boyfriend in the SD, came staggering up the stairs with a crate of beer in her muscular arms. She had long, lank, tarnished fair hair and a perpetual pus-filled spot on the side of her nose.

Gerda fell eagerly upon her, pointing excitedly to Steiner and shouting something about revenge. Gertrude dumped her case of beer and looked down upon Steiner without much interest.

'What am I supposed to do about it?'

'Tell your boyfriend in the SD!' urged Gerda, aiming another vindictive kick into the small of Steiner's back.

'A la bonne heure*,' replied Gertrude, in French.

She had no idea what the expression meant, but it sounded good and she used it frequently. She had picked it up from a French sailor to whom she had once been engaged for eight days, which was the length of time his boat had been in Hamburg. She had been engaged to many other sailors since then, but she had never forgotten 'à la bonne heure'. If you wanted any special favour from Gerda, you had only to remark, in tones of admiration and wonderment, 'Oh, you speak French, do you?' and she would rise immediately to the bait. Unfortunately, the favour was almost always accompanied by a recital of her favourite fairy tale, of how she had been born into a rich French family and of how they had abandoned her at an early age and left her in a fashionable boarding school, the location of which was vague and could never quite be pinned down; but if you were prepared to hear her out, then she in return was willing to grant you all manner of small favours.

* That's the spirit

Porta and Tiny had once strung her along very successfully for a whole evening, when they had eaten half the food in the canteen and drunk themselves into a near paralytic stupor – and all at Gerda's expense. Mind you, Tiny had paid for it afterwards. On returning to barracks he had suddenly taken a notion into his head to demonstrate to Porta the regulation manner in which an infantryman – and in particular an infantryman belonging to the regiment in which he had himself begun his military career – should fall to the ground on all fours and crawl along on his stomach. As Porta stood watching him, he saw Tiny disappear from view, hurtling groundwards, flat on his stomach, and crashed his head straight into a piece of sharp stone. The stone made a hole the size of a pigeon's egg in Tiny's forehead, and the blood ran in rivers down his face, but he picked himself up and linked arms with Porta, and they rolled back to barracks singing at the tops of their voices:

'Soldaten sind keine Akrobaten!'
(Soldiers are not acrobats.)

The idea seemed to amuse them, and they were still trying unsuccessfully to turn cartwheels when they landed up outside the door of the infirmary and Tiny passed out.

He now, however, was very much alive, and he leaned forward over the beer-slopped table and shouted across to Gerda.

'Hey, Beanstick! You want someone to come and kick his face in for you? Stand me a couple of pints and I'll do it like a shot!'

'Watch it,' growled the Old Man, from the far end of the table.

The Legionnaire stretched out a steely hand and closed it round Tiny's wrist. He shook his head, disapprovingly.

'A joke's a joke, but we don't want a corpse on our hands, do we?'

'Don't we?' Tiny considered the matter. 'Why not?'

'Because they're bloody difficult things to get rid of?' I suggested.

'Why? Why not take 'em down and dump 'em in the water?'

Barcelona gave a short crack of laughter.

'You ever tried marching down to the harbour with a corpse tucked under your arm? You'd have the coppers down on you like a ton of bricks before you were even half-way there.'

While Tiny was digesting this piece of information, Heide suddenly took his nose out of his beer mug to inform us that he was in no mood to stand guard duty that night and had half a mind to go down the road to the 'Matou' to see their renowned whore in the green dress. We had all heard of the lady in question, though speaking for myself I had never seen her in the flesh.

'Mark you, she's expensive,' said Barcelona, gravely.

'But worth it,' said Heide.

'You know old Bernie the Boozer?' Porta leaned forward towards us, his eyes gleaming. 'He told me that for 5,000 he'd spent a whole night and half the next day with her. According to him, he was on the job non-stop and did it sixty-seven times.'

'Like hell!'

'It's true,' insisted Heide. 'I saw him the day after, he hardly had the strength to get out of bed.'

'Ridiculous bloody way to spend your money,' said the Legionnaire.

'Oh, I don't know . . .'

With an obscene smile on his lips and his thoughts obviously far away, Porta pulled out a seagull's egg and cracked it into his beer. With the point of his bayonet, he stirred the mixture dreamily round and round.

I watched him, fascinated.

'Is it good?' I asked.

'Sodding awful,' replied Porta, licking his bayonet clean.

'Tell us that story of the girl you asked to marry you,' suggested the Old Man, leaning back in his chair and filling his pipe. He glanced at his watch. 'We've just got time before we go on duty.'

And he hauled his feet up on the table, settling comfortably in his chair and preparing himself to listen to one of Porta's rambling excursions into story telling – part truth, part invention, and, knowing Porta, I should say the more unlikely passages being the ones that actually did take place.

The rest of us followed the Old Man's example and put our feet up on the table. Steiner was lying on the floor groaning, and we left him to it.

'Well, it was right back at the beginning of the war,' said Porta, coaxing the remains of his egg yolk up the side of the glass with one finger and sliding it into his mouth. 'Before all the fighting broke out. I was with the 11th Regiment at Paderborn . . . Don't know if you've ever been to Paderborn? Flaming horrible, it was. Dead as a bleeding doornail, nothing to do from one day to the next except stand and stare at all the po-faced gits that lived there running off to church every five minutes . . . Not only that, but to tell you the honest truth I wasn't all that struck on the idea of fighting this bleeding war from the word go. Seemed proper daft to me. Shells and bombs and Christ knows what . . . nothing to eat, nothing to drink—' He drew in a breath and shook his head. 'Didn't do nothing for me at all. It's not your scene, I says to myself. It's not your scene, Porta my lad . . . you got to get out of this as quick as you can . . . Well, as you know, I'm not one to sit around on my arse doing nothing. No sooner said than done, that's me . . . So the minute I'd made my mind up, I got this rather serious malady what threatened to do me in.'

The Old Man laughed.

'I'll never forget it . . . God knows what he didn't do to himself to try and get sick. The stuff he ate . . . Christ, it would have felled an elephant! But not this lad. Oh, no! The more he tried, the healthier he got.'

'Yeah, I reckon I got so toughened up you could've bounced me all over a perishing minefield and I'd've come out in one piece.' Porta sucked the egg off his fingers, picked up a leg and farted, then settled back to his story. He grinned at us, knowingly. 'I did it all right in the end, though. I was a bit green in them days, but I wangled my way into the infirmary all right.'

'I remember the infirmary!' cried Tiny, in excitement. 'Stuck away round the back of the Cathedral. They shoved me in there when my big toe swelled up. Enormous, it was. Almost had to take it off.' He turned to Porta. 'Here, you remember that sawbones they had in there? Him with the wooden leg? What was his name?'

'Brettschneider,' said Porta.

'Yeah, Brettschneider, that was the bastard! I remember when I was in there—'

'What about my story?' said Porta, coldly.

Tiny looked at him a moment, then blinked.

'All right,' he said. 'I'm not bothered.'

'Thank you ... Well, like I was saying, I got took off to the infirmary, where I saw this bastard doctor you just mentioned. And he was a bastard, I'll grant you that ... First day I was in there, he comes marching up to me with half the bleeding hospital trailing behind him. They screech to a halt at my bed, and he stands there, coughing in my face and asking me what I'm playing at and what I think's wrong with me. So I explains about how I'm paralysed practically all over and can't feel a thing, and how unfortunate it is, on account of the war starting up, and how I wanted to do my bit, and all that, and all the time he just goes on standing there and coughing – and me paralysed all over,' said Porta, indignantly. 'Paralysed all over and couldn't even move out of the way. Might have had TB or the galloping clap for all I knew ... So anyway, after a bit I gives a sort of groan, like—' Porta gurgled hideously in the back of his throat – 'and he agrees with me about it being unfortunate, and then quite sudden, like, he whips off all the bedclothes and leaves me lying there exposed with all these strangers looking on like I was some sort of specimen been tipped out of its bottle. So then he starts kind of prodding and poking and saying can I feel it and does it hurt, and me just lying there and making like I can't feel a damn thing, and all the time I'm thinking, You're not going to catch me, you bastard, you scum, you lousy stinking medico ... Anyway, after a bit he straightens up and tells everyone how sad it is, this poor soldier going and getting paralysed right at the start of the war ... But never mind, he says to me. I reckon we can put you right again. How did you say it come on? he asks. Sort of sudden, like? Just about the time when war was declared? Like a sort of shock?' Porta looked round at us and closed one eye. 'Stringing me along, see? Making like he was easy to con . . . So I thought I'd pile it on a bit, give it a few details . . . You're right, I says. That was just how it come on, like a sort of shock, all through the body, like you said . . . I was standing in line with the others – we was being kitted out, see – and all of a sudden I come over bad. Real bad. Cold sweat and stars and everything turning round and this horrible kind of ringing in the ears . . . I managed to go another few yards and then I got this paralysis, like, and I just blacked out . . . Oh, I tell you,' said Porta, 'I really laid it on thick. Like I said, I was green in them days . . . I even forced a few tears out and carried on about how bad I felt, not being able to fight and earn medals and how chuffed my poor old mum and dad would've been if their son had been a hero . . . Tell me! I cries, all ardent like, Surely there's some way a man what's paralysed can serve his country and his people and his Führer? . . . You know what the bastard said?'

We shook our heads, obligingly, though some of us had obviously heard it all before in one version or another. Porta spat.

'Oh, yes, he says, you can get up and start walking again just like everyone else has to . . . and with that, he bashes me real hard on the knee cap when I'm not ready for it, and my bleeding leg shoots out and knocks his glasses off . . . Jesus, I don't know who was more mad, him or me . . . So anyway, when he's recovered a bit and they've picked his glasses up for him and stopped sniggering behind their hands, he takes some bloody great long thing off a tray and begins shovelling it down my lughole until I think it's going to come out the other side of my head . . . and when he's finished playing with that, he yanks my eyelids somewhere over the top of my head and has a good long look at my flaming eyeballs, till after a bit – thinking maybe he's colour blind, like – I says, they're blue, and he says, what, and I says blue, fancy having a doctor what's colour blind, and he just curses me all over the bed and starts fishing down my throat looking for my tonsils. God, that bastard had a field day! He was in my mouth, down my ears, up my bum, everywhere he could possibly poke something he bloody poked it—'

'So what happened, in the end?' asked Stege, who was new to the story.

'Hang on a minute, I'm getting there!' said Porta, irritably. He couldn't bear to be interrupted, or urged on to the conclusion before he was ready for it. 'Next thing the bastard does, he stands back and says how sorry he feels for me ... It's enough to break your heart, he says, seeing this young man what's so gravely ill and asks nothing more but being able to serve his people and his country and his Führer ... It might be better, he says, to put you in an isolation ward – like maybe a military prison? But we'll see how you go, he says. It wouldn't surprise me if you was to get better quite sudden. It's the way with these maladies like what you've got. They attack people sudden and they go sudden, especially at times like now, when the country's at war. You'd be surprised, he says, how many other brave boys like you have been struck down in the prime of life this past week or so ... and most of 'em, he says, grinning, like, with his dirty great choppers, most of 'em's already up and about and back with their units ... just like you're going to be.' Porta shook his head. 'What a bastard! Next thing I know, he's trying to get me out of bed – trying to get me to walk, like some bleeding miracle in the bleeding Bible. He has four of 'em haul me out and set me upright, and of course as soon as they lets me go I just collapses on the floor and they has to put me back again. He doesn't like that. You can tell he doesn't. For two pins I reckon he'd have put the boot in and walked off and left me to it. Only he couldn't do that, on account of he was supposed to be curing me, so he sort of pulls his face together and starts telling the sister what sort of treatment she's got to give me ... We'll start off gentle, he says. Nothing too drastic ... Put him on a fluid diet, he says, for a start. No solids. No meat. Right? And of course, no alcohol ... Give him emetics every day, he says, to make him vomit ... Purge him every other day, clean his bowels out ... If that doesn't work, try him on quinine ... but nothing harsh, not just at the moment. We'll see if we can't cure him the easy way first ... And then he grins at me, the bastard, and he leans over the bed and he says, we'll have you out of here and serving at the front in record time, you see if we don't ... we'll have you winning medals yet, he says. You'll have your chance to be a hero, lad ... Honest,' said Porta, 'it was more like a threat than a bleeding promise. So I thanks him very kindly with tears in my eyes, and all the time I'm swearing to God he's not going to get the better of me . . .'

'And does he?' said Stege. 'I mean, did he?'

'Course he did,' said Porta, scornfully. 'With half the bleeding Army trying it on? He could spot them a mile off . . . Took him eleven days to get me back on my feet again. Eleven days of sodding purgatory. He drove me out of that place, you know that? They get you to such a state you'd sooner walk through a perishing minefield than let them go on buggering about with you . . . I remember there were four others in the same ward with me. One had rheumatism, one had kidney trouble, one had lost his memory and one was just a sodding nutter – least, I thought he was. He acted like one all right. Old Brettschneider said he was as sane as anyone else. I dunno, though . . . We were all "cured" at the same time and sent back together to the Regiment. Well, we'd only been back a couple of days when this bloke sticks a gun in his mouth and pulls the trigger. Leaves half his brains splattered about on the ceiling . . . I dunno whether you'd really call that sane . . .'

'It's all very well,' said Stege, 'but you can't blame the doctor. He was only doing his job. He never knows, when he sends a malingerer packing, whether he's going to crack up under the strain—'

'Ah, balls!' said Porta.

'I remember that incident,' put in Barcelona. 'Wasn't it that bastard of a sergeant – what was his name, Gerner, was it? Well, wasn't it him that drove the poor sod to it?'

'Just like he drove many others,' agreed Porta. 'Were you there that time he had a go at Schnitius? You remember Schnitius? The one what ended up having his feet amputated? Well, he used to go round in fear and bleeding trembling of Gerner. Were you there that time he shopped him?'

'It rings a bell,' said Barcelona. 'Something to do with an ashtray, wasn't it?'

'Yeah. That's the one. Gerner come round on one of his inspections – you know what he was like about the place being spotless all the time? Well, he comes round one day and we're all standing to attention as neat as you please without a speck of dust to be seen anywhere, when old Schnitius suddenly discovers he's forgotten to empty his ashtray. Now Gerner doesn't smoke and he goes mad about ashtrays full of fag ends and so forth, so without stopping to think Schnitius picks it up and shoves it under the bolster on his bunk. Anyway, it all goes O.K. until Gerner's just about to leave the room, and suddenly something makes him look round and he sees smoke rising up, like the bolster's on fire. So of course he rushes up, screaming like a bleeding maniac, and it's Schnitius' bed and old Schnitius is standing right by it, so he hasn't got much chance, really ... And Gerner turns on him and says, is that you what's left this shit lying round here? And Schnitius can't very well deny it, so next thing we know Gerner's making him eat up all the ash and the fag ends and the crap and lick out the ashtray into the bargain—'

'Jesus, yes!' cried Barcelona. 'And shortly after that the poor devil spewed up his ring all over the floor of the bog—'

'Yeah, and Gerner comes along and catches him at it and tells him he can bloody well get down on his hands and knees and lick it all up again.'

Steiner, who had been slowly and painfully recovering and had taken his seat in our midst, with a handkerchief pressed to his bleeding head, now quite suddenly transferred the handkerchief to his mouth and turned away, heaving.

I leaned forward eagerly to Porta.

'Did he do it?' I demanded. 'Did he actually do it?'

'Sure he did it,' said Porta. 'He was scared stiff of that bloke.'

I sat back again.

'I wouldn't have done it,' I said.

Porta looked at me.

'Schnitius wasn't full of booze like you are. And he was new to the Army. Didn't know how to stick up for himself ... Anyway, he was still down there on his hands and knees, throwing up again as fast as he cleared one patch up, when the C.O. comes along ... Lt. Henning,' he said to Barcelona. 'He was all right, as officers go, but it used to make him mad when he had to deal with squabbles between the men, like. So he hauls Schnitius into his office and asks him what the devil he thinks he's doing, and Schnitius, like the stupid sod he is, goes and shoots his mouth off about Gerner and the way he's been treating him. So then, of course, the Lieutenant gets madder than ever and calls Hauptfeldwebel Edel into his office and tells him to tear strips off Gerner. And the result is that Gerner gets put in the cooler for ten days and the rest of the N.C.O.s gang up together and beat the hell out of Schnitius for dropping Gerner in the cart. If the fool had had any sense, he'd never have mentioned Gerner in the first place. He'd've said he enjoyed eating spew, or he was just doing it for a lark, or something. Only like I said, we was all so green in them days—'

'Hang on a minute,' interrupted the Old Man. 'I thought you were going to tell us about this girl you asked to marry you?'

'Ah, yes,' said Porta. 'Yes ... well, it was after I'd been driven out of the infirmary. While I was in there I'd seen this bird several times and taken a bit of a fancy to her, like. She used to hang about after Brettschneider when he come round the wards with his little band of followers. I was really quite gone on her. When I got out, I started sending her postcards. First one I sent, I'll always remember that, it was one of them old ones they was bringing out, with some Feldwebel dressed up in old-fashioned gear choking the life out of a Polish dragoon or some such thing. And across the top, in large letters, it said "Vengeance". I remember wondering at the time whether she'd get the message—'

'What message?' said Stege.

'Well – that I wanted to slip her a length, see?'

Stege looked at him.

'And did she get it?' he asked, bewildered.

He had yet to learn that when listening to one of Porta's stories you accepted it as it came, without troubling too much about the internal logic.

'No, I don't think she did at first. Any rate, I didn't hear nothing from her. So in the end I sent one with a message wrote on the back of it. It was this airman, see, sitting on this bench with a bird. And the airman's got his hands tucked down between his thighs, and the bird's making these eyes at him, and on the back I wrote a sort of billy-doo—'

'What did you say?' asked Tiny.

'I don't remember after all this time. I just know I took a lot of trouble with it. I didn't write any old thing. I started off saying how I hoped she wouldn't think it a liberty, me writing to a lady like her from the shitty barracks I was in, only I thought shitty mightn't be the right word, so I crossed it out and wrote Prussian, instead. I took trouble, see? I didn't just put down the first thing what come into my head.'

'I hope she appreciated it,' said Stege.

'You bet she did! Very chuffed, she was ... Probably never been courted like that in her life before. Mind you, she was shy at first. I had to wait days before she'd agree to see me. Then she sent some bloke round with a message and said I could go and call on her if I liked. She lived with her family, of course. An old house in the Bismarckstrasse, it was. I knew I had to create a good impression, so I had a shave, like, and smartened up the old uniform and had a bit of a wash down, and it was just as well I did, 'cos strike me when I got there it was one of them posh places and it was the maid what opened the door to me. All toffee nosed, she was. Wanted to know if I'd got a card she could take in. I don't need no card, I says to her. You ask anyone at Paderborn, I says. I'm very well known round these parts ... So off she goes, walking like she's got a poker up her backside, and leaves me standing there in the hall. While she's gone I has a quick gander round to see what's what, and I take the opportunity to clean up my boots on a velvet cushion what they've got on the sofa. Velvet's one of the best things you can get for polishing boots on, and now I've got clean feet and all I'm really beginning to feel like a gentleman, ain't I?'

'Just a minute,' protested Tiny. 'I thought you said you was in the hall?'

'That's right. That's were she left me.'

'So how come you're using velvet cushions off the sofa to polish your feet on?'

'Because they've got this sodding great sofa in the perishing hall, that's why! Jesus, you can tell you ain't never been anywhere classy. I suppose you think the hall's a farting little passage behind the front door, don't you? Well, it ain't, it's a bleeding big space with furniture and pictures and all, like a flaming room. And where they sit and nosh is different from where they sit and natter. And where they sit and natter ain't downstairs, like you and me's used to, it's up on the first floor. And where—'

'And the bog's got a mink cover on the flaming seat!' jeered Tiny. 'Skip the boring details and just tell us the dirty bits ... What happened next? She come down to this hall what's like a room and you pulled her on to this sofa with the velvet cushions and you got the meat in?'

'Pardon me,' said Porta, 'but I refuse to be rushed. Either you listen to the whole story and nothing but the story and get the artistic bits along with the physical ones, or I give up and you can start telling your own perishing tales. Take it or leave it, mate, but I got my pride same as what Schiller and all that had. You want to appreciate the juicy parts, you got to sit through the rest of it first. Like not having cake till you've had the bread and bleeding butter.'

Tiny retired, grumbling, and telling us to give him a nudge when Porta got to the point where he put the meat in. If ever he did. Steiner turned round with a blood- and vomit-covered handkerchief and looked blearily at us.

'What's going on?' he said.

'Nothing!' Tiny sat up again, triumphantly. 'That's just what I'm complaining of ... NOTHING's going on. If that'd been me, now, I'd have raped her ten times before I'd even got as far as the house. And then I'd have had her on the sofa, and on the velvet cushions, and—'

'But what happened?' I said, to Porta. 'What happened, in the end?'

Porta shrugged his shoulders, sullenly. It was plain that Tiny had upset what he conceived to be his artistic soul and now we should never hear the end of the tale.

'Tell her the bit about asking her father if you could marry her,' urged the Old Man.

'Why?' said Porta. 'It's not funny.'

'That's a matter of opinion,' said the Old Man, who had obviously heard the story many times before.

'Christ almighty!' said Porta, angrily. 'I only asked him if I could have her bleeding hand in bleeding marriage so's we could bleeding have it away together all nice and legal, like! What's so funny about that, then? I could've clobbered her one on a park bench, couldn't I? I could've slipped her a length any flaming time I liked—'

'Pity you didn't,' said Tiny, sourly. 'Might have had a tale worth telling then.'

'I suppose,' I said, 'you never did marry her?'

Porta just gave me a contemptuous stare and turned away.

'Course he didn't!' said Tiny. 'He never married her, he never fucked her, he never did bleeding nothing to her!'

At that moment the loudspeakers began crackling out an order for all Chiefs of Section in the Fifth Company to go to the armaments room for distribution of weapons. The Old Man knocked out his pipe and stood up.

'Time we were off,' he said. 'Who's going to carry Steiner?'

We moved to the door, all of us rather the worse for wear. Tiny was furious with Porta and Porta had reverted to being furious with everyone; Steiner had to be supported by Barcelona and the Legionnaire, and Heide appeared to be walking in his sleep. As we filed past the counter, Gerda's head suddenly sprung up from nowhere, her pale eyes contracted with hatred, her lips drawn back over her long teeth.

'I hope you all fry in hell!' she hissed.

It was the end of a good evening's drinking.

'Look, they can do what they bloody well like,' declared the youth, vaingloriously certain of himself. 'I don't give a tinker's damn for any of 'em! Far as I'm concerned, they can go and get knotted.'

He was sitting on the draining board, his feet in the sink, eating pickled gherkins from a jar. As he spoke, his companions solemnly nodded their agreement and approval. The house was full of young people, boys and girls, all very vociferous and very sure of themselves; sure of their ability to stand out against authority and of their willingness to face death rather than fight for a cause they did not believe in. On the chairs and the tables, stretched out on the floor, squatting in the corners, in the kitchen, the salon, the bedrooms and the bathroom, this band of young rebels shouted their agreement.

'It's not our war!' cried a disembodied voice from beneath a table. 'We didn't start it, we don't want it, and we're not going to fight it!'

'People are dying every day, in their thousands, and the poor fools don't even know what they're dying for—'

'They torture them at the Gestapo. People are scared to open their mouths and tell the truth any more,' declared a young girl who was not quite so young as she looked and was doing her best to seduce a nervous youth who was still a virgin.

'Well, I'm not scared!' screamed a fragile-looking creature from his position on top of the unlit stove. 'When my turn comes to be called up I shall tell them exactly what I think of them!'

'Hear, hear,' murmured his companions, while the nervous youth took off his spectacles and vigorously polished them, rather alarmed at his own daring at being in such company.

'What happens if the Gestapo comes?' queried some faint-heart sitting in the passage.

'Let them come!' A young boy seated on the kitchen table, who was in the habit of declaiming dramatic poems that he learnt by heart, threw wide his arms and faced them challengingly. 'Let them come! What do we care? The world is our oyster . . . and this land is our land, because we are the future! They can't force us to fight and destroy ourselves!'

One Sunday evening, five months later, their weekly meetings were brought to an end by the sudden arrival of three men. Three men in leather coats, wearing shoulder holsters.

They encountered a small core of stubborn resistance, but for the most part the proud youth of Germany were swiftly dealt with.

The nervous youth, who greeted their appearance with shrill screams of hysteria, was silenced by one sharp slap across the face.

The young girl who was not so young as she seemed, and who never had succeeded in seducing him, managed to spit out a couple of obscenities before she was kicked in the stomach and pushed to one side.

The boy in the sink had moved to the bathroom and was making love on the floor with his girlfriend. They were separated by a few well placed prods with the butt end of a pistol and sent downstairs to join the others.

The poet wet himself with fright the very moment the intruders arrived. He offered no resistance of any kind.

In a long line, shuffling single file with their heads hanging, fifty-two boys and girls left the house and entered two green coaches that were waiting outside. The world was their oyster, but fear was an unknown quality and they were meeting it face to face for the first time.

For three days they were retained at Stadthausbrücke No. 8. Their treatment was not particularly harsh, but it was enough simply to be there; it was enough to learn the meaning of fear and to understand that courage had no place in their lives. Courage was for those with power.

After three days they were put into uniform and sent off for training. Several died during their preliminary courses of instruction; some through accidents, others because they chose to. And as for the rest, they battled on and tried to come to terms with their new situation and their new selves; tried to grow reconciled to the fact that when it came to the point they were no different from all the other poor idiots whom they so heartily despised.

They didn't want to fight. It wasn't their war. They hadn't started it and they didn't believe in it. But they fought, just the same.

CHAPTER FOUR

On Guard at the Gestapo

WE saw them coming up the steps, pushing an old woman between them. The two Unterscharführer, Schultz and Paulus. Kriminalrat Paul Bielert's most indefatigable head hunters.

We stood at the entrance to the building and watched them go in.

'I wonder what that poor old cow's supposed to have done?' muttered Porta.

I shrugged my shoulders and made no reply. What could I have said? How did I know what one miserable old woman, wearing a coat that stank of mothballs, might have done to offend the Gestapo? It was a perennial wonder to me how your actual average non-influential citizen ever managed to avoid offending them.

As the old woman passed in front of us, she turned and smiled. She half opened her mouth, then Paulus gave her a shove forward and they passed through the doors. I wondered what she wanted to say to us, two strange soldiers standing in the rain with trickles of water dripping off our helmets and down the backs of our necks.

We turned and watched as they walked towards the lifts. The old woman could hardly keep up with the two men and their long-legged strides. Schultz gave her another push.

'Come on, granny. We haven't got all day. You're not the only one that's been invited to the party.'

They pressed the button and stood waiting for the lift to arrive. Paulus suddenly caught sight of Porta and me standing watching from the doorway and he waved an impatient hand.

'Get out of here! You're supposed to be on guard duty, and in any case this isn't a pantomime . . . Go on, piss off!'

'Watch it,' growled Porta, warningly. 'You don't give orders to me, darling!'

'That's what you think!' Paulus came striding towards us, his grey eyes contracting pinpoints. 'You seem to have forgotten that I'm an Unterscharführer—'

'Filthy shit, more like.'

'You dare to talk to me like that?' demanded Paulus, almost as taken aback as I was myself.

'Why not?' said Porta, with one of his evil grins. 'You can't do nothing to me . . . not without I spill the beans about that raid you carried out at No. 7 Herbertstrasse . . . You hadn't forgotten that already, had you? Because I can assure you that I hadn't. In fact, I been thinking, Paulus: we got room for someone like you in our regiment. How'd you like to leave the SD and come and join us, eh? Chaps have come to us for doing far less than what you've done.'

The man's eyes widened, and then contracted again.

'What do you know about Herbertstrasse?' he asked.

'I know you're a thief, for a start—'

Paulus drew himself up very stiff and raised a cold eyebrow.

'Are you presuming to call an Unterscharführer of the SD a thief?'

'You heard,' said Porta, cheerfully. 'And I'll say it again if I feel like . . . whenever and wherever I feel like it . . . Why, anyway? You got any objections, have you?'

Paulus heard the lift arriving. He pursed his lips to a thin line and strode away, not looking back in our direction. Porta watched him, a satisfied smirk on his lips.

'That'll give him a few sleepless nights, the bastard!'

'Why?' I said. 'What went on at Herbertstrasse?'

We turned back again, into the rain.

'To tell the truth,' admitted Porta, 'I don't really know, except it's where they picked up those two whores, a few days ago. The ones that had been hiding a couple of deserters. Apparently they done a raid on the place, and whatever went on there it was enough to make old Paulus think twice, wasn't it? You see the way he changed colour?'

'Yes, but surely to God,' I said, 'you know more about it than that?'

Porta shrugged.

'Only by hearsay. One of the whores that lives at No. 7 – not the two they took away, another one. The place is lousy with 'em – well, she was telling me that Paulus and another bloke nicked the girls' ration cards and walked off with their savings. I wasn't sure it was true until just now.'

'You mean, you tried it on without actually knowing?' I said, aghast.

'Why not? Nothing venture, nothing gain, as some other geezer once said.'

'So what happens? You going to shop him?'

'Not before I've squeezed him dry,' said Porta, callously. 'When he ain't no more use to me, I'll make bloody sure he's sent off to Fuhlsbüttel ... and on the day he finds himself landed in a disciplinary unit, I'm going to go out and paint the town the brightest bleeding red you ever saw!'

I grunted.

'Always assuming you're still alive to do it. One of these days you're going to bite off just a bit more than you can chew. One of these days you're going to meet up with someone who turns round and tells you to get stuffed—'

'Ah, bollocks!' said Porta. 'You think I don't know what I'm doing? They're all the same, these types, right from Himmler downwards. The minute you try a little bit of the old blackmail lark on them, they all get the wind up and start shitting blue bricks ... they've all got something to hide, see? All you got to do is find out what it is.'

We stood in silence a few moments, contemplating the empty street. The rain blew into our faces and got into our eyes and down our necks.

'I wonder what that little old girl had done?' I said.

'I dunno. Opened her mouth too wide, I expect.'

'You reckon they'll give her the full treatment?'

'Why not? Only reason they bring 'em in, to see how loud they can make 'em shout ...'

We tramped along by the side of the building, our heavy boots resounding on the pavements. The pale light of the streetlamps was reflected in our wet helmets and rifles.

'I could fancy a cup of tea and Slibowitz right now,' said Porta, longingly.

'Make it Slibowitz and tea,' I said, 'and I'll join you . . . three-quarters Slibowitz and the rest tea . . . and God in heaven!' I added, irritably, as I felt my shirt flapping damply against my back. 'I'm sick to death of this pissing awful rain! I'm sick to death of the whole bleeding war, and everything to do with it! We're all sick to death of it! They're sick of it, we're sick of it, so why the hell don't we all call it quits and go home again?'

'Some hopes,' said Porta, cynically. 'It's only the people what have to fight the bleeding thing what are sick of it . . . And they're not the people what can call it off. Them as starts it and them as finishes it aren't nothing to do with the likes of you and me. They don't give a fuck what we feel about it, and they're not going to get sick of it all the time they're making so much bleeding money out of it, are they? They'll just go on until we're all dead and buried. Much they flaming well care . . . And them over there,' he said, pointing wildly in the direction which I conceived to be England and the rest of Europe, 'they're just as bleeding bad as them over here. Revenge, that's all they want. Revenge and money, that's all any of 'em bleeding wants.'

'It's like the Legionnaire said the other day,' I agreed. 'They call this the Second World War, but really it's just the same as the First World War and every other war that's ever been fought. It's all one great big war that never ends. We think it ends and then another one starts up, but he's quite right, it's all the same one, just fought on different fronts at different times with different weapons . . .'

I remembered very clearly the Legionnaire saying that.

'It won't ever end,' he said, 'because They don't want it to . . . Why should they? As long as the war goes on, then capitalism can flourish. Stands to reason, doesn't it? So of course they're going to keep it alive. It might die down from time to time, but they'll damn well make sure the fire never goes out altogether. There'll always be someone there to fan the flames.'

'That's treason!' shouted Heide. 'I could denounce you for that! That's Communist talk!'

'Balls,' said the Legionnaire, distastefully. 'Communist, capitalist, Nazi, I hate the whole damned lot of them . . . I'm just a soldier, doing what I'm told to do.'

The Old Man looked at him a moment.

'Do you enjoy being a soldier?' he asked.

'That's irrelevant,' said the Legionnaire, with a shrug. 'It's just a job, same as any other job. No one ever bothered to ask me what I'd ENJOY doing. I didn't have any choice in the matter.'

'So that's why you do it?'

'Well, look at it this way.' The Legionnaire leaned forward towards him. 'Do YOU like being a soldier? Did YOU have any choice in the matter? Does anyone? Why do people go on paying their taxes? Or not driving without a licence? Or paying for their food instead of stealing it? Because they ENJOY doing these things? Or because they don't have any choice in the matter? Effectively, because they don't have any choice in the matter. It's either obeying the law or going to the nick. Or in my case, originally, being a soldier or starving. Or in our case, now -- your case and my case and Sven's and Porta's and Tiny's – being a soldier and doing what they say, or being stood against a wall and having our brains blown out.' He sat back, shaking his head. 'And if you call that any sort of choice, then I don't.'

I sighed and watched the rain falling steadily off my helmet.

'Sodding guard duty,' I said. 'Seems like it goes on for weeks at a stretch.'

'Let's pray for a pussy cat,' said Porta. 'A nice fat black pussy we can shoot at . . . Anything to relieve the mono- tony . . .'

We had retraced our steps and were back near the entrance to the building, at a part where the wall was crenellated, with loopholes and small turrets.

'Let's slip behind there and have a fag,' said Porta. 'We can get out of the way of this God awful rain then. No one won't come looking for us here.'

We slipped behind the wall, settled ourselves in a dry spot and removed our helmets. There was only a quarter of an hour to go before Heide and Tiny would turn up to relieve us. Doubtless they would bring something strong and warming to drink with them.

'Who knows?' said Porta, hopefully. 'We stay here long enough, we might even give some poor sod just the opportunity he's been waiting for to send the whole perishing lot of 'em up in flames . . . In fact, anyone come up to me with a bomb in his hand and asked me to look the other way for a bit, I'd do it like a shot. He wouldn't even have to bribe me . . .'

'Talking of money,' I said, squatting on my haunches, 'what about those steel helmets the Legionnaire nicked from Supplies? What's happening to them?'

'They're with a Swedish concierge in the Bernhard Nachtstrasse at the moment. He says they're safe as houses, but they can't stay there for ever. There's a locksmith in Thalstrasse who's willing to buy 'em, but he wants us to dump 'em all in a depot in Ernst Strasse – just opposite Altona Station. Problem is, getting 'em there. We can't use our own trucks, we'd never get away with it.'

'How much is he willing to pay?' I asked. And then added, 'As a matter of fact, I know where we can lay hands on a quantity of howitzer shells, but again it's a question of transport. We'd have to go early in the morning and we'd have to have an SS truck. Not only that, we'd need a special permit signed by the SS, or they wouldn't let us collect the stuff. They've been a bit jumpy ever since some geezer managed to walk off with a couple of engines that didn't belong to him . . . Still, if we could get the necessary transport it'd be worth a try . . . I was tipped off by a chap I know in the SS. He's got a chip as big as Mount bleeding Everest on his shoulder on account he once tried to do a bunk and they caught up with him.'

'This locksmith,' said Porta. 'He's giving us 67 pfennig a kilo. We'd probably be able to screw him a bit more for the shells. Say 69 . . . Any rate, like you say, it's worth a try. Tiny could manage a nice new set of number plates, and if we took the big Krupp I reckon we might get away with it. That's a twin brother to an SS truck, near as damn it.'

'How about the permit?'

'Couldn't your pal in the SS fiddle it for us?'

'It's a possibility. How much do you reckon we'd have to pay him for it?'

'A kick up the arse,' said Porta. 'We've got a hold on him, don't forget. One squeak out of us and he's for the high jump.'

'Yes, but—' I broke off and closed a hand over Porta's wrist as I heard footsteps approaching. 'Watch it! Someone's coming . . .'

We sat there a moment, our ears strained, and then Porta poked the muzzle of his rifle through the loophole.

'If it's a Gestapo bastard I shall shoot him,' he decided. 'Anyone says anything, we'll tell 'em we thought it was a saboteur. They're always going on about saboteurs.'

'Don't be sodding stupid,' I said. 'We'd never get away with it.'

Porta suddenly lowered his rifle, obviously disappointed.

'It's only Tiny and Heide.'

We peered over the top and saw them slowly approaching. They were talking earnestly and waving their arms about, and Tiny had a bottle clenched in one vast paw.

'Thank you, God, for the Emperor,' breathed Porta. 'And specially for his horse . . .'

We heard Tiny's loud laugh, and then the lower tones of Heide, grumbling and cursing.

'He's a shit, he's a sod, and he's a bastard, and he's going to get what's coming to him. Great finicking stupid queen . . . well, he's pissed his kipper this time, and so I tell you.' He paused, spat on the pavement and ground it in with the heel of his boot. 'You wait till I get my hands on him. You just wait!'

'I don't like him, either,' said Tiny.

'Biggest load of shit I've ever met in the whole of my life,' said Heide, vindictively.

Porta laughed and jabbed me in the ribs.

'That'll be Feldwebel Brandt . . . take a bet?'

'Like hell!' I said. 'It's practically a certainty.'

'Well, it was time he was bumped off. Sounds like Julius might have something in mind.'

'I'm game,' I said. 'I can't stand the bastard.'

'Suppose I jumped up and down on his stomach till he farted his guts out?' we heard Tiny suggest, in a helpful way.

Heide looked at him, a fanatical glare in his eyes.

'Jesus Christ, only to think of the swine makes me feel sick! I still don't know how it happened . . .' He stopped and held out his arms appealingly. 'Tiny, just tell me: aren't I the cleanest, smartest, best-groomed soldier in the whole Regiment? In the whole Division? In the whole damned Army?'

Tiny looked at him and nodded vigorously.

'Yeah. Yeah, I reckon that's right.'

'Of course it's right! Look at my chin strap – look at it, go on, look at it! I'll give you my next five years' pay if you can find even the slightest mark on it . . . well, you can't, I promise you that, so don't yank my bleeding head off!' Heide jerked himself away from Tiny, who had taken the offer literally and was peering closely at his chin strap, clutching it with one big paw. 'You know what,' continued Heide, 'when I was going through training – and this is Gospel truth, so help me God – they used to end up looking at our arses if they couldn't find anything else to get us on. And you know what? My arse was the cleanest bloody arse in the whole company! And it still is! You could look up my arse any day of the week, any minute of the day, and you'd find it as clean as a new pin. I swear to you,' cried Heide, growing ever more excited, 'that I wash the damn thing out three times a day!'

'I believe you!' shouted Tiny, becoming infected with some of Heide's own enthusiasm. 'I believe you, you don't have to show me!'

'Look at my comb!' Heide pulled it out of his pocket and thrust it beneath Tiny's face. 'Cleaner than the day I bought it! And just tell me, what's the first thing I do when we've had to dig ourselves in somewhere? What's the first thing I do?'

'You clean your finger nails,' said Tiny, positively. 'I've seen you do it.'

'Precisely. I clean my finger nails. And what do I do it with?

I do it with a nail file . . . Not with the point of my bayonet, like you and the others.'

'That's right,' nodded Tiny. 'That is quite right.'

'And what about this!' Almost beside himself, Heide dragged off his helmet and pointed to his head. 'Not a hair out of place! All cut according to regulations . . . combed according to regulations . . . even the perishing fleas march single file on the right! But Leopold Brandt, the Feldwebel of the Devil, God rot the balls off him – Leopold Brandt has to haul me up on account of my parting isn't dead straight! Me!' screeched Heide, turning purple. 'Me, of all people!'

'It's a diabolical liberty,' said Tiny, earnestly.

'It's more than that, it's a bloody outrage!'

'It is,' agreed Tiny. 'It's an outrage.'

'The man's a sodding nut!' cried Heide. 'He even had me standing at one end of the courtyard while he climbed up on to the roof of the Third Company H.Q. and looked at me through a bleeding range finder! Just so he could PROVE the bloody thing wasn't straight!'

'That's madness, that is,' said Tiny.

They walked forward, caught sight of us and slipped behind the shelter of the wall to join us.

'What's all this?' demanded Porta. 'You got it in for Brandt, have you?'

'I'll tell you something,' offered Heide, 'only keep it under your hats . . . if we can manage to get friend Leopold as marker on number three next time we have rifle practice with real ammunition—' He paused, significantly, nodded and winked. 'That'll be the end of that creep.'

'How come?'

Tiny turned to whisper in Heide's ear.

'Shall we tell 'em?'

'If they swear to keep their big mouths shut.'

Porta and I instantly swore. Tiny took a jubilant swig of Slibowitz from his bottle and handed it on to Porta.

'It was like this,' he said. 'It was me what thought of it in the first place, and it's me what's arranged it all . . . It was when I was out on the rifle range last week. I suddenly had this idea come to me about how we could polish the bastard off. It was just a question of having the opportunity.' He took back the bottle and had another swig. 'Well, I had the opportunity a couple of days ago. I was sent off with another guy to change the plate on number two. While we was doing it, he had to go off to the bog to have a slash – being as Hinka does his nut if the place starts stinking of urine. He can't stand to have blokes pissing on the Third Reich ... Anyway, while he was gone I took the opportunity to take the plate off of number three and fix it on again a bit too low down, see?' He demonstrated, with one hand beneath his chin. 'Result is, anyone stands on the butt and his head's unprotected and liable to get blown off ... and nobody to say who's responsible for it.'

'Very clever,' I said, 'but how can you ensure that it is Leopold who's on number three at the right time?'

Tiny tapped his head with a finger.

'I'm not as stupid as you might think. I got it all worked out, don't you worry ... First, it's the Legionnaire what draws up the lists, so he can easy arrange for Leopold to be on number three; second, we all know that Leopold likes showing off when he's out there; and third, we always finish up by firing with telescopic sight, and it's always at number three ... Am I right?'

'I guess so,' I said. 'But what's supposed to happen?'

'Well, now, someone—' and he looked meaningly at Heide and Porta – 'someone has to go out and finish the job by fixing a few explosives in the loophole where Leopold's going to stick his pretty head ... and then it won't be your fault if you fire a bit to one side, will it?'

'It's a piece of piss!' Heide rubbed his hands together. 'Can't fail!'

'Only one thing,' I said. 'Suppose the Old Man finds out? There'll be hell to pay ... You realize it's premeditated murder?'

'What, killing a shit like that?' said Porta, in surprise. 'That's not murder, it's a bloody service to your country.'

'Yeah? You just try telling that to the Old Man—'

'Look,' said Heide, coming over to me and holding up a

121

clenched fist by way of warning, 'you don't have to come in with us on this, nobody's forcing you, but one squeak and you've had it—'

I pushed his fist away.

'I'm shedding no tears for Leopold,' I said. 'I just don't fancy swinging for a bastard like that.'

'Nobody ain't going to swing,' said Porta. He took some dice from his pocket, crouched down, blew on them, rattled them in his hand and blew on them again. 'Fancy a game?'

Tiny squatted down to join him. He looked on with interest as Porta repeated his performance with the dice.

'What's all the show for? Everyone knows they're loaded.'

Porta looked up, indignant.

'That's just where you're wrong. I wouldn't dream of using loaded dice with you . . . As a matter of fact, I've got two sets. This is the good one.'

'Ha bloody ha,' said Heide.

Slowly, Porta turned his head to look at him. Slowly he tossed the dice from hand to hand.

'That reminds me,' he said, 'you owe me two litres of Slibowitz and twelve pipes of opium. Due yesterday. Should have kept your mouth shut, I might have forgotten about it . . . and from now on, the interest goes up to 80 per cent. You know, Julius, you'll have to start taking a grip on yourself. Too many debts aren't good for a man.' He pocketed his dice, stood up and took out a small black notebook. He smeared a tongue liberally over his finger and began leafing through the pages. 'Let's have a look, see where we stand . . . here we are. Julius Marius Heide, Unteroffizier, 27th Regiment, 5th Company, 2nd Section, 3rd Group . . . that's what I've wrote down.' He fixed Heide with a stern eye. 'I suppose you won't deny that IS you?'

'You know bloody well it is!' snapped Heide. 'Don't be a damn fool!'

Porta raised a warning eyebrow. He held the book nearer to his face and bid Tiny shine the beam of his torch over it.

'Fourth April – 9 bottles of vodka. Seventh April – 3 bottles of Slibowitz. Twelfth April – I've got that down as your birthday. That's hard, that is. You owe more from that day than any other . . . 712 marks and 13 pfennigs, 21 bottles of Slibowitz,

9 pipes of opium, Danish eau-de-vie, a half-case of Dortmunder, free entry to the brothel for a month . . .'

Porta's voice droned on with the long list of Heide's debts.

'Then we come to the 20th – that's Adolf's birthday, that is.
Let's have a gander what you had on that day . . . should mean
something pretty special to you, Julius.' Porta gave him a
knowing leer. 'After all, you was a member of the Party, if I
mistake not?'

'Was,' agreed Heide. 'You know bloody well I'm not any
more.'

'Only because they threw you out,' said Porta, brutally.
'Couldn't stand the sight of you any more . . . Anyway, on
Adolf's birthday you lost 3,412 Reichsmarks and 12 pfennigs.
And you can add 80 per cent on to the whole lot. The rate
you're going, doesn't look like you'll ever be free of debt, does
it?'

'Hey, I wish I could write!' exclaimed Tiny, suddenly
snatching the notebook from Porta and wonderingly examining
the entries. 'I bet you if I could write I'd be a millionaire by
now . . . Know what I'd do? I'd nobble one of them rich types
and pinch his cheque book! Then all you'd have to do is sign a
few cheques and grab the lolly.'

He beamed round at us with a grin of triumph on his face.
No one had the heart to disillusion him. Porta returned to his
pursuit of Heide.

'Look here,' he said, in friendly tones, 'we've been mates a
long time, you and me. I don't like to feel you're worried about
being in debt to me all the time . . . how about wiping it off?'

'You what?' said Heide, unable to believe his luck. 'You
mean cancel it?'

'Something like that,' agreed Porta, with a sly grin.

Heide turned instantly to Tiny and me.

'You heard him! You bear witness to that!'

'All right,' said Porta. 'No need to get so excited. Wait till
you've heard my conditions.'

'What conditions?' asked Heide, at once suspicious, as well
he might be.

'Well, to start with, I want those three bales of cloth you've
got hidden away in Beanstick's room . . . and then I'll have the

two barrels of Dutch herrings what you left with that dentist in Hein Hoyer Strasse.'

Heide's amazement was pitiful to behold. His mouth dropped open and his eyes widened, and he stammered as he spoke.

'How the heck did you know about that?'

Porta's little baggy pig's eyes sparkled maliciously.

'I know a lot more than you think! I know everything there is to know about you. I make it my business to know, when people owe me as much as what you do.'

'The – the carpets in Paulinen Platz?' asked Heide, too shaken to be circumspect.

'Of course.' Porta hesitated a moment, then, obviously making a shot in the dark: 'Give me the carpets as well and I'll overlook the rest and we'll call it quits.'

His shot in the dark hit its target: it was obvious from Heide's reaction that there was, indeed, something in addition to the cloth, the herrings and the carpets.

'How do I know you won't try blackmailing me?'

'Give you my word.'

Porta raised his arm, with three fingers held up in salute.

'Your word!' scoffed Heide. 'I wouldn't trust you further than I could throw you . . . You can have the herrings and the cloth and I'll go halves with the carpets.'

'Who's calling the tune round here, me or you?' Porta wanted to know. He jabbed a finger into his chest. 'It's me you owe the money to and it's me as says what I'll take for it . . . I'll have all the carpets.'

'That's a bit steep!' protested Heide. 'Eight hundred flaming carpets! That's a hell of a lot more than I owe you—'

'Take it or leave it,' said Porta. 'But you don't play ball with me and I certainly don't play ball with you, mate.'

'You mean you'd shop me?' asked Heide, indignantly.

'You bet . . . over and over, for everything I could bloody well think of! I haven't forgotten what you did to that peasant that time.* I've had it in for you ever since. I don't forget that easy.'

Heide shrugged his shoulders.

* See WHEELS OF TERROR

'Oh, well, if you're going to keep raking up the past . . . But I'll tell you one thing. Both the herrings and the carpets are hot as hell, so don't blame ME if you get picked up for them . . . Just remember that I shan't know anything about them.'

'Don't kid yourself,' said Porta. 'They nab me and I'll make damn sure they nab you as well.'

'Well, now, you just listen to me,' hissed Heide. 'I could shop you right here and now if I wanted . . . You know why? Because I happen to know a bloke who works in one of the SS depots. And I happen to know that they're after someone who's nicked a hefty load of steel helmets . . . they've already got a cell ready and waiting at Fuhlsbüttel.'

'So what?'

'So it's you that stole the bloody things!' screamed Heide.

'For God's sake,' I said, nervously. 'You'll bring half the flaming Gestapo down on us if you go on shouting like that.'

Heide dropped his voice to a venomous whisper.

'You go on pushing your great beak into my affairs and you'll find yourself breaking stones at Torgau before you're very much older.'

It was Tiny, with one of his totally irrelevant remarks, who intervened and prevented probable bloodshed.

'The day we bump off Leopold,' he remarked – quite suddenly, it seemed to the rest of us, though he had doubtless been turning it over in his mind for some while – 'I'm going to have a binge of bangers and Slibowitz.' He licked his lips and rubbed a hand over his belly. 'I'm going to have a real celebration, a real blow out.'

'One thing,' I said. 'Leopold and his pals ought to be bloody proud of us. They're always bawling at us about being hard as Krupp and his flaming steel . . . well, pretty soon they're going to find out that we are . . . They've done a good job on us, I reckon.'

'Krupp and his steel!' scoffed Tiny. 'Soft as butter, that stuff . . . You watch this!'

He sent his fist crashing into the concrete wall: his fist remained unbroken, but the wall shuddered violently and a small crack appeared in the centre and branched out in two directions. We looked at it wonderingly, impressed as always by

Tiny's feats of strength. He was a giant compared to the rest of us, and on many occasions we had seen him split open a brick with his bare hands. He had once broken a cow's neck with one flat-handed blow across its throat. Porta was also able to split open a brick, but it always took him a couple of attempts. Steiner had once tried it and broken every bone in his hand. The rest of us were content to stand by and watch, and Tiny had latterly taken to practising with an iron bar, contemptuously dismissing bricks as child's play.

We heard footsteps approaching, and we stood listening. They sounded like the measured steps of a soldier.

'Who is it?' whispered Porta. 'Tiny, go and have a gander.'

Noisily, Tiny emerged from our shelter.

'Halt or I'll shoot!'

The footsteps stopped abruptly and we heard a well-known voice.

'Stop buggering about, it's only me.'

'Who's you?' demanded Tiny.

'For crying out loud!' said Barcelona. 'If you can't recognize my voice after all these years you need your flaming ears tested!'

'Can't help that,' said Tiny, obstinately. 'Got to have the password before I can let anyone through.'

'Piss off!'

We heard Barcelona's footsteps start up again, then abruptly cease at a wild shout from Tiny.

'Give me the password or I'll fire!'

'Look, you perishing great fool, it's me, Barcelona! Put that rifle down and stop arsing about!'

Heide crept up to Tiny and hissed urgently at him through the darkness.

'What's got into you? Let him through before there's a nasty accident.'

'I got to have the password,' chanted Tiny. 'I'm a good soldier, I am. I know what's expected of me, I can't just let any Tom, Dick or Harry walk past.'

It seemed to be deadlock. Barcelona stood uncertainly a few yards off. I held my breath, wondering what new maggot had got into Tiny, but knowing from past experience that it was asking for trouble to cross him when he was in one of these moods.

'Ah, for Christ's sake!' snapped Barcelona, suddenly losing patience.

He launched himself at Tiny, hurtled past him and fell headfirst into our midst. Tiny lowered his rifle and came in after him.

'That had him worried,' he announced, in satisfied tones. 'Nearly shitting himself, he was.'

Barcelona turned on him.

'What d'you think you were playing at, you brainless ape? What the devil is the flaming password, anyway?'

Tiny shrugged a shoulder.

'How should I know? You're the Feldwebel around here, not me. If you don't know what it is, how can we be expected to?'

'Are you out of your tiny bird-brained mind?' asked Barcelona, witheringly. He saw the bottle of Slibowitz and held out a hand. 'Let's have a swig ... The Old Man sent me round to tell you that with any luck we'll be having a quiet time of it tonight. The Gestapo's busy having a witch hunt through the ranks, and Bielert's putting his own men through the hoop, so they're not likely to have any time to spare for us.'

'What's brought this on all of a sudden?' I asked. 'What's the point of it?'

'It's the great periodic purge,' explained Barcelona. 'They do it now and again, just to keep 'em on their toes ...'

'What are they getting them for?'

'Just about everything you can think of. Everything from first-degree murder to pinching a handful of office paper clips ... thuggery buggery rape and incest ... you name it, they've done it ... Bielert's got half the bloody Gestapo lined up downstairs waiting to go into the cells. I tell you, if he carries on like this all night he'll be the only one left there in the morning.'

'Sodding good job, too,' I began, when Porta suddenly interrupted with a wild cry.

'Hang on! We ought to be able to cash in on this, if we volunteer to give 'im a hand—'

'Who?' said Tiny, looking startled. 'Bielert?'

'Of course Bielert! Who else, for God's sake?'

'But what for?' babbled Tiny.

Barcelona gave a wolfish grin.

'Qui vivra, verra,' he murmured. (Who lives will see.)

Fifteen minutes later the guard was changed and we were free to return to the guard room. Barcelona had already gone back with news of Porta's suggestion, the Old Man had already offered our services to a surprised Bielert, and the scene was already set. We swaggered in together, and Porta at once took command of the situation.

'I'm the one who's going through their pockets.'

'Fair enough.' The Legionnaire nodded his approval. 'You've certainly got a nose for the loot.'

'Just watch your step,' said the Old Man, grimly. 'What you're proposing comes under the heading of misappropriation of funds—'

'Ah, stop whining!' said Porta, with a contemptuous wave of the hand.

There was a knock at the guard room door. The Old Man walked slowly over and a secretary pushed three SD men into the room.

'All candidates for the jug,' he said, abruptly. 'Take good care of 'em.'

He tossed three yellow forms on to the Old Man's desk and left the room. Barcelona opened the register and entered the details, the men's names and ranks and the crimes for which they had been arrested. In the top left-hand corner of the yellow forms it was explained that the prisoner would be referred to an SS tribunal within forty eight hours, but that he was in the meanwhile being guarded by a disciplinary company. In other words, us.

Porta had taken his stand in the middle of the room. He leered a welcome at the three prisoners.

'Take a good look,' he offered, with false bonhomie, 'and see what you think of me . . . We're going to be stuck in each other's company for the next few hours, so we might as well try to get on together. It's entirely up to you, of course, whether we do or we don't. Speaking for myself, I'm an easy enough bloke to get

128

along with. But I'm like a cat, see? Rub me the wrong way and it does bad things to me. My name's Joseph Porta of the 27th Regiment and I'm an Obergefreiter, backbone of the German Army and don't you forget it . . . All right, let's have those pockets emptied!'

Reluctantly, the three men laid out their possessions on the table. Unterscharführer Blank looked understandably anxious as he produced five marihuana cigarettes. Porta picked them up and sniffed at them.

'You ought to be ashamed of yourself,' he said. 'Carrying this sort of trash around with you. You know bloody well it's against the regulations.'

'One of the prisoners gave them me,' muttered Blank, in an attempt to make his crime less heinous.

Porta shrugged.

'Sounds a good enough excuse . . . a prisoner give 'em you, and now a prisoner's given 'em me.' He put them carefully into a pocket and turned his attentions to Scharführer Leutz. 'How about you, then? You had any little gifts given you, eh?' Without waiting for Leutz' reply, he picked up five paper sachets and opened one of them. 'This gets worse and worse,' he said, in tones of outraged piety. 'We only want the pipes and we'll have your actual opium den down here, won't we?' He glared at Leutz. 'How could you bear to use the filthy stuff? You, what's supposed to be one of the protectors of the Fatherland?'

Leutz lowered his gaze to the floor. I guessed he was smarting at his own invidious position, being rebuked by this fool of an Obergefreiter and unable to do a thing about it. He looked up again, his expression defiant. He moved forward slightly and I saw his muscles flex, and at the same moment Leutz, from the corner of his eye, caught sight of Tiny and stopped short. Tiny was idly toying with a spade; a big, sturdy spade with a thick wooden handle reinforced with iron bands. Even as Leutz watched, Tiny nonchalantly broke this spade in half and tossed the pieces away. He glanced across at Porta.

'I'm getting out of practice,' he complained. 'How about lending me one of that crew to have a go on?'

'Later,' said Porta. 'If they don't behave themselves.'

He put the opium away with the marihuana cigarettes and

turned to examine a gold wristwatch, picking it up and listening approvingly to its tick.

'Not bad,' he said, absently pocketing it.

Leutz took a few deep breaths but said nothing. Porta cast an avaricious eye upon Oberscharführer Krug and was at once attracted by the enticing sight of a gold ring on one finger. Two strands of gold were twisted round each other to represent snakes, and the heads were diamonds. Porta held out his hand.

'I'd better take that off of you or you won't get to sleep tonight worrying about it.' Krug protested bitterly, and Porta snapped an impatient finger. 'Keep you're mouth shut when you're addressing an Obergefreiter,' he said, grandly. 'And get a move on with that ring. I'd like to know who you stole it from in the first place.'

Krug changed his tactics. He put his hands on his hips and swelled out his chest. The Old Man wrote studiously at his desk, never once taking his eyes off the register.

'Can you not see,' roared Krug, 'that I am Oberscharführer?'

'I'm not blind,' said Porta, arrogantly. 'But so long as you're my prisoner I don't care if you're a flaming general, I'll treat you like the shit you are.'

Krug grew mottled and crimson.

'I shall make a report of this! I demand that you treat me with respect, according to the Regulations—'

'Respect!' jeered Porta. 'You're not even fit to wipe my arse on! And the sooner you realize that you're no longer in a very healthy position, the better for you.' He held out his hand again. 'I'll tell you who'd like that ring,' he said, to the rest of us. 'Old Hot Knickers down at "The Hurricane". She's given me good service, that girl. It's only fair she gets a little something to remember me by. And if you're a good boy,' he informed Krug, 'I'll tell her it was a present you give me, and whenever we're having it away together we'll spare a thought for you in the Dirlewanger Brigade.'

I saw a nervous tic rippling down the side of Krug's forehead at the mention of the Dirlewanger Brigade. It was supposed to be top secret, but we knew very well, and Krug and his companions knew very well, that it was an SS disciplinary brigade whose unique mission in life was to hunt down and to kill, by any means available, the partisans which swarmed in the thick forests round Minsk. The Brigade was led by SS Brigadenführer Dirlewanger. He had been handpicked for the position from his prison cell, where he had been serving a sentence for crimes of violence, and he had an almost psychopathic streak of sadism in him. In fact, on one occasion he had so overstepped the mark that even Himmler and Heydrich had called for him to be court-martialled and condemned to death. There was a long list of indictments against him, starting with the least brutal, the rape of several Polish prisoners, but the murderer was under the powerful protection of SS Obergruppenführer Berger, who, after more than one hour's talking, was able to persuade Heydrich and Himmler that for the sake of the Fatherland and for the sake of survival it was necessary to tolerate Dirlewanger and his coarse methods of warfare. Heydrich, particularly, was impressed by his argument, since it coincided very largely with his own precept of opposing terror with worse terror and violence with worse violence.

Dirlewanger ultimately met the death he deserved, though unfortunately not until 21st January, 1945. It was he himself who had originally introduced the barbaric form of torture of roasting men slowly over an open fire, and one day in Poland he had a chance to be on the receiving end. A party of German soldiers discovered him hanging by his feet from a tree, his head, dangling a few inches above some smouldering ashes, done to a turn like a piece of roast pork. According to some Polish partisans, the operation had been carried out by eight of his own men, who had circled about him singing joyously as he suffered and died.

He had screamed for four and a half hours. Today, in the War Museum at Warsaw, there is a picture recalling the event, with Dirlewanger's hated face plainly discernible amidst the leaping flames of the fire.

Krug glared up at Porta from beneath lowered brows. He had no illusions about his probable fate, he could guess only too well what was in store for him. He had seen a great many men, old comrades, some of them, sent off to the Dirlewanger Brigade, but it was a fact that he had never seen a single one of them come back again. Rumour had it that not only the men themselves vanished for ever, but that all traces of their identity, their papers, their possessions, their very names in the records, were expunged at the same time.

Krug had but one chance, and that was a slender one, being totally dependent upon the whim of the Governor of Torgau military prison – and that one-armed bastard, reflected Krug, grimly, was known to have no love for the Gestapo. Only one thing for it, and that was to be on his best behaviour as a prisoner and to take every possible opportunity to declare his own loathing of the SS. The Governor was bound to have his spies everywhere, and sooner or later word would be sure to reach him regarding the prisoner Krug's behaviour. Perhaps, with any luck, he would then be able to avoid the Dirlewanger Brigade . . .

'Well?' said Porta.

Krug shook his head free of forebodings and looked defiantly at Porta. With two swift, soft steps Tiny was at his side, standing mountainous and threatening by his elbow. In the circumstances it doubtless seemed a trifle futile to continue his protests. Krug took off the ring and sullenly handed it over.

'That's better,' said Tiny, giving him a shove through the door, out into the passage and towards the cells. 'Let's go and lock you up for the night. You'll be nice and cosy here until your pals come to pick you up tomorrow morning.'

'God help him,' said Porta, cheerfully. 'Doesn't stand a chance, poor bastard. Good as dead already.'

Tiny opened a door and they pushed Krug into the bare cell. Tiny stood swinging a bunch of keys, while Porta was lost in admiration of his ill-gotten ring.

'How's it feel,' asked Tiny, curiously, 'to be a living corpse?'

Krug found himself starting to sweat. He mopped at his brow with a dirty handkerchief, in the corner of which could be seen a set of initials that certainly did not belong to him.

'P.L.,' read out Porta, slowly. He was referring to another set of initials – those engraved on the inside of the ring. 'Who's P.L., Krug?'

A hectic rash of sweat broke out on Krug's forehead.

'Paula Landau . . . she died at Neuengamme.'

'And she gave you the ring for looking after her so nicely?' suggested Porta, with a sneer.

Krug waved the handkerchief helplessly to and fro, his entire face now drenched in a dew of perspiration. Paula Landau . . . The fear of discovery had been with him ever since he had taken the ring from the dead girl's finger . . . the almost dead girl's finger . . . It was not his fault that she had died. She had been more corpse than living human being from the very day they had brought her to Neuengamme. There was nothing Krug could have done to save her, and no one would have thanked him if he had. It was not death he had on his conscience, it was the ring. He had stolen that ring, and that in itself was considered an act of treachery punishable by death. Of course, if he hadn't purloined it someone higher up in the hierarchy would certainly have done so, but it seemed unlikely that any tribunal would accept this as a valid argument in his defence.

Krug flashed a furtive glance at Porta, then swiftly bent and unscrewed the heel of his boot. With flushed face he stood up and thrust two fifty-dollar bills at his tormentors.

'It's all I've got . . . you're welcome to it, it doesn't look as if I shall be needing it any more.'

It was a tacit plea for the subject of Paula Landau to be dropped, and Porta accordingly dropped it; not from any motives of sympathy, but simply because it seemed that there was nothing of any particular advantage to himself to be gained from pursuing the matter.

'What they got you for, anyway?' asked Tiny. 'Whatever it was, I hope you didn't admit to it?'

Silently, Krug bowed his head. Tiny looked at him incredulously.

'Jesus!' he said. 'They make 'em thick in the Gestapo, don't they?'

Krug shrugged his shoulders.

'There wasn't any point in denying it. They'd set a trap for me, they had all the evidence they needed. There was nothing I could have said.'

'Always deny everything,' chanted Tiny, as if reciting a lesson he had learnt by heart. 'So what they pinch you for, then? Caught you nicking things, did they?'

'No. I was just trying a bit of – er – well – blackmail, I suppose. I guess I went too far. Overstepped the mark.'

'There's always some silly bugger that has to get himself nabbed,' said Tiny, philosophically. 'It's a question of knowing when to stop. Like me, for instance, if I could lay my hands on ten pipes of opium, I'd only take eight of 'em ... Pays off in the long run.'

'That's all very well,' protested Krug, feebly, 'but as far as I'm concerned here and now you've taken every damn thing you can lay hands on.'

'Ah, well now, you're different,' said Tiny, comfortably. 'Dead men can't talk, see? And you're as good as dead, mate ... I know, because I've had a gander at your papers. And I may not be able to read, but I'm not colourblind, and I know as well as the next man what a dirty great red mark means ... It means Dirlewanger, and Dirlewanger means death ...' He leaned forward and spoke confidentially to Krug. 'You ever seen what happens to blokes when Uncle Jo's partisans get hold of 'em?' Krug shook his head, mesmerized by horror, and Tiny turned triumphantly to Porta. 'Tell him ... Go on, tell him what we seen! Tell him about that chap what had been eaten alive by ants—'

'That's nothing,' said Porta, scornfully. 'They know all about that trick in the Gestapo ... But what about that one where they string you up from a couple of trees and leave the birds to peck your eyes out?' He turned to Krug and addressed him in conversational tones. 'You heard of that one, have you? Tie you up by the legs, each leg to a different tree, and just leave you there to rot ...'

'Nasty,' said Tiny. 'Very nasty ... I only remember one person ever surviving. That was that bird, Nadasja de Mogilef. You remember her?'

'I remember the mess she was when they cut her down afterwards,' said Porta. 'They'd carved two bloody great swastikas

134

into the cheeks of her arse and strung her up stark bollock naked and the birds had had a go at her face.'

'Mind you, she asked for it,' said Tiny. 'She was selling information to our side and shopping her own people right and left.'

'Threw herself under a train in the end,' mused Porta. 'But what about that SS bloke they done in? What was his name? Ginge?'

'That's right! They stuck him on a pole and roasted him like a pig!' cried Tiny, enthusiastically.

'And he wasn't even in the Dirlewanger bunch. Just an ordinary Waffen SS officer . . .' Porta looked kindly towards Krug. 'You want a piece of advice?' he asked. Krug nodded, his face pale and clammy. 'First chance you get there, down there at Fuhlsbüttel, climb into a noose and hang yourself . . . It's no good hoping they'll let you off the hook, because you don't stand a cat in hell's chance. And don't start imagining they'll send you to an FGA*. The only SS men we ever get are the ones what've done something pretty small, like nicking the office blotting paper or pissing on the CO's pot plants, but you've really gone and shit your copybook, you have. Far better do away with yourself while you've still got the chance . . .'

Porta and Tiny left the room. The heavy door clanged shut behind them. Tiny's key grated in the lock and their footsteps crashed back along the corridor. Krug stood a moment where they had left him, then slowly collapsed to the ground and lay there, staring at the concrete in blank desperation. All his life he had been told he would come to a sticky end, and now it seemed as if he had. He felt that Porta's advice had probably been good, but he knew he could never follow it. Even now, he could not quite bring himself to believe in his own misfortune. And yet, as he stared round the cell, the nightmare grew clearer, closer, more realistic. The room was bare and clinical and quite incredibly clean. There was an abundance of cold air, yet no bed, no blankets, no stool. And if this was the Army for you, how much worse would the Dirlewanger Brigade be!

Krug fell at last into a troubled half-sleep, but was woken

* FGA – Feldgefangenabteilung (Disciplinary Company)

every twenty minutes or so by someone tramping up the passage in heavy boots, or by the banging of cell doors. The cells were all full, and from the amount of activity throughout the night it appeared that Bielert was continuing his frenzied purge through the ranks. Not that that was any comfort to Krug, shivering on the bare floor of his cheerless cell. He found the prospect of dying in the company of his former SD comrades scarcely any more inviting than the prospect of putting his head in a noose.

Back in the guard room work had slackened off and Heide and Porta had settled down to a game of cards. Inevitably, the peace was soon shattered by loud oaths and venomous shouts of accusation and counter-accusation flung back and forth across the table. On this occasion, it seemed proven beyond any reasonable doubt that Porta was the culprit: he had been holding the Ace of Spades up his sleeve and had somewhat maladroitly introduced it into his hand at a point when the kitty had assumed worthwhile proportions.

Heide jammed his knife hard into the table, only centimetres away from Porta's arm.

'You're cheating again!'

'So what?' said Porta, brazenly.

Cheating was, after all, an accepted hazard of card-playing.

'You had the Ace of Spades!' screamed Heide. 'I saw it!'

'Well, one of us has to have it,' retorted Porta. 'What makes you think you've got sole claim to it?'

Heide grew stiff and pale. While Porta unconcernedly laid out his hand, for all to see the incriminating card, Heide pulled his knife out of the table and brought it crashing down into Porta's shoulder. Porta moved just in time. Quick as a flash, his hand shot out in a sharp chop across Heide's throat. Heide, too, just avoided the blow. When it came to a fight, they were well matched.

Porta snatched up a bottle, smashed it against the wall and hurled what was left of it into Heide's face. Heide saw it coming and had time to duck. He gave a shriek of triumphant laughter and rushed in with his knife. I saw it poised to strike, and then there was a scream of pain from Heide as Porta jammed a knee hard into his crutch. The knife clattered to the floor. Heide rocketed backwards, propelled by Porta's hands closed tight round his throat. We watched, with interest, as Porta got Heide up against the wall and began bashing his head to and fro, Heide crumpled slowly to the ground and Porta followed him, plainly out for blood.

'That's enough!' The Old Man's voice cut sharply into the sudden silence. 'Give it a rest, for God's sake!'

'I'd like to kick his ugly face in!' panted Porta.

We looked at Heide's face. Far from being ugly, it was, in fact, the only presentable, respectable, unmarked face amongst the lot of us. We could all, except Heide, boast more or less permanent disfigurements. Tiny had lost an ear, I had a broken nose, Barcelona a glass eye, the Legionnaire a puckered scar, and so on, but Heide's face was fresh and clean and carefully shaven, and I could suddenly understand how Porta felt about it, and why he had this urge to kick it in. Why, after all, should not Heide too have a few reminders of the war to carry him through the rest of his life?

'Kick him to death!' urged Tiny, recklessly.

'Hold your mouth!' snapped the Old Man. 'How many more times do I have to tell you that it's me that gives the orders round here?'

He took up his sub-machine gun and perched on the edge of the table with it, swinging a leg and watching us. We eyed him uncertainly. We felt pretty sure he would never use it, the Old Man just wasn't that sort of person, but nevertheless when he was really serious we always took good care to humour him.

Heide came slowly to his senses. He held his aching head in both hands and looked up at Porta with the light of hatred still in his eyes.

'Bloody cheat,' he hissed, between his nice white teeth.

And then he spat out a mouthful of blood and gingerly felt his throat, which was bruised and purple with the marks of Porta's fingers still standing out clearly.

'Think yourself lucky you've still got a head on your shoulders,' sneered Porta. 'One of these days I'm going to really go to town on that lovely face of yours. When you've lost an ear and an eye and a mouthful of teeth you won't have quite so high an opinion of yourself.'

Heide slowly got to his feet, dragging himself up by the wall.

'Just because you're as ugly as sin,' he said, haughtily, 'it doesn't mean to say you have to be jealous of other people's good looks . . . You ought to try washing and shaving once in a while, it would do wonders for you.'

He had a point there; he really did have a point. But before Porta could make one of his usual obscene rejoinders we were interrupted by the arrival of two SD men and the old woman we had seen earlier on in the day. She had aged by several years in the few intervening hours. From an upright and fairly well preserved elderly lady she had turned into a bent and wrinkled old crone, with black hollows beneath the eyes and a mouth wrinkled up like a prune. They stood her in a corner and handed over the usual sheaf of papers to the Old Man.

'For you. Just fill 'em in in the normal way.'

'Hang on a minute, don't be in such a hurry.' The Old Man looked at the prisoner, looked back at the papers and then up at the SD men. 'You've come to the wrong place. We don't have any dealings with civilians. We belong to the Army, not the Gestapo.'

One of the men bent down and spoke a few words into the Old Man's ear. The Old Man frowned, looked again at the prisoner.

'I see . . . Well, in that case—'

The man shrugged a careless shoulder.

'Please yourself, of course. I just thought she'd be better off with you . . . Not that I give a damn either way. It's all in a day's work as far as I'm concerned. Mind you—' He passed a weary hand across his brow, as if he had the cares of the world upon his shoulders – 'it's not an easy job. It takes it out of you more than you always care to admit. There are moments when I find myself wishing I could do something slightly less taxing, but—'

He shrugged again, eloquently. Porta at once hooted and Tiny made a loud farting noise.

'Bring on the violins!' jeered the Legionnaire. 'Nobody obliged you to be a copper, did they? The Army's crying out for men, in case you're interested—'

'What, him?' said Porta. 'Him in the Army? Don't make me laugh!'

Before the object of their scorn could retaliate, they were interrupted by an unexpected voice from a forgotten quarter.

'Children, children, don't fall out with each other! Harsh words can never be taken back and you'll only regret it later.'

Startled, we turned to regard the old lady in her corner. She smiled gently and forgivingly upon us.

'There is already so much unhappiness and discord in the world,' she informed us, in her tremulous bleating tones. 'I beg of you, not to add to it ... You're all good boys at heart, but war is a trying time and it plays upon the nerves and makes one behave as one would never dream of doing in times of peace.' She paused, but we were far too flabbergasted to speak. 'You must try to follow the example of your excellent chief,' she told us. 'Herr Bielert. Such a gentleman, and so very kind. He insisted on arranging for a car to take me home.' She gave us a charming smile from her puckered old mouth. 'He was so horrified when I suggested I might walk!'

Tiny opened his mouth to speak, but Barcelona gave him a hard kick in the leg and he closed it again.

The two SD men stood by the door looking foolish. One of them waved a hand at the sheaf of papers.

'Now perhaps you can understand why we brought her to you?'

'All right,' said the Old Man, curtly. 'Leave her and get out of here.'

The old woman politely shook hands with her two guards, as if she had been paying a social call.

'Thank you so much for looking after me. And remember, any time you happen to be near Friedrichsberg, drop in and see me. You know my address. I always have a supply of sweets and illustrated magazines to offer my visitors ... Young people always enjoy my magazines.'

Muttering uncomfortably, they shuffled out. At the foot of the stairs one of them turned.

'Good-bye, Frau Dreyer.'

He blushed scarlet as he said it. Frau Dreyer raised a gracious hand as the Legionnaire closed and locked the door behind them, putting a barrier between our two worlds: they were the Gestapo, we were the Army, and as far as we were concerned that was the way it was going to stay.

The little old woman opened her bag and pulled out a packet of sweets. She offered them amongst us and we nodded our appreciation and helped ourselves avidly. Tiny, in fact, helped himself twice.

'Don't you worry,' he told her. 'You're with the Army now.' He nodded and winked, and we looked at him apprehensively. You never knew, with Tiny, what he was liable to say next. He was not the ideal companion for a sensitive old lady. 'We know how to deal with these bastards in the Gestapo,' he continued, boastfully. 'Why, I remember once I—'

He broke off with a loud howl of pain. Barcelona looked at him.

'I don't think Frau Dreyer's really very interested in that sort of thing.'

'What sort of thing? Why not?' demanded Tiny, instantly aggressive. 'I was going to tell her about that time in Pinsk, when we helped those three whores get away from the Gestapo—'

'Well, sodding don't!' snapped Barcelona.

Frau Dreyer herself intervened.

'Let the poor boy speak. He's just a big overgrown child, I'm sure he couldn't harm a fly and I should like to hear his story.'

Tiny looked at her with wide open eyes. Porta sniggered.

'He's nothing but a ruddy great liar. He tells lies like you and me eats or sleeps. He does it natural, like. Can't help himself, if you know what mean. Like for instance, say today was Monday the 19th, he'd tell you it was Tuesday the 20th. Not for any reason. Just out of habit. You can't ever take what he says to be true.'

'He'd sell his soul for half a farthing,' added Steiner.

Tiny was about to protest, in the way which came most naturally to him. He picked up a chair and prepared to bring it down on Porta's head, but the Legionnaire caught him by the arm and whispered a few words into his ear. The Legionnaire could always work wonders with Tiny. He put the chair down and retired muttering to a corner.

The rest of us, smiling vaguely at the old woman, sat down to play dice. Frau Dreyer watched us a while, and then, to our intense relief, settled herself in a chair and went to sleep.

For half an hour she slept, and then Porta's loud braying laughter woke her up again. We tried not to notice, but her quavering tones soon floated across to us.

'If you don't mind,' she said, 'I think I should like to go home now. Do you suppose my car would be ready yet?'

Porta gave a wild yell of glee as he threw six aces.

'Herr Bielert did promise me a car, you know.'

We gritted our teeth and did our best to close our ears. She was just a stupid old woman who had no idea what the hell was going on. Perhaps she was a congenital idiot, or perhaps she was in an advanced stage of senility. She certainly didn't seem to appreciate that she was now in the hands of one of the world's most pitiless judicial systems.

Heide scooped up the dice, shook them energetically, making as much noise as possible, and shot them elegantly across the table. Six aces. As Porta before him, he gave a loud whoop of joy. Then, in silence, he picked them up from the table and prepared for another go.

'Herr Feldwebel,' went on the thin piping voice, which was beginning to grate on all our nerves, 'would it be too much trouble to ask you to see if my car is ready? I really am becoming extremely sleepy sitting here. I should like very much to be taken home now.'

Heide sent the dice flying over the table again. Another six aces. No one said a word. I could feel the tension mounting. Porta licked his lips, picked up the dice and looked at them suspiciously. Heide smiled.

'Sorry to disappoint you, but they're not loaded. What you have yet to learn is that it takes intelligence to play this game. An intelligence which some of us have and some of us don't. And just to prove it, I'll throw you another six . . . double or quits.'

'Don't be a fool,' said Barcelona. 'It won't turn up again.'

'Take a bet?'

Heide grinned, collected up the dice, raised his arms above his head like a prize fighter and gave the leather dice box a good long shake before bringing it down on to the table. He left it there, his hand firmly holding it down, for at least a minute, calmly taking time off to light a cigarette. It was one of Porta's, but Porta was staring so hard at the dice box he never noticed.

'Oh, dear, how my poor feet do ache!' sighed Frau Dreyer, a note of the dreaded self-pity creeping into her voice. 'I put on my best shoes to come here, and they do pinch me so . . . and I've been here since early this morning, you know . . .'

Heide blew out a mouthful of smoke and drummed his fingers on top of the dice box.

'Come on, come on,' muttered Steiner. 'Let's be having it!'

'There's no real need for all this suspense,' said Heide, smoothly. 'I can tell you what's under there without looking: six aces . . .'

'Like hell!'

Heide smiled sweetly.

'You don't believe me? Well, now, I'll tell you what I'll do. We won't make it double or quits, we'll make it ten times or quits.'

Porta began chewing frantically at a finger nail. He ran a hand through his red hair and screwed up his face in a frenzy of indecision.

'This is lunacy,' declared the Legionnaire. 'You can't possibly KNOW that there are six aces under there . . .'

The voice droned on from its corner.

'It's two o'clock, Herr Feldwebel. There's another three hours to go before the trams start up again. What shall I do if the car doesn't come?'

Slowly, Heide began tightening his grip on the leather dice box. His voice had been quite steady, but I saw the sweat standing out in his hairline. We all leaned forward with him. Tiny had a cigarette hanging forgotten from his lips. Porta had chewed his finger almost to the bone. Any minute now we should know the truth.

'Are you so sure?' said the Old Man, not daring to take his eyes off the box and look at Heide. 'Are you really so sure?'

'I'm sure,' confirmed Heide, and a bead of sweat trickled down his top lip and splashed on to the table.

Someone's rifle clattered to the floor, but our concentration was intense and the noise scarcely penetrated the outer edges of consciousness.

'I can hear a car. I can distinctly hear a car. Perhaps it's come for me at last.'

Frau Dreyer rose from the chair and began buttoning her threadbare overcoat.

Slowly, very slowly, Heide lifted the dice box.

He had thrown six aces.

The tension broke abruptly. Tiny hurled his chair against the wall and pounded both fists on the table. Steiner shouted aloud. The rest of us leaned back and let out our breath in great sighs. Porta tore his fascinated gaze away from the dice and looked up almost pleadingly at Heide.

'How d'you do it, Julius? Tell us how you do it . . . six aces on the trot! I've never seen that in my life before.'

'Like I said, it takes intelligence.' Heide wiped the back of his hand across his brow and resumed his usual air of arrogance. 'If you count up what you owe me, I reckon you'll find it wipes out my debts to you.'

Porta frowned.

'I'll play you one more throw.'

The sweat at once broke out again on Heide's face. He stared into Porta's small and greedy eyes and was plainly tempted. But at last he stood up and threw back his chair.

'Not interested. I've done it three times, that's quite enough. You do it too often, it gets boring.'

'Balls!' said Porta. *You* know bloody well you couldn't do it again, not if you tried all night!'

Heide shrugged. He could afford to. He looked across at Frau Dreyer.

'Why did the Gestapo come for you?' he asked, coldly.

Not that he really cared, but it was one way of silencing Porta.

'Oh, my dear, it was my neighbour,' said Frau Dreyer, in

hushed tones. 'She wrote them that I had insulted the Führer.'

We turned round, our attention caught. Insulted the Führer! That could be interesting. Stege leaned towards me and whispered gravely in my ear.

'The poor old girl could be shot for that.'

We all looked at Frau Dreyer, who had become, quite suddenly, an object of quite incredible wonderment. Not because she was liable to be condemned to death – God knows, we were well accustomed to that – but because she could sit there in all innocence and not realize the enormity of her crime and its probable consequence.

'How had you insulted the Führer?' said Heide.

Frau Dreyer touched delicately at her nostrils with a small handkerchief that smelt of lavender.

'Well, it wasn't anything really, you know. Or at least, only what everyone else has been saying . . . It was during that very bad air raid we had last year. You remember, they bombed Landugsbrücke and the boarding school behind Bismarck's statue . . . Frau Becker and I – Frau Becker, that's my neighbour – we went along to have a look at the damage. And it was then I made the remark which so upset poor Herr Bielert, though really how was I to know, when everyone else had been saying it for days? It was better under the dear Emperor, I said. At least they didn't fly over in their aeroplanes dropping bombs on us. And in any case—' she looked at us, sternly – 'a man like Adolf Hitler, what does he know of running a country? I'm sure he tries his best, but he was born in poverty and he knows nothing of the ways of the world.'

We stared at her in a shocked, incredulous silence. Barcelona swallowed once or twice before speaking.

'Did you – did you repeat all that to Herr Bielert?'

'Of course,' said Frau Dreyer, with a proud lift of her head. 'He asked me my opinion, and I gave it. I am not yet too senile to have an opinion, I should hope.'

'No, but you – you shouldn't have – you really shouldn't have—'

Words failed Barcelona. He opened his eyes helplessly at the rest of us, and Porta hunched a careless shoulder.

'Let's see what the dice have to say about it . . . will she or won't she?'

And he ran a finger across his throat and winked ghoulishly at us.

We sat round the table and each one pressed his left thumb against the edge. Heide shook the dice.

'What'll it be?'

'The little bird on the park railings,' suggested Tiny.

'O.K.'

'One,' said Steiner.

'One to six,' said Porta.

'One to six,' we chanted, in chorus.

The dice rolled across the table.

Eight soldiers playing at dice in the cellars of the Gestapo, much as the Roman soldiers, in their time, had played at the foot of a hill near Jerusalem.

'This is disgraceful,' said the Old Man, suddenly. 'Pack it up, for heaven's sake.'

And he turned his chair round, facing Frau Dreyer, and began speaking energetically about God knows what; anything to keep her attention away from the macabre game that was in progress.

The dice lay on the table: four aces, two sixes . . .

'She's had it,' muttered Barcelona 'The dice are always right.'

'Everyone agreed, one to six?' asked Heide.

Porta nodded.

'Six for life, one for death . . .'

We looked across at Frau Dreyer. She was earnestly telling the Old Man the history of her late husband.

'He was killed at Verdun,' we heard her say. 'He was in the 3rd Dragoons at Stental. It was nice at Stental, I liked it so much. We had such a good time there . . . My husband was in the Dragoons from 1908 until his death. He fell on the 23rd December 1917. He'd gone out to find a fir tree for Christmas and he was killed by a stray bullet on the way back . . . He was a good soldier and a very brave man. He was with Hauptman Haupt and Oberleutnant Jenditsch, when they took the fort of Douaumont—'

'Douaumont!' cried Tiny, his face wreathed in smiles. 'I know all about Douaumont! The Prussians was only in there for about five minutes before the Froggies threw 'em out again, arse over tit to the other side of the Rhine . . . and you fuck off!' he added angrily, in Heide's direction. 'What are you trying to clobber me for? Keep your sodding great feet to yourself.'

'Frau Dreyer's husband was killed at Verdun,' Heide reminded him. 'Couldn't you choose your words more carefully?'

'It's only the truth, what I'm saying.' Tiny stuck out his lower lip, mutinously. 'You ask anyone if it ain't.'

'He's right,' said Porta. 'The Frogs knocked 'em about so bad at Douaumont that the Crown Prince himself was given a right bollocking from the old Emperor.'

Barcelona frowned at him and turned back to Frau Dreyer.

'What did Herr Bielert say to you, exactly?'

She sighed and frowned and dragged her eyes away from a photograph of Himmler, which seemed to mesmerize her. Across the foot of the photograph, printed in gold letters, were the words:

HEINRICH HIMMLER, Reichsführer of the SS
   Chef der Polizei (Head of Police)
      Minister des Inneren (Minister of the Interior).

'Herr Bielert was so kind. He listened to all that I had to say, and I could tell it upset him, and I thought perhaps I'd been offensive in some way, but then he told me it was all over and done with and I wasn't to bother my head over it any more.'

And she looked back up at Himmler and smiled at him.

'Did he tell you what was going to happen to you?' asked the Old Man. 'Did he write down what you said about Herr Hitler?'

'Oh, yes, indeed, he was most punctilious. He dictated it all word for word to another gentleman who was sitting in the room with him. I'm afraid I became rather sleepy, I think I must have dozed off, but when I opened my eyes again I found they'd written quite a book between them . . . and then Herr Bielert told me I was to go to Berlin.'

'To see the Führer?'

'Oh, dear me, no. I'm sure he's far too busy to bother with people like me . . .' She looked again at the photograph of Himmler, and her forehead puckered. 'I can't quite remember . . . there were some initials, I know, but—'

'RSHA?' suggested Barcelona, into the cold silence that had fallen upon us.

'Ah, yes! RSHA! That was it!' Frau Dreyer clapped her hands together and looked at Barcelona. 'Do you know it, Herr Feldwebel?'

Barcelona looked round at the rest of us for help, but we turned away and left him to it.

'Yes, well – it's a – well, it's a – a big department in Berlin.'

'What do they do there?'

'They – ah—' Barcelona scratched desperately in his hair. 'Well, it's a sort of cross between a – a registry office and an employment bureau.'

'I like it!' approved Porta, boisterously. 'I like it, I like it! But you left out the most interesting bit.'

'What's that?' asked Frau Dreyer, innocently.

'Well, now, I'll tell you. The RS—'

'For God's sake!' said the Old Man. 'Hold your tongue!'

'I wonder if they wish to offer me employment?' Frau Dreyer sighed and kicked off one of her shoes. 'I fear I'm rather useless. I suffer from my feet, you know . . . I should have gone to the chiropodist this morning, but of course I had to miss the appointment because of coming here to see Herr Bielert.'

We nodded, solemn and awkward and wishing she could be spirited away, struck dead, turned to stone, anything to save us this embarrassment. She leaned back in her chair and began talking, rambling on in that way old people have, more to herself than to us.

'I was out when they came for me. I'd gone to settle up with Herr Berg in the Gänsemarkt. Once a month I go. I was early, of course – I always am. I like to sit down in the station for a bit and watch the people go by. And then at this time of year they have such a splendid show of flowers to look at. I know Herr Gelbenschneid, the station master. I know him very well. He

147

has green fingers, his roses are some of the best I've ever seen. I wish I could grow them like that, but there you are, if you don't have the touch there's nothing you can do about it.'

She shook her head, resigned, and Tiny shook his with her in sympathy.

'Well, now, I knew as soon as I got to the top of my road that something had happened. I saw the car, you see. A big grey one, and I knew it belonged to the SS because I'd seen them before. At first I thought they'd come to see my neighbour. Frau Becker. She has a son in the SS. He's an Untersturmführer in the "Reich" division. She's very proud of him, naturally. Before he was made an officer he was in another regiment . . . what was it? SS Westland, I think. My youngest son was in the SS, you know. I didn't want him to be, but he would have his own way. Attracted by the uniform, I shouldn't wonder. Young boys are so easily swayed by these things . . . Anyway, he's dead now. They sent me his Iron Cross. I remember he was very angry with me when I told him his father wouldn't have been at all pleased at him going into the SS. You ought to wait, I said to him. Wait till you're called up, like your brothers . . . Three brothers, he had. Two of them went into an infantry regiment, and the oldest went into the Pioneer Corps. He's dead now, as well. The other two were reported missing. They might still be alive, I don't know, I try not to think about it too much . . . But the youngest boy, he was always one to have his own way. When I told him to wait for the call-up and not go throwing his life away, Mother, he said to me, Mother I should by rights report you for spreading defeatist talk, but just for this once I'll pretend not to have heard you. Never again, mind you. Next time I shall report you whether you're my mother or not . . . Oh, dear, he was so angry with me . . . didn't even want to kiss me goodbye when he went . . . and now he's dead, like all the rest of them, and I've nothing left save his Iron Cross. I keep it in the drawer along with all their baby clothes. Their little vests and their little knitted shoes . . .'

She suddenly looked across at us and smiled. Tiny smiled back, in a rather sickly fashion, I thought.

'But anyway, you see, as I walked down the road I realized that the car was parked outside my door, not Frau Becker's, and

I thought for a moment it was Paul come back from the grave ... Paul was my youngest son, of course. The one I was telling you about ... Well, the young man that got out of the car, he looked just like him, I'm sure. Six feet tall, wide shoulders, narrow hips, blond hair, blue eyes ... he was always the most handsome of the four ... And this young man was so like him it gave me quite a turn. And when he spoke, he was so gentle, so polite, so obviously well brought up. He must have come from a good family, you know ... The only thing I didn't take to was the black leather he was wearing. He seemed to be all black leather from head to foot ... so cold, I always feel. So very impersonal ... But then, perhaps it's a uniform?'

Smiling now at Tiny, now at the photograph of Himmler, she took us through the entire scene. I was able to picture it so well: the blond young god from the SS, with his arrogant blue eyes and his black leather boots, and the silly old lady, faded and trusting and too busy comparing him with dead baby Paul to notice the menace lurking behind his façade of polished charm.

'Frau Dreyer?' he had politely inquired, as he stepped out of the car.

And the old woman, all of a flutter, had presented herself to him and held out her hand and had it crushed in a big black gauntlet, and the young man had gone on to verify the fact that she was indeed the Emilie Dreyer who lived at Hindenburgstrasse No. 9. And all the time standing there with a suave smile on his face and a Walter 7.65 in his pocket, and old Frau Dreyer never suspecting a thing. He turned and opened the car door, to usher her into the back seat. They wanted her at headquarters, there were matters that had to be talked about.

'Oh, I'm so sorry, but I can't possibly manage today! I have an appointment with Dr Jöhr, to have my feet seen to, you know. I suffer very badly with my feet.'

And the SS man had laughed aloud at that. A visit to the chiropodist! That was the poorest excuse he had ever heard.

Frau Dreyer never knew why he found her innocent statement of fact so amusing. She went on to explain, in case he might not have appreciated the seriousness of the problem, that Dr. Jöhr was a busy man with a large practice, and if you didn't cancel an appointment at least twenty-four hours in advance you still had to pay for it.

The SS man laughed even louder. He at least had a good sense of humour.

'Don't you worry about your feet, old lady. We'll get in touch with Dr Jöhr and see that he doesn't charge you.'

'But you see,' she said, 'it might be weeks before I can make another appointment. He's such a very busy man . . .'

Losing patience with the daft old bag, the SS man had taken her by the shoulder and pushed her towards the car. As he did so, she had suddenly realized that his left arm was missing, and this had completely sidetracked her from the problem of her feet. Such a dreadful thing to have happened! Such a tragedy, such a disaster, such a—

'Do you mind if we don't discuss it?' he said, curtly.

She showed him the SS ring that had belonged to Paul. She told him about Paul, about his Iron Cross and how he had died for his country, but the young man seemed curiously uninterested. He had bundled her into the back seat of the car and slammed the door on her, and they had driven off at full speed to the Gestapo. They went everywhere at full speed, those people.

The driver was a very different type from the other young man. A rough, tough, crude type of person. No manners, no breeding. He had a glass eye, which had been ill made and looked more like a blood alley than a glass eye. And his face was thick and coarse, and Frau Dreyer felt from the beginning that he was out of sympathy with her.

'Watch it, grandma!' were the first words he had addressed to her, as she was hustled into the car; and then, turning to his companion: 'I hope the old bag behaves herself in the back.'

'You get on with the driving and leave everything else to me,' was the young man's retort.

Frau Dreyer felt that the implied rebuke had been justified.

'It was not up to a man of that class to address me as grandmother,' she told us. 'And as for calling me a bag, I find that to be totally lacking in respect towards one's elders and betters.'

'Yeah, I know what you mean,' said Tiny. 'But if I was you I wouldn't get too hot under the collar about it. I mean, it's not like calling someone a—'

Just in time, Porta clapped a hand over his mouth.

'In future,' he begged him, 'just confine your remarks to a simple yes or no and then we'll all rest a lot easier.'

'Get out of it!' shouted Tiny, indignantly breaking free. 'I'll say what I flaming like and it's no concern of yours . . . And I'm certainly not saying yes any more, I can tell you that for nothing. First time I ever said yes it got me two months in the nick. I swore blind after that I'd stick to no.'

'So long as you do,' said Porta. 'That's all we ask.'

And he turned back to the bench on which he was stacking up one of his marked packs of cards. He always put them away very carefully in their original wrapping paper, sticking it down with an application and regard for detail that was totally missing from the more official tasks that were given him.

Barcelona and Heide were idly playing dice again. Frau Dreyer went on with her tale as if there had never been any interruption.

'I couldn't help feeling he was rather an unpleasant man altogether. He drove so fast, you know, really quite dangerous, and on several occasions I swear it was a miracle that people escaped. But he just laughed, as if it were a great joke . . . Then at Harverstehude they stopped to pick up a young girl. I don't know why they wanted her, but I must say that even the young man who was so charming to me behaved in a VERY ungallant way towards her. Perhaps she may have done wrong, I wouldn't know, but I really cannot see that there was any need for them to hit her as they did. A gentleman should never hit a woman, never! And if he does, he only shows himself to be no gentleman, and so I said to the young man. Don't you agree with me, Herr Feldwebel?'

'I do indeed,' said the Old Man, gravely.

'I wouldn't have hit her,' said Tiny. 'What'd be the point of it? I can think of something I'd far rather do. What's the point of clobbering 'em if you can—'

This time, it was the Legionnaire who shut him up. Frau Dreyer blandly continued.

'When we arrived here,' she explained to us, 'they showed me in to a sort of waiting room up on the third floor. There seemed to be a great many other people there who had come from interviews, and they left me in with them for some time. Not very polite, I thought. After all, I hadn't ASKED to see Herr Bielert, you know. It was he who had sent for me. So I do think they might have made a little more effort . . . However, I suppose they are busy men and there is a war on. I think an apology is all I would have asked . . . Well, even when they took me out of the waiting room I still didn't get to see Herr Bielert. Instead, they insisted on going through all my pockets and my handbag and taking away a great many letters of a personal nature. I know they were only doing their job, I know there is a war on and we all have to beware of foreign agents, but I still can't help feeling that they were overreaching themselves just a little . . . and I am still at a loss to know what right they have to read my letters . . . Anyway, when they had searched me they took me off to a second waiting room. I didn't like it in there at all. An old man with a gun sat on a chair and wouldn't let any of us speak. It was most boring, and not only that, I was hungry.'

They had left her there for several hours, and then the blond one-armed Oberscharführer had collected her and taken her to a small room elsewhere in the building, where two men in civilian clothes had asked her if she had ever said the Führer was a fool.

'Well, of course,' she told us, 'I denied it at once. I said to them, someone has been spreading horrid lies about me. And then they asked me if I wouldn't please try to help them, because you see it was their job to look into all this sort of thing and make sure no one had ever said anything bad about the Führer, and really in the end they were quite nice about it all and told me I should take my time and try to remember exactly what it was I'd said . . .'

'Didn't you ever tell your neighbour, Frau Becker, that you thought the Führer had been foolish ever to start the war?' Bielert had asked her.

'Oh, yes,' she said to him. 'I did say that and I'd say it again. I think this war is a piece of sheer folly.'

And then, to her bewilderment they had all laughed heartily and the one man had written down her words on a sheet of paper.

'You see, Frau Dreyer, it's just as we said . . . you called the Führer a fool.'

She had been taken aback, then. Assured them that by saying the war was a foolish action, she had not intended to imply that the Führer was a fool. She wouldn't – hadn't – couldn't—'

'But surely,' Bielert had insisted, 'anyone who commits a foolish action is a foolish person, and hence a fool?'

She had to admit the logic of it.

'But, as I told him, I wasn't the only person who said such things. Everyone was saying them. I was only repeating what I'd heard . . .'

Of course, Bielert had at once jumped in to ask who, and where, and when.

'Well, there's Herr Gelbenschneid, the station master, for a start. I have frequently heard him say that this war is the worst thing that's ever happened to Germany . . . And then there's Frau Dietrich, the nurse at the chiropodist's. She told me only the other day she wished the war had never been started and the sooner we were defeated the better as far as she was concerned. And then—'

In her ignorance, she had dictated a whole list of names to Bielert's avid note-taking companion, who had promptly passed them on to the Oberscharführer – presumably for immediate action.

'And then,' said Frau Dreyer, wonderingly, 'they wanted to know if I'd ever been in a mental home . . .'

'As a matter of interest,' said Porta turning round, 'have you?'

'Well, no, I haven't, and it seemed such an odd question that I quite took fright and began to cry . . . To tell you the truth,' confessed Frau Dreyer, confidentially, 'I was scared they were going to fine me. For saying things I shouldn't have, you know. Even though I didn't realize they were wrong . . . I asked them if I mightn't apologize rather than pay a fine, because all I have is my widow's pension, you see, and I simply couldn't afford it . . . Well, they were really very nice about it all. They said I shouldn't have to pay a fine, so not to worry about it, and they would accept my apologies on behalf of the Führer ... And then, I remember, they grew very friendly and began asking me questions about my boys. They were so interested in them, it quite took my mind off everything else! And we talked of this and that, and it turned out that Herr Bielert was a good friend of Bent, who used to be my Kurt's closest companion in the old days. He became an SS Obersturmführer, and quite often he used to come round and visit when Kurt was on leave. Now, he was a brave boy, such a row of medals on his chest, and yet, you know, he didn't believe in the war, either. I remember once, it was just before Kurt's birthday, just before the battalion was sent to the front, I remember Bent telling me that the Führer was only a man, not a god, and that like all men he sometimes made mistakes ... And as for Himmler! I can't tell you how angry he and Kurt became whenever one mentioned Himmler! You would have thought the poor man had done them some personal injury! Why, I remember—'

'Hang on, a second,' said the Old Man, frowning. 'You didn't tell him all this, did you? You didn't tell Bielert?'

'Oh, yes,' she said, blithely. 'They were so interested, you see, and Herr Bielert told me that Bent had always been an intelligent boy and that he was wasted at the front, so they were going to call him back to Hamburg and promote him. I wanted to write and let him know straight away, but they said not to, because they wanted it to be a surprise for him.'

'Of course,' agreed the Old Man, solemnly. 'And what else did you talk about while you were there?'

'Well, now—' She gathered up the wrinkles in her forehead, trying to remember. 'We spoke of my nephew, Dietrich. He's a student of theology, you know. For some reason Herr Bielert seemed to think that he might have said bad things about the Führer. He asked me to tell them what Dietrich had said, and I told them, I can't recall that he ever said anything ... And then Herr Bielert grew quite angry and shouted at me, couldn't understand what it was that I'd done to displease him, and the other man kept shaking his head at me and I grew so confused I really don't know what I should have done if Herr Bielert's telephone had started to ring. And they all ran out with their revolvers and I was left alone for some while until another man came and took me away.'

'Brought you down here?' asked the Legionnaire.

'Oh, no,' she said. 'They shut me up in a little room, and then they came for me again and took me back to see Herr Bielert. And that was when they wrote down everything I'd told them and I had to sign it for them.' She smiled. 'When I'd done that they were pleased with me again. They gave me coffee and cakes and told me I should be taken care of.'

We looked at her, silently. It was incredible that anyone could be so naïve.

'I wonder if my car will be here soon?'

She addressed her appeal to the Old Man, who made vague noises of encouragement and looked across at the rest of us. We shuffled our feet and stared at the floor.

'One day when you can spare the time,' said Frau Dreyer, graciously, 'you must drop round to visit me. Let me know beforehand and I'll see if I can't make one of my fruit cakes for you. All the boys like my fruit cake . . .'

We mumbled our thanks and she smiled upon us and nodded her head up and down on its frail neck, and then, to our unspeakable relief, her eyelids drooped and she drifted off into an exhausted sleep, snoring gently and rhythmically.

Porta had finished stacking his marked cards. He suggested a game and we agreed, provided we play with Barcelona's pack.

Two hours later we were still playing, so engrossed in the game that we could hardly bear to leave the table for long enough even to stagger across to the handbasin for a piss. Frau Dreyer slept on.

We were disturbed by an impatient rapping at the door. Barcelona went across to answer it and found himself confronted by two SD men carring sub MGs.

'Heil Hitler!' they greeted him, severely. 'You got an Emilie Dreyer down here?'

At the sound of her name, the old lady woke up. She stumbled across the room, heavy with sleep.

'Is that my car?'

'That's it, lady. Your car . . . Get your things together and come with us. We're taking you to Fuhlsbüttel.'

'Fuhlsbüttel?' She hesitated. 'But I don't want to go to Fuhlsbüttel, I want to go home.'

The SD man laughed.

'Don't we all?'

'But Herr Bielert said—'

'Herr Bielert said he'd lay on a car for you, and he has. And we're all going off in it together for a nice little ride to Fuhlsbüttel. So be a good lady and hurry along, I don't want to have to get rough with someone old enough to be my grandmother.'

For the first time, Frau Dreyer began dimly to perceive something of the truth. She turned, trembling, to the Old Man and held out her hands.

'Herr Feldwebel—'

'God will protect you,' said the Old Man, very low and almost as if he were ashamed of himself. 'Go with them, Frau Dreyer. It's all you can do. All any of us can do . . .'

'Yes, of course,' she said, doubtfully.

She stood a moment, helpless, her old lined face quivering. We handed her her bag and her coat and silently she pattered after the SD men. One of her shoe laces was undone and both her thick wool stockings were crumpling round her ankles. The heavy door slammed behind her. We heard the other doors slamming, as well, as the prisoners were taken from their cells. They were led into the courtyard, packed into the big green vans that would transport them to Fuhlsbüttel.

In one of them sat a little old lady who even now could not understand the crime she had committed.

In the guard room, no one spoke and we avoided looking at each other. We were ashamed of ourselves and the uniforms we wore.

After a while, Tiny left the room. Still without a word. We returned half-heartedly to our cards, but before we could deal out another hand Tiny was back again.

'Krug's still in his cell!' he panted, excitedly. 'Hanged himself with his braces!'

The tension was now broken. We crowded out of the room and along the passage to witness the scene. Krug swung from the ceiling like a misshapen rag doll. His face was blue and bloated, and his protruding eyes looked glassily upon us. His neck seemed quite incredibly long. Beneath him, on the floor, lay his kepi.

'Best thing he could have done, really,' said Barcelona.

We looked up dispassionately at the swaying body.

'No need to feel sorry for that rat,' declared Tiny.

I don't think any of us did. Not even Stege attempted to speak up in his defence.

'We'll have to put it in the report,' said the Old Man. 'There'll only be repercussions if we don't.'

We trooped back up the passage to the guard room. While the Old Man seated himself at his desk and took up a pen, the rest of us now quite happily returned to our interrupted game of cards.

'Pity he couldn't have had the decency to wait till he got to Fuhlsbüttel!,' said Porta, rapidly shuffling the pack while the rest of us watched him like hawks. 'Still, some people just naturally have bad taste . . .'

They were black marketeers, the pair of them. Born to get themselves constantly into trouble and always to get themselves out of it again, respecting each other's treachery and cunning even as they sought to outdo one another. They stole everything they could lay hands on, sold everything that came their way, from women to spent cartridges.

The SS driver weighed the cigarette in the palm of his hand a moment, regarding it thoughtfully. He then raised to to his nostrils and gave a suspicious sniff.

'I think you're a filthy liar,' he declared, at last. 'Take it to pieces and let me see for myself.'

'Do you doubt my word?' demanded Porta, arrogantly. 'If I tell you there's opium in each fag, then there is opium in each fag.'

He spat contemptuously at the SS pennant flying from the big grey Mercedes. The driver at once returned the compliment of those soldiers who had given their lives in the first world war.

With these exchanges of formalities complete, they returned to business.

'I've got a nice little haul of car tyres,' offered the SS man. 'Just do you . . . Only trouble is, they're a bit hot at the moment.'

'You'll be a bit hot,' said Porta, 'if ever they lay their hands on you . . . Bet you a pound to a pinch of pig shit you'll end up with us one of these fine days!'

The SS man hunched an indifferent shoulder.

'Chance you take,' he said, laconically. 'If you're interested, I can let you have the address of a good strip show.'

'I know plenty of strip shows.'

'Not like this one. Not round here. Not with stark naked lovelies in it.'

Porta licked his lips. A hot splash of colour fell across his cheek bones.

'Completely naked?'

'Near as damn it. Shoes, stockings, suspender belts . . . just enough to titillate. Can't complain of that, can you?'

Porta scraped his throat a few times.

'Can you hire 'em out for an evening, like?'

'Why not?'

They put their heads close together and began to discuss terms.

CHAPTER FIVE

Porta and the SS

ONE day, quite suddenly and with no warning, Lt. Ohlsen was arrested. He was accused of having associated with a group of officers who had come under suspicion and of having himself uttered defamatory words against the Führer. We later discovered it was his wife who had denounced him.

They came for him one morning, two military police and a lieutenant, slinking silently into camp in a manner so furtive that they at once drew attention to themselves. Doubtless their aim was to pick him up with the minimum of fuss and smuggle him out before too many questions could be asked, but fortunately we had wind of their presence and were able to alert Colonel Hinka. Not that there was much anyone could do, but at least we could put up a good fight. Some officers we should gladly have seen arrested, but Lt. Ohlsen was not one of them. He had been two years with the Company and had served with the Regiment since 1938, and we had no mind to stand by and watch as they marched him off.

On hearing the news, Colonel Hinka at once sent his Adjutant to arrest the two MPs as they left Company Headquarters. The guards were alerted and all exits closed. No one was to leave the building.

The Adjutant smiled suavely upon the officer who was with the police.

'Colonel Hinka would like to have a few words with you, Lieutenant ... If you'd care to come with me, I'll take you to his office.'

The Lieutenant and the two policemen followed him, stubbornly dragging Ohlsen along with them. He was the prey that

159

they had been sent to fetch, and they had no intention of letting him go at this stage of the proceedings.

In Hinka's office, the storm burst. Hinka, furious that any upstart policeman should try arresting one of his officers without first asking his permission, swore that no one should leave the premises until the matter had been sorted out to his own satisfaction. He picked up the telephone and rang through to the Kommandantur in Hamburg. They swiftly denied all responsibility. He tried Hanover, with no success. He tried the Abwehr (Counter Espionnage), who wanted nothing to do with it. Finally, in desperation, he got through to the Army Personnel Bureau in Berlin and demanded to speak with General Rudolph Schmudt.

Needless to say, such an abnormal amount of activity on what should have been a morning like any other morning did not escape the ever-watchful eyes of the Gestapo.

It was not long before a familiar grey Mercedes drew up with two SS-Unterscharführer and a small dapper civilian, dressed all in black. The civilian looked at one and the same time seedy and sinister. Like a bank clerk going off to his grandmother's funeral, with his shiny black bowler, his big black overcoat, his gloves, his scarf, his umbrella and his cramped rounded shoulders and shuffling footsteps; like a weasel after a rabbit, with his small close-set eyes shifting furtively from side to siden bright as diamonds and as hard, missing nothing and ceaselessly on the alert . . .

Captain Brockmann could hardly believe his eyes when he passed this curiously clad creature creeping up the stairs. He stood a moment, staring after him, then hurried across to the sergeant in charge.

'Who the hell was that clown?'

'I dunno, sir. I asked him for his pass, but he just walked right on up the stairs like he never heard me. Like he was a ghost or something.'

'A ghost!' The Captain gave a short bark of laughter. 'An escaped lunatic, more like. No one who was even remotely normal could walk round in that ludicrous get-up.' He snatched the telephone from its hook and dialled a number. 'Klaus, there's a chap dressed in black from head to foot wandering about the place if he owns it. Have him picked up and brought straight to me under escort.'

He laughed and rubbed his hands together as he replaced the receiver. Whoever this little black maniac was, they were going to have some fun with him. Captain Brockmann had something of a reputation in the Regiment as a wit and a wag, though he occasionally went too far for everyone's liking. Only a month earlier he had succeeded in pushing Lt. Köhler to suicide. But nobody was likely to care what happened to this funereal non-entity creeping round the building with his rolled umbrella and his stooped shoulders.

Borckmann rang up one or two of his particular friends amongst his fellow officers and invited them along to the party.

The intruder was stopped in the corridor by a Feldwebel and taken down to Brockmann's office. He went without a murmur, only a twisted smile on his lips and a gleam of anticipation in his diamond-bright eyes.

Brockmann was waiting for him, legs straddled, hands on hips, while his friends lolled about in easy chairs and smoked and prepared to watch the fun.

'Well?' bawled Brockmann, swaying forward slightly on the balls of his feet so that his boot leather creaked. 'What the devil do you think you're doing, wandering about the barracks as if they're a public amusement park? Civilians aren't allowed on the premises without a special pass . . . and even if they've got a special pass they're expected to show it to the sergeant on duty and not just stroll in without so much as a by your leave.' He swayed a bit more, until he was creaking all over like a sail boat at sea. 'Are you deaf and dumb or something? Why didn't you reply when the sergeant asked to see your papers?'

The civilian stood with bowed head, looking down with interest at the floor. Brockmann took his riding crop from the desk and brought it lashing down against the side of a boot. He then held it behind his back, rocking back and forth on his heels and swishing the crop gently to and fro so that his spurs jingled. As he did so, he sucked industriously at a hollow tooth and rolled a comical eye at his fellow officers. They grinned encouragingly as they smoked their cigarettes.

'Do you realize I could have you locked up and left to rot – and no questions asked? An old black crow like you, you could be dangerous. For all I know you've got your pockets stuffed full of time bombs, eh? Planning to blow up the whole barracks . . .'

The civilian looked up. He stared mildly into Brockmann's face, and his expression was far-away and calculating, as if this present moment were of no concern whatsoever and he was deliberating upon more important matters.

Brockmann jerked his riding crop at the big black umbrella.

'Have you got a licence for that thing?'

'Of course not, the chap's a saboteur!' declared Lt. Berni, stubbing out his cigarette and coming across to have a closer look. 'Sticks out a mile. Traditional saboteur's outfit, that.'

Everyone laughed. They began circling round the man, examining him from all angles, noting the greenish sheen of his bowler, the sunken neck and the rounded shoulders, the ridiculously long overcoat and the enormous gloves that hung puppetlike from the sleeves.

'Do him good to be in the Army,' declared Lt. Reichelt. 'See a bit of action, get some of that tension out of him.'

Not that Reichelt had ever seen any action. Before the war he had been a wine and spirit merchant, and now he bought his safety with cognac and champagne. Reichelt was having a good war. He had built up a reputation as a ladies' man, and he never ran less than three mistresses at a time, discarding them all after a few weeks and finding himself three new delights.

'Brockmann, I think you ought to examine his papers,' said Schmidt, who was the Commissary General and whose war was going as smoothly as Reichelt's.

Instead of women, Schmidt had food. He lived for food. He not only ate it, he also stole it and sold it to a butcher in Lübeckerstrasse. The butcher in Lübeckerstrasse traded almost exclusively in food stolen from the barracks. Schmidt was not his only supplier.

'You'll probably find,' added Schmidt, 'that he's lied his way out of military service. He ought at least to be in the

Territorials. You'd like that,' he told the impassive civilian. 'Do you no end of good.'

The man remained silent. Schmidt wrinkled his brow in perplexity.

'You don't think the chap's touched in the head, do you?'

There was a rap on the door and before anyone could say 'come in' it had been opened and an SS Unterscharführer had entered the room. He was big and brutish and well over six feet tall. On his sleeve were the letters SD: on his kepi, pushed carelessly to the back of his head, gleamed a silver death's head. He ignored Brockmann and walked straight up to the civilian. He saluted smartly.

'Heil Hitler, Standartenführer! We've just had a message from the RSHA over the car radio. Said to pass it on to you immediately, sir ... Number 7 command has just completed operations successfully.'

The Standartenführer nodded his head, as if well satisfied. His eyes glittered behind his spectacles.

'Very well, Müller. Tell them that I want the prisoners to be held in the strictest secrecy. No one is to interrogate them before I arrive. I'll be with you in a moment.'

Müller saluted again and left the room. The civilian turned to the assembled officers.

'I thank you, gentlemen, for the entertainment. It has been most enlightening ... I have to be going now, but I feel sure we shall meet again ... Heil Hitler!'

He followed Müller from the room. The officers looked at one another apprehensively, no longer so sure of their own omniscience.

'What the hell was all that about?' demanded Brockmann. He strode across to the door, opened it and shouted. 'Sergeant!'

'Yes, sir?'

'Find out who that man was and let me have the answer within five minutes if you don't want to end up in trouble.'

'Yes, sir.'

Brockmann came back into the room and laid down his riding crop with a hand that was not quite so assured as it had previously been. Schmidt licked his lips.

'Gestapo?' he suggested, nervously.

From the silence, he knew that he was right. It had to be the Gestapo. Schmidt wiped a plump pink hand over his brow and felt a sudden constriction across the chest. There were some sausages and some cases of ham, Italian haricot beans and one or two other little bits and pieces that he had been hoarding up, ready for the butcher in Lübeckerstrasse ... and with the Gestapo on the premises, one never knew ... one never felt quite safe ...

Muttering his excuses beneath his breath, Schmidt left the room and hurried on trembling fat legs to his own department. Within a matter of moments the whole depot had been turned upside down, as Schmidt's staff dropped whatever they had been doing and rushed to carry out new orders. Twenty minutes later, two trucks left the barracks full to overflowing with ham and haricot beans. They were deposited in a safe place with Schmidt's opposite number in an artillery regiment, and the whole operation cost Schmidt several pounds in weight and nineteen cases of champagne. The nineteen cases of champagne cancelled out all the profit he would make on the ham.

Not everyone in the barracks knew that the Gestapo had been there. And even amongst those who had heard rumours, not everyone flew into a blind panic. A certain Obergefreiter, supposed to be on guard duty at the time, was even chatting quite amiably with the driver of the Mercedes. They were discussing business together, and had been doing so ever since the Standartenführer had entered the building.

'Well, come on!' urged the SS driver. 'Out with it! How much do you want for the—' He glanced round suspiciously and lowered his voice. 'For them?' he substituted.

On his right sleeve he wore a white armlet with the letters RSHA.

'They're worth quite a bit,' said Porta. 'How much are you prepared to offer, that's more to the point?'

The man hesitated. A crafty expression appeared in his eyes.

'A thousand?'

He plunged a hand deep into his pocket and came out with a bundle of notes. Porta laughed in his face.

'You lost your marbles?' he jeered. 'What do you think this place is, a bleeding charity home? A thousand! You must be joking!' He pushed back his helmet, settled his rifle more comfortably and pushed both hands into his pockets. 'You know, nobody ain't forcing you to buy the goods,' he said, kindly. 'I mean, you don't HAVE to have them if you don't want 'em . . . I only offered 'em to you on account of I thought you might be smart enough to handle 'em. No good letting an amateur get his mits on them, he wouldn't know how to get rid of 'em and like as not he'd land us all in trouble. But being as you're obviously a chap what knows his way around . . .'

'Look, I could get the bleeding things for free if I really wanted 'em that bad!'

The driver turned and spat contemptuously upon the memorial for the glorious dead of the first world war.

'How do you reckon that?' sneered Porta. 'I wasn't born yesterday, mate, it's no good thinking you can take me for a ride!'

And by way of retaliation he took a hand from his pocket, bent over the Mercedes and vigorously blew his nose on the SS flag which fluttered from the bonnet of the car.

The SS man pretended not to have seen. He simply turned and spat for the second time on the glorious dead of the 76th Infantry Regiment.

'Seems to me,' he said, 'seems to me you don't know who I am or who I work for.' His chest swelled out as he spoke. His face glowed with simple pride. 'That's my boss that's gone in there just now. Gone to speak to your CO, he has.'

'So what?' said Porta, coldly.

'So you'll change your tune a bit when I tell you who he is. I reckon you'll be so shit scared you'll give me your precious fags for free.' The SS man smiled unpleasantly and held out his right arm, displaying the letters RSHA for Porta to see. 'I can be bought – at a price,' he admitted. 'Say, twelve pipes of opium?'

'Bought?' Porta leaned forward and spat on the SS flag. 'Why the hell should I want to buy a creep like you?'

'Silence, pal. You don't buy me, you buy my silence.'

'Sod that for a laugh!' Again Porta spat. The swastika pennant, flying so bravely a few moments ago, was beginning to sag

165

under the weight of so much moisture. 'You can keep your flaming silence! You think I care two hoots for an idiot like you?'

The SS man curled up his top lip in a self-satisfied sneer. He felt very sure of himself. He leaned out through the window of the Mercedes.

'You'd better care, that's all I can say ... Because if you don't watch your step you're liable to land yourself in real hot water ... My chief is none other than Standartenführer Paul Bielert!'

A note of triumphant reverence entered his voice as he pronounced the name. His eyes blazed with the devout fervour of a missionary telling a bunch of habitual drunkards about Jesus Christ.

Porta walked up very close to the car and spat yet again on the pennant.

'I don't give a monkey's crutch piece for Paul Bielert!' he declared. 'Paul Bielert can go and get stuffed ... Sod Paul Bielert!'

The SS man narrowed his eyes and regarded him in stupefaction.

'You dare to say that about the Standartenführer?' He shook his head, bewildered. 'You must be a raving nut ... a certifiable bloody lunatic ... you can't go round saying sod Paul Bielert and get away with it! Bielert's just about the biggest bastard in the whole of Germany! He'll have your guts for garters if he ever gets to hear of it ...' His voice took on a note of pious wonderment as he spoke. 'Even SS Heinrich shits blue bricks whenever he hears the name Bielert. Only one man I ever heard of what could stand out against him and that's Gruppenführer Heydrich ... and we all know what HE's like.'

Porta leaned against the side of the car and looked down at the earnest driver.

'How about you, then?' he said, casually. 'If he's as bad as you say, you must be pretty scared of him yourself?'

'Everyone's scared,' retorted the driver. 'And so would you be, if you had any flaming sense ... And just remember this, pal: it's all very fine and grand standing out here cursing and blinding, but you won't be so bloody cocksure when the time comes!'

'Time?' said Porta, innocently. 'What time?'

'The day of your reckoning, that's what time, mate ... the day when you have to stand up and face the Standartenführer.'

'What makes you think I ever will have to?'

'I don't think, I know ... because I can go to the authorities any time I damn well feel like it and spill the beans about your drug trafficking. And when you're standing in front of Bielert you'll wish you'd never tried to push your luck so bleeding hard ... Only the other day he had nine men executed, just for the hell of it. When I say executed, I mean heads off, down on the old chopping block ... Nine at a blow! Nine heads rolling about in the basket! I'm telling you – you get in his hands, you don't stand a chance. He doesn't have men butchered because they've committed crimes, he has 'em butchered because it amuses him!'

'Christ,' said Porta, scornfully, 'that's nothing. I had a CO once, he was practically a homicidal maniac. Lindenau, his name was. Papa Lindenau, we used to call him ... as a mark of our affection, like.'

Porta grinned, as if savouring some particularly delightful memory.

'He was burnt to a cinder at Kiev Pavlo. I watched it happen.' He laughed uproariously for a few minutes, then looked down again at the SS man. 'I tell you, Bielert's a babe in bleeding arms compared with Papa Lindenau.'

'How do you know?' asked the man, jealously. 'You've never had anything to do with the Standartenführer.'

'That's what you think. You'd be surprised the people I've had dealings with in my time ... the people I happen to be on personal terms with.'

The driver frowned.

'Personal terms?' he repeated. 'What do you mean by that?'

'People in my position,' said Porta with dignity, 'have dealings with both them at the top and them at the bottom. And when we have dealings with people, we tend to get on personal

167

terms with them . . . you have to, otherwise you couldn't have dealings, could you? I mean, you know too much about each other, see? Like if I offer you something and you buy it, you could say we was on personal terms with each other . . . If you get my meaning?'

The driver remained silent a moment, reluctant to believe what Porta was saying yet not quite able to dismiss it outright. Porta closed one eye, took careful aim, and for perhaps the tenth time scored a bull's eye. The driver leaned farther out of the window and stared accusingly at the bonnet of the car.

'You keep your bloody spittle to yourself!' he screamed. 'Look at my flag! It's ruined!'

Porta looked at it and slowly smiled.

'Yeah . . . looks like it's been out in a rainstorm,' he agreed.

Red-faced, the driver stormed round to the front of the car and tried unsuccessfully to dry the pennant on his sleeve.

'You do that again,' he told Porta, returning to the driving seat, 'and you'll be asking for trouble.'

'Think I care?' jeered Porta.

The SS man slammed the door shut and put his head out of the window. He looked up suspiciously at Porta.

'Have you really had dealings with the Standarten-führer?'

'Wouldn't you like to know?'

'Well, I'm asking you . . . have you?'

'You think I'd tell you? Why don't you try running to him like you said and telling your little tales. You'll soon see whether I've had dealings with him or not . . . But one word of warning.' Porta bent down and put his face very close to the other's. 'I don't advise you to try it unless you fancy a good long stay in Torgau.'

'Who said anything about Torgau?' The driver withdrew his head and stared up at Porta in hurt innnocence. 'Who said anything about running to the Standartenführer?'

'You did. Just now. Remember?'

The driver hunched a shoulder.

'Forget it. One says these things . . . just a load of bull, really. Didn't mean a word of it.' He attempted a laugh. 'I thought you were going to tell me about your old CO? Papa Lindenau who got burnt to death at Kiev Pavlo?'

'How about the fags?'

'I'll have them, don't worry, I'll have them!' said the driver, eagerly. 'Just name your price . . . and I'll tell you what, I'll throw in the address of a place I know, as well.'

'What sort of place?'

'Very classy. Very superior establishment.' The driver closed one eye. 'Take it from me, it's a cut above the usual.'

'Well . . . I'll consider it,' said Porta, graciously. 'But no more talk of running off to Bielert, eh? Little men like you didn't really ought to meddle with this sort of thing. You don't know what you're getting yourself into. Now take me, for example—' He puffed out his chest. 'You don't get into a disciplinary regiment for nothing, you know. You people in the SS, you have it too easy. Makes you soft. I'm not at all sure I'm doing the right thing, offering you this stuff. How do I know you're not going to balls it all up? And if you do, you mark my words, your pal Bielert ain't going to be very happy about it. He's a professional, I'll give him that. But you—' Porta pulled a face – 'you're just an amateur. Like as not you'll lose your nerve at the last minute and drop us all in the shit.'

'I never have before!' protested the man, indignantly.

'No, but this is pretty hot stuff. I've never sold you stuff like this before.'

The driver licked his lips.

'Look, I'll make it 3,000 instead of one . . . and I'll throw in a case of powdered milk, as well. How about that?'

'Where's it come from, this powdered milk?'

'Denmark,' said the man, proudly. 'Nicked it from the Todt Organization over there, didn't I?'

'Is it safe?'

'As houses . . . And I'll let you have that address I promised you. Can't say fairer than that, now can I?'

Porta seemed to reflect a while. He scratched under one arm, stretched between the cheeks of his bottom, pushed his helmet from the back of his head to the front. Thoughtfully, he sucked at one of his few remaining teeth.

The SS man, now coveting the opium above anything else in the world, grew desperate.

'Just remembered something else,' he said. 'I got a whole bundle of photos you can have, if you like.'

'Photos?' said Porta, disdainfully. 'What would I want them for?'

The driver gave a sly wink.

'They're worth having. You take my word for it.' He made a few vaguely obscene shapes with his hands. 'Not the usual sort of crap, believe me! Real arty farty sort of stuff. Everything you've ever dreamed of. All tastes catered for. Enough to make a castrated monkey take himself in hand.'

'Don't know any castrated monkeys,' objected Porta; but nevertheless he seemed drawn to the idea. 'Where are these photos?'

The driver grinned craftily.

'I got 'em on me . . . not the sort of stuff you can leave lying around just anywhere.'

'Let's have a gander.'

Porta held out a dirty hand and the driver shook his head.

'Come off it! You think I was born yesterday?'

'O.K. Stuff your sodding pictures. Much I care.'

Porta withdrew his hand and stood up. He shouldered his rifle and prepared to depart. The driver at once leaned out of the car and clutched at his arm.

'Don't be in such a hurry . . . we can come to some arrangement.'

They eyed each other warily.

'Let me see the pictures.'

'I'll hold 'em up and let you take a dekko from a distance,' temporized the driver.

'You know something?' said Porta, contemptuously. 'I could sell this stuff elsewhere for treble the price you're offering. 'I'm only letting you have first option because I got a kind of funny idea you're liable to become one of us pretty soon.'

'One of you?' The driver shot him a quick look of alarm. 'What d'you mean, one of you?'

'One of our lot . . . Well, look at it this way. You've dabbled

170

your dirty little hands in too many pies to get away with it for ever. You just ain't smart enough. Sooner or later they're going to catch up with you, and the rate you're carrying on it's going to be sooner rather than later. And when that happens, mate, I reckon we're going to have the pleasure of your company ... marching along beside us, hiding in the trenches with us ... And then you'll know you've really arrived. After a short spell in Torgau, of course.'

'Yeah? You think so? Well, that's just where you're wrong, mate. If the day ever comes when they chuck me out of the SS and into a disciplinary regiment, it won't be with your scrubby lot, it'll be with the cavalry. They've got their own mob, and that's where I'll be heading.'

'Ah, now you're talking about the 37th Uhlans,' said Porta. 'Only trouble is, you're all out of date. They don't exist no more. The 49th Kalmykrytterdivision made mincemeat out of 'em some time ago. Only about ten survived and they didn't bother to re-form the Regiment, so you're out of luck.'

The driver stared at him, his eyes almost starting from his head.

'Is that the truth?'

'Would I tell you a lie?'

There was a long silence. Porta stood by the side of the car, nonchalantly picking dirt from beneath his finger nails.

'So if I – ah – came to you, then,' said the driver, at last, 'how do you reckon I'd make out?'

Porta shrugged.

'Hard to tell. Some last, some don't. Some go under, some come to the top.'

'Do you have any buglers in your Company?'

Porta looked down at him and grinned.

'Fancy being a bugler, do you? That's a change of heart, ain't it? A minute ago you wouldn't even look at us. Not quite so cocky now, are we?'

'I never was cocky,' declared the driver, vehemently. 'I wouldn't be such a fool. It never does to be too damn sure of yourself in this sodding awful world. Everyone knows you don't make old bones, being under the Standartenführer. I'd probably stand just as much chance with your lot ... Suppose they did send me to you – is there anything you could do to help me?'

'Help you?' said Porta, at once suspicious.

'To be a bugler . . . Hang on a minute, I'll show you.'

He plunged a hand into the glove compartment and emerged with a bugle, brash and shining, with the gold ribbon of the cavalry.

'Look here.' He pointed to four rosettes fixed to the instrument. 'See those? I won them at competitions. I've played this bugle all over the place. I played it at one of Adolf's blow-outs, when all the nobs came to nosh with him . . . I played it for old King Carol . . . I played it back in 1938 when Chamberlain came over and had his head talked off. There was even a picture of me in the English newspapers. They had my name and all. People paid more attention to me than what they did to Adolf and Chamberlain.'

'Not surprising,' said Porta, dryly. 'Who'd want to listen to them two clowns drivelling on?'

'Look, if you don't believe me—'

'I believe you, for God's sake!' Porta pushed the bugle angrily away as the man raised it to his lips. 'Don't blow the bloody thing, we'll have the whole flaming barracks running out to take a look.'

'Well, but I just wanted you to know—'

'Don't worry. Wait till it happens and I'll see what I can do.'

'Will you have a word with your CO about it?'

'Look,' said Porta, 'you got the wrong idea, mate. I don't have to have words with no CO. It's me what practically runs this bleeding Company. I say you're going to be a sodding bugler, then you're going to be a sodding bugler and that's all there is to it.'

The driver looked at him doubtfully, and Porta clapped a suddenly friendly arm about his shoulder.

'Come down to Bernard the Boozer's some time and bring the blower with you. Show us what you can do . . .'

'And what about the fags?'

'Well, what about 'em? You want 'em or not?'

'I want them all right. It's just a question of the price . . . If only you'd take my photos, I swear you wouldn't regret it. I'll tell you this for nothing, you'll never find any as good as this little lot. They're worth twelve pipes of opium on their own. Look – just take a look.'

He pulled a small folder from his pocket and selected a picture. Porta stared down at it coldly, apparently unmoved. Only the glittering of his small eyes betrayed his eagerness to lay hands on the photographs, and this did not pass unnoticed by their owner. Slyly he pushed back the photograph and drew out another, depicting a scene of such pornographic boldness that it took even Porta by surprise. Unable to contain himself any longer, he stretched out a hand towards it. The SS man grinned and at once moved it out of reach.

'Not bad, eh? And that's one of the milder ones . . . You wait till you've seen some of the others!' He licked his lips and winked. 'Give you wet dreams for a month on end!'

Porta groped for some of his lost dignity. He stepped back a pace and sniffed.

'I can get plenty of the real thing,' he said. 'What do I want with pictures?'

The SS man smiled.

'Wait till they send you back to the trenches. I bet it's not so easy there . . .'

'There are ways,' said Porta, darkly.

'Yeah? Well, if that's the way you feel . . .' He flipped quickly through the photographs, dwelling here and there upon one that specially took his fancy, titillating Porta still further with a rooty chuckle or a prim downturning of the lips. 'Mind you, you're passing up a good investment. Should have thought you were smarter than that . . . After all, you get tired of looking at 'em, you can always trade 'em in for a new set or sell 'em off to someone else for a good price. Still, if they don't do nothing for you that's all there is to be said . . .'

'Wait a minute.' Porta held out a hand. 'Let me have a quick dekko, make sure they're all genuine and what you say they are. I been caught that way once already and it ain't going to happen again.'

'How was that, then?'

'Some bloke sold me thirty-five photos. He showed me the

first four and I was mug enough to take his word for the rest. when I got 'em back home I found I'd been done ... the others was all pictures of bleeding scenery and bits of building and suchlike. I spent eight days looking for that bastard. I'm still looking ... I even promised Tiny a couple bottles of vodka if he could lay hands on him for me. And I'll catch up with him one day, don't you worry. I never forget a face. And when I lay my hands on him—' He bent down to the car window, and suddenly there was a knife in his hand. He ran it swiftly through the air, only centimetres away from the driver's throat. 'He won't live to sell any more dirty photos, you can take my word for that.'

'I do,' said the driver, his top lip twitching. 'There's no need to demonstrate.'

'I just thought you'd like to know.'

'You surely don't think I'd be fool enough to try the same trick? Not on a pal? Not on someone like you?'

'Why not?' growled Porta. 'I'd try it on you fast enough, if I thought I'd get away with it. I'd try it on with anyone what was fool enough to let me. And you and me, mate, we're blood brothers, we are. What I'd do, you'd do, and we both know it. So let's have a gander at those snapshots before we decide anything.'

'Well, I dunno ...' The driver scratched thoughtfully at the lobe of his ear with the ignition key. 'I'll make a bargain with you: I let you have a quick whip through the photos and you let me have a fag while you're doing it. Just to hold it. As a security, like.'

'O.K.'

The exchange was effected. Porta could hardly get his hands on the photographs fast enough. The driver sat holding his opium cigarette, watching Porta's face change as his little elephant's eyes gobbled up one piece of pornography after another.

'Like 'em?' he said, casually.

Porta swallowed a few times, cleared his throat, made an attempt to speak in his normal register.

'Not bad,' he allowed. 'Some of 'em were quite horn-making ... I suppose,' he said, grudgingly, 'I could always let 'em out

174

for hire when I've had an eyeful ... Tiny's fool enough to promise me a year's pay just to have 'em in his hands for a while ... Yeah, all right, it's a deal.'

The remaining eleven cigarettes were handed over. Porta put the photographs in his pocket and the driver produced three bundles of bank notes, each with a band round it. Porta stood stolidly counting them.

The driver sat and sniffed his opium cigarettes. They were firm and well packed, the best he had seen in a long time. He wondered if it would be worth the trouble and expense to get Porta drunk one day and try to discover where he obtained his supply of opium—

'Hang on,' said Porta. 'I'm a hundred marks short.'

'You can't be. There's a thousand in each pack, I counted them myself.'

'Count again, then.'

He did so. Three times. One hundred marks short. He shook his head in bewilderment, but the call of the opium was strong and he had no mind to jeopardize his chances for the sake of a hundred marks. He handed over another banknote.

'That's better.' Porta slipped an elastic band round the three bundles and buttoned them away in a pocket. 'And don't forget that address you promised me.'

'I'll give it you right away. It's near the Alster. A white house with a black roof, you can't miss it.' He scribbled something on a sheet of paper and handed it over. 'It's a strange-looking place, it used to belong to some Chinks.'

'Did they leave any of their birds behind? I could just fancy a nice little bit of Eastern Promise ... They say,' said Porta, carelessly, 'that they can do it standing on their heads with their feet in the air.'

'I wouldn't know about that, but you'll get your money's worth all right. Just tell 'em you've come from Rudolph. Rudolph Kleber. They know me. They—' He broke off, suddenly stiffened. 'Watch out, he's coming back!'

Instantly, Rudolph was transferred into the perfect chauffeur, sitting patient and upright behind the steering wheel, his opium cigarettes disappearing into a hidden pocket by some practised sleight of hand.

Porta stepped back a pace or two and snapped into the regulation guard position. He looked as if he had stood without moving for a hundred years. Only his eyes swivelled round, watching as three men came out of the building. Paul Bielert, dressed in black from head to foot; the SD Unterscharführer, one hand on his holster; and Lt. Ohlsen walking between them. They stepped into the car and the long low grey Mercedes rolled majestically from the barracks.

Porta watched until it had disappeared. He wondered for a moment where they were taking the Lieutenant and why, but he had more pressing matters on his mind and he soon deserted his post, left the barracks to look after themselves and slipped away to the garages. There, crouched behind a pile of oil drums, he gloated over his spoils. He went through the photographs, studying each one in minute and luscious detail, until the excitement became unbearable and he had to put them away for a more auspicious moment. He took out his bundle of banknotes and counted them again. Then, from another pocked, he took out an odd hundred mark note. With a satisfied grin, he slipped it under the elastic band with the rest of the pile. That would teach that fool Kleber not to keep his eyes open!

Eventually, he deigned to return to his post, where he found Heide waiting for him.

'Where the devil have you been?' he snapped. 'Tiny's been along twice already and both times you weren't here!'

'Piss off,' said Porta, in his usual amiable fashion. 'You give me a pain in the arse . . . I had more important things to do than bugger about playing at toy soldiers.'

'Sod that!' cried Heide, growing excited. 'You're supposed to be on guard and you'll bloody well BE on guard! You take your orders from me, you don't make them up yourself!'

'Who fucking says?' jeered Porta.

'I do!' shouted Heide. He paused, took a deep breath, and continued. 'Perhaps you didn't know it, but we've had the Gestapo here today. They've just run through the barracks like a dose of salts. Looking for you, I shouldn't wonder. I always said you'd end up with a rope round your neck.'

'Not this time, chum. They've come and they've gone, and it wasn't me they was after.'

'Well, anyway,' said Heide, sullenly, 'I'm sick and tired of continually having to cover up for you. Next time it happens you can bloody well take the consequences and go hang for all I care.'

'O.K. Suits me. I can look after myself.'

Nonchalantly, Porta slipped a hand into his pocket and brought out the photographs. Nonchalantly, he began to study them. He passed through them just fast enough to whet Heide's appetite; just slowly enough for him to have a glimpse of the subject matter. Heide momentarily forgot his grievance. He leaned towards Porta, craning over his shoulder.

'Where'd you get that lot from?'

'Mind it,' said Porta, at once shuffling the photographs together and holding them out of sight. He laid a finger on the side of his misshapen nose. 'None of your business.'

Heide breathed avidly down his neck.

'Let's have a dekko.'

'With pleasure. You can have them for an hour, if you like.'

Heide at once stretched out a hand, two patches of colour spreading fast across his cheek bones. Porta flipped casually through the photographs once again.

'Smashing, ain't they? Take a look at those tits . . .'

'Well, come on, let's have 'em, then!'

'Mind,' said Porta, judiciously, 'it'll be a waste unless you got time to enjoy 'em properly . . . If I were you, I'd take 'em down to the bogs and shut yourself up for an hour or two. Quick one off the wrist and you'll be well away . . .'

Heide was beginning to sweat.

'How much do you want for them?'

'Nothing. They ain't for sale. Only just got 'em, didn't I?'

'Well, then, what – what do you—'

Heide's mouth was twitching so much he could hardly speak.

'You can hire 'em, if you want. Hundred marks an hour for the whole lot, or five marks for singles.'

'You what?' Heide's speech abruptly returned to him.

'Hundred marks an hour to look at a load of scabby old whores? You must be bleeding joking!'

Porta hunched a shoulder and put the photographs away inside his empty gas mask case.

'Take it or leave it, nobody's forcing you.'

He strolled away again, leaving Heide in an indecisive heap of desire and indignation. It was not long before Heide had caught up with him and was muttering hotly into his ear.

'Give them to me. Here's your hundred marks. And I suppose you know that it's daylight robbery?'

Porta looked round at him.

'Well, if you're so oversexed you can't stop yourself looking at dirty pictures, it's hardly any fault of mine, is it?'

His face livid with lust and burning with shame, Heide snatched at the photographs, thrust them deep into a pocket and walked off without a word. At the end of his guard duty he disappeared into the latrines and was seen no more for a full hour.

'They've taken Lt. Ohlsen off with them,' announced Barcelona, as Porta returned to the guard room.

'Yeah? So what?' said Porta. 'He can take care of himself . . . What they nabbed him for, anyway?'

'Nobody knows, but I can tell you one thing: all the top brass is up in arms about it.'

'Fat lot of good that'll do.'

'Old Hinka's foaming at the mouth, and the Adjutant's flat out on the carpet. According to Feldwebel Grün, we shan't be seeing Ohlsen back here again. Looks like we'll have a new CO pretty soon.'

'It's obviously something serious,' said the Legionnaire, who had just come in and had caught the tail end of our remarks. 'I saw them as they drove off. An SS Mercedes with Auntie Bielert in the back of it. And you know what means . . . Section IV/2a. They're only concerned with the big stuff there.'

'What can he have done?' I demanded.

Porta lifted one indifferent shoulder and pulled a face.

'Trouble with flaming officers, they never know when to stop talking . . . Clack clack clack, here there and bleeding everywhere, anyone could be listening to 'em . . . But they're so much in love with the sound of their own voices yapping on they don't care if people do do a bit of the old eavesdropping. They LIKE 'em to eavesdrop . . . blimey, they sometimes talk so flaming loud you can't HELP but eavesdrop . . . And then they sit back on their great fat arses with their chests covered in bits of tin and they think they're safe and that nobody can't touch 'em, just because they're sodding officers . . . don't seem to realize that when it comes to dealing with people like Bielert you might just as well be a private as a lieutenant for all the bleeding good it'll do you.'

'I'll bet you a pound to a pinch of pigshit,' said Steiner, 'we won't never see Ohlsen again.'

'That's for sure,' agreed the Legionnaire.

Tiny suddenly clattered into the room, making more noise than usual and plainly spoiling for a fight. He tossed his rifle into a corner, bounced his helmet on to Barcelona's feet and spat, en passant, into someone's cup.

'What's eating you?' grumbled Barcelona, kicking the helmet to the far side of the room.

Tiny swung round on him.

'I'll tell you what's flaming eating me!' he roared, like a bull in its death agony. 'I've only spent the whole of my perishing guard duty chatting up a bird along by the electric fencing—'

'What were you doing along by the electric fencing?' demanded the Old Man, suspiciously.

'Chatting up this bird, like I said. I—'

'You had no right to be there,' objected the Old Man.

'Well, I was, so balls to that!' retorted Tiny.

'And what happened?' I asked. 'Wouldn't she play?'

'Oh, she'd play, all right,' said Tiny, bitterly. 'Only trouble was, just before I got started on the job I had this mad urge to have a piss . . .'

'So?'

'So I pissed . . .' He turned and held out his hands, appealingly. 'You ever pissed on an electric fence?'

A great roar of laughter went up. Tiny scowled.

'It's not flaming funny! I damn nearly got myself burnt to a cinder . . . and her just standing there sniggering, with her knickers in her hand, laughing fit to bust, and me trying to

stop pissing and not being able to . . . Jesus Christ almighty!'
He smote a fist heavily on to the table, furious at the injustice of
it all. 'A bird all ready and waiting to be screwed, and I couldn't
do nothing with it . . .'

'Very frustrating,' said Porta. 'Accept my commiserations,
mate. I know what it's like, I've had it happen to me. Not
because of an electric fence, of course, we're not all that stupid,
but the same sort of situation—'

'And now I feel as randy as a goat!' bellowed Tiny.

Porta put a hand on his arm and winked at him.

'I've got the very thing you need to help you out of a fix . . . a
set of photographs . . . all genuine, all unique . . . better than the
bluest films you ever saw . . . I'll let you have 'em for an hour
for one hundred marks. Just as soon as Heide's finished wan-
king over 'em . . . What do you say?'

Tiny abruptly forgot his accident with the electric fencing.

'Can I have 'em on credit?'

Porta's expression at once changed.

'On credit?' he said. 'On credit?' he repeated, his voice rising
by half a horrified octave. 'What d'you think I'm running, a
bleeding charity or something?'

'All right, all right,' said Tiny, hastily. 'No need to get your
knickers twisted . . . Hundred marks, you say?'

'A hundred marks,' confirmed Porta.

'I'll get it!' Tiny made for the door. 'I'll get it, I tell you!
Just don't let 'em out to anyone else before I get back!'

'I wonder if I could get some photocopies made?' mused
Porta, returning to his seat. 'That way, I could lend 'em round
the whole barracks . . .'

'Let me see,' said the Legionnaire, 'I was nineteen when I saw my first execution. It was at Casablanca, I remember. Some idiot who'd been twelve years in the army and suddenly gone berserk. Taken it into his head to go galloping off God knows where . . . Thought he could get away with desertion, poor fool . . . Of course, I've seen hundreds of others since then, but somehow you never manage to forget the first one.'

'I was only eighteen,' said Barcelona. 'It was in Madrid, when I was with the Thälman Battalion.* We had to shoot a kid of about my own age behind the abattoirs. He hadn't done anything, poor sod. He just had a rich father, that was all. So we shot him . . . and Christ, what a hash we made of it! No training, no experience . . . we blew half his head away!'

Heide shrugged a contemptuous shoulder.

'Personally, I never trouble my head over executions. Can't see the difference between shooting a man who's standing up against a brick wall and shooting a man who's hiding in the trenches. It all comes to the same thing. It's all war.'

'You remember that time we had to shoot that telephonist bird?' demanded Tiny, with his usual eagerness for recalling gruesome spectacles. 'That was a right farce, that was! It was Sven's fault. Him and Stege. Wanted to act the gentleman and save her unnecessary suffering . . . and while they was buggering about she took to her heels and scarpered.'

Porta gave a loud crack of laughter.

'I remember! We had to chase her back into the building and all up and down the bleeding corridors—'

'Yeah, and old Gustav bleating along behind us telling us not to shoot or we'd bugger up his books—'

'That's right, she had to be done away with proper, according to the regulations, else her papers wouldn't be in order.'

'She was a murderer,' said Heide, coldly. 'I saw her file in Hauptfeldwebel Dorn's office. She killed her best friend.'

'Yeah, but only because her best friend happened to have pinched her fiancé,' I objected.

Heide looked at me.

'Fiancé, my arse! She just slept around with him and took presents off of him . . . he was a rich bloke, remember?'

*German battalion of Communist volunteers

'Next week we're on duty at Fuhlsbüttel,' said Steiner, suddenly. 'I've arranged to be sick that week. I've already seen the Feldwebel down at the infirmary. It's costing me two cartons of fags, but I reckon it's worth it. I know for a fact they've got at least five executions laid on for that week.'

'Don't worry me none,' declared Tiny. 'So long as they give us a bit of extra cash for being there. I don't care how many flaming executions they got going. Way I see it is, if we didn't do it there'd be a hundred others who would.'

'Precisely,' said Heide. 'And in any case, we're supposed to be soldiers. We just do what we're told to do ...'

CHAPTER SIX

In Preventive Detention

In the offices of the Gestapo, 8 Stadthausbrücke, Lt. Ohlsen sat facing Paul Bielert across a wide desk.

Lt. Ohlsen was holding a document in his hand. Bielert was thoughtfully smoking a big cigar. With a smile on his lips, and his eyes narrowed, he watched the smoke as it twisted and curled on its way to the ceiling. Ohlsen was his 123rd arrest that week. Gruppenführer Müller in Berlin could hardly do otherwise than express his satisfaction with Bielert's industry. Though, mind you, Müller was a fool and a swine. Not a patch on Obergrüppenführer Heydrich.

Bielert shifted his position slightly and thought about Heydrich. They had assassinated him, the fools. And yet he was one of the best men they had had. A man Bielert had not objected to working for. Intelligent, self-assured and unscrupulous. A very angel of the devil. Even SS Heinrich had thought twice before crossing swords with him. And who knew, wondered Bielert, as he had often wondered before, who knew if Himmler and the Führer himself had not had a hand in his murder? Scared that the man was growing too powerful, and hence dangerous? Certainly the whole affair had been handled in a highly unsatisfactory manner. There were still far too many unanswered questions for Bielert's liking.

Why, for instance, had none of Heydrich's assassins been allowed to survive to tell their tale? The order of SD Gruppenführer Nebe, who was in charge of the mopping-up operation, had made it very clear that death and not capture was what was required: 'Take no prisoners. They must all be killed, by whatever means available – even if it means violating the sanctity of a church, should they attempt to take refuge in one. Burn the church if necessary, but let none escape.'

The last of the assassins had been run to earth in Prague. He had given himself up without a struggle, and instead of shooting him on the spot they had taken him back with them. He seemed perfectly willing to speak, but strangely enough he had never been given the chance: he had been shot in Nebe's office. According to the official report in the newspapers it had been suicide, and most people had readily believed it. Even the English had swallowed the story and had put it out on the BBC.

Bielert slid open a drawer in his desk and looked down upon the pistol he kept in there. It was the pistol he had used to shoot the last of the assassins, there in Nebe's office. He had been glad enough to do so at the time, thinking only of revenge, but now he sometimes found himself wondering what the man might have said, had he been given the opportunity to talk.

Shortly after the inquest, Nebe had been removed from office. He had grown cocksure and over-zealous since Heydrich's death and was evidently considered to be an embarrassment. At first Bielert had been puzzled, but his cunning brain had soon put two and two together and he had begun to wonder if he might not be the next on the list. He had instantly put in for a transfer and been sent to Hamburg.

By way of a so-called reprisal for the murder of Heydrich, they had burnt down the entire village where it had happened, just outside Prague. It was the military police who performed the operation. A rumour was spread about that the SS had been responsible for it, but in fact there were no more than five SS men in the whole commando. The liquidation had been entirely the work of MPs from Dresden and Leipzig.

Bielert laughed softly to himself. It had originally been proposed that the Waffen SS should perform the task, but SS Obergruppenführer Berger had strongly opposed the idea on the grounds that it would he harmful to the current recruiting campaign for volunteers from Bohemia and Slovakia. He had probably been right, in theory. In practice, as it turned out, the recruiting campaign was in any case dealt a blow from which it never recovered.

The idea of burning the village had come from Himmler

184

himself, and it seemed an excellent one. An act so terrible, on such a scale, would set the whole world by the ears. They would understand at once that it was a reprisal: an act of revenge against the Tchechoslovak resistance movement, which had supposedly assassinated Heydrich. And in the face of such an orgy of slaughter, of burnings and shootings and hangings, all for the death of one man, the people would surely turn and curse the resistance movement for bringing such misery upon them?

The only trouble was that the English almost immediately became suspicious. They lost no time in broadcasting their views on the affair, with the result that many hundreds of volunteers from Bohemia and Slovakia at once deserted and joined the Resistance movement instead, while the recruiting offices fell suddenly silent and empty. Heydrich had been exterminated, certainly, but the rest of the plan had gone sadly astray. One might even say, thought Bielert, closing the drawer again, that it had backfired. And serve them right, too.

He turned his attention to Lt. Ohlsen, who was frowning as he read through the warrant for his arrest. Bielert leaned back in his chair and smiled contentedly through a cloud of cigar smoke. It was a good idea – and his own – to give these intellectual types the chance of acquainting themselves with a few of the facts before the interview began. It unsettled them, made them less sure of their ground and more disposed to open their mouths and try to talk their way out of trouble. And in Bielert's experience, the more a man talked the more trouble he made for himself.

He waited patiently. Ohlsen was now reading through the warrant for the third time, going through it with desperate care, to make sure he had missed none of it. They always did that. The first time they skipped through it and only half understood it; the second time they slowed down sufficiently to grasp a few of the essentials, although even then their minds still refused to accept the hard fact of their arrest; but the third time round, their nerve began to go and they began to be far more malleable. So Bierlert sat back and bided his time, looked at his well-kept fingernails and savoured the aroma of his excellent cigar.

Lt. Ohlsen appeared to be no exception to the general rule. He was reading the document with painful slowness, still tending towards incredulity and yet with a growing horror of awareness which spread from the deepmost pit of his bowels and steadily up through his body, making his palms sweat and the hair follicles prick at the back of his neck.

'To the President of the People's Tribunal,
People's Tribunal, 7.J.636/43 (52/43 – 693)

Hamburg, 3rd April 1943
8 Stadhausbrücke
Hamburg 2.

Warrant of Arrest

Lieutenant Bernt Viktor Ohlsen, born 4 April 1917 at Berlin-Dahlem, currently serving with the 27th Armoured Regiment, is required to be interned by the State Secret Police. The 27th Armoured Regiment is at present stationed at Hamburg, at the Altona Barracks.

An official inquiry is to be held into the conduct of the said Bernt Viktor Ohlsen. He is accused of seeking to disrupt public order by spreading alarm and despondency and by generally encouraging acts of sabotage and insurrection. The facts are as follows:

1) On 22nd January 1943, while the Regiment was at the Eastern Front, the Accused made the following declaration to a fellow officer:
   'If you ask me, the Third Reich won't even see its centenary, let alone the millenium ... everyone knows the war's as good as lost. It's not going to be long before the English and the Americans come up through the Balkans and Italy and invade Germany herself ... and then Adolf and his pals can go jump in their ovens and burn themselves to cinders, and the sooner the better as far as I'm concerned.'

2) On or about the same date, the Accused showed to a junior officer some Russian propaganda inciting German soldiers to desert.

The offences committed are in violation of Paras 5 and 91, Article I of the Penal Code. The arrest and preliminary investigation of the Accused shall be carried out by the State Police, 8 Stadthausbrücke, Hamburg 2.

The arrest and detention of the Accused are subject to appeal before the President of the People's Tribunal.

(Sgd) Dr Mickert
President of the Court of Appeal.'

Lt. Ohlsen came to the end of the document for the third time. He laid it on the desk and looked across at Paul Bielert, with a gesture of resignation.

'What am I supposed to say?'

Bielert blew out a cloud of smoke and hunched an indifferent shoulder.

'That, of course, is entirely up to you,' he said, smoothly. 'I am only the person in charge of the preliminary investigation. It is not up to me to tell you what you should say. However, there is one word of advice I can give you.' He leaned forward across the desk, gesticulating towards Ohlsen with his cigar. 'Remember always that we at the Gestapo are not idiots. We know what we're about. We never arrest anyone without very good reasons ... and we never make mistakes. We check the facts most carefully before we even go to the lengths of bringing in a suspect for questioning. In a case such as yours, therefore, you will only make it worse for yourself if you attempt to deny any of the charges ... particularly since, in the final analysis, you will end up by saying just whatever we wish you to say.'

He smiled, and leaned back again. His eyes glittered with malevolent enjoyment behind his thick-lensed spectacles.

'If I were you, I shouldn't worry your head too much about the details. When it comes to it, it resolves itself quite simply into a question of choosing whether you walk out of this room on your own two feet or whether you're dragged out like a sack of potatoes ... it is entirely up to you. But whatever you decide, it makes no difference to me. Either way, you don't leave until you've made a full and satisfactory confession.'

He held his cigar under his nose a moment, delicately twitching his nostrils as the smoke curled up. He looked across at Ohlsen and smiled amiably.

'Of course, you can make things far easier for yourself if you do decide to be sensible. If you're willing to make a confession straight away, it saves both your time and ours. We don't have the bother of going through all this rubbish—' He disdainfully tapped a finger on a pile of papers and documents that lay before him on the desk – 'and you will probably be detained in Torgau no longer than two to three weeks, which I think you will agree is quite reasonable. After Torgau, of course, you'll either be sent to a disciplinary regiment as an ordinary soldier or possibly put in an FGA* for a few months.'

Lt. Ohlsen ran a hand through his hair, making it stand on end like a brush. He met the glittering grey eyes of Bielert, and he refused to flinch.

'Everything you say sounds perfectly straightforward,' he allowed. 'Even, in the circumstances, quite tempting . . . I suppose most of the poor fools you have sitting in this chair would be gullible enough to believe you. The only thing is, I've already served three years in a disciplinary regiment and I'm perfectly well aware of the fact that no one – I repeat, no one – has ever survived more than two months in an FGA.'

Bielert hunched a shoulder.

'You're exaggerating, of course. I have personally known several people who have been through the ordeal and are still very much alive to tell the tale . . . naturally, they are the ones who have been sensible and co-operative, I will grant you that. But anyone who is willing to be reasonable is always given a fair deal. And frankly, Lieutenant, I don't see that you have any real choice in the matter. Owing entirely to your own lack of discretion you have succeeded in landing yourself in your present position, so why not confess to your crimes and have done with it? I have, I can assure you, sufficient evidence against you to have you executed if you don't choose to co-operate with us.' He picked up his pen and pointed it towards the Lieutenant. 'When I say executed, I mean – executed. Decapitated . . . Have you ever seen anyone decapitated, Lieutenant? It's not a wholesome experience, even for the audience . . . Anyway, that

* Feldgefangenenabteilung – disciplinary camp

188

is the position in which you find yourself and it's up to you to take your pick. But whatever you do, don't underestimate the Gestapo. I don't exaggerate when I tell you that our information services are so efficient that we even know what people say in their sleep . . . My men are all over the place. And I make no bones about it, some of them are pretty unscrupulous people. I don't care who they are or where they've come from, whether they're generals or whether they're prostitutes, whether I've met them at society dinner parties or in the urinal of some stinking bistrot, so long as they can do the job, that's all I ask . . . If I felt so inclined, Lieutenant, it would take me no longer than a couple of weeks to have the whole of your life history from the moment you were born, even down to the minutest details that you yourself have probably never known . . . I daresay I could find out the colour of the very first dummy you ever sucked, if it were of any interest or importance to me.'

Lt. Ohlsen made to interrupt, but Bielert held up a hand.

'One moment before you speak. You shall be given all the time in the world very shortly. Let me first tell you some of the more salient facts as I have them. We know, to begin with, that you have frequently spoken to your men of treason and of sabotage and of desertion. You've treated the Führer's name with disrespect and you've read and discussed prohibited literature – in particular, "All Quiet on the Western Front", from which you've often quoted long passages. All this in direct violation of Paragraph 91. In addition, your wife is ready to make depositions as to other treasonable acts of yours . . . We have far too much against you, Lieutenant, there's no point in trying to fight us. Why not take up your pen and make a full confession, and we can be done with the whole unfortunate business within the hour. You can cool off in the cells for a week or two, and then I imagine your sentence will be six to eight weeks in Torgau. After that, as I said, a disciplinary regiment. Stripped of your rank, of course, but at least a very much wiser man.' He smiled. 'You'll know better than to open your mouth too wide in the future.'

'It all sounds eminently reasonable,' murmured Ohlsen. 'Only one thing worries me: what guarantee do I have that everything will take place just as you've promised? I have heard of people being shot for lesser crimes than I'm supposed to have committed.'

'One hears so many tales,' said Bielert, carelessly. 'Just as one should guard against talking too much, so, perhaps, one should guard against listening too much . . . As for a guarantee, of course, I'm afraid that's not possible. As you will appreciate, I am not the person who will ultimately sit in judgement upon you . . . However, you can rest assured that I have had a great deal of experience in cases such as yours, and I do know what I'm talking about. Whatever sentence is passed has to come through to me for confirmation, and I am able to modify it as I see fit. If I find a judge has been too lenient, it is in my power to have both him and the accused put in a security camp. Equally, I can, if I wish, tear up an order for execution and have the prisoner released immediately. It all comes back to this question of willingness to co-operate. We are constantly on the look out for new talent, and to this end we are always interested in those who wish to co-operate with us. You, for instance, could do both of us a good turn if you chose to come and work for me. I should be particularly interested to learn certain details regarding your commanding officer, Colonel Hinka. Also, you have a cavalry captain by the name of Brockmann in your regiment. I have a very special interest in Captain Brockmann. I will be honest with you, Lieutenant: it would give me positive pleasure to see Captain Brockmann's head severed from his shoulders . . . Still—' He sat up very straight and squared his narrow shoulders – 'let us get your affairs in order to begin with. Make your confession, serve your time in Torgau, and I can promise you that within three weeks I shall send an order for your immediate reinstatement in your company, with your present rank of lieutenant. It will all be made to appear perfectly normal to your colleagues, and once back you can quickly prove to me that you have regretted any past errors . . . Not, of course, that we ever force men to collaborate with us against their will. It is your own decision entirely.'

Lt. Ohlsen gave a cynical smile.

'It's all very well,' he said, 'but there's one flaw in it . . . You see, in the first place, I categorically deny all the charges made against me—'

Bielert sighed.

'Ah, Lieutenant, I thought you had more intelligence than to start running your head against brick walls! Whether you deny the charges or whether you admit them is totally irrelevant. You yourself are irrelevant, if it comes to that. I have nothing against you in particular – it was more chance than anything which made me pick on you. It could have been any member of your family. I could, if I'd wished, have arrested the whole lot of them while I was about it, but I don't require the whole lot of them, I require only one ... One member of each family in Germany. That's what I must have.'

Lt. Ohlsen stiffened.

'I'm afraid I don't follow you. What does my alleged behaviour have to do with my family?'

Bielert tossed the butt of his cigar negligently through the open window and shuffled a few papers on his desk.

'Nothing,' he said. 'Nothing at all. The point I am trying to make is that it might just as well have been your father or your sister or your brother as you ... It was mere chance that you happened to be the one who was chosen.' He looked across at Ohlsen with a cordial smile. 'We could just as well have arrested your father.'

'On what grounds?' demanded Ohlsen, coldly.

Bielert glanced down at the papers before him.

'Twenty-sixth April 1941,' he read out, crisply. 'At a few minutes past eleven ... he was discussing politics with two friends. During the course of the conversation he made the following statements: 1) that he no longer believed in the possibility of a Nazi victory, and 2) that he considered the State to be an idol with feet of clay. That may not seem to you a very grave crime, Lieutenant, but you would perhaps be surprised what we can do with it if we choose! And then, of course—' He pulled out another sheet of paper – 'there's your brother Hugo. He's serving at present with the 31st Armoured Regiment at Bamberg. We have information on him as well, you see ... He has been known on several occasions to make some very curious remarks on the men who run the Third Reich. We could certainly issue him with an invitation to come along here for a chat ... And then again, there is your sister.' He selected a third sheet of paper and ran a finger down it. 'Here we are ... a nurse in an Air Force hospital in Italy. In September 1941 she was on a hospital ship in Naples. On the fourteenth of that month she was heard to remark that she held Herr Hitler directly responsible for ... let me see ... "for all this shameful and senseless slaughter" ...' Bielert collected his papers together and looked across at the Lieutenant. 'And there you have it,' he said, simply. 'We possess similar information on virtually every citizen who has a tongue to speak with. I have here—' He indicated a wire tray containing a bulky file – 'a case against a top official at the Ministry of Propaganda. A man in his position, and he knows no better than to pour out his heart to his mistress! However, he was sensible enough to make a full confession and offer his services the moment I taxed him with it. He could well be very useful to me. I've long had my eye on Dr. Goebbels and his waste-paper Ministry! You see, Lieutenant, I believe in aiming high ...'

He laughed, brushed a few ashes off the lapel of his jacket and tightened the knot in his tie.

'You have an odd sense of humour,' remarked Lt. Ohlsen, dryly.

Bielert abruptly pulled down the corners of his thin mouth. The grey eyes narrowed to slits.

'I am not interested in having a sense of humour, Lieutenant. My work is far too serious for such frivolities. I do what has to be done and it takes up twenty-four hours of every day. The security of the entire country rests on my shoulders. Mine and my colleagues' ... We have a duty to perform. Anyone who is unable to fit into our society must be exterminated for the good of that society. I think you will agree it is no laughing matter.'

'Not if you put it like that,' murmured Ohlsen.

'Hm.' Bielert cracked all his knuckles one after another, then tapped a hand impatiently on the table. 'Well, I can't afford to waste any more time talking to you, Lieutenant. Sign the declaration and I shan't bother with the rest of your impertinent family. They deserve to be locked up, but as I said, I can't be doing with the whole lot of them. One from each family, that's all I require. It was Reinhard Heydrich's idea, and like most of his ideas it's fundamentally sound . . . Just wait until the war is over, Lieutenant. You'll see the day when the entire population of Europe raise their hands in salute whenever an SS officer goes by. As they do in Japan, you know. I was in Japan for several months. It was a most enlightening experience. Dutch and English officers prostrating themselves before their Japanese masters . . .' He leaned back luxuriously in the depths of his leather chair, his small, neat hands resting lightly on the arms.

Lt. Ohlsen tried to suppress a shiver and failed. It needed only a pair of glittering black crows to transform the chair into a devil's throne, and Bielert into a creation dragged from the depths of Grimms' fairy tales.

He turned and looked out of the window. A steamer hooted mournfully on the Elbe. Two pigeons puffed and strutted on the ledge. From the flagpole hung the red flag with its swastika, limp in the still air. A flight of seagulls rose up, squalling in a fretful heap over a crust of bread. Lt. Ohlsen turned his eyes away. He had never been able to bear the sight of seagulls since the day in the Mediterranean when he had been on board a boat that was torpedoed. Himself, lying wounded and unable to help, he had watched in horror as a pack of ravenous birds had alighted on the dying ship's captain and torn out his eyes. He had loathed seagulls ever since. At least the birds of prey, the crows and the vultures, even rats and hyenas, had the decency to wait until their victims were dead before tearing them to pieces. But not seagulls. Seagulls tore the eyes out of their living prey. They seemed to him to be the Gestapo of the bird kingdom.

He looked back at Bielert, little grey man hunched in his armchair, indescribably evil, with a power that was terrifying, and he suddenly saw Bielert as a seagull: crouching over a warm body, sucking out its eyes and cramming them into his mouth . . .

Ohlsen stretched out a hand for the pen. He signed the declaration without even looking at it. He no longer cared. And besides, it was true. He had said far harsher words about the Führer than Bielert had accused him of. Perhaps, after all, he would be dying for a good cause . . . But he wished to know who it was that had denounced him. He wished there were some way of getting word to Porta and the Legionnaire. They would take his revenge for him, no matter who it was, and revenge would be sweet even by proxy.

Paul Bielert leaned forward with a slight grunt and took the declaration. He looked at the signature and nodded, then offered the box of big cigars to Ohlsen.

'There! It's done . . . and it wasn't really so difficult, was it?'

Ohlsen said nothing. There was really nothing to be said. He knew he could have prolonged the matter, denied all the charges, refused to sign, but he knew also that it would have been futile. The Gestapo had all the power and there was nothing the individual could do.

Ten minutes later, two SD Unterscharführer entered the room. One laid a heavy hand upon Ohlsen's shoulder.

'We're just going for a spin in the car, Lieutenant. We've come to take you with us. You'll enjoy the outing.'

They laughed uproariously. Unterscharführer Bock was reputed to be something of a joker.

Lt. Ohlsen left the room in silence, continued in silence through the building and out to the car. Unterscharführer Bock sat in front, next to the driver, and kept up a running commentary as they passed through the city. Down Mönckebergstrasse, across Adolf Hitler Square; détour on account of the bomb damage, along the Alster, past the hotel 'Vier Jahreszeiten', across the Gänsemarkt; down the Zeughausalle and into the Reeperbahn. The Reeperbahn was crowded. It seemed to be full of people who had nothing better to do than drift from one bar to another growing progressively and squalidly drunk as they did so.

'Pity we're in such a hurry,' said Bock. 'We could have stopped for a beer.'

Along the length of Kleine Maria Strasse stretched a long queue of people.

'They're waiting to try out the new whores,' explained Bock, hanging over the back of the seat and addressing Lt. Ohlsen, who made no attempt to show any interest. 'We've just installed another twenty of 'em. There's service for you! Don't never let me hear anyone say the Third Reich isn't well organized ... Tell me, Lieutenant, have you ever stopped to think exactly what National Socialism really is?' Ohlsen kept his head turned away, staring bleakly through the window. 'Well, I'll tell you,' said Bock. 'It's the one and only workable form of Communism.'

Ohlsen turned slowly to look at the man.

'How do you make that out?' he asked, wearily.

Bock laughed, flattered that he should at last have gained Ohlsen's attention.

'Well, now, the way I see it is, over here we're what I call *national* communists. We want to make Germans out of the whole world. Anyone got the wrong shape nose, the wrong type of hair, the wrong colour skin, he's out. And that's as it should be, because they're not Germanic ... Right? Now, the Russians, they're not nearly so choosy. They don't care what you look like, it's enough for them just to tap you on the shoulder and say, from now on you're a Bolshevik and you've got to think like a Bolshevik. And that's all they care. No feeling of nationality at all ... Mind you, I've got to admit it, in some respects the Russians know what they're doing a damn sight better than we do. Take priests, for example. Over here, we let 'em walk about quite freely, don't even make 'em wear a swastika ... Over there, they hang the bastards. Hang 'em and be done with it. And I say that's the way we should treat 'em. Because otherwise we're just storing up a parcel of trouble for ourselves, you mark my words. A parcel of trouble ... It doesn't pay to be too soft, and they're stronger than what you probably think they are. People are suckers for that sort of thing, all the jiggery pokery and the bowing and the scraping and the going to confession and all the rest of it. For myself I wouldn't have nothing to do with any of it. Catch me going anywhere near a bleeding priest!'

He laughed, and the driver laughed with him.

'Why is that?' asked Ohlsen, mildly. 'Do you have so much on your conscience?'

195

Bock looked out at the Königin Allee, with its church lying in ruins.

'I've not got nothing on my conscience, don't you worry. All I've ever done is carry out orders. Done what I been told to do. It's no concern of mine what the orders are, nor who gives 'em, so don't you try blaming me for anything.'

The car drew up outside Headquarters and a sentry bent down and spoke to the driver.

'Where from and where to?'

'Gestapo IV/2a, Stadthausbrücke 8. We're going to the garrison prison.'

'Let's see your pass.'

The sentry glanced for a moment at Lt. Ohlsen, and his thoughts were written clearly on his face:

'Last time he'll ride in the back seat of a car, poor devil ... probably the last time he'll ride anywhere at all ...'

He walked round to the front of the car to check the number plate. Resolutely, he saluted Ohlsen.

The big Mercedes drove on into the barracks. Lt. Ohlsen caught sight of a group of officers in white jackets walking up the broad steps to the casino. He himself had been to that casino, in earlier, happier days which now seemed a lifetime ago.

They drove on across the square and pulled up outside the prison. Bock laughed.

'Here we are, Lieutenant! A five-star hotel, all for your delight ... private bathroom and a soft bed, what more could a man ask? Don't be alarmed that the doors are locked and barred. That's not to keep people from getting out, it's to keep 'em from getting in ...'

He pressed a button at the side of the door, and far away in the depths of the prison could be heard the faint ringing of a bell. Soon there were heavy footsteps and the sound of keys turning in a lock. The door was swung slowly open by an Obergefreiter. Bock announced the arrival of Lt. Ohlsen as if he were the Queen of Sheba in person, and the Obergefreiter accepted delivery in phlegmatic silence as if he were taking receipt of a crate of vegetables.

'Is he one for the chopper?' he asked, laconically, as he handed back the official forms, duly signed.

'Who knows?' laughed Bock.

He saluted and turned away, leaving Ohlsen standing help-less on the wrong side of the stout iron-clad doors. He was marched along to a reception office, where an artillery Stabs-feldwebel lorded it behind a large empty desk. He was short and squat, with a bald head and an enormous chest, an over-hanging forehead and small round eyes like boot buttons. He took his time reading through Lt. Ohlsen's papers, either be-cause he had difficulty in reading or because he enjoyed wall-owing in a sense of self-importance before a disgraced officer.

'Crimes against the state,' he said, slowly running a square-tipped finger along the line of print. 'Crimes against the state ...' He looked contemptuously across at Ohlsen. 'I don't like people that commit crimes against the state. I'd rather have your real honest crook than scum like you. You can trust the green uniforms, but you can't never trust the red. I'd even rather have a yellow than a red. They might drive you bleeding barmy reading the bleeding Bible all day long, but at least they don't give no trouble. You people, though – you're just a load of idiots that won't never learn. Tilt at windmills,' he said, scorn-fully. 'That's what you do. Tilt at windmills ... Now, you listen to me.' He abruptly changed his tone to one of official barking. 'Empty your pockets and lay everything out upon the table. And when I say everything, I mean everything ... and that includes all the little goodies what you've tried stuffing up your arsehole. You can just hook 'em all out again. I wasn't born yesterday, you know: I've seen it all before ...' He leered. 'That's right, put 'em on the table. Work from left to right and make sure you keep 'em in a straight line. Use the edge of the table as a guide ... space 'em out proper, two fingers between each item ... lighter and matches over on the right, money down at the end on the left ... and get a move on, can't you, we haven't got all day, there is a war on, you know!'

Lt. Ohlsen stood back and looked at his personal belongings spread out in a straight line along the edge of the table: lighter, pen, watch, pipe, notebook, and all the other oddments that a man normally keeps in his pockets. At the end, on the left, were 32 marks and 67 pfennigs.

Stabsfeldwebel Stahlschmidt noted every article, in detail, on a sheet of paper, and then attached a label to each one. On Lt. Ohlsen's notebook was a red star: the cockade of a Russian commissar, and a souvenir of Kharkov. Stahlschmidt tore it off with an oath, hurled it to the floor and trampled it vigorously underfoot.

'We don't keep that sort of trash here. I should have thought that was a crime against the state in itself, carrying about rubbish that belongs to the enemies of Germany.'

He looked across at Lt. Ohlsen, his eyes gleaming with malicious anticipation: they had now arrived at the point where the Lieutenant must be stripped of his medals and his uniform and be subjected to a search. Stahlschmidt always enjoyed that more than anything.

He licked his fleshy lips and rubbed his sweating palms down the side of his legs, regarding Ohlsen through half-closed eyes. This one, he estimated, was not likely to give him any trouble, although prisoners in the past had been known to produce the most unlikely reactions and it never did to take too much for granted. The essential, as far as the Stabsfeldwebel was concerned, was to push the prisoner over the borderline, where rage or panic or general desperation would prompt him to lash out against his tormentor. Then, and only then, could the Stabsfeldwebel really begin to savour the joys of his position; then, and only then, could he pass to the counter-offensive. With Obergefreiter Stever standing foursquare and solid like a human Mount Everest at the door, blocking any possible escape route and complacently witnessing the fact that his superior was acting purely in self-defence, Stahlschmidt could work out all his problems, all his neuroses, on the hapless prisoners.

Still watching Lt. Ohlsen, he picked up a long slender riding switch and began tapping it pensively against his calf. He was remembering the scene that had been played out only a few days ago, with a fool of a colonel from the 123rd Infantry Regiment, who had been accused of sabotage. The man had borne all manner of insults and rough treatment with soldierly dignity until it came to the point where he was ordered to remove his clothes. And there he had stalled, and, indeed, had lost his head and become completely hysterical. That had been an unexpected turn-up for the books!

Stahlschmidt's thick wet tongue flicked out again and moistened his lips as he remembered the apoplectic colonel.

'You may be an officer and the commander of a regiment,' Stahlschmidt had sneered, secure in the safety of his own position; 'you may be covered in bits of tin and honour and glory and all the rest of the gubbins, and you may come from a bleeding blue-blooded family, but by Christ, as far as I'm concerned you're nothing but a lousy stinking bastard that's broken the law and that's here to be punished! And if you live long enough you'll be taken out and shot, and nobody's going to give a damn if your blood's as blue as the bleeding Med . . .'

At this, the Colonel had exploded. Obergefreiter Stever, watching from the door, had leaned forward and pushed him neatly in the small of the back, so that he lost his balance and cannoned into the waiting Stahlschmidt. For a few moments they had tossed him back and forth between them, punching him in the stomach, jabbing him with the butt of a rifle, until the Colonel, seizing his chance, had shot through the door and gone galloping up the passage with his shirt tail flapping against his stringy old thighs. They had chased after him, up and down the corridors, and finally cornered him with the aid of Greinert, otherwise known as the Vulture. While Greinert and Stever had held him between them, Stahlschmidt had pulled out his pistol and forced him to take it in his right hand, pressing it against his temple.

The Colonel had died badly. He had begged and pleaded and babbled hysterically, with tears down his cheeks, of the favours he could arrange for them if only they would spare his life. His last despairing words had been to offer them free use of his wife and daughters . . . Stahlschmidt had laughed as he forced the Colonel to press the trigger and blow his brains out.

Naturally, one could not expect all prisoners to put on such a good show, nor to commit suicide, but looking at Lt. Ohlsen Stahlschmidt found himself hopeful that this young man might also prove an entertaining proposition.

He scraped his throat and swallowed hard in anticipation.

'Will the prisoner now please remove his garments and lay them out on the two chairs provided. Undergarments on the left, all the rest on the right. Boots to be placed half way between the two.'

He scraped his throat again, waited a second, then looked up to see how the Lieutenant was taking it. To his acute disappointment, the Lieutenant was taking it quite indifferently. His face was unchanged. The lines round the mouth had perhaps hardened, the expression in the eyes perhaps grown a little bleaker, but it was evident that he was not going to crack easily. The Stabsfeldwebel had seen the signs before. The signs of a man who could no longer find the energy to fight or to set himself up against the system. And they were the most tedious of all prisoners. They would do whatever they were told, accept all manner of insults and injuries without so much as raising an eyebrow; just sit quietly in their cells and wait to be interrogated, wait to be tried, wait to be found guilty and shot. All this without a flicker of emotion to indicate that they cared. And perhaps they didn't care, and it was this which so irked the Stabsfeldwebel. Because a man who didn't care was a man who was invulnerable, and a man who was invulnerable was a man without interest. You could jeer at him, taunt him, humiliate him all you liked, and it was only a waste of time and a source of frustration, for you might just as well pour a flood of scorn upon a brick wall and expect it to fall to pieces as expect a man who no longer cared to show any stimulating reactions.

Lt. Ohlsen slowly and impassively undid his jacket and hung it over the back of the chair.

'Don't take all day about it!' snapped Stahlschmidt. 'You're not getting changed for a fancy dress ball!'

The Lieutenant obediently pulled off his shirt and trousers and flung them after the jacket. His expression was still blank. He showed no signs of shame, or anger, or humiliation. Stahlschmidt chewed at his meaty underlip with a set of yellowing teeth. Wait till the bastard was up before the Governor! That would shake him out of his lethargy. That would teach him to sing a different tune. That would—

Lt. Ohlsen stepped out his boots and stood naked between

the two chairs. Stahlschmidt turned to regard him. His top lip curled up in a hoop of derision.

'What a loathsome sight! Eh, Stever? What a horrible, loathsome sight ... There's something very disgusting about naked bodies ... You didn't look so bad with your uniform and all your lovely medals, but believe me, if you could see yourself now you'd want to crawl into a hole and die ... Look at you! Look at those great bony knees! Look at those horrible hairy legs! Look at those huge horny toenails! Jesus Christ, what a specimen, eh?'

He winked at Stever and began pacing round the Lieutenant, casting derisory glances at him, every now and again poking or prodding him. The Lieutenant bore it all with an air of weary patience, as if the Stabsfeldwebel were a child to be humoured and tolerated.

'All right!' roared Stahlschmidt, coming to a stop. 'Let's have you down on your hands and knees ... down on the floor, down you go! Ten press-ups, and no cheating ... Stever, come over here and take a quick dekko up his backside, make sure he's not got nothing hidden there ...'

Obergefreiter Stever willingly left his post at the door and walked to the far end of the Lieutenant. As he reached the last of his prescribed number of press-ups, Stever suddenly placed one heavy booted foot on his rump and gave him a shove that sent him flying. Stahlschmidt did his best to get in the way — even the lightest touch by the prisoner and he could claim to have been attacked by him — but annoyingly the Lieutenant managed to control his fall. He crashed into the door, but he avoided the Stabsfeldwebel.

He staggered to his feet and stood patiently by the side of one of the chairs, awaiting the next absurd order. His eyes were blank, staring not so much at the Stabsfeldwebel as straight through and past him, and by his very indifference he remained aloof and impregnable.

Stahlschmidt breathed deeply. If this insolent Lieutenant persisted in his present course of action, his stay in prison was likely to prove very uncomfortable indeed. It was Stahlschmidt who for all practical purposes actually ran the prison. The Governor came round occasionally on a tour of inspection, but it was Stahlschmidt who made all the decisions and organized the general treatment of the prisoners. Whatever he chose to do, Major Rotenhausen would close his eyes to it. Too close an inquiry into their affairs would have pleased neither man, and so long as Stahlschmidt remained reasonably circumspect the Governor was content to leave matters in his hands.

'Right!' Stahlschmidt stepped forward to the chairs. 'Belt and braces are left down here. We don't want you taking them off to the cells with you and getting bad ideas into your head.' He leered into the Lieutenant's face. 'We don't have suicides in this establishment . . . not unless I personally arrange for them. Just remember that. I daresay there's nothing you'd like better than to put an end to your lousy miserable existence before you have to face the tribunal and take the just punishment what's coming to you . . . I daresay you'd like to deprive society of the pleasure of having its revenge, wouldn't you? I know: I've met your type before. Think you can get away with things without paying for them. Well, you can't, and I'm here to see to it that you don't.'

He rubbed his large misshapen hands together and took a turn about the room.

'It'll either be Torgau or Glatz. One of the two. That's where you'll end up . . . I hope it's Glatz – eh, Stever? You've got your actual Colonel Remlinger at Glatz. He knows how to deal with people like you. He knows how to break you, he knows how to make you grovel . . . he runs that place with a discipline that would have made even old Fritz* turn pale. I've seen your actual death or glory boys fresh from the trenches and covered from head to foot in scars and medals, I've seen 'em walk in there proud as peacocks one day and snivelling like kids the next . . . They make you go up and down the stairs, four flights of 'em, on your hands and knees, you know that? They treat you like you deserve to be treated, lower than beasts of the field . . .'

As the Lieutenant remained in his impassive trance, Stahlschmidt took a pace backwards and tried a new tack.

'Still, maybe I'm wrong at that. Maybe it won't be Glatz and it won't be Torgau. Who knows, eh? It might be the old chop-

* Frederick the Great

202

ping block . . . I seen 'em do that to a bloke. Just once, I seen 'em do it and I couldn't bear to watch no more . . . Bloodthirsty, it was. Very. They don't always come off clean at the neck with the first blow . . .'

A slight, involuntary ghost of a smile flickered across Ohlsen's lips. It seemed to Stahlschmidt as if he were laughing at him: laughing kindly and trying not to show it, as at a child's naïve exaggeration.

Stahlschmidt stiffened.

'All right, that's enough of the talking! Get your clothes back on, and at the double before I lose patience! I'm a busy man, I've got things to do. It's all right for you, you're a nothing, you're a nobody, you got no responsibilities, but I got a position to keep up, I can't hang around all day telling fairy stories to the likes of you.'

Lt. Ohlsen quickly dressed himself again. He was obliged to keep one hand on his trousers, now that his braces had been confiscated. He was about to put his tie round his neck, when Stahlschmidt suddenly yanked it violently away from him.

'No ties allowed! What do you think this is, a fashion house? And do your jacket up properly, I won't have slipshod ways in my prison!'

The Lieutenant silently folded the wide lapels of his jacket across his chest and buttoned them down. Stahlschmidt nodded approvingly.

'Good. That's better. I can see you're quick to pick up new ideas . . . We'll make a man out of you yet. You'd be surprised the number of officers who've come in here like you and been sent out again as real soldiers . . . Right! A little gentle exercise before you go to the cells. Arms above your head, jumping on the spot . . . starting – now!'

The Lieutenant put his arms above his head and began jumping on the spot. As he did so, his trousers fell about his ankles and threatened to trip him up.

Stahlschmidt and Stever threw back their heads and roared with coarse laughter. Lt. Ohlsen went on jumping. He seemed almost unaware, and certainly uncaring, that his trousers were round his ankles and that he looked ridiculous.

Stahlschmidt stopped laughing, dug Stever in the ribs and

glared at him. Stever also stopped laughing. Lt. Ohlsen had ruined the joke: it simply wasn't funny any more.

Together they stood watching him, bewilderment and rage writ large on Stahlschmidt's face. He found himself wondering whether in fact the prisoner's mind had given way completely. Certainly there had been others whose spirit had broken and who no longer cared what became of them, but this idiot Lieutenant was holding out far longer than most. It was conceivable that a man could be left unmoved by thoughts of his ultimate fate, the chance of imprisonment or execution, but sooner or later Stahlschmidt had never failed to produce a spark of reaction by subjecting them to the smaller humiliations of life, the handing over of their possessions, the stripping, the searching, the jumping on the spot ... Was this stubborn fool of a prisoner completely insensitive? Had he no proper pride or sense of shame?

Stahlschmidt moved on to his next charade.

'Right! Down on the ground, flat on your stomach! Five turns to the right, five turns to the left, and don't take that belly off the floor or there'll be trouble!'

Lt. Ohlsen obediently fell flat upon his stomach. Obediently he began pulling himself round in a circle.

Stahlschmidt moved across towards him and deliberately stood on his fingers. Lt. Ohlsen winced. He bit his lips until they bled. Stahlschmidt renewed his efforts, walking back and forth over the prisoner's hands. Ohlsen saw a red mist of pain before his eyes, but no more than a low groan of protest was wrung from him.

After that, they gave him a rifle, a heavy Belgian rifle of antiquated design, and led him out in the corridor, where they called up Greinert the Vulture and had him assist them in putting the Lieutenant through his paces.

'Rifle drill!' bawled Stever. 'Down on your knees, prepare to fire!'

Greinert walked round with a critical eye, ready to jump on the smallest of faults, but he lacked the imagination to invent any and unfortunately for him Lieutenant Ohlsen appeared not to have any faults. He knew what he was doing when it came to handling rifles.

'On your feet, ready to fire!' yelled Stever.

Lt. Ohlsen was on his feet in an instant, the rifle in regulation position. Stever at once began shouting out a new string of orders.

'Down on your stomach! On your knees! On your feet! Present arms! Stand at ease! Fix bayonet! Down on the ground! Stand to attention! Stand at ease! Ready to fire! Half-turn to the right! Face front! Running on the spot, start now!'

Lt. Ohlsen took it all in grim silence. They kept him at it until he was almost, but not quite, at dropping point.

'Stand to attention!' roared Stever, whose voice was growing hoarse.

The Lieutenant stopped running on the spot. He pulled himself upright and stood stiffly to attention. For a second the building swayed before his eyes and he thought he was going to pitch forward, but the sensation passed and he retained his stance. Not, however, before the lynx eyes of Greinert had noted the slight movement. He stepped forward in a lather of excitement.

'He moved! He's supposed to be standing to attention, and he moved!'

Stever and Stahlschmidt, who had not noticed anything, handed over the field of battle to Greinert.

'Look at him!' screamed Greinert. 'Shaking all over like a wet dog! And him an officer! Supposed to train new recruits, and doesn't even know how to stand to attention! Doesn't even know how to obey an order!' He moved closer to the Lieutenant. 'I said stand to attention, not dance an Irish jig! When I say stand to attention, you stand to attention. That means you freeze to the spot, you grow like a statue, wild horses couldn't drag you away and earthquakes couldn't shake you . . .'

Lt. Ohlsen spoiled this fine burst of poetry by involuntarily swaying forward again. The Vulture stepped back a pace, pulled down his jacket, pushed back his helmet. His breath came snorting indignantly down his nostrils.

'Things have come to a pretty pass,' he said, bitterly, 'when a simple sergeant has to take an officer in hand and start training him in basic discipline.'

Suddenly, and with no warning, his right fist shot out and

crashed into the Lieutenant's face. Ohlsen staggered backwards, knocked off balance by the blow. He took a few uncertain steps, then regained his equilibrium and came once more to attention, standing stiff and straight and staring ahead, despite the blood that was pouring from his nose and dripping on to his tunic.

The Vulture at once launched into a fine display of histrionics. He raved and he roared, he mocked, he jeered and he intimidated, and he accompanied the whole tirade with a non-stop string of vitriolic obscenities. He raced off into a positive frenzy of fresh instructions, spitting them out one after another until the Lieutenant was several moves behind him and would have had no hope of keeping up even under the best of conditions.

When Ohlsen was finally standing to attention once again, his face streaked in blood, his nose swollen, his chest heaving and his ears ringing, Greinert embarked upon a new set of tactics. He began by standing a few paces away and studying the Lieutenant intently from head to foot, now and again giving a small scornful laugh. When he had finished with this amusement, he walked closer and stared direct into his face, trying to make him lower his gaze or blink. When Lt. Ohlsen did neither, Greinert set off on a circular tour, walking very silently round and round, and round and round, in never-ending circles . . .

It was a well-known trick. Most people broke after the first five minutes. Some, the toughest and most experienced, held out for ten. Very very rarely did a man last quarter of an hour.

Lt. Ohlsen survived for thirteen minutes. His head was beginning to swim and his arms to grow lead weights. His knees were trembling and he had cramp in his fingers. Greinert had been watching and waiting for this moment. He took up his position behind the Lieutenant and waited a while longer; and the, very gently, he stretched out a hand and gave a sharp push at Ohlsen's rifle. The rifle slipped from his numbed fingers and fell to the floor with a crash that rang startling loud in the silence.

'So now we come to it!' screamed Greinert. 'An officer who can't even hold on to his rifle! Drops it to the ground like a toy he's got tired of!' He walked round to face the Lieutenant. 'Get down on your stomach and grovel!'

Ohlsen fell thankfully to the ground. Greinert gave him a kick.

'Pick that rifle up and crawl forward! At the double, we don't want to be here all bleeding day! And lick the rifle while you're doing it ... I said lick it, damn you, lick it! Crawl and lick, crawl and lick, one – two, one – two ... keep it up, no flagging, I didn't tell you to stop!'

And so the Lieutenant crawled up and down the passage, licking his rifle till his tongue was sore. Each time he passed in front of Stahlschmidt and Stever they trod on his fingers and abused him. Each time he passed in front of Greinert he received a kick in the face, in the head, in the groin. He was bleeding from both nose and mouth. His hands were almost raw. His eyes were clouding over.

Someone dragged him to his feet and began using him as a punch ball. They pushed him to and fro between them, battering him until he fell limply from one to another and finally slid unconscious to the floor. Greinert aimed one last vicious kick into his crutch, but fortunately the Lieutenant was no longer capable of feeling pain. He lay on his back with his head to one side, a thin trickle of blood coming from his mouth and dripping to the floor.

'Hm.' Stahlschmidt grunted and stood looking down at the inert form. He had been unable to break the man's mind, but at least he had had the satisfaction of breaking his body. 'All right,' he said, turning back down the corridor. 'Throw him into number nine and forget about him.'

Happily he returned to his office. It had, on the whole, been a good day. This stubborn fool of a lieutenant was the fourth prisoner he had passed through the initiation ceremony. Stahlschmidt rubbed his hands together and trod with jaunty step to the window. If only, one day, a certain Lt. Hans Graf von Breckendorf could be passed through the initiation ceremony! If he could only have von Breckendorf crawling naked and shivering before him, jumping with his trousers round his ankles, lying in a heap with blood trickling from his mouth ... his joy would be complete.

Stahlschmidt swallowed and forced himself to sit down, before the excitement of the prospect should overcome him. He prayed nightly to a god he didn't believe in for von Breckendorf to be delivered to him. He hated von Breckendorf with a hatred that could only partially be appeased by the constant humiliation and brutality that he practised on all the other officers who came his way. Never, as long as he lived, would he forget the way that he had been made to suffer at von Breckendorf's hands.

It was a Saturday afternoon, a hot, bright day in the middle of July. The Stabsfeldwebel had just come off duty and had gone straight to the canteen for a beer. He had undone his collar and pushed his cap to the back of his head, and he remembered even now the anticipatory saliva suddenly flooding his mouth as he walked towards the steps.

At the foot of the steps, barring his entrance to the canteen, was Lt. Graft von Breckendorf. He had been made a lieutenant on the eve of his nineteenth birthday and he was arrogant and insufferable on account of it. He was sitting astride a magnificent dapple horse when Stahlschmidt came up, and as Stahlschmidt drew near he extended a langorous arm and poked the tip of his riding crop into his throat.

'What's the meaning of that, Stabsfeldwebel? Do your collar up immediately, I will not tolerate men wandering about half undressed for all to see . . .' And as Stahlschmidt did up his top button, von Breckendorf's eyes had narrowed and he had lowered the crop and pushed Stahlschmidt in the abdomen with it. 'How disgustingly fat you're becoming! Locked away in that prison of yours, it's not good for you, I don't believe you have nearly enough exercise. It's not healthy for a man to sit hunched over a desk all day. Come along with me and I'll put you through your paces.'

Stahlschmidt had had no alternative but to obey. The horse set off at a trot, and he had to run along behind to keep up, breathing in the sweet, suffocating smell of hot horse and saddle leather and human sweat.

Von Breckendorf had sent him through every obstacle on the obstacle course. Stahlschmidt had emerged from the barbed wire with his uniform in shreds and his face torn to ribbons, but von Breckendorf had appeared not to notice. He had immediately dragged him off to the stables, sent him into the ring and made him run round it several times while he rode behind him cracking his whip and saying 'Hup!' each time they came to a jump. Even then von Breckendorf had not wearied of the entertainment. He had given Stahlschmidt ten minutes to go away and change and to come back dressed in full combat uniform, including his gas mask, and he had then run him round the ring thirty-six times, von Breckendorf on horseback. Stahlschmidt on a leading reign. Any time Stahlschmidt staggered he felt the cut of the riding crop across his shoulders. He had been on the point of passing out when finally von Breckendorf had let him go.

'I think you'll find that's got some of the loose flab off you,' he had said, smiling benignly. 'Good day, Stabsfeldwebel. I feel sure we shall meet again some time.'

Stahlschmidt hoped so. With all his heart, he hoped so. Each morning he woke to a new day full of new expectations. Each morning he hurried to his office and ran a febrile eye through the sheaf of papers that had been left on his desk. One day, please God, he would see the name of Hans Graf von Breckendorf amongst them . . .

Nobody had ever seen fit to tell Stahlschmidt that Lt. Graf von Breckendorf had been killed over a year earlier at Sebastopol. Had he ever found out, it would almost certainly have broken his heart.

During the following days the prison staff were kept more busy than usual, and several happy inmates were locked away in their cells without first having to undergo the initiation rites. A large-scale offensive had been launched against those officers who entered into over-friendly relations with the people of occupied countries, and as a result the number of arrests was increasing daily by leaps and bounds. Anyone who was even heard to say a good word for an enemy nation came under the gravest of suspicion, and one indiscreet infantry officer at Oldenbourg, chancing to remark that he found Winston Churchill a great deal more inspiring than certain other people, found himself under arrest almost before he had finished speaking.

A cavalry officer who chose to salute with two fingers raised in the V for Victory sign was rushed straight away to see Herr Bielert: infringement of the famous paragraph 91. The cavalry officer was never seen again.

The vast majority of those accused not only made full confessions within the hour, they also volunteered the names of friends and relations, whether they were guilty or not. Paul Bielert was having a most gratifying war.

As for Lt. Ohlsen, in cell number nine, he found himself a regular visitor to Bielert's sparsely furnished office, with its inevitable vase of pinks from which Bielert helped himself to a buttonhole every day. He soon grew so accustomed to these visits that they ceased even to be a diversion.

For the rest of the time he lay huddled in his cell, pressing his aching head against the stone wall in an attempt to find some relief from the pain. He thought back to the trenches, and they now seemed a model of comfort compared with his bleak prison cell. He wondered often why no one from the Company had come to see him. Possibly they thought he was already dead. It would be quite typical of the Gestapo if they had announced his execution days or even weeks before it took place.

He was strictly guarded, and isolated from the other prisoners save during the exercise period, but even then it was impossible to exchange more than the odd snatched word here and there. Both Stahlschmidt and Greinert were ceaselessly on the watch, prowling to and fro, and Stever and some of the other guards were in the habit of sitting on the wall to watch the fun. The exercise period, far from being a relief from the cramped monotony of the cells, was in fact a nightmare. The prisoners were obliged to run in circles for a full half hour, with their hands clasped behind their necks and their legs held stiff. It was most amusing to watch, most exhausting to perform. It jarred the entire body and cramped the muscles of the leg. But it was Stahlschmidt's very own personal invention and he was naturally proud of it.

When the SD had come the first time to collect Lt. Ohlsen for interrogation with Bielert, they had taken one look at his battered face and swollen nose and laughed until they almost cried.

'What's happened to you, then? Fell down the stairs, did you?'

Stahlschmidt had earnestly explained that the Lieutenant was subject to bad dreams and had thrown himself out of bed in a fit one night, which only increased the general hilarity.

'It's an odd thing,' remarked one of the Unterscharführer, wiping his eyes, 'how many of your prisoners manage to fall out of bed . . . I wonder you don't start tying them in at night. For their own protection, of course . . .'

On the wall of Ohlsen's cell, a father had scratched a few pathetic lines to his son, bidding him farewell and commending him to the care of the world. Erich Bernert, Colonel, 15.4.40 . . . Lt. Ohlsen wondered what had happened to Erich Bernert, Colonel, and whether his son was old enough to be told about him. And then he fell to thinking about his own son, Gerd, whose mother and her family had placed him in a National Socialist Education Camp near Oranienburg. Lt. Ohlsen was very well aware that once he was dead the leaders of the Hitler Youth would lose no time in taking Gerd to one side and poisoning his mind against him. Probably they had already begun on the task. Your father was a traitor, your father was an enemy of the people, your father betrayed his country . . . Yes, and then there were his in-laws, the proud-faced stiff-necked Länder, who never had approved of him. He could hear Frau Länder's voice, ringing out rejoicing, as she heard the news of his death. A traitor to his country, he had spoken out against the Führer, and in her mind he would be no better than a sexual pervert or a murderer. She would tell her smart friends all about him, in hushed tones over the afternoon tea cups. She would revile him for having brought such shame upon the family, and yet at the same time she would dine out on the story for weeks to come.

Lt. Ohlsen began to feel that he was already dead and forgotten. He no longer cared what became of him, he was not scared of death, he almost welcomed the idea as a release from pain; and yet it was hard to sit alone in his cell and think of the world outside, laughing and crying, fighting and playing, totally unaware of his existence. How easy it was to cease to be! How swiftly people forgot, how little they cared . . .

And then, one day, he had some visitors. The Old Man and the Legionnaire came to see him, and at once the curtain lifted and he was no longer a ghost, he was part of the world again. He might not be able to walk out and join them, but at least they had remembered him. And although, obviously, neither the Old Man nor the Legionnaire could set him free or change his ultimate fate, he knew now that his treatment would not go unrevenged. And that made it easier. There was a certain satisfaction in knowing that those who had sneered at you, humiliated you, beaten you half to death, were themselves under sentence of revenge and never even knew it.

The little Legionnaire had looked upon all three of them, Stahlschmidt, Stever and Greinert, and the Legionnaire would remember. The Legionnaire always remembered.

Stever was present throughout the visit, and he found himself strangely troubled by the sight of the Legionnaire. He had tried, at first, to join in the conversation, but the Legionnaire had coldly rebuffed him. Swallowing this treatment, Stever had then handed round his cigarettes, even though smoking was strictly forbidden. They had all looked the other way without even saying thank you.

At the end of the visit, the Legionnaire had looked up at Stever with narrowed, calculating eyes.

'You're Stever – that right? And the big fellow in the office, the one with three stars on his shoulder, that's Stahlschmidt? And your pal I saw you with before we came in – the one with the crooked nose – he's called Greinert?'

'Yes,' said Stever, wondering why it mattered.

'Good.' The Legionnaire nodded his head and gave a most unpleasant smile. 'Good. I shall remember that. I never forget a name – or a face . . . Good day.'

And he had strolled away down the passage singing a song under his breath. Just loud enough for Stever to catch the words: Come, come, come, oh Death . . .

Stever returned slowly to Lt. Ohlsen's cell. The Legionnaire had upset him. There was something unnerving about the man. Stever sat down on the edge of the bunk and looked across at Ohlsen.

'That little chap,' he said, warily. 'That little chap with the scars all over his face . . . he a friend of yours?'

Lt. Ohlsen silently inclined his head. Stever picked nervously at an ear lobe.

'Nasty piece of work,' he observed. 'Looks like he'd knife his grandmother in the back for half a fag . . . Gave me the cold shudders, he did. Wouldn't surprise me if he was some kind of a nut. Probably certifiable . . . I don't know how an officer like you can bear to have him around you.'

Lt. Ohlsen shrugged his shoulders.

'I don't "have him around me". No one "has the Legionnaire around him". He's what you call a loner . . . He's only got one real friend, and that's death.'

Stever shivered.

'What do you mean, death? I don't know what you mean. Is he a murderer or something?'

'Upon occasion. If he feels like it. He has been known to kill those who offend against his own personal code of morals. It's a bit different from yours or mine, you see. Not nearly so elastic, for a start. The Legionnaire won't accept any excuses. He sets himself up as his own judge and his own executioner. That's part of his moral code: a man shouldn't sit in judgment unless he's prepared to carry out himself the punishment that he decrees . . . and the Legionnaire always is prepared.'

Stever wiped a hand across his brow.

'People like him shouldn't be let loose. He's enough to give you the creeping willies . . . I tell you, I've met some bastard types in the R.S.H.A. before now, but that pal of yours really takes the biscuit. Makes your flesh creep just to look at him.'

Lt. Ohlsen smiled.

'He's not pretty, I'll grant you that. But I think he has a certain sort of charm, don't you find?'

'Charm be buggered!' said Stever. And then, suddenly fearful: 'Here, you don't think he's got anything against me, do you?'

'Why ask me?' said Lt. Ohlsen. 'He doesn't let me into his secrets. No one ever knows, with the Legionnaire, until it's too late . . . You may have remarked something else about him,

Stever: he walks like a cat. No sound at all. He wears rubber boots, of course, but it's more than that. It's a skill he's acquired over the years. He could walk up behind you on a gravel path covered in twigs and bits of broken glass and you'd never hear him coming . . . until it was too late.'

'Well, anyway,' said Stever, rallying a little, 'I don't see that I've done anything to upset him. I've never seen him in my life before, and I've no wish ever to see him again.' He took off his helmet, wiped his head, put the helmet back on. 'I'm only an Obergefreiter,' he said, fretfully. 'It's not up to me to give the orders round here. I'm just the poor cunt that has to carry them out.'

'Of course,' agreed Lt. Ohlsen, with a comforting smile. 'You don't have to explain. You don't enjoy kicking people in the guts, but you have to do it none the less . . .'

'Exactly,' said Stever. He leaned forward. 'I'll tell you something, Lieutenant. It's Stahlschmidt, he's the dangerous one round this place. He's the Stabsfeldwebel, he's the big wheel. So if the little guy with the scars feels like carving anyone up, do me a favour and tell him to go for Stahlschmidt, will you? Marius Alois Joseph Stahlschmidt, that's his name, and he's a bastard. You're quite right, Lieutenant: I can't stand to see men beaten up and smashed to pulp. Specially not officers. But what can I do? I'm only an Obergefreiter. And as a matter of fact, I'm thinking of putting in for a transfer. I tell you, I can't take this place much longer. Not only that, but it's asking for trouble, ain't it? I mean, some of the blokes that come here are let out again. Not very often, but it does happen. And what about the ones that are sent off to disciplinary regiments? Stands to reason SOME of 'em are going to survive, doesn't it? And one day they're going to come back here, I reckon, looking for Stahlschmidt. And when that happens, I'd rather be somewhere else, thank you very much. I mean, they're not to know that I'm just doing my job and carrying out my orders, are they? I mean, you didn't until I told you, did you?'

Lt. Ohlsen gravely shook his head. Stever suddenly stood up.

'Look, I'll show you. I was transferred here from a cavalry regiment in Paris.' He pulled out his military notebook and thrust it at the Lieutenant. 'See that? The 12th Cavalry, I was. And then the lousy sods sent me to this shithole ... I didn't want to come, make no mistake about that. Only thing was, I didn't have no say in the matter, did I? I've often asked for a transfer, believe you me, but what can I do, Stahlschmidt doesn't want me to go, he's got used to me and he needs me ... like when he goes too far and clobbers people too hard and they die on him, he's got to have me to give him an alibi. Be a witness, like. Explain how it was only in self-defence and all that crap.'

'I see.' Lt. Ohlsen handed back the notebook. 'Tell me Stever, don't you believe in a God?'

Stever looked alarmed, as if he suspected some kind of trick, some kind of double meaning.

'No, not really. Can't say I do.'

'Have you ever tried saying your prayers?'

'Well—' He shuffed his feet, uncomfortably – 'once or twice I did, yeah. When I was in the shit up to my neck and couldn't see no way out, like ... But I can't say it does much good, myself.' Stever buttoned his pocket and turned with sudden enthusiasm to Ohlsen. 'Now, you listen here, Lieutenant. I'm going to take good care of you from now on. Now we've had this talk and we understand each other ... You want something to read, maybe? Most officers seem to get a kick out of reading. Well, I'll nick a few books from somewhere and let you have 'em. Only take care Stahlschmidt don't see 'em, for God's sake ... As for Greinert, you don't need to worry about him. He's got his own cells to look after. This lot down here, they belong to me ... And just before I go, Lieutenant, I got a little present for you. Brought it specially for you, I did. I've had one or two, but these'll last you a few hours.' He slipped a packet of cigarettes under the mattress on the bunk and winked conspiratorially at Ohlsen. 'You and me can be pals, eh? Only smoke 'em near the air vent, so's the smell don't hang around, there's a good lad.'

He moved towards the door, and then turned.

'We get our chocolate ration this evening. You like chocolate, Lieutenant? I'll bring you my ration. I'll put it behind the water tank in the bogs, then next time you go for a crap you can pick it up, O.K.? And you will speak to your pal about me, won't you? Tell him what I said about Stahlschmidt being the bloke he really wants. I don't need to tell you, Lieutenant, I'm risking my neck for you, what with the fags and the chocolate and the books and all. Even talking to you like this, I could be nabbed for it . . . But somehow I liked the look of you right from the first moment I saw you. Don't you remember I winked at you behind Stahlschmidt's back? Don't you remember that?'

'I can't say I do,' admitted Ohlsen.

'Well, I did,' said Stever. 'And another thing: don't you worry about me getting the wind up, or nothing like that. I'm not scared of nothing and no one. Anyone knows me'll tell you that. I got my two Iron Crosses in Poland, and it was tough out there. Really tough. Talk about the Russian front, that's got nothing on Poland . . . I was the only man in all the Company that got the Iron Cross. You tell your friend that. And tell him I haven't always been stuck in this dump. I been at the front, as well. At Westa Plata, for instance. I wiped out a whole section single-handed. That's as true as I stand here, so help me. I got the EKII* for that. And in Warsaw I destroyed four air raid shelters full of partisans. I destroyed four air raid shelters single-handed with a flame thrower. Not a single one got out alive. That's when they give me the EKI. So you see, I know what's what, and I can't be accused of not doing my bit. I was mad to get to Stalingrad, only the bastards wouldn't let me.'

He opened the door, went out, turned and put his head back in again.

'Tell me,' he said. 'This friend of yours with the ugly mug . . . he looks like the sort that would use a knife?'

Lt. Ohlsen nodded.

'That's right. He's a dab hand with a knife, the Legion- naire . . .'

Stever slammed the door and tottered on weak legs down the passage to the lavatory. He ran the cold water tap over his head for a few minutes, feeling suddenly sick and faint.

Lt. Ohlsen, alone in his cell, contemptuously brushed the blanket where Stever had been sitting, then stretched out full

* Iron Cross 2nd Class

length on the bed, his hands behind his head, staring up at the ceiling with a smile on his lips. The revenge had already begun and he himself was able to take a hand in it.

Stever left the lavatory with his hair dripping water and hurried back along the passage to Stahlschmidt's office. He burst in without troubling to knock at the door.

'Did you see number nine's visitors, Stabsfeldwebel? Did you see that little guy with the scars? Did you see the look in his eyes? Did you—'

'Calm down, Stever. Calm down.' Stahlschmidt gazed across at his subordinate through eyes that had narrowed to two calculating slits. 'I saw them, but there's nothing whatever to worry about. They're people of total non-importance. And as for the one with the scars, in my opinion he was quite obviously drunk. Stark raving drunk. I watched him going down the passage. He was singing some sentimental rubbish about death.'

'Death?' whispered Stever.

'Well, either he was drunk,' said Stahlschmidt, 'or else he's suffering from shell shock. I shouldn't wonder if that was it. He was practically bent double under all the decorations he was wearing. These front line heroes are usually pretty unstable types.'

Stever wiped his sleeve across his forehead and sank into a chair.

'I don't know about unstable . . . sodding mad, if you ask me . . . and dangerous with it! That man is dangerous, you mark my word! Christ almighty, with a face like that, he ought to be locked up . . . Did you see that scar he had? Running right down his face? It kept changing colour, I swear it did! And his hands, I've never seen anything like them!'

Stahlschmidt shrugged his shoulders.

'You have a very vivid imagination, Stever. They just looked like hands to me.'

'Hands that were made for strangling,' said Stever, hoarsely.

Stahlschmidt made an impatient noise somewhere down the back of his throat and picked up the visitors' permit that was lying on his desk.

'Willie Beier and Alfred Kalb,' he murmured.

'That's it!' cried Stever. 'Alfred Kalb! That's him, I recognize the name!'

'All right, there's no need to shout.'

Stahlschmidt sat down and examined the permit through his magnifying glass. His face suddenly twitched.

'Take a look at that signature,' he said.

'What's the matter with it?' asked Stever, squinting slightly.

Stahlschmidt looked up in annoyance.

'Obergefreiter Stever, I have always regarded you as a reasonably intelligent person. Not brilliant, but not altogether moronic. You do have a certain semblance of brain. If you hadn't, I'd have had you sent packing to a disciplinary company long ago. However, that's beside the point. The point is, I don't like working with idiots. They dull the intellect and they slow the reactions. And if you're going to start fumbling and muttering and scratching your arse every time I put a simple question to you, then you might just as well get out of here right now before I throw you out.'

Stever licked his lips, nervously.

'Let me have another look,' he begged. 'I'm – I'm not quite myself today.'

He snatched up the paper and examined it under the glass. He turned it this way and that, he took it to the window, he closed each eye in turn, he almost stood on his head, but still he could see nothing very remarkable about the signature.

'Well?' said Stahlschmidt.

'Yes!' Stever laid down the paper and the magnifying glass and stepped back a pace. 'Yes, now you come to mention it there is something rather odd about it. I'm afraid my eyes aren't quite as quick as yours. I'd never have noticed it if you hadn't pointed it out to me.'

'Hm! It's taken you long enough to get there. Either you need glasses or your brain's starting to go soft . . . You'll have to get to bed earlier at night. Have a good eight hours' sleep and don't drink so much. Make sure your bowels are in good working order.'

218

Stahlschmidt opened the bottom drawer of his desk, took out a bottle of whisky and filled two glasses.

'Still, I'm glad you tumbled it in the end. The signature has almost certainly been forged. It's a good thing you spotted it.'

Stever's eyes widened. His hand, which had automatically been stretching out for the whisky glass, wavered a moment, then changed direction and picked up the permit once more. For the life of him he could still see nothing wrong with the signature.

'Out of all the permits we've had in this office,' continued Stahlschmidt, 'have you ever seen one that's been signed by Standartenführer Paul Bielert in person? Not printed or rubber stamped, but actually written by him in pen and ink?' He shook his head. 'Of course you haven't! The Standartenführer wouldn't so degrade himself as to sign his name in person to every fiddling farting little bit of paper that came his way . . . Even I don't, so I'm quite sure he wouldn't. Even I use a rubber stamp.' Stahlschmidt looked up at Stever and his lips twisted in what might have been a smile. 'And so do you on occasion, don't you, Stever? A rubber stamp with my signature on it . . .'

'Me?' gasped Stever, in tones of outrage. 'I've never done that in my life!'

Stahlschmidt raised one derisive eyebrow.

'No? Well, perhaps you've not been aware of it at the time . . . perhaps you suffer from amnesia? Sudden blackouts? Dizzy spells? I give you the benefit of the doubt, you see, because it's obviously a very serious offence to use another man's signature without his knowledge and authorization.'

'Of course it is!' exclaimed Stever, self-righteously. 'That is why I would never, never—' He broke off. 'I mean, why on earth should I?' he demanded.

'Oh, my dear Stever, I can think of a dozen reasons.' Stahlschmidt sprawled back in his chair with his legs spread out under his desk, enjoying the sensation of having Stever at his mercy. 'Perhaps you had some gambling debts? Perhaps you wanted to requisition some article that you could sell on the black market? I'm sure you don't need me to tell you all the things a rubber stamp can be used for! As I already said, you're a person of fair intelligence, and people of intelligence are the biggest scoundrels on earth.'

'But Stabsfeldwebel, you're a person of great intelligence yourself!' burst out Stever, triumphantly.

This time, Stahlschmidt raised both eyebrows together, as high as they would go.

'Watch what you're saying, Stever. Just remember your position. You're only an Obergefreiter, don't go putting on airs and graces . . .' He reached out for the permit again. 'Let's have another look at this forged signature. With a bit of luck, Willie Beier and Alfred Kalb will soon be joining their friend the Lieutenant in our cells.'

Stever rubbed his hands together and snatched eagerly at his whisky glass.

'God, if that happened I swear I'd mend my ways! I would, really! I'd feel that Him up There was kind of saying, Well, I do exist, this is proof of it . . . Know what I mean? And I'd go to mass at least once a – once a month. Yes, I would. Once a month I'd go. To EARLY mass,' said Stever, impressively.

'You don't think that's rather excessive?' murmured Stahlschmidt.

'I'd do more than that, I'd go down on my knees and pray!' shouted Stever. 'God, if I had that little scarred bastard in here I'd – I'd put his eyes out for him!'

'You mean, like Greinert did to that Major he took such a dislike to?'

'Exactly! I'd do it with my thumbs, just like he did . . . stuff a bit of rag into his mouth so's nobody would hear, and dig both his eyes out . . .'

'It sounds too delightful,' murmured Stahlschmidt. 'But I wonder, would you really have the guts to do it, when it came to the point?'

'With that rat, yes!' Stever tossed off his whisky and set the glass back on the table with a jaunty flourish. 'I feel more like myself again, now . . . I can already see those two being marched through the doors under escort . . .'

Stahlschmidt nodded and smiled. He looked again at the forged signature and he felt very sure of himself. And even if he were proved wrong, he could always blame Stever. He picked up the telephone and dialled a number.

'I want the Commissariat. Feldwebel Rinken. This is Stahlschmidt here, Stabsfeldwebel Stahlschmidt of the garrison prison ... oh, that is you, is it, Rinken? Why don't you announce yourself, for God's sake? I could be talking to anybody, couldn't I? Listen, I've got a job for you, I want you to — What? What's that you say?' He remained silent a moment, then exploded down the receiver. 'You'll bloody well do what I tell you and no questions asked! I don't doubt you're busy, and so are we, working our bollocks off doing all the stuff you should have done and haven't, so don't try that one! In any case, it's perfectly simple and straightforward, a piece of piss, I just want you to arrange for two men to be picked up and brought over here as soon as possible. You got a pencil? Good. Make a note of their names ... Willie Beier and Alfred Kalb ... all right? You got that? Good. They came to visit one of the prisoners here and I don't like the look of them. Particularly the Kalb man. He's either suffering from shell shock or else he was as pissed as a newt. Anyway, the point is, they got in here on a forged pass, so I want them brought in for questioning as soon as possible, and—' He broke off, suddenly suspicious. 'What are you laughing at?'

'You!' Rinken's loud gaffaws could he beard at the far side of the room,' and Stever looked up, inquiringly. 'Really, Stahlschmidt, have you lost your grip or something? What the devil have these two madmen got to do with me? They're your pigeon and you're welcome ... under Heeresarmeevorschrift* number 979 of 26th April, 1940, para. 12, clause 8, it's exclusively your concern if something like that occurs in your territory, and you're obliged to make a report on ... And until we've got your report our hands are tied ... All I can say is, I hope for your own sake you've made a mistake. It's not going to sound too good, is it? A couple of men allowed to walk into your prison as bold as brass with forged papers that no one checks? Visiting a prisoner under your very nose when they had

* Army Bulletin

no right to be there . . .' He made a soft clucking noise of disapproval with his tongue. 'I shouldn't care to be in your shoes right now, and that's a fact! You ought to have pinched 'em before they left the prison.'

Stever, who had crept up to the desk and been listening, sprang away at these words and stood, white and trembling, by the door, as if prepared for instant flight.

Stahlschmidt drummed his fingers on the desk and screwed his neck a few inches out of his collar.

'Look here, Rinken, don't be bloody absurd! There's no need to throw a tantrum over this thing! Strictly off the record, I only rang you up because I'm not altogether SURE that the pass was forged . . . I THINK it is, but I want to check, and I want you—'

'Like hell! A second ago you were telling me to have them picked up because they'd quite definitely got in on a forged pass—'

'No, no, I said I THOUGHT they had—'

'Thought, my anus!' said Rinken, crudely. 'No use trying to wriggle out of it, Stahlschmidt, I've got a witness who'll testify if necessary. He's listening in on the extension.'

'Sod the witness!' roared Stahlschmidt. 'You don't think I care for any lousy witness, do you?'

'Whether you do or not,' said Rinken, darkly, 'I've already explained that the affair is nothing to do with us. You'll have to put in an official report. Time and again you've told us that what goes on in your nick is your business and no one else's. If you'd had any sense at all you'd already have this couple under lock and key. But since you haven't, and since the matter has now been brought to my notice, I suppose I shall have to get in touch with Lt. Col. Segen and put him in the picture. We'll have the two men brought in for questioning and we'll soon get to the bottom of the story . . . but I still want a written report.'

Stahlschmidt kicked savagely at his waste paper basket and forced himself to speak calmly. Perhaps he had been a trifle precipitous. The affair was not progressing as he had anticipated.

'Look, upon reflection, Rinken, you're quite right. It's my

affair and I shouldn't have bothered you with it. I'm sorry, I wasn't thinking, I—'

'That's quite all right.' Rinken's voice purred down the receiver, full of cream and honey and general complacency. 'We all make mistakes. I don't mind having a word with Segen about it. Just let me have your written report, that's all I ask.'

'Well, but look, it's really not worth your while—'

'One thing I should be interested to know,' interrupted Rinken. 'Whose signature had they forged?'

'Bielert's.'

'Bielert's? I see. In that case, the matter really is serious. I'll take it up without delay, written report or not.'

'But look here—'

'Incidentally, Stahlschmidt, did you know they're forming a new disciplinary infantry regiment? I hear they're crying out for experienced N.C.O.s. Why don't you put your name forward?'

'Rinken, please!' Stahlschmidt forced himself to be humble. With a great effort of will, he induced a note of supplication to enter his voice. 'Don't go bothering Colonel Segen about it. Let the matter drop. To be perfectly honest I don't really have any idea whether or not the damned pass is forged, it was just an idea that occurred to me. But in any case, the two men are no longer in the area, they—'

'No longer in the area?' repeated Rinken, joyously. 'Really, Stahlschmidt, don't you have any method of controlling people's exits and entrances? It sounds to me as if the public at large can wander in and out as if you're running an art gallery rather than a nick ... Who let these men in, in the first place? Who let them out again? Who checked their credentials?'

'I did,' said Stahlschmidt, irritably. 'You know I did. You know it's me that sees to all that sort of thing. God knows, there's no one else I can rely on ...'

Rinken laughed, sardonically.

'Speaking of relying on people, I've been relying on you, Stahlschmidt, to pay me back that 100 marks you owe me. You hadn't forgotten it, I hope? One hundred marks, plus 24 per cent interest.'

'I hadn't forgotten it. I never forget my debts, especially to friends. But the thing is, Rinken, I'm not too flush at the moment. I've – I've had a lot of extra expenses. A couple of new uniforms and a pair of new boots. You know how it is ... you can't go round in rags. Not when you're a Stabsfeldwebel. And then the prices they charge these days are ridiculous! I had to pay four times more for those boots than I should have done ... And in any case, you know, you lent me that money as a friend. Without interest. You never said anything at the time about 24 per cent.'

'Really, you astound me,' said Rinken, coldly. 'First of all you ring me up with wild tales of forged passes and two raving mad criminals running in and out of your prison with no one even asking their names, and then you start babbling about new uniforms and outrageously expensive boots and expecting me to pay for them, and finally you try to deny ever borrowing any money from me!'

'No, no, only the interest!' protested Stahlschmidt.

'You owe me 100 marks plus 24 per cent interest,' said Rinken, stubbornly. 'You deny the interest and you refuse to pay me back the 100 marks. That's more than enough for me. I shall speak to Colonel Segen about you. You can't expect to do that sort of thing and get away with it, you know.'

There was a click and the line went dead. Rinken had hung up. Stahlschmidt sat a moment, staring aghast at the telephone, wondering how it was that the affair had backfired so disastrously.

'What did he say?' asked Stever, taking a few hesitant steps away from the door and back into the room.

'Mind your own bloody business!' snarled Stahlschmidt.

He paced furiously up and down a few times, kicking any object that was unfortunate enough to lie in his path, smashing his fist into the filing cabinet, spitting on the photograph of Himmler. And then he suddenly lunged back towards his desk and clawed up the telephone again.

'Paul? Is that you, Paul? It's Alois here.' His voice flowed gently, sweetly, coaxingly down the line. 'Listen, I'm sorry about that money I owe you. You're quite right about the 24 per cent, of course you are, but you know how it is ... one protests as a matter of principle! We all do it, don't we, Paul?

It's just habit, it doesn't mean anything, it doesn't mean I'm trying to wriggle out of it . . .'

'That's as may be,' said Rinken, coldly. 'All I'm interested in right now is getting my money back. I'll give you until mid-day tomorrow and not a moment longer. One hundred marks plus the interest.'

'Look, I swear to you,' said Stahlschmidt, 'I swear to you, Paul, you'll have it all back. I'll put it in a plain envelope and send Stever round with it.'

From the far corner of the room, Stever shook his head violently to and fro. Stahlschmidt ignored him.

'All I ask, Paul, is that for the sake of our friendship you tell me how the devil I'm to get out of this fix! It's all been a ghastly mistake, but there must be some way out.'

'As far as I can see, there are only two things you can do,' said Rinken, still very cold and curt. 'You can either go to your C.O. and make a clean breast of it, and hope he's fool enough to swallow it – which he probably won't be, and then he'll start poking around and asking questions and you'll be worse in the shit than ever. Or else, of course, you can take the bull by the horns and ring straight through to the Gestapo. Only thing is, you'll need to be very very careful what you say to them. Have a rehearsal first, I should, if I were you. And even then, of course, you'll have had it if the pass turns out to be genuine. Bielert will come down on you like a ton of bricks. And then again, on the other hand, if it IS a forgery you'll be in even worse trouble, because then they'll want to have a word with the two guys you let in, and you can imagine how pleased they'll be when they've discovered you've let 'em go . . .'

There was a moment's silence. Stahlschmidt sat chewing a pencil, holding it between his back teeth and gnawing at it.

'Paul,' he said, at last. 'Are you there, Paul? I just had a new idea. Mightn't it be simpler if you just forgot I ever rang you in the first place? Come round tonight for dinner. I'll invite one or two of our pals. Feldwebel Gehl might be able to dig up some girls from somewhere. Come round about eight and we'll—'

'Hang on,' said Rinken, suspiciously. 'Did you say FORGET it? A man in my position?'

'Well, you could,' urged Stahlschmidt. 'Couldn't you?'

'I don't know,' said Rinken, slowly. 'I do have my situation to think about, you see. I have no desire to be sent off to a disciplinary company at this stage of my career . . .'

'But nobody would know,' whispered Stahlschmidt.

'Well . . . well, no, perhaps you're right. Except that I still want an official report, mind . . . However, I accept your invitation to dinner. Eight o'clock, I think you said?'

'Eight o'clock,' confirmed Stahlschmidt. 'I'll provide the wine, the food, and the entertainment . . . You're a good chap, Paul, I've always said so . . . I think I'll just tear up this damned pass and forget it ever happened.'

'I shouldn't do that,' said Rinken. 'I don't think that would be at all wise. If it is official, there'll be copies galore all over the place. And if it isn't — well, quite honestly, I think you should do a bit of discreet checking. Otherwise there'll be hell to pay if ever the story comes out.'

'You're right,' said Stahlschmidt, sweating heavily round his collar. 'You're quite right. I'll telephone my C.O. He's as thick as pigshit, he won't ask any questions.'

'I think you ought to get it cleared up once and for all,' said Rinken. 'I'll keep quiet at this end until I hear from you.'

'That's good of you,' murmured Stahlschmidt, hating Rinken more with every minute that passed.

'Mind you,' said Rinken, in jocular tones, 'I shouldn't fancy being in your shoes right now. It would never surprise me if tonight's blow out didn't end up as a farewell party . . . you might even end up in one of your own cells!'

'My God,' said Stahlschmidt, 'if that's your idea of a joke, I don't think much of your sense of humour. With friends like you about, I don't need enemies.'

Rinken's happy laughter rang down the telephone.

'And anyway,' said Stahlschmidt, irritably, 'they'd never do a thing like that.'

'Why not?' asked Rinken. 'In any case, it's always nice to be with old friends . . . you could talk about the good old days when you were in charge of the prison and they were as the dust beneath your chariot wheels . . .'

Chuckling to himself, Rinken put down the receiver. Stahlschmidt sat staring at the telephone, wondering for a moment if he were sickening for some disease. The room was spinning about his ears, he felt sick and giddy and a cold perspiration had broken out all over his body. And you never knew, in these days of war. So many odd diseases seemed to be going round . . . He groped for his pulse and turned to Stever.

'I think I shall have to pay a visit to the M.O. I feel really quite ill . . . You can take over for a few hours. Or a few days, it might be, if they keep me in bed.'

Stever began to tremble.

'I don't think that's a very good idea, Herr Stabsfeldwebel. Surely Greinert is more qualified than me? In any case, he's been here longer than I have.'

'Greinert's a fool.'

They sat staring at each other a while, then quite suddenly Stahlschmidt picked up the telephone and asked to speak to Major von Rotenhausen, the prison governor.

'Sir? Major Rotenhausen, sir? It's Stabsfeldwebel Stahlschmidt here, sir.'

'Well, Stahlschmidt? What is it?'

I have to report, sir, that two men of the 27th Armoured Regiment – a Willie Beier and an Alfred Kalb – visited one of the prisoners today on a pass that I now think might be a forgery.'

There was a long silence, while Rotenhausen tried to take in what had been said to him and tried to think of a pertinent question to ask. At last he found one.

'Who did they visit?'

'Lt. Bernt Ohlsen . . .'

'Who's he? Whose prisoner is he?'

Stahlschmidt closed his eyes. He sank in upon himself, huddling up in his chair.

'The Gestapo . . . IV/2a . . .'

His voice was the barest whisper.

'And who signed the pass?'

'Standartenführer Paul Bielert,' said Stahlschmidt, and almost fell off his chair.

Rotenhausen hung up. He gave no indication of what he intended to do, or even if, indeed, he intended to do anything at all. Once again Stahlschmidt was left with a silent telephone receiver in his hand. He replaced it helplessly in its cradle.

'Well,' he said to Stever, in tones of bracing joviality, 'we're in the shit and no mistake ... What the devil do we do now?' Stever looked at him, a hump of immovable misery. 'That bloody Rinken!' railed Stahlschmidt. 'Who does he think he is, jumped up bag of skin and bones! Just because he helps his sodding C.O. put on his overcoat every day ...' Stahlschmidt turned and spat vehemently in the direction of the over-turned waste paper basket. 'You know what he used to do before the war, don't you? He was a bloody milkman, that's what he was! And you can bet your sweet life that's what he'll be again as soon as the war's over ... Ah, come on, Stever, get your brain to work, man! Don't stand there like a solidified turd, start thinking!'

Stever elaborately cleared his throat before speaking.

'Herr Stabsfeldwebel,' he said, 'I'm quite sure you'll be able to find a way out.'

And he looked Stahlschmidt straight in the eye, very firmly throwing the ball back in his court. Stever intended to make it quite clear that he had had nothing to do with the affair.

Stahlschmidt outstared him. He waited until Stever dropped his gaze, then grimly smiled.

'If I go under, you'll be coming with me,' he murmured, too soft for the other to hear. 'Make no mistake about that ... I don't drown alone!'

For ten minutes more he paced about the room, watched furtively by Stever, who had no desire to stay but was too scared to go.

The monotony was broken by the sudden screaming wail of the sirens. The two men looked at one another.

'Here they come again,' said Stever.

'That'll be the Canadians,' said Stahlschmidt.

They stood listening a moment, then Stahlschmidt jerked his head towards the door and picked up the whisky bottle.

'Come on. Down in the cellars and pray like heck they drop a bomb on the Gestapo.'

'And Major Rotenhausen?' suggested Stever.

'And Major Rotenhausen,' confirmed Stahlschmidt. 'And

Rinken, as well, if it comes to that . . . I should send a personal note of thanks to the head of the Candian Air Force.'

They hurried down to the cellars, stayed there for the duration of the air raid, approximately twenty minutes, and finished off the bottle of whisky between them. When they emerged, it was only to discover that the attack had concentrated on the southern area of the port and had been nowhere near the Gestapo. Or Major Rotenhausen, or Rinken.

'Not even an indirect hit,' mourned Stahlschmidt, as they returned to his office.

He looked at Stever and Stever looked back at him. There was no hope in that direction. Stever was not a man to come up with bright ideas.

'Well, there's only one thing for it . . . I'll have to take a chance and ring the bastards . . . see if I can't explain it to them . . . It'll be worse in the long run if they find out for themselves.'

The trembling of his hand as he dialled the dreaded number of the Gestapo – 10 001 – belied the bravado of his voice.

'State Secret Police. Stadthausbrücke Section.'

Stahlschmidt swallowed a mouthful of saliva. Stumbling over his words, stammering, stuttering, gasping for air, he managed to stagger through his report.

'Just one moment, Stabsfeldwebel. I'll have you transferred.'

Stahlschmidt moaned gently and ran a finger round the inside of his collar. A new voice came on the telephone; crisp and sharp and authoritative.

'Hallo, yes, can I help you? This is the Executive Service here, IV/2a.'

Once again Stahlschmidt tripped and tumbled through his story. Even to his prejudiced ears, it no longer seemed to have any ring of truth or probability about it.

'So who signed this pass?' the voice demanded.

'Herr Standartenführer Paul Bielert,' croaked Stahlschmidt, and he humbly inclined his head to the telephone.

'You can drop the "Herr"!' snapped the voice. 'We gave up that plutocratic fawning a long time ago.'

Stahlschmidt at once let loose a flowing string of apologies and excuses, almost prostrating himself across the desk as he did so.

'If you've quite finished?' said the voice. 'I'll hand you over to the Standartenführer himself.'

Stahlschmidt gave a terrified yelp. The telephone went dead. He looked at the hated instrument and knew a moment of intense desire. If he could only wrench it away from the wall and hurl it into the courtyard, might not all his troubles be ended? Or perhaps if he were to be taken suddenly ill . . . he felt ill. He did feel ill. He felt very ill—

'Hallo?'

Stahlschmidt clutched in terror at his throat.

'H – hal – hallo?'

'This is Paul Bielert speaking. What can I do for you?'

The voice was low and agreeable; kind and soft and somehow inviting. For one rash, mad moment Stahlschmidt was almost tempted to make a full confession of his folly, to grovel and to sob and to go down on his knees. Instead, he opened his mouth and began jabbering the utmost futilities into the telephone. The story fell out pell mell, disjointed and rushing forth at a hectic pace. At one moment he was declaring on oath he had known straight away that the signature had been forged; the next moment he was flatly contradicting himself by saying that even now he was unsure on the point and wanted only to check up. He denounced Rinken, he denounced Rotenhausen, he denounced the entire prison staff. They were all lazy, useless, deceitful bastards and hadn't a clue. He, Alois Stahlschmidt, was left to carry the can for everyone. He was left to—

'One moment, Stabsfeldwebel.' The voice broke in, persuasive and almost apologetic. 'I dislike to interrupt you in full flow, but has anyone ever told you that you are not, perhaps, as bright as might be desirable?' Stahlschmidt gulped noisily into the telephone and his neck grew slowly scarlet. 'If this pass really were a forgery,' continued Bielert, still in his soft, persuasive voice, 'does it not occur to you that the names of the visitors might also be assumed for the occasion? Have you already checked on this? Have you checked on their company?

Have you searched the prisoner since the two men left him? Have you searched his cell?'

'Ah, yes! Now that was Obergefreiter Stever's job, Stand-artenführer.'

'And has Obergefreiter Stever done it?'

'Oh, yes! Yes, yes, indeed yes! I saw to it myself!'

'And what did he find?'

'Ah – well – nothing, actually, sir.'

And Stahlschmidt turned to look accusingly at Stever, who was staring with bulging eyes, sheeplike and incredulous.

'In that case, it must surely have been a very superficial search?'

'The trouble is, sir, you see, as I was explaining, it's quite impossible to trust anyone in this place to do a job properly. I find myself quite unable to delegate. Unless I set to and—'

The voice again broke in upon his frenzied explanations. It was no longer quite so gentle as it had been.

'Now you listen to me, Stabsfeldwebel! I hold you and you alone to be responsible for the whole of this miserable affair, and if the prisoner is found dead in his cell because of it you may rest assured that I shall personally arrange for your execution.'

Under the desk, Stahlschmidt's kneecaps began to bounce and his legs to knock together. For the first time in his life, he wished he were out fighting at the front.

'As for the pass,' continued Bielert, 'you can bring it round to my office yourself. I suppose by this time you'll have managed to alert half Germany?'

Slowly and brokenly Stahlschmidt recited the list of people who knew of the affair.

'One can only be thankful,' said Bielert, sarcastically, 'that you haven't yet written to the newspapers about it ... Or perhaps you were on the point of doing so when you decided to telephone me and ask for my permission?'

An odd sound, a strangulated yelp of panic, forced its way out of Stahlschmidt's mouth. Stever looked at him in awe. He had never seen his chief in such a pitiable state. Thank God he himself was only a miserable Obergefreiter!

Stahlschmidt slowly let fall the receiver and stared round the room with red-rimmed eyes. Who knew but that fool of a prisoner might not even now be in the act of swallowing smuggled poison in his cell? He turned wildly to Stever.

'Obergefreiter! What are you standing there for? Get a move on, for God's sake! I want the prisoner's cell searched from top to bottom ... I want the PRISONER searched from top to bottom ... Jump to it, man, don't just gawp!'

Stever made a sudden dive for the door. He shot through it and sprinted up the passage, crashing headlong into Greinert, who was coming in the opposite direction at a more leisurely pace.

'So what's up with you?' he asked. 'What's all the mad rush all of a sudden?'

'You'll know soon enough!' panted Stever. 'Get a couple of men and bring them along to number nine. We've got to search the bastard inside and out.'

Greinert shrugged his shoulders and sauntered off. A few moments later he returned with two companions and together the four men began the search. They tore off Lt. Ohlsen's clothes, they ripped up the mattress on his bunk, they heaved at the iron bars on the window, they broke everything that was breakable, including the chamber pot. They tapped the walls, the floor and the ceiling, and the Lieutenant sat naked on the bunk, watching them with an amused smile.

Stever did a disappearing trick with the packet of cigarettes he had pressed on the prisoner earlier in the day. Greinert ran howling and shouting up and down the cell. The other two men took hold of the Lieutenant and searched him thoroughly, peering in his mouth and down his ears, forcing his legs apart, examining his body in minute and unscrupulous detail. Lt. Ohlsen bore it all with weary patience. He opened and shut his mouth a dozen times for them, but they failed to discover his false tooth where the little yellow phial was secreted. There was enough poison in that phial to kill ten people. The Legionnaire had brought it back with him from Indochina.

All the time the search was going on, Stahlschmidt was pacing back and forth across his carpet, and had soon blazed a perceptible trail from the door to the windows, from the windows to the bookshelves, from the bookshelves back to the door.

The bookshelves were full of fat legal volumes, most of which Stahlschmidt had 'borrowed' from libraries or smuggled out of shops and other people's offices. He fancied himself as something of a lawyer. He always told his mistresses that he was a prison inspector, and in his local bistrot, 'Le Chiffon Rouge', he was known as Herr Inspektor. He had learnt a number of legal paragraphs by heart and he was accustomed to quote them parrot fashion whenever the occasion arose. He had quite a following in the Chiffon Rouge and his advice was frequently sought on legal matters – though rarely by the same people twice. Too many had been disappointed in the past to go back for a second helping. The fact was that Stahlschmidt never could bear to confess to his own ignorance on a subject: whenever he found himself at a loss he simply quoted an imaginary precedent, invented on the spur of the moment, and based all subsequent advice upon it.

As Stahlschmidt paced past the windows for the sixth time, the telephone rang. He stopped in his tracks, staring distrustfully at the instrument. He blamed all his sudden misfortunes upon the telephone. Slowly, he walked across to the desk; warily he picked up the receiver. He spoke in a voice that was low and reluctant.

'Garrison prison . . .'

As a rule, he would snatch up the receiver and scream, 'Stabsfeldwebel Stahlschmidt speaking! What do you want?' But not any more. Never again. That wretched pass had ruined all that for him.

'You sound a bit down,' said Rinken's voice, maddening and full of cheer. 'What's up? Spoken to the Stapo, have you? Any luck?'

'Get knotted!' snarled Stahlschmidt. 'I'm sick to death of this place, and so I tell you! I've a good mind to put in for a transfer. You work hard, you do your best, you're a damn sight more conscientious than anyone else, INCLUDING your commanding officer – and what happens? I ask you, what happens? You get kicked in the teeth for your pains, that's what happens!'

'Ah, well, we live and we learn,' said Rinken, in an annoying, jollying-up sort of voice. 'But look here, don't give up hope. If you really want a transfer, I'm sure I can arrange it: that disciplinary company I was telling you about still wants N.C.O.s. They'd welcome you with open arms ... Shall I give 'em a ring?'

'Sod that, I'd sooner you gave me some good advice for a change! I've had Bielert himself on the phone to me. He wants me to take the pass round to him personally.'

'So? You're not scared of Bielert, are you? There's no need to be, unless you're suffering from a bad conscience ...'

'Don't come the innocent with me, Rinken! You know bloody well there's no one in the whole of Germany with a completely clear conscience. Even the SD guards at Fuhlsbüttel and Neuengamme shit blue bricks when they have to go anywhere near Stadthausbrücke.'

'Best put your brown trousers on!' joked Rinken.

Stahlschmidt swore violently and slammed the receiver down.

Of course, what he could not possibly realize was that there was far more to the affair of Lt. Ohlsen's visitors than met the eye. For a start, he did not know that a few days ago the Legionnaire, the little Legionnaire with his scarred face and his hard eyes and his supple hands with their long fingers, had paid a visit to Aunt Dora at the 'Ouragan'. (That was the very day before Aunt Dora had disappeared. Officially, it was understood that she had gone to Westphalia to visit a sick friend, the widow of a Gauleiter. Unofficially – well, unofficially, one wondered ...)

However, the Legionnaire had visited her at her establishment and they had sat down at a table in the corner and pulled the thick curtains together until they were in a private alcove of their own. Before them, on the table, were two glasses, a bottle of Pernod and a bowl of roast chestnuts. They gnawed the chestnuts open with their teeth and carelessly spat the skin to the floor. Aunt Dora bent her head to her glass and sucked up a mouthful of Pernod.

'So, Paul's nabbed your little Lieutenant, has he? For opening his big cakehole too wide ... Well, all I can say is, he must be a bit soft in the head, going round blabbing like that to all and sundry. I mean, it's asking for trouble, isn't it? Might just as well climb on to the roof tops and shout it through a megaphone, eh?'

The Legionnaire shrugged his shoulders and picked up his glass, squinting at it through narrowed eyes.

'You're quite right, of course. Some people just aren't fit to survive ... Now you and me, we know how to look after ourselves, but Ohlsen—' He shook his head. 'A babe in arms! Gestapo could run rings round him ... Still, I've known the fool for a long time, I can't just leave him there to rot. I've got to do something for him.'

'If you say so.' Aunt Dora spat out a mouthful of chestnut and looked at it in disgust. It was brown and bitter. 'Bloody woman! Can't even roast chestnuts, now. You'd never believe the trouble I had getting a cook. And now that she's here I'd almost sooner do without her and get on with the work myself. She's useless. Quite useless!' She tossed off the remains of her Pernod and poured another glass. 'It's the same with all the staff these day. Even the girls aren't what they used to be. Just lower-class whores, most of 'em. Straight off the street, no style at all ... And you can't rely on them, you know. Take that slut, Lisa. The one that's supposed to be at the check desk ... She's been off sick four times already this month ... Sick, my fanny!' Dora picked out another chestnut and crammed it into her mouth. 'I know what she's up to, thank you very much! There aren't no flies on old Dora!'

'I'm quite sure there aren't,' agreed the Legionnaire. 'The thing is, why on earth don't you get foreign girls? I thought they were two a penny these days?'

'They are, but I wouldn't let them anywhere near the place,' said Dora, bitterly. 'Half of them are Gestapo spies. You think I want foreign trash breathing down my neck, reporting my every moment? I'd be whisked off to Stadthausbrücke in no time!'

The Legionnaire smiled.

'Why, now, Dora, I'm sure you don't have anything on your conscience!'

Dora cackled and punched him amiably in the chest. She leaned across and poured out more Pernod.

'How about this lieutenant of yours, then? What have they got him for? One of their famous paragraphs?'

'Ninety-one b,' said the Legionnaire, taking a chestnut and grimly surveying it. He sank his teeth into it and ripped off the outer shell. The long scar which ran down the length of his face looked red and painful. 'I'm afraid he's for the high jump,' he said, briefly.

'Just for shooting his mouth off?'

'You say "just",' said the Legionnaire, 'but you know as well as I that's fast becoming the number one crime of the century . . . And in any case, they wanted someone to hold up as an example of what happens to people who talk too much. They've got it all planned out, I managed to have a look at his papers . . . Porta introduced me to a rather seedy character who works in the Commissariat. Goes under the title of "Doctor", but almost certainly isn't . . . Anyway, I succeeded in finding his weak spot—' The Legionnaire gave Dora a wink and a charming grin – 'and that's how I got to see the papers. Easy when you know how. Some people will do anything to get what they want . . .'

'So what do they plan to do to your lieutenant?'

The Legionnaire frowned.

'Execute him . . . Read out the list of his crimes in front of the execution squad . . . They reckon that way they'll break even the bravest of them. It's no fun, seeing a man executed. It's not a question of shooting, it's a question of—' He chopped a hand into the back of his neck. 'Takes a lot of courage to go away after that and commit any crimes on your own account.'

'Courage!' said Dora, scornfully. 'Everyone talks about courage all the time! What's courage supposed to be? Something you've got when your head's safe on your shoulders and your belly's full and you've got a glass in your hand . . . Don't talk to me about courage! You try being in the hands of those bastards for more than ten minutes and see how far courage takes you . . . There's only one way to deal with the Gestapo, and that's to know something about them that they don't want anyone else to know. You've got a hold over them, you're all right. Without one, you're buggered.'

'I couldn't agree with you more.' The Legionnaire leaned across the table and spoke confidentially. 'How about Bielert, Dora? You know things about Bielert, don't you? Enough to help Ohlsen keep his neck on his shoulders?'

Dora shook her head.

'I doubt that, love ... I might be able to manage a pass for you, so's you could go and see him, but anything else and I'd be risking my own neck. I know a thing or two about Paul all right, but even a lap dog'll bite if you kick it hard enough. And you know Paul ... He's unreliable. Like a wild beast. So long as you've got the upper hand he'll behave himself and do what you want. But you try pushing him too far and he just loses control of everything. Goes mad and hits out in all directions ... Besides, I can't help feeling this lieutenant of yours has gone and stuck his neck out. It's asking for trouble, carrying on like a mad thing like he did, shooting his mouth off to every Tom, Dick and Harry ... Anyway, I don't know him from Adam. If it were someone like you, I might consider taking the risk, but not for some unknown idiot that can't keep his mouth shut. And it's playing with fire, interfering with Paul's prisoners.'

'Yes, I know.' The Legionnaire pursed his lips and looked down into his glass. 'That man collects prisoners like other people collect butterflies.'

'He's a dangerous bastard, that one.' Dora picked out another chestnut and thoughtfully dipped it into the melted butter at the bottom of the dish. 'I've half a mind to lie low for a bit myself, as a matter of fact. Just disappear, like. Give the keys to Britta and go into retirement until the Tommies arrive ...'

The Legionnaire laughed.

'Never tell me they're on to you, Dora? Not you, of all people!'

'I don't know.' Dora scratched in her tangled hair with a dirty fork. 'But there's a voice at the back of my head keeps saying, "Pull your knickers up, Dora, and do a bunk" ... I've noticed, just recently, we've had rather too many visits from a certain type of person ... Know the ones I mean?'

'I believe I do,' murmured the Legionnaire. 'The sort of chap who comes in for a Pernod and nearly chokes himself to death over it?'

'Exactly,' said Dora. 'Beer types. Spot them a mile off. Hats pulled down over their eyes like something out of a bleeding spy film.'

'Pernod has its uses.' The Legionnaire picked up his glass and smiled. 'It sorts out the wheat from the chaff . . . the man in the street from the man in the Gestapo . . . Hey, Dora, you remember that one whose throat we cut?'

Dora shuddered and began scratching compulsively between her hanging breasts.

'For God's sake don't remind me of it! It brings me out in goose flesh even now . . . I still remember the mess my garage was in. Blood all over the bleeding floor . . .'

At that moment, the ghostly wail of the air raid sirens started up.

'Shit!' said Aunt Dora. 'That means the cellars.'

'With a couple of bottles?' suggested the Legionnaire. 'You never know how long we're going to be there . . .'

A table was pushed back and a trap door opened. Clients and staff arrived at a run, jostling each other down the narrow steps into the cellar. A supply of bottles was passed down from hand to hand, the trap closed, and the assembled company stretched themselves out and prepared to enjoy the enforced intimacy. Only Gilbert, the porter, remained upstairs. It was necessary to have someone on guard to watch for looters.

The raid lasted an hour. Dora staggered up the steps and tottered back to her table in the corner. Her glass of Pernod was still where she had left it. She picked it up and stared at it with slightly glazed eyes.

'Tell you what,' she said, as the Legionnaire rejoined her. 'I'll give Paul a ring and see what I can do for you. Come round here tomorrow morning, if you're able to get out of the barracks. About eleven o'clock. If I can dig a pass out of the old sod, then I will. If not—' She shrugged. 'If not, it means I'm losing my grip and I'll probably be joining your lieutenant on the scaffold.'

The Legionnaire laughed.

'The day will never come, Dora! I'll be round at eleven, and you'll have the pass, don't you worry.'

He went out into the street and was immediately approached by a girl on the look-out for trade.

'Got a cigarette, darling?'

The Legionnaire brushed her out of his way and walked on. She hurried after him, panting endearments down his neck. The Legionnaire suddenly stopped. He swung round on her, his face contorted and his eyes blazing.

'Piss off out of it and leave me alone! I'm not interested!'

He took one step towards her, but that was enough: the girl fled, and for the next two days she hardly dared set foot outside the front door.

A couple of hours later, Dora kept an appointment with Standartenführer Bielert on the corner of the Neuer Pferdemarkt and Neuerkamp Feldstrasse, along by the side of the abattoirs. Bielert enjoyed the abattoirs. He often passed an afternoon there, watching the slaughter.

He and Dora walked together across the Pferdemarkt and entered the restaurant of the Hotel Jöhnke, taking their places at a table set somewhat apart from the rest. Dora went straight to the point.

'I had to see you, Paul. I need a pass, a visiting pass or whatever you call them, and I need it in a hurry.' She ran her fingers through her hair and looked at him distractedly. 'I'm always in a hurry these days, it's dreadful. Honestly, you've no idea the trouble I'm having with staff. Rush here, rush there, do this, do that ... you can't get them for love or money, I'm having to do half the cooking and housework myself now.'

Bielert smiled.

'That's nonsense, Dora. I've told you often enough, I can supply as many people as you need.'

'Foreigners!' scoffed Dora. 'Thank you, no. I'd rather go down on my knees and scrub my own floors than have Gestapo agents running loose about the place. But I must have my visiting pass!'

'Whom do you want to visit? And where?'

'Someone in prison. A lieutenant.'

239

'I see.' Bielert pulled out his cigarette case and thoughtfully inserted a cigarette into his long silver holder. 'You know, my dear, you're really becoming very demanding just lately. A pass is a valuable commodity these days. Greatly in demand.'

'Don't come that crap with me!' said Dora, scornfully. 'You can get me a pass just by snapping your fingers, if you feel like it.'

'In that case,' he murmured, 'I suppose it all depends upon whether or not I do feel like it . . .'

'You'd better,' said Dora. 'And buy me a rum, will you? A nice hot one.'

They sat in silence until the drinks arrived. Bielert looked consideringly at Dora.

'Suppose you begin by telling me who it is that really wants this pass? And just who it is they want to visit?'

'Here you are. It's all written down there.'

She handed him a piece of paper. Bielert studied it a moment and raised one almost non-existent eyebrow.

'Lt. Bernt Ohlsen?' he said, slowly. 'Imprisoned for crimes against the State . . . and you want me to allow him to receive visitors?'

Dora shrugged.

'Why not?'

'Why not? Why not, you say? I'll tell you why not!' Bielert screwed the paper into a ball and threw it angrily to the floor. 'Because the man is a criminal and a traitor and a danger to his country! I have nothing but scorn and hatred for men of his type! If I had my way, they'd be exterminated wholesale. Them and their families. Their wives and their children and their mothers and their fathers! All of them!'

His face had twisted itself into an abrupt mask of white, trembling hatred. Dora watched him, dispassionately. She had heard it all before. At the far end of the room, several people quietly stood up, called for their bills and disappeared. Bielert ranted on regardless.

'I have a list of names so long,' he boasted, 'that even Gruppenführer Müller was taken by surprise . . . It's not only that we're at war. It's more than that. We're living through a revolution, and I count myself as one of its chief engineers. I have a loathsome job, I know. A filthy, degrading job. But a very necessary job and one that I believe in. The end will justify the means, and without men such as myself to carry the thing through to its conclusion the revolution would suffocate on its own vomit tomorrow.'

'Yes, you're so right,' murmured Dora, vaguely; and then, her eyes lighting up: 'Talking of Müller, I saw him only the other day! He came into my place, quite unexpectedly, just out of the blue, like that! We got as pissed as newts together, I can tell you . . . it was quite a reunion, after all these years!'

'Müller?' said Bielert, his nose twitching anxiously as he stared at Dora. 'Which Müller are you referring to?'

'Why, Gruppenführer Müller, of course . . . the one you've just been telling me about . . . My God, I hadn't seen him since the day he got his promotion to Untersturmführer! We did have a laugh together!'

'I wasn't aware that you knew Heinrich Müller,' said Bielert, frowning at her. 'How did you meet him? You've never been to Berlin in your life, that I know for a fact.'

Dora looked at him and laughed.

'Oh, Paul, don't tell me you even keep tags on ME? On your old friend Dora?'

'Who said anything about tags?' demanded Bielert, irritably. 'I just have your safety in mind, that's all. One never knows what unlikely turn events may take these days.'

'You're so sweet to me!' Dora smiled and raised her glass to him. 'But surely you mean YOUR safety, rather than mine? After all, if anything should ever happen to me – if events ever should take an unlikely turn – it would rather put you on the spot as well, wouldn't it?'

'We live in troubled times,' replied Bielert. He took a small sip of cognac and knocked some ash off his cigarette. 'Tell me, Dora, what did you and Müller talk about?'

'Oh, this and that and old times,' she said, airily. 'And strangely enough, at one point, people who had committed crimes against the State . . . like this Lt. Ohlsen, only far worse. Müller was asking me about some Communists I used to know once. He was specially interested in any that had left the Party and gone into the Gestapo.'

241

Bielert's eyelids flickered just slightly.

'I see. And were you able to help him?'

'Well, I was and I wasn't,' said Dora, frankly. 'I gave him one or two little titbits to be going on with, but it wasn't till after he'd left that I remembered this.'

'What is "this"?' asked Bielert, a shade too smoothly.

Dora pulled up her dress, plunged a hand up the leg of her thick wool knickers and brought out a letter.

'Here you are,' she said. 'Funny thing, I was turning out my cupboards a while back and I came across a whole heap of old junk. And in the junk I found this letter. All about some cell or other—' She unfolded the letter and frowningly read it. 'Cell 31 – a Communist cell, you know the sort of thing . . . It talks about a Paul Bielert, who was head of this cell. It's quite a coincidence, isn't it? Someone having your name, I mean.'

'Quite,' said Bielert. He took the letter from her and glanced through it. 'Very interesting. Do you mind if I hang on to it?'

Dora smiled at him.

'Do what you like with it. Matter of fact, I've got one or two others that might interest you . . . All on the same subject, of course.'

Bielert coloured slightly.

'How is it you've managed to lay hands on correspondence that dates from 1933 and earlier? Who did you get it from?'

Dora looked down into her glass and shrugged a shoulder.

'You've still got a lot to learn, haven't you, Paul? You've still got a good way to go before you catch up with me. You've done well for yourself, but you always were inclined to be backward . . .' She put out a hand and patted his arm, consolingly. 'Poor old Paul! When you were learning how to milk cows in the reform school, with all the old monks doddering about and driving you mad and you just muttering under your breath about revenge, I was already taking steps to make sure of my future. I picked up everything I could lay hands on and stored it away for a rainy day. By the time you started playing little kids' games with your pals in Cell 31, I'd already acquired the magpie habit. It was a piece of cake, getting hold of your letters. Of course, I didn't know then if they'd ever be any use, but I thought I might as well keep them. Just in case . . .' She squeezed his arm a moment, then sat back in her chair. 'Why do we have to rake all this up? I don't want to get you into trouble. All I want is one simple little pass with your signature on it.'

'Come round to the office tomorrow. I'll have it ready for you.'

Dora laughed.

'You must be joking! Me set foot in your office? I'd never be allowed out again! No, thank you, I'd rather you sent one of your men round to my place with it.'

Bielert looked coldly at her. His fist clenched and unclenched on the table and his eyes narrowed, but his voice remained soft and low.

'You know, Dora, I'm beginning to wonder if it might not be a good idea for me to send several men round to your place . . . They could bring you back with them in the car and you could pay us a little visit. I'm sure it would be quite enlightening for both of us.'

'I'm sure it would,' said Dora, matching his tone. 'And I'm quite sure it's not the first time the idea has occurred to you.'

'Well, no, but now and again it does come upon me more forcibly than usual . . .'

'The only trouble is, Paul, that you couldn't possibly have me shut away in a cell without having yourself shut away in another one only a few hours later. There's an awful lot I could tell . . .'

They smiled at each other in mutual hatred and understanding.

'Well, well,' said Bielert, carefully extracting his cigarette stub from the holder. 'You shall have your pass. I'll send Grei round with it at three o'clock.'

'All right, that suits me fine. Grei and I get on with each other very well. Did you ever know him before the war, I wonder? I can still remember the time when he used to sing nothing but the Internationale. Of course, he's changed it to the Horst Wessel now, but who can blame him? Only a fool tries to swim against the tide.'

Bielert stood up.

'One word of warning, Dora: watch your step. You have many enemies.'

'You too, Paul. I hope you follow your own good advice . . .'

Stever had been in the Army for five years, and he was a good soldier. Stahlschmidt, on the other hand, had been in the Army almost thirty years, and he was a very bad soldier. And as for Rotenhausen, who was an officer and the Governor of the prison, it was arguable whether he could be called a soldier at all. It was not, in any case, thought Stever, the length of service that counted so much as whether a person had the aptitude.

'And I have the aptitude,' said Stever to himself.

He looked at his reflection in the glass and smiled and saluted. He enjoyed being a soldier. Both Stahlschmidt and Rotenhausen were too busy lusting after power. Neither of them realized that they were but tools in the hands of the Nazis.

'I realize it,' thought Stever, prancing and posturing before the long mirror. 'That's why I shall survive.'

Stever had no particular desire for power. Power brought not only increased prestige but increased personal risk, and Stever could well be doing without it. He was happy with his present position and his present way of life. He was paid regularly, was nowhere near the front line, and had a regular supply of women and clothes.

The clothes were supplied free by a tailor who lived in the Grosser Burstah and whose son had once been a prisoner in one of Stever's cells. All Stever's suits and uniforms were hand-made and the envy of his comrades.

As for his women, he chose them carefully and had a semi-permanent entourage. In Stever's mind, human beings fell into four categories: men who were soldiers and men who were civilians; women who were married and women who were single. Stever despised civilians and found single women more trouble than they were worth. He always went for the married ones. At the age of fifteen he had made the discovery that most married women were sexually undernourished, and he had taken upon himself the task of easing their lot.

There was something very satisfying about married women. For a start, they never wanted to become emotionally involved, they never made any demands other than the purely physical, and this suited Stever down to the ground: he found it impossible to imagine existing for anyone but himself and for anything but his own gratification. The idea of being expected to

244

consider another person's wishes was terrifying and alien to his nature.

Secondly, he found that married women were always very anxious to be pleased. In nearly all the marriages he had encountered the batteries had seemed to run dry after two or three years, and then Don Juans such as Stever were able to step into the breach and make good the deficiencies.

He found young girls too much of a responsibility, too much of a trial, while virgins were a positive menace.

'Shove a hand up their clout before they're ready for it and they'll scream the place down and have you arrested,' he gravely explained to Obergefreiter Braun, who found it difficult to get hold of a woman, though he was far better looking than Stever. 'Have to spend bleeding hours touching 'em up and whispering at 'em and telling 'em how bleeding lovely it's going to be and how much you want them, and all that kind of balls . . . and half the time,' he added, 'you're in such a hell of a state when they finally drop their drawers that you bugger the whole thing up anyway. And half the time they don't like it and keep complaining you're taking advantage of 'em and go on bleeding moaning all the time you're on the pissing job . . . game's not worth the flaming candle,' said Stever, in disgust. 'You stick to the married ones, chum. They know what it's about and there's no bleeding rigmarole to be gone through before they let you have it.'

'I see,' said Obergefreiter Braun, puckering up his forehead. 'I'll try one of them next time.'

'Yes, you do that,' said Stever, cramming his cap on his head and stepping smartly out of the barracks.

No one seeing Stever outside the prison, with a pleasant smile on his lips and a helping hand for little old ladies who couldn't cross the road, would ever have taken him for the same man who casually battered prisoners half to death before throwing them into their cells to rot. And if anyone had asked Stever himself about it, he would have been quite puzzled.

'Look, I'm only an Obergefreiter,' he would have said. 'I'm only carrying out my orders . . .'

And besides, he had never actually killed a man. He prided himself on that. He had been through the entire war without firing a shot at anyone. And that was a record to boast of. Stever had no man's blood on HIS conscience . . .

CHAPTER SEVEN

Prison Discipline

MAJOR ROTENHAUSEN turned up once every month to introduce himself to the latest batch of prisoners and to take his leave of those who were departing. He never said farewell to those who had been condemned to death, since as far as he was concerned they no longer existed; only to those who were leaving to serve their sentences in one of the military prisons, Torgau or Glatz or Germersheim.

His favourite visiting hour was eleven o'clock at night, when all the prisoners had settled down and were asleep. He enjoyed the inevitable panic and confusion as guards raced round the cells shaking unwilling men into wakefulness in order that they might be presented to the prison Governor. It gave him a pleasurable sense of his own position and importance.

He made one of his surprise visits four days after the affair of the forged pass. It was a few minutes before midnight and he went to the prison straight from an evening's play at the casino. He was in particularly good humour. He had dined well, he had drunk a little too much and he had passed an entertaining evening. He was the picture of sartorial elegance, and he knew it. His grey cape, lined with white silk, billowed gently in the breeze. His leather boots creaked energetically as he walked across the courtyard. His long legs looked superb in their sleek grey trousers, and his epaulettes gleamed golden in the darkness. Major Rotenhausen was one of the garrison's best-dressed men: three years earlier he had made a marriage of money, and he was now president of the casino. Men looked at him and envied him, and Rotenhausen held his head high and felt himself to be the pride of the German Army.

Most people who came to the garrison accepted Rotenhausen at his own value, assuming automatically that he was a man of influence and a power to be reckoned with. There had been only one occasion, that the garrison could recall, when some stranger, some upstart officer from God knows where, had walked into the place and upset all the accepted rules of etiquette, had ignored Rotenhausen and set all the other officers by the heels.

He was a young colonel, no older than thirty at the very most. He had lost an arm at Minsk and was stationed temporarily in Hamburg, a half-way halt between hospital and a return to the front line. He had received virtually every decoration that was available, and his chest was a blaze of medals. His uniform itself caused several disdainfully raised eyebrows. Apart from the tunic, which was tailor made, the rest had all very obviously come straight from the stores. Men looked at his boots, his trousers, his kepi, even his leather belt and holster, and silently sneered. His pistol was a P.38. All the other officers carried the Walther, a neat little job which they felt to be more becoming to their status, but the unknown colonel was apparently indifferent to such niceties.

He belonged to an Alpine Regiment, the edelweis flash stood out boldly on his left sleeve, and although at first the garrison had no idea who he was or why he was there, this fact in itself was enough to put them on their guard.

Only half an hour after his arrival, the Colonel called a meeting and informed the startled company that he had provisionally taken over the command of the garrison.

'I am Colonel Greif of the 9th Alpine Regiment,' he announced, into the horrified silence. 'I am here for a temporary period.'

He shook hands with no one; merely fixed them all with his bright unblinking gaze and continued with his introductory lecture.

'I've always got on well with the men under my command, and I expect to do the same with you. Just pull your weight as I pull mine and we shall all do fine together. Only one thing I cannot stand and will not tolerate, and that's a shirker.' The steady brown eyes flickered back and forth across the ranks of the assembled officers. 'I suppose you must be aware, gentlemen, that the units at the front are crying out for replacements? I'm sure you don't need me to tell you, but if for some reason you haven't been out there for a while you might not be quite aware how desperate the situation has become: there are men in my regiment, for instance, who have had no leave for the last three years . . .'

He asked every officer present how long he had been in the garrison, and his eyebrows rose ever higher and his lips turned down at the corners as he heard the replies. The number who had ever been anywhere near the front was but a minute percentage of the total.

'I can see, gentlemen,' said Greif, 'that things are going to have to change round here . . .'

And change they did; and abruptly. Within three days of the Colonel's arrival all the fantasy uniforms, the capes and the cloaks and the stylish kepis, the highly polished boots and the neat little pistols, had been reluctantly packed away and exchanged for more regulation attire. The garrison became a place of hard work, filled with sweating hurrying men and drab uniforms, instead of presenting its more usual aspect of a fancy dress ball in full swing.

'We're at war, for God's sake!' was Greif's constant cry. 'This is a military establishment not a toy-soldier fort!'

Even the officer commanding the 76th Infantry Regiment, old Colonel Brandt, had to bend before the storm and abandon his lorgnette.

'If your sight is defective, then go and get yourself some spectacles,' said Greif, curtly. 'But don't ever let me see any more of this affectation.'

And Brandt had to stand there and take it. Had to stand to attention and suffer insults from this strip of piss, this one-armed ribbon-bedecked jumped-up colonel from nowhere who was young enough to be his son . . .

The garrison suffered not in silence but in a continuous state of low dissatisfied muttering. Men gathered together in small secretive groups and spoke in veiled tones of various accidents that might possibly befall the Colonel. One lieutenant even had the brilliant idea of denouncing him – anonymously, of course

– to the Gestapo. While they were still trying to work out what to denounce him for, the garrison as a whole received a shock from which it never quite recovered: Colonel Greif had a social call from no less a person than Heydrich.

Heydrich of all people! The devil's adjutant! The idea of denouncing Greif to the Gestapo was tacitly abandoned and men began to grow suddenly restless and to seek after change. Requests for transfer began to pour in. No man in his right senses would wish to stay on in Hamburg under someone who was a friend of Heydrich. Even the front line was preferable to the Gestapo . . .

Rotenhausen was not amongst those who joined in the first mad scramble to get out. He stayed his hand a while – not through any low cunning but simply because his reactions were slow. And God protected him, thus confirming his own exalted view of himself. Only a few days after Heydrich's visit to the Colonel, Greif was advised by telegram of a new posting. He packed his bags and set off within hours for the Russian front. He was never to see Germany again. He died in a snowdrift just outside Stalingrad, and when the Russians discovered him, on 3rd February, 1943, he was stiff and cold and had been dead for some time.

The garrison celebrated his departure for four days and nights non-stop. The champagne flowed and the old carnival uniforms were pulled out of their hiding places. Men strutted and peacocked to their hearts' content and Colonel Brandt bought himself a new lorgnette.

Greif's replacement was a Brigadier General of doubtful intelligence and possibly suffering from a premature onset of senility. The garrison were charmed by him. A most delightful old fool, even if he would insist on slobbering over their wives' hands and whinnying like a horse whenever he presented himself to them.

'General von der Oost, Madame . . . of the Infantry, of course!' And then he would straighten himself up, creaking and grunting, tug at his jacket, heave at his collar, clear his throat and trot out one of his standard jokes. 'I'll venture to guess you don't know why I'm in the Infantry, eh?'

Obviously no one ever did, and no one ever cared, but the answer came just the same.

'Well, I'll tell you ... I'm in the Infantry for the simple reason that I'm not in the Artillery, d'you see ... never could stand the Artillery, matter of fact ... dreadful business, all that noise all the time, gives me a shocking bad head ...'

One day he staggered into the casino and stopped the whole proceedings with a great roar of delighted laughter.

'Gentlemen, I'm happy tonight! Do you know why I'm happy?'

By this time his officers had grown accustomed to his simple turn of wit. They did know why, but he was a brigadier general and he suited them very well, so they shook their heads and humoured him.

'I'll tell you why!' The General held out his arms, delighted. 'I'm happy because I'm not sad!'

Even when they had all politely fallen about in deferential amusement, von der Oost was not satisfied. Beaming, he advanced upon them and cracked another witticism.

'Yesterday I was damnably sad ... simply because I wasn't happy, d'you see ...'

Better an old fool like van der Oost than an objectionable young hothead like Greif. The garrison and their new commander were on excellent terms. Von der Oost asked no more than that he be allowed to keep them in a state of constant amusement. Men quickly found that if they laughed at his jokes he would blindly sign any piece of paper that was set before him, whether it be an illegal requisition for a crate of margarine or an execution order. There was even a rumour in the garrison that the Brigadier General was unable to read.

'Well, well,' he always remarked, after scrawling his signature across a document. 'Well, well, well, there you are, d'you see. Always up to date, eh?' And he would lean back in his chair and wave a hand at his empty trays. 'In tray, out tray, pending ... nothing in any of 'em, d'you see ... That's the way to do it, gentlemen. Keep up with the work and it never gets on top of you.'

'They executed three infantry soldiers at Fuhlsbüttel

yesterday,' said his Adjutant one morning, by way of making conversation.

'Ah, yes,' said van der Oost. 'They have to, don't you see ... each war demands its sacrifices. Without sacrifices there wouldn't be any war, you know. Wouldn't be any war ...'

He always slept during the Kriegspiel*. He would drop off at the beginning and wake up half-way through with loud cries of encouragement and advice.

'The foreign armoured divisions must be destroyed, gentlemen! Must be destroyed before they manage to reach Germany and cause a congestion ... The essential in a battle of this kind, d'you see, is to make sure the enemy run out of munitions ... What's a tank without shells? Eh? Like a railway without a train ...'

And the officers would nod their agreement and conscientiously begin moving the pieces as he directed. But somehow, no matter how hard they tried, they never were able to devise any scheme for cutting the enemy's supply line. In the end they hit on a solution, and at the start of each game they would solemnly announce to the General that the enemy lacked munitions, whereupon, quite contented, he would rub his hands together and beam his approval.

'Well done, gentlemen. That means we have won. All we need do now is bomb the enemy's factories and then we shall have them at our mercy.'

And off he would fall to sleep, convinced of his own brilliance as a military strategist.

One day the garrison cat upset the whole field of battle by depositing a litter of kittens in the middle of Hill 25. All the little tanks, all the little field guns and all the little armoured cars, were scattered pell mell about the table, some upside down, some on their side, some even on the floor. It looked as if a miniature bomb had scored a direct hit. And the cat, as is the way of cats, had chosen a particularly inapposite moment to give birth, as the garrison had invited their neighbours in to partake in a game.

Van der Oost lost his temper for the first time since he had been there. He demanded that the cat should be hauled up

* War game

252

before a court martial. There was nothing for it but to humour him and join in the fantasy. Two Feldwebels cornered the cat and held her throughout the trial. It was the nearest they had come to danger during the whole of their military careers. The cat was sentenced to death on the grounds of having sabotaged the officers' instructions course in the art of warfare. However, the next day found the General in a better temper. He reprieved her on condition that his batman attached her to a collar and lead and looked after her. Some time later the cat disappeared: the General's batman had sold it to a butcher and the General fretted his heart out until another cat was found to take her place.

Two years had passed swiftly and pleasantly since the terrible advent of Colonel Greif and his brief reign of terror. The garrison was a happy and hedonistic place, and Major Rotenhausen increased his sphere of influence from day to day. He had discovered that the Brigadier General had a passion for cognac, and he had also discovered where he could lay hands on a continuous supply of it. Major Rotenhausen and General von der Oost understood each other very well.

Humming briskly to himself, Rotenhausen marched across the dark courtyard to the prison – to his prison, the prison he commanded and where he kept his prisoners. He smiled and flicked his riding crop against the side of his leg. He never went riding, he was terrified of horses, but the crop looked good and was useful for bringing recalcitrant prisoners to heel.

Stabsfeldwebel Stahlschmidt had been warned by telephone of the visit, and he came to meet him. Rotenhausen rather distantly returned his salute. Stever was also there. They had had to search half the town for him and had eventually run him to earth in a private club, where he had been watching an obscene film in which naked people of various shapes and various sexes committed atrocities upon one another. Stever had still not completely returned to the mundane world of the prison.

'Very well, Stabsfeldwebel. I suggest we get down to business straight away,' said Rotenhausen, vigorously switching at himself with his crop. 'I'm a busy man, as you know, so let's waste no time.'

Stahlschmidt led the way to his office. It was not only clean, it was not only tidy, it was impeccable in every detail: every single object in it was placed according to the rule book. Rotenhausen walked about it a few times, peering into hidden corners for patches of dust, examining the wire baskets for papers that had no right to be there, taking out a metal rule and measuring the distance between the edge of the desk and the edge of the in-tray, the edge of the desk and the ink well, the ink well and the out-tray, the out-tray and the blotting pad. Stever stood stolidly at the door watching him. Stahlschmidt walked about behind him and every now and again closed an eye in Stever's direction. What fools these officers were! He knew that Rotenhausen had long cherished a desire to fault him on some small point of order. Had he himself been an officer, thought Stahlschmidt, he would not have taken so long about it. But then, he was smarter than Rotenhausen and that was why Rotenhausen would never catch him out.

Having measured everything on the desk that was even remotely measurable, Rotenhausen sighed with weary boredom and demanded to see the list of the prisoners. Smiling, Stahlschmidt handed it over to him. He read it through with the aid of a monocle, which he had great difficulty in keeping in his eye.

'Stabsfeldwebel, this list is deficient. I see no mention of the number of new prisoners . . . I see no figure for the number of men who are to be transferred . . .'

'There we are, sir.' Stahlschmidt jabbed a fat red finger at the foot of the page. 'I think you'll find these refer . . . seven new prisoners, sir. One lieutenant colonel, one cavalry captain, two lieutenants, one Feldwebel, two privates. Fourteen to be transferred, sir. All of them to Torgau. There's one brigadier general, one colonel, two majors, one captain, one Hauptmann, two lieutenants, one Feldwebel, three corporals, one marine, one private. There are also four men condemned to death. Their appeals have been rejected and all necessary arrangements have been made for their execution.'

'Well done, Stabsfeldwebel.' With a twist of the lips, Rotenhausen dropped his monocle and laid the paper on the desk. 'It gives me great pleasure to find everything so well organized. You obviously know your work and take care over it.

You're a man in whom one can have all confidence. Hm.' He beat himself hard with his riding crop. 'No slovenly ways here like there are at Lübeck, eh? Everything goes like clockwork with you, doesn't it, Stabsfeldwebel?'

'I do my best, sir.'

'Let me just give you one word of warning, however: watch out for accidents . . . You know the sort of thing I mean? If a prisoner happens to break an arm or a leg, that's perfectly all right by me, but do try to avoid breaking their necks!'

'Me, sir?' Stahlschmidt frowned. 'Me break their necks, sir?'

'You know what I mean!' said Rotenhausen, irritably. 'Just take great care, that's all I'm asking . . . If not, we shall both find ourselves in trouble. There's a man called Bielert at Stadthausbrücke. You may have heard of him. A most disagreeable type. He's started taking rather too much interest in our affairs these past few weeks. Nosing about the garrison, asking questions about the prison, the way it's run, how many people in it, you know the sort of thing . . . He even had the infernal nerve to come bursting into the casino at two a.m. the other day. Such behaviour would never have been tolerated in the days of the Emperor. A man like that would have been thrown out on his ear . . . A lieutenant who didn't know him took him at first for a priest. I ask you! Strange type of priest . . . He was one of Heydrich's disciples, you know. Not a man we should be wise to cross, Stabsfeldwebel. We know better than that, don't we?'

'Well, if I'm to understand you correctly, sir—'

'If you are to understand me correctly, Stabsfeldwebel, just remember this: that unless you want to end up in the forests of Minsk fighting partisans, you will behave with circumspection and do nothing that might bring this man Bielert down on our heads . . . If you want to hit the prisoners around a bit, I've already said that's all right by me. God knows they deserve it, and in any case I should be the last person to interfere with a man's pleasures . . . But use a bit of discretion, that's all I ask. There are plenty of parts of the human body you can bash to your heart's content and nobody any the wiser. Remind me to show you when we start on the interviews . . .'

In the corridor, the guards had lined up all those who were to have the honour of being presented. First of all, the newcomers. And to start with, a forty-eight year old lieutenant who had been sent there on a charge of refusing to obey orders. His introduction to Rotenhausen took exactly three minutes and four seconds, and he was then carried away almost senseless by two Gefreiters. There was hardly a mark on his body.

'Well, you didn't last long, did you?' sneered Stever, jabbing the groaning man in the belly. 'Three minutes! Hardly a record, is it? We had a Feldwebel here once, he held out for two hours. Still on his feet at the end of it. Rotenhausen had to give up and take a rest in the end, before he could get strength enough to finish him off.'

Lt. Ohlsen was in the corridor with all the other guests. They were standing in a line with their faces to the wall, their hands clasped behind their necks.

Two heavily armed guards marched up and down, ready to fire on the least provocation. It had occasionally been known for a prisoner driven to desperation or blind rage to leap at the Major and attempt to throttle him. No one, of course, had ever survived such a foolhardy attack. They always ended up as lifeless bodies in one of the discipline cells, down in the cellars, trussed like chickens with a label tied round one ankle.

Stever yelled out Lt. Ohlsen's name. Ohlsen jumped round, marched into the office where Rotenhausen conducted his interviews and sprang smartly to attention.

The Major was enthroned behind the desk. Before him lay his riding crop. Stahlschmidt stood at his elbow. He was holding a rubber truncheon, coated with the crusted and coagulated blood of ages past. Stever stood inside the door, just behind the prisoner.

'Heil Hitler,' remarked Rotenhausen.

'Heil Hitler,' responded Ohlsen, tonelessly.

The Major smiled. He leaned forward and picked up a sheaf of papers.

'I've been reading through your file,' he told Ohlsen. 'To me, your case doesn't look to be too good. In fact in the light of my past experience I can confidently predict that you will be sentenced to death. Probably decapitated . . . unless you're lucky, which I doubt. If you are lucky, of course, you'll be shot, but I shouldn't hold out too much hope if I were you. I have a feeling for these things.' He looked across at Ohlsen. 'Death by decapitation is both dishonourable and unaesthetic. There's too much blood, and a headless body is not a pleasant sight ... absurd and revolting at one and the same time ... Do you have any comments you wish to make? Do you want to ask me for anything? Do you wish to lodge any complaints?'

'No thank you, sir.'

'I see.' Rotenhausen leaned back in his chair and squinted at Ohlsen. 'The prisoner is not holding his head straight,' he observed.

Stahlschmidt at once stepped forward with his right arm raised and his fist clenched. Stever moved in to help with the butt of his sub-machine gun.

'Better,' said Rotenhausen, appraisingly. 'But still not quite right ...'

A pain ripped its way through Lt. Ohlsen's body. It came so suddenly and was so intense that he felt it must surely be tearing his inside to pieces. He staggered and swayed and only just managed to remain on his feet.

Rotenhausen turned with raised eyebrows to Stahlschmidt.

'He moved!' he said. 'Don't they teach people how to stand to attention these days?'

Stahlschmidt bunched his fist again. Stever moved in with two ramrod blows from the butt of his sub MG hard into the kidneys.

Lt. Ohlsen fell forward on to his knees. Tears sprang from his eyes and he felt as if red hot pokers were being rammed up the muscles of his back.

Rotenhausen shook his head.

'This is too bad,' he remarked, gently reproving. 'Does the prisoner now refuse even to stand up? Must he grovel on the floor in that obscene fashion?'

He nodded at Stahlschmidt. Lt. Ohlsen lay on the floor, screaming. Stever was hitting out with the frenzy of a maniac. Stahlschmidt concentrated on kicking. After a few moments a thin trickle of blood oozed from the prisoner's mouth. Rotenhausen at once banged on the table with his crop.

'Obergefreiter, get that man on his feet!'

Stever dragged him up. Lt. Ohlsen groaned then shouted as new pains tortured his broken body. Thoughts of his son suddenly flitted through the dark mists of his mind and he muttered to himself.

'Is the prisoner daring to complain?' asked Rotenhausen, outraged.

They didn't know what he was doing, but they beat him up a bit more, just to teach him a lesson. They then disposed of him, throwing him back senseless into his cell.

From the new prisoners they passed to the old; to those who were to be transferred to Torgau. Each man had to sign a declaration to the effect that he had been well treated and had no complaints to make.

One brigadier general refused to sign.

'I suggest, for a change, that you listen to my point of view,' he said, very cold and calm and reasonable. 'I'm being sent off to Torgau for a maximum period of two years. It might very well be less, and it certainly won't be more. If I choose to tell the authorities of the things I've seen in this prison – two cold blooded murders, just for a start – you'd be sent down for about twenty-five years. Now just reflect a moment what that means. It means, first, that after I've served my sentence I shall be transferred to a disciplinary regiment. I shall almost certainly be given back my old rank of brigadier general and end up in command – they're short of experienced officers, so they've really no alternative. And once I'm back in a position of authority, I can promise you I shall move heaven and earth to have you people sent to my division.'

His words fell into a shocked silence. Stever looked hopefully for guidance at Stahlschmidt, but Stahlschmidt made no move. It was plain from his expression that for once he was nonplussed. He had met stubborn prisoners, foolhardy prisoners, prisoners who tried insulting him or even attempted physical violence; but never in all his career had he encountered one who dared to threaten. Prisoners were not in a position to threaten, and he wished Major Rotenhausen would explain as much to the Brigadier General.

Rotenhausen lolled nonchalantly in his arm chair. He took

his time lighting a cigar, then picked up his riding crop and flexed it gently across his knee. He looked up thoughtfully at the Brigadier General.

'Do you really suppose,' he drawled, 'that a man of your age would last six weeks in a disciplinary regiment? I guarantee that after you'd been there three days you'd be looking back on your spell with us as one of the cushiest times of your life.'

He smiled. The Brigadier General met his eyes and Rotenhausen looked away.

'I'll make you an offer,' he said. He took his pistol from its holster, leaned across and laid it on the desk, within the General's reach. 'There you are. It's all yours. Take it and use it.'

There was a long silence. The General made no movement. Rotenhausen suddenly rose from his arm chair, walked round the desk and cracked his whip only inches away from the General's face. Stahlschmidt caught his breath. If the idiot went berserk and the General arrived at Torgau with purple bruises all over his face and half the bones in his body broken there would be hell to pay. Let Rotenhausen talk his way out of that one, if he could. At least Stahlschmidt would have had no part in it.

'You'd like it, wouldn't you, if I were to beat you black and blue?' Rotenhausen threw back his head and laughed. 'Just suit you fine, wouldn't it? Then you really could go bleating to Colonel Vogel at Torgau about the nasty way we've treated you here ... Well, I'm sorry to disappoint you, but we're not such fools as all that. In fact, we're not fools at all, as you'll very soon discover. We go strictly according to the rule book here. There are other ways of breaking a prisoner's resistance besides using violence.' He turned to Stever. 'Obergefreiter, in ten minutes' time I want the prisoner standing ready in the courtyard in full combat dress. Fifty kilos of damp sand in his rucksack, and try to find a couple of nice sharp stones to slip in his boots. And while you're about it, make sure they're old boots — old and stiff and preferably half a size too small. All right?' He smiled, and Stever nodded enthusiastically. 'We'll start him off with a couple of hours' gentle exercise. See how he gets on.'

'Yes, sir!'

Stever's round, amiable face split wide open with a grin of anticipation. Stahlschmidt laughed aloud, appreciative of the joke. Not quite such an idiot after all, old Rotenhausen!

Only the Brigadier General remained impassive, giving no hint as to his thoughts. He was not a young man and it seemed unlikely he would survive two hours of Rotenhausen's 'gentle' exercise, with or without boots that crippled him and a rucksack full of sand on his back. Even if, by some miracle of will-power, his heart held firm, Rotenhausen would almost certainly invent some new diversion to finish him off. And the General knew that under Prussian military law Rotenhausen was well within his rights. There was no rule against killing a man by such treatment.

'Prisoner . . . about – turn!' Stever held the door open and jerked his head at the General. 'Forward – march! At the double! One-two, one-two . . .'

As the unfortunate General disappeared down the corridor at a fast trot, Major Rotenhausen picked up his cape and swung it carelessly over his shoulders, put his pistol back in its holster, settled his kepi on his head, tilting it saucily over one eye. He had studied the effect in the glass and he knew that it made him look dashing and fearless.

'Come with me, Stabsfeldwebel. I'll teach you the best way to deal with a recalcitrant prisoner without incurring any awkward complications or giving rise to too many questions. It's all a matter of technique.'

Stahlschmidt snatched up his own cape and followed the Major from the room. He automatically set his kepi on his head at the same rakish angle as Rotenhausen. He always wore it like that and it was more than possible that Rotenhausen had copied him. It occurred to Stahlschmidt in the nick of time, however, that the Major might just think it was the other way round, and silently cursing he re-adjusted it, so that it sat at the regulation angle low on his forehead. He knew that he looked the complete idiot, like an ape done up in its Sunday best, but better that than incurring a jealous scene.

Rotenhausen strode in front of him. He had thrown his cape over his shoulders and had drawn on a pair of gauntlets. The gold braid of his epaulettes gleamed in the darkness of the prison. Stahlschmidt regarded him with contempt.

'Bloody Prince Charming poncing off to a masked ball,' he thought, scornfully, and he began to imitate Rotenhausen's walk, tossing his own cape over his shoulders and gesticulating right and left to an imaginary crowd.

They went out into the covered courtyard. Stever had performed a quick-change act on the General, and they were already standing there waiting.

'Just looking for a couple of suitable stones, sir,' panted Stever, who had obviously thrown himself heart and soul into the job and was more exhausted than the prisoner.

'Very well, Obergefreiter. It's good to see such enthusiasm, but no need to kill yourself.'

'No, sir.'

While Stever crawled about in search of his stones – 'Nice and sharp,' said Rotenhausen, pleasantly – Stahlschmidt inspected the General, checking his kit, testing the weight of his rucksack.

The stones were found and accepted and inserted into a pair of dilapidated boots: the uppers were stiff and unyielding, the soles were into holes. They were at least one size too small. The General was scarcely able to cram his feet into them, and the red-faced Stever had to expend yet more energy heaving them on.

Rotenhausen took his place at the top of the steps and prepared to conduct the proceedings. Stahlschmidt stood beside him, while Stever positioned himself at the far end of the courtyard, his sub-machine gun at the ready.

'Keep your eyes skinned, Stabsfeldwebel.' Rotenhausen rubbed his gauntleted hands together and smiled. 'Should anything untoward occur during the course of the exercise, should the prisoner suffer a heart attack or a stroke, let us say, it will be no fault of ours.'

'Naturally not,' agreed Stahlschmidt.

'Of course, a man has to be physically in first-class shape to stand up to such rigours. I myself should certainly not care to endure it. But then, there is no question of my entering a disciplinary unit and fighting at the front. And nor, might I add—'

and Rotenhausen grinned, showing all his top teeth and fillings – 'do I possess quite the same foolhardiness of spirit as the prisoner.'

He turned to face into the courtyard, standing legs apart and hands on hips, and began barking out the first of a long string of orders. Right turn – stand to attention – left turn – running on the spot – forward at a run – faster, faster, faster! – knees up, up I said! – no flagging, keep it up – halt! – down on your stomach – forward crawl! – twenty times round the court-yard . . .

The Brigadier General was sweating under his heavy load. His eyes beneath his helmet were bulging from their sockets, as he gasped for breath and fought to carry out each fresh order as it came. He knew only too well that the least hesitation, the least sign of weakness, would give Rotenhausen the opportunity to pounce. He would doubtless be shot for refusing to obey orders. The Brigadier General had served forty-three years in the Prussian Army. At the age of fifteen he had entered the military academy at Gross Lichterfelde. He had worked his way up, he knew all the tricks in the book, he knew his own rights and he knew those of others. And at the moment, Major Rotenhausen was within his rights.

'Prisoner – halt!'

The General staggered thankfully and incredulously to a stop. But there was to be no respite. Down in a squatting pos-ition he went, and round the courtyard he began painfully to hop like an arthritic frog. His body cried out in protest but his brain refused to listen to its urgent appeals. He went on hop-ping, and the stones in his boots cut his feet and the unyielding leather, a size too small, stubbed his toes and rubbed blisters on his heels.

Stahlschmidt was openly laughing at the sight. Stever shouted words of encouragement each time the General passed him at the end of the courtyard.

The hopping came to an end and the jumping began. Long jumping, high jumping, jumping on the spot; jumping feet apart, jumping feet together; jump up, fall to the ground, crawl forward; jump up, fall to the ground, crawl forward; jump up, fall to the—

After twenty minutes of this treatment, the General quite suddenly fainted. It was against the rules to shoot an unconscious man for refusing to obey orders, but it took Stever barely two minutes to revive the prisoner.

The exercise continued as if the interruption had never been. Rotenhausen finished his first cigar and lit another; he finished the second cigar and lit a third; and then the Brigadier General began to break. At first they noticed only a low moaning as he toiled round the courtyard. It seemed that he was moaning in spite of himself, without even realizing it. Later, the moaning raised its pitch and grew in intensity. Later still it became a wail, which rose and fell and died away and came again and again with ever increasing urgency. And then the wail became a shriek of protest, a shout of agony, a long inhuman scream of a man tortured beyond the limits of his endurance and reason.

All over the prison men woke up and heard this mindless call of despair and ran with dread to the windows of their cells. Only a few, those who had been inmates for a long time, remained in their bunks and resisted the temptation to respond to the summons of the tortured man. They knew what was happening out there. They had seen it before. Special Training, they called it . . .

The cry was broken now at intervals. And at each interval there came a long, shuddering breath and a rolling rattle in the throat. Stever was in the centre of the courtyard, his sub MG pressed hard against the General's abdomen, just above the navel and just below the dome of the diaphragm. Stever knew what he was doing. You left no traces that way. You might rupture the stomach, perhaps, but who was to say that that might not have occurred spontaneously during the normal course of a rigorous exercise? And since when had rigorous exercise been frowned upon in the Army?

Rotenhausen was no longer smiling. He was enjoying himself too much and concentrating too hard to smile. His mouth was drawn back over his teeth in a thin and twisted line. His eyes shone with the gleam of the fanatic.

'Prisoner! On your feet!'

With Stever assisting with his sub-machine gun, the General staggered upright. He swayed forward as if he were drunk.

Stever ran alongside him round the courtyard, jabbing him gently with the butt of the gun.

'Halt! Five minutes' rest! The prisoner can sit down ... Have you anything you wish to say?'

The General, an old man now, with palsied limbs and shrunken cheeks, stared unseeingly ahead out of eyes that were covered in a milky film. He had the air of a corpse enclosed in a diseased but still living body. Slowly he shook his head. His lips silently framed one word: no. He had nothing he wished to say.

Stever stared down at the General in contemptuous amazement. Was the man a complete fool? Where was the point of setting himself up in opposition to authority? What could he possibly hope to gain by it? Another half hour of suffering and he would be dead – and all for nothing, as far as Stever could see.

The five minutes came to an end. The prisoner was hauled to his feet. He made another two laps of the circuit and then pitched forward, head first, and lay still. Stever was on him in an instant, beating him wantonly about the head and shoulders, kicking at his feeble old legs, reviling him for being a fool.

Again the General staggered to his feet. Stever looked at him with hatred. Why couldn't the old sod give up and die? Any more of this and there would be no sleep for any of them tonight. As it was, there were only three hours to go before reveille. He promised himself that the next time the General faltered he would give him such a blow as would finish him off once and for all.

The prisoner stood upright – or as upright as he could. His shoulders drooped, and the straps of the rucksack cut deep into them. He was trembling from head to foot. His helmet was askew, his white hairs were plastered in wisps over his forehead, and tears were streaming from his half-closed eyes. Painfully, he ran a swollen tongue round his lips, which were torn and bleeding. In a voice that was no more than a feeble croak, he gave Rotenhausen best: he had no complaints to make of his treatment and he wished to sign a declaration to that effect ...

'I assumed you would, sooner or later,' said Rotenhausen,

simply. 'Everyone else does, so why not you?' He took out another cigar and paused to light it. 'I trust, by the way, that you are not sufficiently small-minded to regard this period of exercise as in any way being connected with your previous refusal to sign the declaration? That of course would be quite contrary to all my principles ... The fact is, we do occasionally select a prisoner at random and put him through the hoop, so to speak – purely for his own good. It gives him a taste of what to expect in a disciplinary camp, and therefore a far better chance of ultimate survival ... Why do you keep gasping like that? Are you thirsty?'

The General nodded.

'Well, now you know the sort of thing you're likely to have to put up with, don't you? I hear that in Russia the men are expected to march for half a day or more without a drink.'

There was still a further twenty minutes to go before the stipulated two hours were up, and even though the General had capitulated Rotenhausen saw no reason to cut short the exercise period.

The old fellow set off yet again round the courtyard, with the faithful Stever plodding and prodding at his side. He weathered another ten minutes, and then, quite suddenly, he stopped and heaved and vomited blood. Stever butted him violently with his gun.

'Get on, damn you! Get on!'

The final minutes of the drama were played out in slow motion, with the General dragging himself round the ring at the pace of a tortoise and Stever walking with him and meditating upon the possibilities of a sly blow that would put an end to all their miseries, allow the General to die in peace and himself to get some sleep.

Back inside the prison, the General collapsed. This time it took Stever almost five minutes to revive him. Rotenhausen ordered that he should remove his clothes and be taken for a shower, so Stahlschmidt and Stever led him away between them, stripped him naked and held him beneath the cold water for ten minutes. They then put his clothes back on him, dripping wet, and marched him off to the office to sign his declaration.

265

They had to hold the paper for him, and support his arm and hold the pen in his hand before he could do so. Rotenhausen watched in some amusement.

'Why couldn't you have signed it right at the beginning?'

The General seemed not to hear the question. He stared blankly ahead, and the light of life in his eyes was barely flickering.

'I'm speaking to the prisoner!' snapped Rotenhausen. 'I expect an answer!'

The answer came, but it was both unexpected and involuntary: the General quite suddenly began to relieve himself, there in Stahlschmidt's impeccable office, standing there unconscious with the urine running down his leg and on to the carpet.

Rotenhausen gave a shout of indignation and jumped back. Stahlschmidt was almost beside himself. He forgot the presence of the Major and knew only that some filthy swine of a prisoner was daring to spoil his carpet. He ran at the General, shaking him back and forth and pouring abuse over him. Stever stepped in with the truncheon and began methodically, and with a certain lack of enthusiasm, to beat the prisoner in the stomach and the back and across the shoulders. He was sick of the old man's pointless resistance, he wanted him to die, quickly and quietly, and let them all get to bed. But still he made sure that he hit him only where no tell-tale marks would be left. He finally pushed the prisoner to the floor, bent him forward and rubbed his nose in the mess.

Major Rotenhausen shook his head.

'This is a most disgraceful happening. To think that an officer could behave in such a fashion! You have my full permission to do what you like with him from now on, Stabsfeldwebel. I have totally lost interest. He is evidently not a gentleman. Only remember what I told you earlier: no traces. That is all I ask.'

Stahlschmidt clicked his heels together.

'I'll see to it, sir!'

Rotenhausen picked up the inspection register, wrote a few words in a large, plain hand and signed it with a flowing signature:

'Inspection of garrison prison carried out. All in order. Prisoners due for transfer called for final interview: no complaints made.

P. ROTENHAUSEN
Prison Governor.'

He raised two laconic fingers to the rim of his kepi and left the office, very well contented with his night's work. He went straight round to see his mistress, the wife of a lieutenant, who lived at Blankenese. While he was there, enjoying the delights of the house, Brigadier General von Peter quietly died.

Obergefreiter Stever launched a few languid kicks at the inert body, but it no longer moved. Stahlschmidt bent over it.

'Thank Christ for that! Now perhaps we shall have a bit of peace.'

'I thought he'd never go,' grumbled Stever.

'Pissing on my carpet! To think they make officers of pigs like that ... The very idea!' Stahlschmidt turned to Stever. 'There's no need to go spreading the story round the prison, by the way.'

Stever smothered a yawn.

'I shouldn't dream of it, Stabsfeldwebel.'

'As well for you ...' Stahlschmidt waved a hand at the old grey body lying limp on the floor. 'Get rid of that rubbish, I don't want stinking corpses cluttering the place up. And tell that lieutenant in number nine to come and scrub my carpet. That's the sort of work fit for an officer.'

'What do we put in the report?' asked Stever, carelessly picking up the Brigadier General by one of his legs.

'I don't know ...' Stahlschmidt scratched at his chest a moment. 'Has he got any marks on him?'

Stever let the leg drop and closely examined the body.

'A few bruises, that's all ... They could have come from anything.'

'Good. I'm glad to see you know your job ... What would you say to taking over from me when I leave?'

Stever goggled at him.

'Are you leaving, Stabsfeldwebel?'

'Not just yet awhile, but I shall be.' Stahlschmidt flexed his arms and did a casual knees-bend. His long leather boots creaked impressively. 'I aim to move on to Potsdam. To the garrison prison at Potsdam. And then, my dear Stever, you'll be able to have this lovely office all to yourself as your very own. How would that suit you?'

'It sounds like a bit of all right,' said Stever, 'but could I get to be promoted?'

Stahlschmidt tapped the KV*I on his chest.

'You, too, could wear one of these . . . You don't have to go and beard the Russians in their den to get one, you know.'

'No,' said Stever, 'but how could I – I mean, how would it – well, frankly, I don't care too much for the idea of going off to a training school for two years just to learn how to be an N.C.O.'

'Who said anything about going off to a training school? You don't think I bothered with all that sort of nonsense, do you? Use your brain a bit and it's not necessary.'

'But how do you get round it?'

Stahlschmidt shrugged.

'Impress people. Make your mark. Pressurize them. Take the trouble to learn by heart some bit of rubbish by Goethe or Schiller or some other daft old sod. Bring it out whenever you get the opportunity. Con people. Play the game right and you'll get wherever you want . . . Like I'm going to get to Potsdam.'

Stahlschmidt laughed happily and flexed the muscles of his arms. Stever looked doubtful.

'Easier said than done,' he muttered.

Stahlschmidt smiled.

'Some of us can, some of us can't . . . Let's get that filthy corpse out of here. Go and find Gefreiter Hölzer, ask him to give you a hand. Arrange a suicide in the prisoner's cell – you know the sort of thing, you've done it before.'

'Stool by the window?' said Stever.

'That will do. And twist the old fool's sheet round his neck and tie a knot . . . at the back of the neck, mind you. Not at the front. I knew a stupid bastard at Innsbruck made that mistake. Deserved a rope round his own neck, if you ask me . . . While

* Knegsverdienstkreuz I Klasse–Medal for Military Merit, 1st Class

you're doing that I'll give the M.O. a ring and tell him what's happened. This time of night, he'll sign a death certificate without even looking at the corpse.'

They had a quick glass of cognac from Stahlschmidt's secret cupboard and then each went about his work. Stever and Hölzer carried the corpse out of the office and back to its cell, where they arranged a squalid and effective suicide.

At the door of the cell they paused and looked back at the hanging body.

'Let's wait outside,' suggested Hölzer.

Stever laughed.

'You know, it creases me . . . it really creases me when people start going on about heaven and God the Father and the angels and all that kind of crap. Look at him hanging there! Can you imagine a sight like that ever flying round heaven with a bare arse and a couple of wings and a halo and all?'

Hölzer shivered slightly.

'Don't tempt providence. Just lately, I get cold fingers all up my spine every time I see a bleeding priest in the street. I have to cross over the other side of the road, you know that?'

'Superstitious clap trap,' said Stever.

'No, it's not. It's more than that. I'm not superstitious and I'm not religious, but I sometimes get the feeling that one of these days it's going to be our number what turns up.'

'So? We all got to die, haven't we?'

'Yeah, but not like that.' Hölzer looked at the General's limp body and looked away again. 'That's what I'm scared of. And we've had so many of 'em pass through here, I can't help feeling it's going to be like – well, like a sort of retribution, like.'

'Ah, piss off!' said Stever, closing the cell door.

'I mean it,' insisted Hölzer. 'You know what, I was in a club down town the other day, I met these three guys from a disciplinary regiment what's in Hamburg – tank corps or something. Real tough lot. Slit your throat as soon as look at you – and they very nearly did. Pissed to the eyeballs, of course. So just to amuse themselves, pass the time away, like, they tie a bit of rope round my neck and shove a pistol in my belly . . . Know what they said? They said, this is just a dress rehearsal. Next time it'll be the real thing . . . And God help me, I believed them! I still do, matter of fact. And so would you, if you'd been there.'

Stever's air of patronizing superiority had faded slightly at the mention of a disciplinary regiment. His hand went up and plucked nervously at his throat.

'What were they like, these three? One of 'em wasn't a little chap with a dirty great scar down his face, was he? Smoked fags all the time?'

'Yes, he was,' said Hölzer, astonished. 'You know him?'

'Yeah, he visited one of the prisoners just the other day. Nasty piece of work.'

'You're not kidding,' agreed Hölzer, earnesly. 'He put the shits up me, I don't mind telling you ... In fact, the whole place is beginning to put the shits up me. This prison, this town, everything ... There's a club where I go – Aunt Dora's place. You ever been there? Only just lately it's been swarming with Bielert's men. Like flies round a heap of turds. Dora don't care, they can't touch her, she's well in with Bielert, but what about the rest of us?' He moved close to Stever. 'Last night, I opened my mouth a bit too wide – said something stupid to her, I was drunk, didn't know what I was on about – and before I knew whether I'm on my arse or my elbow I'm being flung out of the door by a couple of Gestapo types.'

Stever forced a laugh.

'Why? What'd you do to annoy the old cow? Not fucking enough?'

'Come off it!' protested Hölzer, indignantly. 'I'm there every night of the week when I'm not on duty. I have a go at everyone, I do. Regulars and casuals. She gets her money out of me, I'm not fussy, so long as it's the right sex. The end of last week, I tell you, I was so shagged I couldn't hardly move ...'

'So what's she bawl you out for? What's your trouble? What's all the bellyaching?'

Hölzer shrugged his shoulders.

'I dunno. I reckon I just feel the writing's on the wall. Every where I go I keep seeing these blokes from the 27th ... they've got it in for me, I can feel it in my bones. To tell you the honest truth, I don't think I can take much more of it. I'd sooner be at the front than here.'

Stever looked at him.

'You gone bleeding mad?' he inquired, mildly. 'If you think those types from the 27th are like wild animals here in Hamburg, you just try imagining how they'd be at the front.'

'They wouldn't be at the front,' muttered Hölzer.

'Well, perhaps not that particular lot,' agreed Stever. 'But others just like 'em . . . or worse. And that's the type you get out there, you mark my words. They're bad enough when they're back here in civilization, but stuck out there in the trenches with 'em you'd be a goner and no mistake. They're psychopaths, the lot of 'em! Bleeding psychopaths running about with their pockets stuffed full of hand grenades and God knows what else . . . blow you up as soon as look at you . . . knife you in the back on the slightest provocation . . .' He shuddered. 'No thank you very much! I'd rather spend the rest of the bleeding war in this shit hole than get tangled up with a bunch of homicidal nut cases . . . The thing is, you see, you don't want to let it get you down. Don't take it to heart so much. I mean, the prisoners and all that . . . Whatever they get, they've asked for it. In any case, it's none of your business. You just do what you're told and don't worry about the rest.'

'Yeah.' Hölzer heaved an almost rib-breaking sigh. 'Yeah, I guess you're right . . . but I'm buggered if I know what to do about it. You ever walked round day after day feeling sort of – well – sort of sick with fear?'

'What d'you mean, sick with fear? What kind of fear?'

Hölzer hunched a shoulder.

'I dunno . . . fear of what's going to happen next . . . it just gets worse and worse. Every day there's some new horror I can't seem to cope with. Like tomorrow, for instance . . .'

Stever wrinkled his brow.

'What's happening tomorrow?'

'That bloke in number twenty's for the chopper . . . He's quite a decent sort of chap, really. His family came to say goodbye to him the other day. I had to stand and listen to 'em all weeping and wailing over him . . . fit to make your stomach curdle. And then afterwards they ask me if there's nothing I can't do for him, if there's nothing I can't do to save him . . . Why pick on me? What can I do? What can I say?'

'Nothing,' Stever told him, firmly. 'Not your job, is it? They want anything like that, they got to go direct to Adolf or Heinrich.'

'That's what I tell them. But even if they did it, what good would it do? No bloody good at all, and they know it and I know it ... And night after night,' said Hölzer, bitterly, 'I drink myself silly trying to forget it all. I screw some bird until we're both fucked out, then I booze until I'm paralytic, and then for a couple of hours I'm dead to the world and it's like being in bleeding paradise, you're unconscious, you don't know nothing, you don't have to watch blokes die or listen to kids screaming ... and then it's morning again and you're back where you started, only worse ... because it gets worse all the time ...'

'Listen, you got to watch it,' said Stever, seriously. 'You're in a bad way, you are. You got to try to be logical about these things. There's a war on – right? Whether you like it or not, you didn't start it, so it's no bloody good you worrying about it. Second, how many prisoners do we kill off per week? Half a dozen? Maybe less, maybe a bit more. But some weeks we don't have any executions at all – right? Now, out at the front they're killing off whole battalions in the space of an hour ... all day and every day ... and you think people are losing any sleep over it? Course they're bleeding well not! And just remember this: most of them poor sods out in the trenches are there because they can't bleeding well help it, because the bastards up at the top have sent 'em out there, but the scum we got locked up in these cells are here because they sodding well DESERVE to be here. They done something, they got to pay for it. So there ain't no call for you to go weeping no crocodile tears over them.'

'Yeah, but the thing is,' confessed Hölzer, nervously, 'I can't stand the sight of that axe coming down ... It's bad enough being in a firing squad, but just having to stand and watch while some bloke's head's hacked off his shoulders ...' He shivered. 'And it's not even as if most of the chaps here have done anything really wrong—'

'That's all you know,' said Stever, severely. 'It's not up to you to say. In any case, if you've broken the law you've broken the law and you got to pay for it, and that's all there is to it, and in this country there's a law that says we've not got to think. It's as simple as that, and no one but a fool would ever let on he'd got anything but cotton wool stuffed inside his head ... Am I right?'

'I guess so.'

'There you are, then. You and me are good citizens. We know the law and we keep it. We watch which way the flag's flying, and we fly with it until it starts to change ... And as far as I'm concerned, I don't give a sod whether I'm saying Heil Hitler or Long Live the Party, it's all one to me.'

Hölzer shook his head.

'It's no good, Stever. I still want to get out of this place. I tell you, the sand's running out, and I reckon it's not going to be so long before the flag does start to change. And when it does, Stahlschmidt's going to be one of the first to go to the wall – and I don't want to be in here with him. I want to get out while there's still time.'

'Don't be a fool, Hölzer. There's an easier way round it than that. Nothing simpler than choosing one or two of the right sort of prisoner, helping half a dozen or so to do a bunk, some of 'em are bound to survive ... and bob's your uncle, there's your guarantee for the future! But as for going off to the front to be a bleeding hero, that's just sodding stupid. You go down to the barracks where the 76th are stationed. Go down there some time tomorrow. They're sending off a company to the front. You take a good long look at them as they set out, and I'll promise to give you a bottle of booze for every happy smiling face you see.' Stever spat, contemptuously. 'You won't see none! They'll all look as miserable as bleeding sin, like they're marching off to be buried, because they all bloody well know it's as good as a death sentence. You stay here, on the other hand, and you got a fighting chance. Just say yes whenever it's demanded of you, crawl up Stahlschmidt's arse, lick the Major's boots, and there you are, safe as bleeding houses! And when the final showdown comes, you've only got to remember one thing: you carry out orders, you don't give 'em. You didn't make the laws, you didn't ask to work here, you had no choice in the matter.'

'That's a fact,' said Hölzer. His eyes suddenly gleamed. 'If I had my way, I'd be in the Navy,' he confessed. 'The Army's not my scene, never was. But the Navy, now . . . and that gear they wear . . .' He rubbed his hands together. 'All the birds go for it, you noticed that?'

'Yeah.' Stever turned back to the cell and opened the door. 'Let's see how Auntie's getting on.'

The Brigadier General's corpse swung sadly in slow circles, back and forth, round and round, on the end of its rope of knotted sheet.

'Changing colour already,' observed Stever. 'Well, if we're to believe what they tell us in church the old boy'll be up there perched on a cloud and playing his harp by now. No rules and regulations, not a care in the bleeding world.' He looked across at the body and grinned. 'He wasn't such a bad old sod at that. Old enough to be my granddad and he didn't half take a beating. I thought he'd never go.' He closed the cell door again and they took up their position outside, awaiting the arrival of the doctor. 'I did a good job on that one,' remarked Stever, with a self-satisfied nod. 'Not a mark on his body, even Stahlschmidt agreed I knew what I was doing.'

'Yeah.'

They stood in silence a few moments.

'I am, of course, a specialist in my own field,' said Stever.

'Yeah.'

'The number of people that have passed through my hands since I been here is nobody's business . . . the number of people I've given the treatment to . . . know what I mean?'

'I know what you mean.'

'You get a sort of feeling for it. A sort of knack, like. You know what you can do and what you can't do. Some people never learn, they just get into a frenzy and beat a bloke to pulp. Now to my way of thinking, that's butchery pure and simple. No skill in it, see? No art. Anyone can do it. But—'

Stever's monologue was interrupted by the arrival of the doctor. He swept like a whirlwind into the cell, took one cursory glance at the body, shrugged his shoulders and signed a death certificate with no more ado.

'Here you are.' He thrust the paper at Stever and headed fast for the door. 'If only these wretched people would contain themselves in patience until the morning,' he said, irritably. 'What do a few hours more or less matter to them, after all? Dragged out of my bed at all times of the day and night . . .' He turned and waved a hand towards the body. 'Get that thing cut down and dispose of it.'

He disappeared along the passage and Stever closed the door behind him. He looked at Hölzer with a grin.

'See what I mean? I did a grand job on the old bloke . . .'

They set the stool upright and Hölzer clambered on to it to untie the deceased Brigadier General.

'It's so bloody stupid,' he complained. 'One minute we're stringing the poor bastard up and the next minute we're taking him down again. Up and down, up and down, like a sodding see-saw.'

'There's worse things than see-saws,' observed Stever, sagely. 'I'd sooner go up and down on a see-saw than in and out of the bleeding trenches . . .'

They cut the body down and dragged it the length of the corridor, down the stairs to the cellar. As they opened the door they both let go of it at the same moment and it slid from top to bottom of the stone steps. With joint recriminations they clattered after it, caught it up again and heaved it by the legs behind them. There was a sharp crack as the head ran into something.

'Sod my uncle!' screamed Hölzer, exasperated. 'What they want is undertakers, not flaming soldiers! This is my lot. I tell you, this is my lot. I'm going. I'm putting in for a transfer first thing tomorrow. I'm—'

'For Christ's sake,' snapped Stever, 'will you shut up bleeding moaning? On and on until you drive me bleeding bonkers!'

'Well, I mean it,' said Hölzer. 'I've had a belly full.' He let fall his leg of the body. 'Carting perishing corpses around, collecting up the pissing heads after an execution, they'll have us wiping their arses next, that'll be the next step!'

'Well, all right, then!' Stever threw down the second leg and turned angrily to face Hölzer. 'Go and get yourself transferred if that's what you want. But don't come bleeding whining to me when you're lying head first in the mud at the bottom of some stinking trench with your balls blown off!'

'Don't you worry,' said Hölzer, between his teeth. 'Your number'll be up long before then, you see if it isn't . . .'

Obergefreiter Stever planted his elbows on the bar of the 'Matou' and settled down to be argumentative. He pointed to finger towards Emil, the owner of the bistrot.

'Just shows how little YOU know about it,' he declared, witheringly. 'As a matter of fact, most of 'em go like lambs to the slaughter . . . you don't even have to show 'em the way . . . they get down on their knees and they put their heads on the block just like as if they was saying their bleeding prayers. It's quite a lovely little sight. No screaming, no shouting, no—'

'Do you mind?' said Emil, coldly. 'I have no desire to hear the details of how you murder people. I run a bistrot, not a slaughter house.'

Stever picked up his glass, not at all discouraged.

'We've got a tank lieutenant with us at the moment. Quite a decent type, as officers go. Takes whatever's coming to him and never a murmur. He's for the high jump pretty soon and I'll bet you a pound to a pinch of the proverbial that we don't hear a squeak out of him.'

'That's as maybe. I still don't wish to hear about it.' *Emil wiped a damp rag angrily across the counter.* 'You're a sadistic swine, Stever.'

'What, me?' *Stever finished his drink and pushed his glass across for a refill.* 'What makes you say that?'

He sounded quite hurt. Emil poured out his drink and banged the glass back at him.

'Because it's flaming well true, that's what makes me say it! Because you so obviously love your work . . . you stink of war and death and torture and you wallow in it like a pig in shit . . . you're not a man any more, you're just a degradation!'

'Look here,' *said Stever, earnestly,* 'you've got it all wrong! I know the job I'm doing might seem lousy to some people—'

Emil cut him short with a derisive cackle of laughter.

'That's the understatement of the year! Listen to me, you rat—' *He leaned across the counter and spat the words into Stever's chubby pink face* – 'one of these days you're going to find yourself swinging from the wrong end of a rope, and when that day comes I shall be the first to open the champagne!'

Stever frowned. He withdrew slightly and called across to a girl sitting alone in the corner. She was waiting for clients, but it was too early in the evening: few people ever came to the 'Matou' before ten o'clock.

'Hey, Erika!' Stever snapped his fingers at her and she slowly looked up. 'Did you hear what he said? You don't think I'm a – a sadistic swine and a rat, do you?'

His tone was appealing. He seemed genuinely in search of information. Erika raised an eyebrow and regarded him with bitter distaste.

'You're a swine, all right,' she said. 'Dunno about a rat . . . a sewer rat, perhaps.'

'But why?' Stever held out a hand in bewilderment. 'What have I ever done to you?'

'What wouldn't you do,' said Emil, 'if we ever ended up in one of your cells?'

'No, no, no!' Stever shook his head. 'It's not what I'd do, it's what I'd be made to do . . . You've got me all wrong. I feel sorry for the blokes we got in there. But what can I do for 'em? I haven't got no authority, no more than what you have.'

'You don't have to work there!' hissed Erika, from her corner.

'So what should I do instead? Put in for a transfer and run the risk of getting my head blown off? Would that suit you better? Look,' said Stever, growing desperate, 'I didn't ask for this job, did I? It was all decided over my head by some pen-pushing blimp sitting on his fat arse in an office: Obergefreiter Stever's got to be a jailer . . . It could have been different. It could have been the Russian front. But it wasn't, it was Hamburg. So that's what I call fate, that is, and I don't believe in fighting against fate. And as for what goes on – well, I ask you, is it my fault? Do I make the laws? Do I decide who's going to live and who's going to die? Do I hell! Some fat slob passes the order down the line and I'm just the poor cunt that has to carry it out.'

'My heart bleeds for you,' said Emil.

'I'll tell you what,' said Stever, turning back to him. 'You got to bend with the storm, in this life. When the war comes to an end and the wheel turns full circle – which it will, make no mistake – I'll be sitting pretty with a stack of prisoners to look after. Only thing is, they'll be a different lot of prisoners.*

278

*The old bunch'll be let out, and the new bunch'll be brought in.
And people like you—' He jabbed a finger into Emil's chest —
'people what haven't been forced to carry out orders like I've
been, people what've made a profit selling drinks to the chicken
lovers* — they're going to find themselves laughing on the other
side of their faces. And that, my friend, is what those as are
intellectual call Nemesis.'*

*Stever scornfully tossed two marks on the counter and
walked out of the bar.*

CHAPTER EIGHT

Execution

THE following day, Lieutenant Ohlsen was called to
Stahlschmidt's office and there presented with his Bill of Indictment, which he was required to sign in three places. He was
graciously permitted to take the document back with him to his
cell and was given an hour in which to read it through and note
its contents.

Left alone, Lt. Ohlsen solemnly unfolded the paper and
began to study it:

'State Secret Police
Hamburg Division
Stadthausbrücke 8

BILL OF INDICTMENT

'Wehrmacht Kommandantur, Hamburg
Altona Division

'To: General van der Oost,
Garrison Commander,
76th Infantry Regiment, Altona

* Chicken — a term of derision for the Nazi eagle

279

'Council of War 391/X AK against Lt. Bernt Viktor Ohlsen of the 27th Tank Regiment.

'On 19th December, 1940, Lt. Ohlsen was sentenced to five years' detention for failing in his duty as an officer when serving with the 13th Tank Regiment. After eight weeks in the prison at Glatz he was transferred to a disciplinary armoured regiment. He is at present being held in preventive detention at the Altona Garrison on the order of the Gestapo, Section IV/2a Hamburg. He has no Counsel.

'I accuse Bernt Ohlsen of planning to commit high treason, as follows:

1. On several occasions and using veiled words he has attempted to incite men to the murder of the Führer Adolf Hitler.

2. On several occasions he has made remarks injurious to the good name and reputation of various of the officials of the Third Reich, including the Führer Adolf Hitler. (Details of the above-mentioned remarks are attached to this Bill and marked Exhibit "L".)

3. In spreading gossip and false rumours the Accused has aided and abetted the enemies of the Third Reich and acted in such a manner as to undermine the morale of the German people.

'I ask that the Accused be condemned to death in accordance with Article 5 of the Law for the Protection of the People and of the State dated 28th February, 1933; and in accordance with Article 80, Para. 2; Article 83, Paras. 2 and 3; and Article 91b, 73 Stbg.

'Incitement to murder of the Führer carries the penalty of death by decapitation under Article 5 of the Law of 28th July, 1933.

'The following documents are enclosed:

1. Confession of the Accused.

2. Voluntary Statements by three Witnesses:
   (a) A Garrison cleaner, Frau K;
   (b) Lt. P. of the Military Political Department;
   (c) Gefreiter H. of the Political Service of Military Security.

'The above-named witnesses will not be called to give evidence at the trial. Their Statements shall be destroyed as soon as judgement has been passed, in accordance with Article 14 of the State Security Bill.

'The entire matter is classified GEKADOS (secret) and all documents pertaining to it shall be finally lodged with the RSHA, Prinz Albrecht Strasse 8, Berlin.

'The preliminary investigation has been carried out by SD-Standartenführer Kriminalrat Paul Bielert.

(Sgd.) F. WEYERSBERG
Prosecutor General.'

Lt. Ohlsen walked across to the window. He stared through the bars, through the grey unwashed panes of glass, through to the unimaginable freedom that lay beyond. Seeing it in print for the first time, that monstrous request that he should be beheaded, he found himself suddenly unable to face the reality. It must surely be a black joke, one of the Gestapo's sick attempts at humour. At Torgau, he knew, it was frequently their pleasure to arrange for ten executions to be staged and only eight to be carried out. They worked on the not unreasonable assumption that by the time the last two men on the list had witnessed their companions' heads rolling into the basket, they would be willing to go to any lengths of collaboration to avoid the same fate for themselves. It was small comfort, but all he could think of.

That same day a letter from the Wehrmacht Kommandantur in Hamburg was sent to the Kommandantur at Atlona:

'Wehrmachtkommandantur, Hamburg

TOP SECRET

'This correspondence must be read by two officers and then destroyed. Receipt must be confirmed by telephone.

'Subject: Executions following Sentence of Death.

'It is anticipated that sentence of death will tomorrow be passed on the following four soldiers:

(a) Infantry Oberleutnant Karl Heinz Berger of the 12th Grenadiers (*b*) Lieutenant Bernt Viktor Ohlsen of the 27th Tank Regiment

(*c*) Oberfeldwebel Franz Gernerstadt of the 19th Artillery Regiment

(*d*) Gefreiter Paul Baum of the 3rd Alpine Regiment.

'Two of the above-mentioned will suffer death by shooting, the 76th Infantry Regiment to provide two firing squads, which shall comprise two Feldwebels and twelve men. A medical officer shall be present at the executions.

'The two other accused shall suffer death by decapitation, and the 76th Infantry Regiment is instructed to call the executioner Rüttger from Berlin to carry out the sentence, which shall take place in closed courtyard B of the Garrison prison.

'A minister of religion shall be present at the request of the accused.

'It is the responsibility of the 76th Infantry Regiment to provide the necessary four coffins.

'The bodies shall be buried in the special cemetery, Dept. 12/31.

(Sgd.) A. ZIMMERMANN
Oberstleutnant.'

Lt. Ohlsen was not to know it, but arrangements for his execution had therefore been made well in advance, even before the trial had started, even before the court had passed sentence.

Humanitarianism was a quality unknown and unacknowledged in the Third Reich, whose code of behaviour was based firmly upon a multitude of paragraphs and sub-paragraphs, and upon nothing so flimsy as humanity. The least infringement of any one of these myriad paragraphs carried a rigid penalty, taking no account either of the situation or of the individual. The term 'extenuating circumstances' was altogether too vague for even a sub-sub-paragraph and was therefore not recognized.

The room where the trials took place was as usual filled from floor to ceiling. All the public benches were occupied by soldiers, who came not for vicarious thrills, nor through a wish to learn, nor out of academic interest, but purely and simply because they were ordered to be there. The witnessing of military trials was held by those in authority to have a beneficial effect upon servicemen.

Gefreiter Paul Baum of the 3rd Alpine Regiment, white and terrified, was waiting to hear his fate. The court had retired to deliberate.

The Prosecutor rearranged his papers, preparing for the next case. He had already lost interest in the trembling Gefreiter.

Counsel for the defence sat playing with his gold propelling pencil. With his elbows on the table, he was twisting the lead in and out, and his thoughts were far from the courtroom. He was thinking of his mistress; and not so much of his mistress but of the meal she had promised him that night. A meal of beef and sauerkraut. Mistresses were ten a penny these days, but meals of beef and sauerkraut were something of a luxury.

A female shorthand-writer sucked the end of her pen and thoughtfully regarded the ashen Gefreiter: a sad, squat, peasant type, with thick features and great red hands. She could never sleep with a man like that. Not if all the rest were killed, she couldn't. She would sooner retain her virginity.

The peasant Gefreiter sat staring at the floor. He began to count the boards with his feet: condemned to death, not condemned; condemned to death, not condemned . . . He finished up with an unfavourable verdict and for a moment he grew stiff with terror. Just in time, he remembered that there were more floorboards beneath the bench. He felt cautiously with his feet. Three of them . . . that made 'not condemned'. Feeling slightly happier he raised his head and looked across to the white-painted door in the corner of the court. Through that door would come the three judges when they had decided on his fate. He sat with his eyes screwed tightly shut, willing them to listen to the verdict of the floorboards.

The whole of the proceedings against this boy of eighteen had taken no longer than ten minutes. The President of the Court had asked a few laconic questions. The Prosecutor had spoken a great deal and Counsel for the Defence had contributed one speech of a few seconds' duration:

'Law and order must, of course, be maintained at whatever cost, without regard for human emotions or human frailty. Nevertheless, I would ask the Court to show indulgence and understanding towards my client in this difficult situation in which they find themselves.'

From the point of view of military ruling, the case against the Gefreiter was cut and dried. There were no loopholes, no grounds for argument, and Counsel for the Defence made his brief speech and sat down again to dream of his beef and sauerkraut.

The Gefreiter was growing too nervous to sit still. He shifted up and down the bench, clattering his feet, tearing at his finger nails, clearing his throat. Why didn't they come? Why didn't the white door open? How much longer would they keep him in suspense?

And then it occurred to him – if they were taking so long to decide, it could surely mean but one thing? They were unable to agree on his case. And where there was disagreement, there was hope. That was why there were three judges, to make sure that the decision did not rest solely upon the whims and fancies of one man. Each prisoner must be given a fair chance.

In their antechamber, the three judges sat back in their easy chairs drinking kirsch. Kriegsferichtsrat Burgholz was coming to the end of a very funny story. They had been exchanging stories ever since they had retired to discuss the case. But the case was hardly worth discussing and none of them had even bothered to listen to the evidence. Their verdict had been decided for them in advance.

After half a dozen glasses of kirsch they reluctantly decided to return to the courtroom.

The white door opened.

The Gefreiter began shaking violently. The crowded ranks of soldiers craned their heads for a better view.

The President and his two fellow judges seated themselves with due majesty, smelling strongly of kirsch, behind their horseshoe table. The President delivered their verdict: found Guilty of desertion and sentenced to death by shooting.

The Gefreiter swayed forward in a faint and was jerked upright by the rough grip of a court Feldwebel.

The President calmly continued his speech, rejecting in advance any appeal that might be made against either the verdict or the sentence. He then patted his brow with a perfumed handkerchief, threw a quick glance of indifference at the condemned man and turned to the next case.

Number 19 661/M.43H, the State versus Lt. Bernt Ohlsen. The Gefreiter was led away and Lt. Ohlsen was sent for. The stage management was good and the show was being run with a precision to be proud of.

Obergefreiter Stever threw open the door of Ohlsen's cell and called him out.

'You're wanted!'

'Why? Is it time?' Lt. Ohlsen walked slowly to the door, feeling as if his stomach had suddenly collapsed.

'That's it,' said Stever, cheerfully. 'You're on next. Room 7, under Oberkriegsferichtsrat Jackstadt. He's a fat stinking pig, if ever there was one,' he added, by way of a snippet of interesting information. 'He'll be one of the first to go when the wheel's turned full circle.'

Stever pushed Ohlsen along the corridor and down the stairs, where he was taken in charge by two military policemen outside the entrance to the courtrooms. Stever walked away, humming. Lt. Ohlsen was handcuffed and marched off through the long tunnel that led to room number 7. On their way they encountered the Gefreiter, making the return journey. He was screaming and struggling, and it required three men to hold him in check.

'Will you flaming pipe down and stop bawling?' shouted one of his guards irascibly. He fetched him a cuff round the ear. 'Who the devil d'you think you're impressing, anyway? Certainly not me, I've seen far too much of it already. In any case, what the hell, you'll probably be far better off where you're going than stuck here with the rest of us.'

'Just think,' added another, twisting the Gefreiter's arm behind his back, 'little lord Jesus is probably all ready and waiting for you. Probably got a party going in your honour. What's he going to think when you turn up in this state? Bloody ungrateful if you ask me!'

The boy suddenly caught sight of Lt. Ohlsen, and in spite of his guards he fell to his knees and called out to him.

'Lieutenant! Help me! They want me to die, they're going to shoot me, I was only gone two days, I swear it was a mistake! It was a mistake, I didn't mean it, oh God, I didn't mean it, I didn't mean it! I'll do anything they want me to, I'll go to the Russian front, I'll learn how to fly a Stuka, I'll go down in a U-boat, I'll do anything, I swear I will! Oh, Mother of God,' he babbled, tears making rivers down his cheeks, 'Mother of God, help me, I don't want to die! Heil Hitler, Heil Hitler, Heil Hitler, I'll do anything they want me to, but let me live, please let me live!'

He lashed out with arms and legs and succeeded in throwing one of his guards to the floor. The other two closed in on him and he screamed penetratingly as he struggled.

'I'm a good National Socialist! I was in the Hitler Youth! Heil Hitler, Heil Hitler, oh, God, help me!'

He disappeared beneath three heavy bodies. There was the unpleasant sound of a head being thumped against the stone floor, and when the guards picked themselves up and continued on their way through the tunnel they were dragging an unconscious Gefreiter behind them.

Lt. Ohlsen hesitated a moment and turned to watch.

'What's the matter with you?' One of his own guards jabbed him in the back, pushing him forward. 'The court's not going to wait all day, you know.'

Lt. Ohlsen shrugged his shoulders.

'Getting squeamish?' jeered the guard.

'Call it that if you like ... but that was a child they were dragging along by his hair just now.'

'So what? He was old enough to know what he was doing, wasn't he? They let one off, they got to let them all off, and before you knew it the whole bleeding Army'd be up and away.'

'I suppose so.' Ohlsen turned to look gravely at one of the men. 'Do you have any children of your own, Oberfeldwebel?'

'Sure I got children of my own. I got four of 'em. Three's in the Hitler Youth and one's at the front. SS regiment – Das Reich.'

'I wonder how you'd feel if one day he was dragged out to be shot?'

The guard laughed.

'That's not very likely to happen. He's an SS Untersturmführer. Safe as bleeding houses.'

'Even houses fall down in war time.'

The man frowned.

'What d'you mean by that remark, then?'

'Whatever you like.'

'And suppose I don't like?'

Lt. Ohlsen shook his head, wearily.

'Please yourself. All I know is, I can't stand to see them drag kids like that away to the slaughter house.'

'Well, if I was you, mate, I'd save all your pity for yourself, because the way things are going you're likely to need it.' He nodded significantly and tapped the holster of his pistol. 'And no talking once we get in there, eh?'

Lt. Ohlsen took his place in the courtroom with an air of apparent indifference, and his trial began. Dr. Beckmann, the Prosecutor, turned to him to ask whether or not he intended to plead guilty to the charges brought against him.

Lt. Ohlsen stared down at the floor. It was polished to a high gloss and he experimentally slid a foot across it to test whether it was slippery.

Slowly he raised his head and looked across at the three judges behind their horseshoe table. Two of them seemed to be asleep. The President, enthroned on his big red chair, was lost in contemplation of a fly buzzing round the lamp. Admittedly it was no ordinary common or garden house fly. It was a cleg, or gadfly. A blood-sucking fly. Not very pretty to look upon, but doubtless very interesting from an entomologist's point of view.

Lt. Ohlsen drew his gaze away from the gadfly and turned slowly towards the Prosecutor.

'Herr Oberkriegsgerichtsrat,' he began, respectfully, 'since I've already signed a full confession for the Secret Police, your question is surely superfluous?'

Dr. Beckmann pinched his thin lips together in a sarcastic smile. He stroked a blue-veined hand caressingly over his pile of documents.

'Perhaps the prisoner will be so kind as to leave it to the court to decide whether or not a question is superfluous?'

'Oh, by all means,' agreed Ohlsen, with a slight lift of the shoulders.

'Very well, then. Let us leave aside for the moment the crimes of which you are accused in the indictment.' The little doctor turned and addressed the judges in a loud high-pitched voice. 'In the name of the Führer and of the German people, I beg leave to add to the list of crimes of which the prisoner is accused those of desertion and cowardice and in the face of the enemy!'

The two sleeping judges opened their eyes and looked round guiltily, dimly aware that they had missed something. The President gave up his contemplation of the gadfly. Lt. Ohlsen sprang forward.

'That's a lie! I've never been guilty of either!'

Dr. Beckman picked up a sheet of paper and smiled slyly into it, sucking in his cheeks and making them more hollow than ever. This was the type of combat in which he excelled: a quick barb, a surprise attack, a well-placed arrow.

'I've never in my life even thought about desertion!' shouted Ohlsen.

Dr. Beckmann inclined his head.

'Let us study the matter together. That is, after all, what we are here for, is it not? We are here to prove either your innocence or your guilt. If, of course, you are able to prove the accusation to be false, then you will be allowed to walk out of here a free man.'

'Free?' murmured Ohlsen, raising a cynical eyebrow.

What is a free man? Had there ever been such a person, in his lifetime, in Germany? Certainly there was none now, in the Third Reich. From new-born babies to old men on their death beds, Germany was a nation of prisoners.

'Naturally,' went on Dr. Beckmann, leaning menacingly across his table, 'if you are proven guilty your fate will be very different.'

'Naturally,' said Ohlsen.

The President nodded his head in approval. Dr. Beckmann turned back to the judges.

'With the court's permission, we will disregard the accusations contained in the original indictment in order to concentrate on the fresh charges that I have brought. These charges were made possible only this morning, when I received certain documents—' He held up a bulky bundle – 'from the Secret Police Special Service. The facts contained therein are quite clear, and if I may be allowed to question the prisoner for a few moments I believe I shall be able to convince the court that there is no necessity for a preliminary investigation.'

The President nodded again.

'Very well. The court gives its permission. We shall disregard the charges in the indictment and you may proceed to question the prisoner.'

Dr. Beckmann made a servile inclination and swung round to Lt. Ohlsen.

'On 2nd February, 1942 you were the officer commanding the 5th Company, 27th Tank Regiment? Is that correct?'

'Yes.'

'Will you please tell the court where you were then fighting?'

'I will if I can remember.' Ohlsen stared ahead, frowning, at the enormous photograph of Hitler behind the President's chair. Not a very inspiring sight. 'It was probably somewhere near the Dnieper,' he said, at last. 'But I couldn't swear to it. I've fought in so many places . . .'

Dr. Beckmann tapped a thin finger on the table.

'Somewhere near the Dnieper. That in fact is correct. Your division had been sent to the Wjasma Rshew area. You had received orders to take up a position with your Company near Olenin, to the west of Rshew. Are you able to remember?'

'Yes. The division was on the point of being surrounded. The 19th and 20th Russian Cavalry Divisions had outflanked us on the south, and more of them were coming up on the north.'

'Thank you, thank you, thank you!' said Dr. Beckmann, crisply. 'The court is not in the least interested in hearing of the activities of the Russians. And as for your Division being surrounded—' He looked up at the gallery, full of high-ranking and powerful officers – 'since the Division is still in existence this seems to me a highly unlikely story.'

A loud murmur was borne down from the gallery. It was, of

course, accepted teaching that no German armoured division could ever be surrounded by the troops of an inferior nation such as the Russians. Doubt was therefore at once cast upon the veracity of Lt. Ohlsen's version of the facts. Dr. Beckmann smiled upwards to his audience.

'Tell me, Lieutenant, are you able to recall that period of the war with any clarity?'

'Yes, certainly.'

'Good. Let us see if we agree with each other ... You had received an order, verbally, from your commanding officer Colonel von Lindenau, to occupy a position near Olenin because the enemy had at one point broken through and there was now a gap in the defences. That gap, to be precise, was along the railway line two kilometres to the east of Olenin—'

'Which railway line?' asked one of the judges.

It was not of the least importance and he had no interest whatsoever in the answer, but it created a favourable impression if one asked a question every now and again.

'Which railway line?' repeated Dr. Beckmann, for once at a loss.

He tore furiously through his papers, muttering, '*Which* railway line', to himself in tones of disgust and impatience.

Lt. Ohlsen watched him a while.

'Actually, it was the Rshew–Nelidowo line,' he said, helpfully.

Dr. Beckmann turned with an irritable gesture.

'The prisoner must speak only when he is spoken to!' he snapped. He looked towards the judges and bowed. 'It was the Rschew–Nelidowo line,' he told them, and shrugged his shoulders. 'A branch line merely.'

'Excuse me,' said Lt. Ohlsen, 'but in point of fact it was the main line from Moscow to Riva.'

A suspicion of colour entered the Doctor's pale pinched cheeks.

'I have already explained to the prisoner,' he said, 'that he must speak only when spoken to.'

Lt. Ohlsen pulled a face.

'Just as you wish, but I thought we should have the facts right.'

'We do have the facts right! The line in question may have seemed of large importance to you, but in our eyes it is totally insignificant.'

'Nevertheless,' persisted Ohlsen, 'it's a pretty outstanding branch line that has two tracks and runs for about 1,000 kilometres.'

'We are not interested in how far it runs nor in how many tracks it has,' replied the Doctor, tapping on his documents. 'If I say it is a branch line, then rest assured that that is what it is. You're in Germany now, you know; not in some Soviet bog. And here in Germany we have very different standards from those obtaining in Russia ... But let us pass over this wretchedly unimportant railway line and return to the facts! You received an order from your commanding officer to take up your position to the east of Olenin, and you were told that nothing – I repeat NOTHING, neither God nor the devil nor the entire Red Army – was to shift you from that point. You were to dig yourselves in there and make sure of your position both in front and on both flanks. Is that correct?'

Ohlsen hunched his shoulders and muttered some words too low to be heard.

'Yes or no!' cried Dr. Beckmann. 'Will the prisoner please answer!'

'Yes,' said Ohlsen.

Dr. Beckmann smiled triumphantly.

'Very well. So having established agreement on the orders you received, we may now go on with the tale in order to give the court an example of your extraordinary cowardice and failure to do your duty ... Your company was fighting as infantry, but it was by no means an ordinary company that you commanded. It was a company which had been very much reinforced – you may correct me if I am wrong. Obeying written instructions, a section of tanks fitted with anti-tank guns had been sent to you, and also a section of sappers armed with both light and heavy flame-throwers. Perhaps you would care to tell the court in your own words what the exact strength of your company was at that time?'

'Certainly,' said Ohlsen. 'We had 250 men in addition to the reinforcements you just mentioned. Say 300 men in all.'

'And I think no one would call that a small company,' murmured Dr. Beckmann. 'On the contrary, rather on the strong side, would you not say?'

'I wouldn't argue with you,' agreed Ohlsen.

'Suppose you tell us something of the armaments you had?'

Lt. Ohlsen sighed. He vaguely began, now, to see where the Prosecutor's questions were leading him. He looked across at the judges. One had his eyes closed again, and the President was drawing ranks of dinosaurs on his blotting pad.

'We had two anti-tank guns, 7.5 cm., two mortars of 8 cm. and three of 5 cm. – they were Russian, by the way. Then we had two heavy machine guns, four heavy flame-throwers, four light flame-throwers. All section leaders also had sub-machine guns. Some men had rifles. And the sappers, of course, had mines and grenades and that sort of thing.'

Dr. Beckmann listened to this recital with his head on one side.

'I congratulate you. You have a very remarkable memory. That is exactly how your Company was armed. I have only one comment to make, and that is that your allocation of sub-machine guns was very much higher than average. You had over one hundred, in fact, and yet despite this you behaved in a manner which can only be described as gross cowardice.'

'That is not true,' muttered Ohlsen.

'Oh?' Dr. Beckmann raised an eyebrow. 'I beg to differ, Lieutenant . . . Who was it who gave the order for the Company to retreat? Was it one of your men? A non-commissioned officer? Or was it you yourself, the head of the Company?'

'It was I who gave the order,' admitted Ohlsen, 'but only because by that time the Company had been wiped out.

'Wiped out?' repeated Dr. Beckmann. 'You have a very bizarre notion of the meaning of that expression, Lieutenant! In my book, it is used to signify annihilation – total destruction. And yet your presence here today proves beyond any possible shadow of doubt that the Company most certainly was NOT annihilated! And your orders, Lieutenant, if I may recapitulate a moment, your orders were quite definite, were they not? Neither God nor the devil nor the entire Red Army . . .'

Lt. Ohlsen looked without much hope towards the judges.

'Do I have the permission of the court to relate the events that took place on 2nd February, 1942?'

The sleeping judge woke up and looked about him in alarm: things were happening again and he was not aware of them. The President finished off the last of his dinosaurs and glanced at his watch. He was hungry and bored. He had sat through too many of these trials, they were trivial and irrelevant and a total waste of his judicial intelligence. It was high time such matters were dealt with backstage, by the office staff, without going through all this absurd rigmarole in court. And as for Beckman – he glared at him over the horseshoe table. What did the fool think he was playing at, dragging the case on into his lunch hour in this tedious fashion? All this nonsense about cowardice in the face of the enemy. Nobody wanted high drama when the outcome of the trial had been settled beforehand.

'You have the court's permission,' he grudgingly allowed. 'But kindly be brief.'

'Thank you. I'll make it as short as possible.' Ohlsen looked back again at Beckmann. 'After four days and nights of continuous fighting my Company of three hundred men had been reduced to nineteen. All our heavy guns had been destroyed. We had run out of ammunition. Only two light machine guns were still in working order. It would have been suicide to hang on with nineteen men and no weapons. We were fighting at odds of five hundred to one. Both before and behind us were the Russians, and we were under constant attack. To have stayed on when there wasn't a hope in hell would have been an act of lunacy and an act of sabotage . . . throwing away nineteen lives for no purpose at all, when they could still be of value to Germany.'

'An interesting hypothesis,' admitted Dr. Beckmann. 'But may I interrupt you one moment, Lieutenant. The order of the day from the Führer himself for all troops in the Wajsmo area was to fight until the last man and the last bullet, in order to stop the advance of the Soviets. And you – you, a mere lieutenant – you dare to call that an act of lunacy and sabotage? You dare to insinuate that our Führer, who is under the direct protection of God, is a lunatic? You dare to sit in judgement upon him? You, who are so insignificant that your life could be extinguished this very moment and no one in Germany would even notice, you dare to set yourself up against the Führer and countermand his orders?'

Lt. Ohlsen watched with a mild and detached curiosity as this self-contained and precise little lawyer worked himself into a rage of fanatical self-righteousness on the Führer's behalf.

'Herr Oberkriegsgerichtsrat,' he at last calmly interpolated. 'I can assure you that I had no intention of implying that the Führer was a lunatic, nor of countermanding his orders, which I imagined were to be taken as a form of encouragement to the troops rather than to be followed literally down to the last man and the last bullet. When I said an act of lunacy, I was referring to myself. I was taught that an officer should use his own initiative where the situation calls for it, and in my opinion it called for it then. You have to remember, if you will, that our position had altered radically since Colonel von Lindenau first told me to hold the—'

'We are not interested in what your position had or had not done!' cried Beckman. 'We are interested only in the fact that you were specifically ordered to fight to the last man and yet you pulled out with nineteen! Why did you not get in touch with your regiment?'

'Because the whole combat area was in such a shambles that we weren't able to contact the regiment again until four days later.'

'Thank you.' The weary voice of the President droned into the court. 'I think we have heard enough. The accused has admitted giving the order to retreat from his position near Olenin and the branch railway. The charge of cowardice and desertion is quite clear.' He looked directly at Ohlsen and tapped on the table with his pencil. 'Do you have anything else you wish to say?'

'Yes, I do!' rejoined Ohlsen, heatedly. 'If you will take the trouble to look in my papers you will see that I have received many decorations in recognition of deeds requiring courage over and above the call of duty. I submit that this is proof in itself that I am not guilty of cowardice. On the occasion we were talking of I was not concerned with my own safety but with that of my few remaining men. Nineteen of us – and 270 of our comrades lying dead in the snow all round us. Many of those 270 had shot themselves rather than fall into the hands of the Russians. Of the nineteen that were left, every single one was wounded – some badly. We had run out of ammunition, we'd run out of food. We were eating handfuls of snow because there was nothing else to slake our thirst. Several of the men were suffering hideously from frost bite. I was wounded in three different places myself, and yet I was one of the more fortunate ones. Some of the others couldn't even walk unless they were supported by a companion. And because I valued their lives, I gave the order to retreat. We destroyed everything of value before we left. Nothing fell into the hands of the Russians. We blew up the railway line in several places – and I repeat, it was not a branch line but the main line from Moscow to Riga. We also planted mines before we pulled out.'

Dr. Beckmann laughed sardonically.

'A likely tale! But whether it's true or not, the fact remains: you disobeyed an order to stay at your post and you are therefore guilty of cowardice and of desertion.'

Lt. Ohlsen bit his lip and remained silent, realizing the futility of further protestation. His eyes flickered briefly over the crowded courtroom, but he felt it to be hostile towards him, and he knew – as he had known from the beginning – that the verdict had been delivered long before the case had even come to trial. In the back row of spectators he saw a thin sliver of a man, dressed all in black with a red carnation in his buttonhole: Kriminalrat Paul Bielert, come to witness his final downfall.

The President had also caught sight of Bielert. The flint eyes behind the spectacles flickered and danced, sweeping the court like twin radar beams. The man was openly smoking a cigarette, despite all the notices forbidding this activity. The President leaned forward to tap on the horseshoe table and have him arrested, but just in time one of his fellow judges sent him a warning look and whispered a name in his ear. The President frowned and sat back again, breathing heavily and indignantly and not daring to lift a finger.

Dr. Beckmann, also, had remarked the arrival of Bielert. He developed a sudden series of nervous twitches, awkwardly shuffling his feet and dropping half his papers to the floor. It always bode ill, when the chief of IV/2a appeared on the scene. The man was dangerous and you never knew where or when he was likely to strike next. And was there anyone who could stand up and say, in all confidence, 'I have nothing to fear?' Dr. Beckmann certainly could not.

There was an affair he had been mixed up in four years ago – but surely no one could now discover the details of it? He had been uncertain at the time as to the wisdom of it – but Bielert would hardly go digging that far back? And besides, they were all dead except him. All those who had been in it with him – even Frau Rosen had been hanged in the end. There was no one save himself who could know anything of it. Only you never could tell with Paul Bielert. Four years ago he had been a mere Kriminalsekretär of no importance whatsoever. Who could have prophesied that he would rise to such heights in so short a time? Of course, the man had had the good sense to be a friend of Heydrich's. That had been a shock, when they had discovered that.

Dr. Beckmann pulled out his handkerchief and with trembling hand mopped at his brow. On its way back to a pocket his hand paused involuntarily to clutch at his throat. Dr. Beckmann stared in rabbit-like fascination across the court and into Bielert's eyes. A cold seizure took hold of his spine. What was the man doing here? Why had he come? They were trying no one of importance, every case was straightforward and routine. So why was he here? In whom was he interested?

Dr. Beckmann shook himself out of his petrified stupor, put his handkerchief away and attempted to square his hunched shoulders. Who was the rude uneducated little man, after all? No one. Simply a no one. A rat that had crawled out of a sewer and still had the odour of putrefaction clinging to him. This was a court of Prussian law and he, Dr. Beckmann, was a barrister at law. And a former university lecturer. A respectable citizen, ranking far above Bielert in the social and intellectual hierarchy.

He decided on an instant to take the bull by the horns. Forcing his lips into what seemed to him a smile, though anyone else might well have taken it for an arrogant leer, he nodded at

Bielert across the courtroom. Bielert stared back coldly at him, eyes glittering, narrow lips compressed, cigarette smoke curling from his nostrils. Dr. Beckmann slowly froze. With the arrogant leer still painted meaninglessly on his lips, he turned back to the judges' table. He could feel the hard eyes boring into his neck.

He realized suddenly that the court was waiting for him to speak. He sprang forward and shouted defiantly, determined to demonstrate his patriotism beyond any possible shadow of doubt.

'I ask the court that the accused be sentenced to death by decapitation under article 197b and Article 91b of the Military Penal Code!'

Dr. Beckman sat down and began with abrupt industry to search through his papers. Heaven knew what he was searching for. Composure, perhaps. He wished only to impress Bielert with his devotion to duty.

The President rose and walked with his fellow judges out of the court and back to the ante-chamber. They seated themselves comfortably round the table, where a thoughtful minion had left a carafe of red wine. The President pushed it to one side and called for beer. Someone else wanted sausages, and sausages were accordingly grilled and delivered on a tray with cutlery, plates and mustard.

'Well—' the President stuffed his mouth with hot sausage and swilled it round with beer – 'in my opinion we should grant the request of the Prosecutor and have done with it.'

'I couldn't agree more,' said Kriegsgerichtsrat Burgholz, mopping beer off his chin.

There was a moment's comparative silence while they all concentrated upon their sausages. The youngest of the three judges, Kriegsgerichtsrat Ring, made a half-hearted attempt to speak up on behalf of Lt. Ohlsen.

'I confess I have my doubts about the decapitation,' he murmured. 'It seems unnecessarily harsh, and it's hardly an aesthetic way to kill a man. Besides, we should surely take into account the fact that the prisoner has never previously shown any inclination towards cowardice? In view of his decorations and so forth, could we not perhaps show a certain amount of clemency and change the sentence to death by shooting?'

The President narrowed his eyes as he held up his beer mug and stared into the depths of it.

'I think not,' he said. 'You must remember it's not only cowardice the man's guilty of. He has also plotted against the Führer and made dubious jokes about him. If we allowed that sort of thing to go unpunished, I shudder to think what the outcome would be.'

Burgholz cleared his throat and affected an air of indifference.

'What – ah – what were these dubious jokes, anyway?' he asked. He picked up his fork and drew tramlines through a pool of mustard. 'They can't have been so very bad, surely?'

'That is a matter of opinion,' said the President, gravely.

He looked over his shoulder towards the door, opened his file of papers, selected a sheet and pushed it secretively across the table to his colleagues.

Ring was the first to laugh. He smiled, and then he sniggered, and finally he threw back his head and bellowed. Burgholz at first attempted a more suitable reaction, drawing his brows together and pulling down the corners of his mouth, but Ring bent forward and pointed out one particular gem and Burgholz was soon laughing so much his belly bumped against the edge of the table. Even the President gave a sly smile behind his hand. Ring beat in a frenzy on his thighs. Burgholz overturned a full mug of beer. The tears rolled down their cheeks.

'Upsetting your beer is surely not as amusing as all that, gentlemen?'

With reproof in his voice, the President stretched across and took back the offending sheet of paper. The other two rearranged their faces into lines more becoming to a judge.

'Of course not, of course not,' murmured Burgholz, blowing his nose.

'This document,' continued the President, 'is an outrage of obscenity and propaganda at its most dangerous and vile. In my opinion it is our bounden duty to accept the Prosecutor's plea for death by decapitation. An example must be made of this man. We must act according to the best interests of the State, and not according to the emotional dictates of the heart.'

And picking up his pen he wrote the word 'decapitation' at the foot of a document and signed his name with a legal flourish. He pushed pen and document across the table to his colleagues. Burgholz signed at once, without even pausing for thought. Ring hesitated, drummed his fingers on the table, frowned and sighed and finally with great reluctance wrote his name. Each letter seemed wrung from him by force. The President watched him with growing dislike. This man Ring was coming daily to be a bigger thorn in his flesh. He would have to see what he could do about having him transferred to a more dangerous theatre of war. The Eastern front, perhaps.

The document signed, they relaxed in their chairs and drank a few more beers, ate a few more sausages. Burgholz opened his mouth and gave a gentle, rolling belch. He looked up in mild surprise as he did so, staring wonderingly at his two colleagues as if trying to decide which of them was the culprit.

The President called in the clerk of the court and dictated the verdict and sentence with all the solemnity called for by the occasion. The three judges then picked themselves up and proudly goosestepped through the door and back to the court, followed by the clerk at a respectful distance. The press-ganged audience at once shot to its feet. Only Paul Bielert remained seated, leaning against the wall and smoking.

The President looked across at him and scowled. The insolence of the man was beyond all credibility. But the Gestapo were full of their own importance these days. It was their hour of glory and they were making the most of it in a power-crazed frenzy of terrorism. Their hour would soon pass, reflected the President, as he seated himself. The Russians and the Americans were stronger than anyone had ever suspected, and the time was not far ahead when the Gestapo would find their power evaporated and themselves in the position of their present victims. One day, thought the President, rolling a hand back and forth across the table, as if he were kneading a breadcrumb, one day he would have the pleasure of condemning Paul Bielert to a death by decapitation. It never crossed his mind that he himself might by that time be removed from the bench. Who, after all, could attach any blame to a judge? A judge did not make the laws, he only carried them out.

He looked again at Bielert, and this time there was a thin, sarcastic smile on the man's lips. With an uneasy frown, the President turned away. He began speaking very quickly, in a flurry of words.

'In the name of the Führer Adolf Hitler and of the German people, I hereby pronounce the verdict of the court in the case of the accused Lt. Bernt Viktor Ohlsen of the 27th Tank Regiment.' He paused a moment and took a deep gulp of air. Bielert's glassy eyes were still upon him, and for a moment the President had a queasy sensation at the pit of his stomach, as if – absurd idea! – it was his own sentence he was pronouncing. 'After considering the matter, the court considers that the prisoner is guilty on all counts in the original indictment and is in addition guilty on the extra charges of cowardice and desertion. He is therefore dishonoured and shall be sentenced to death by decapitation. All his worldly goods shall be seized by the State, and the expenses of the trial shall be at the prisoner's own charge. His name shall henceforth be expunged from the registers. The body shall be buried in an unnamed grave. Heil Hitler!'

The President turned gravely to regard the condemned man, standing stiffly to attention before him.

'Does the prisoner wish to say anything?' He repeated the question three times, with no response from Lt. Ohlsen, whereupon he shrugged his shoulders and gabbled out the statutory advance rejection of any appeal that might be contemplated. 'All right.' He nodded to the Feldwebel standing at Ohlsen's side. 'Take the prisoner away.'

As Lt. Ohlsen was being marched back through the tunnel, they met the next prisoner coming down. Twenty-three minutes later the President pronounced his fourth sentence of death that day and left the court room. He exchanged his judicial robes for his pearl grey uniform and made his way home to a dinner of tomato soup and boiled cod. Four death sentences. It was raining outside, a persistent drizzle, and he had passed four death sentences and was going home to eat tomato soup and boiled cod. A typical day in court. Four death sentences. A persistent drizzle. Tomato soup and cod. The President buttoned his coat and walked briskly towards the waiting car.

Oberfeldwebel Stever was waiting for Lt. Ohlsen down in the cells. The heavy door clanged shut behind them. Stever groaned as he pushed back the bolts.

'Well, so what's it to be?' he asked, as he straightened up. 'Another case for the chopper? That makes the third today, and the one that's just gone down there, I reckon he'll be the fourth. Not that that's anything to get excited about. A month ago, we had sixteen in one day . . .' He looked at Ohlsen and grinned. 'Don't take it to heart, Lieutenant. It's happened to better men than you . . . In any case, we all have to come to it sooner or later, one way or another. And you won't be the first or the last to go like that . . . And if the Padre's to be believed, it's a better world you're going to and Jesus will be there to meet you.'

Lt. Ohlsen looked at him.

'Well?' he said. 'Is the padre to be believed or isn't he?'

Stever hunched his shoulders uncomfortably.

'You know more about that than I do . . . I haven't really thought about it too much. I suppose when the time comes I'll have to . . . But as for all this stuff about Jesus and suchlike – well, yeah, I suppose it's always possible.' He scratched his head and frowned. 'You can't say you don't believe in it, like, just in case it does turn out to be true. But the old Padre, he believes in it all right.' Stever paused to assume a suitable expression and a priestlike voice. ' "Mm – pray and the Lord will hear you," he says. "Mm – the Lord will receive you . . ." He always says "mm" before everything. They call him Mm-Müller in the prison. A filthy old shit, mind you – always blowing his nose in his cassock – but I suppose he knows what he's doing.'

'I hope so,' said Lt. Ohlsen, quietly, 'because I intend to say my prayers with him.'

'Go on?' Stever cocked an eyebrow. 'Well, I don't blame you. I mean, you can't afford to take any chances really, can you?'

'It's not a question of taking chances.' Lt. Ohlsen shook his head and smiled. 'I happen to believe in it.'

'Go on?' said Stever, again. 'What are you, if you don't mind me asking? RC or something else?'

'I'm a Protestant.'

'Well—' They reached the door of the cell and Stever flung it open – 'it's all one to me, to tell you the honest truth. The minute I set foot in a church I get the feeling they're all just a load of great gabbling idiots. Don't do nothing for me . . . know what I mean? Still, that's not to say that when my turn comes I won't feel a bit different.'

'Very likely,' agreed Ohlsen, with a faint smile.

He walked across to the window and looked out between the bars at the falling grey drizzle.

'Look here,' said Stever, consolingly, 'you're OK for the rest of today. They won't have set it up yet. They have to get the bloke down from Berlin and I don't think he's even arrived. In any case, he has to have a gander at you first – work out how he's going to . . .' Stever trailed into silence and demonstrated the meaning of it by raising an imaginary axe above his head. 'Know what I mean? It's a skilled job, after all. Not something anybody could do. Not if they want a good clean cut, that is . . . Anyway, there's the Padre'll have to come and see you, as well. It won't be old Müller, though, he's the RC. It'll be the other bloke. Dunno his name, but he'll be along all right, don't you fret . . . Then there's the nosh. They'll give you a good nosh-up, give you a good send-off . . .' He winked. 'Don't want to meet St. Peter with a rumbling belly, do you?'

He raised his hand in a sign of farewell and closed the door behind him. Lt. Ohlsen began a distracted pacing of the cell. Five steps one way, five steps another. He tried walking the diagonals. He tried walking round the perimeter. He walked in squares, he walked in circles, he traced geometrical patterns all over the place.

The hours slowly passed. It was still raining when he heard the garrison clock strike six. He braced himself to expect a visit from the executioner at any moment.

All night he had listened to the striking of the garrison clock. The hour, the quarter hour, the half, the three quarters, the hour, the quarter hour, the half hour, the three quarters, the hour, the—

Despairingly, he began thumping his head against the wall. No use listening to clocks, no use thinking, no use anything any more. His life was over. Let them come and take him when they liked, and the sooner the better. He felt that spiritually he had died on earth already.

Morning came and prison life pursued its normal course. A company of young recruits swung past his cell, singing at the tops of their voices, and Lt. Ohlsen watched them go by and tried to remember if he himself had ever been young. He knew he must have been, everyone was young once, and yet he couldn't remember it. Before the war, it must have been. He tried to work it out in his head. He was born in 1917, and now it was 1943. He was twenty-six. Twenty-six didn't sound very old when he said it aloud, but it certainly felt very old.

They fetched him from his cell for the exercise period. He was treated differently now. He wore the red badge of a condemned man on his breast and he took his exercise with the other condemned men, fourteen of them, marching endlessly in circles. They all had red badges, but some had a green stripe across them, which meant they were to be hanged, and others had a white stripe, which meant they were to be shot. Some had a black spot in the middle. The black spots were due for decapitation.

While the condemned men were marching in circles, Stever was standing at the door of the prison whistling. It was a faint approximation of a dance tune he had heard at the 'Zillertal'. With one finger he beat out the measure on the butt of his rifle.

'Du hast Glück bei den Frauen, bel ami . . .'*

After a while, even Stever realized that the tune he was whistling had parted company from the tune he had heard at the 'Zillertal'. He looked at the exercise party and his whistling abruptly changed course:

'Liebe Kameraden, heute sind wir rot, morgen sind wir tot.'†

The prisoners broke into a trot. Single file round the courtyard, three paces between each man. Hands clasped behind the

* You're lucky with women, my friend . . .

† Dear friends we're fine today, but tomorrow we die . . .

neck. Let them have no chance of communication before they died.

Stever suddenly took an interest in the proceedings. He slammed his PM firmly against his shoulder and bawled at the top of his voice.

'Get a move on, you load of lazy sods! Pick your feet up, put some vim into it!'

He encouraged the men passing by at that particular moment with sharp jabs in the ribs from his PM. The prisoners picked their feet up and began running. Some of them inadvertently shortened the gap between them and the man in front.

'Keep your distance!' screamed Stever, flourishing his PM above his head. 'What do you think this is, a reunion party?'

The PM came crashing down on the nearest head. The condemned men quickened their pace and kept their distance. Stever began beating the rhythm with his foot.

'Out of time! Out of time!' he shrieked. 'Watch the beat, can't you? No use running hell for leather like a pack of mad dogs, you'll never manage the return journey ... and who knows? Some of you might be reprieved at the last minute and then you'll need to be in good nick if you're going to survive in a disciplinary company ... work you bloody hard there all right! One two three, one two three, one two three ... keep it up there! No flagging!'

Several of the prisoners had turned their heads to look at him, the last despairing gleam of hope flickering even now in their eyes. Was Stever tantalizing them or could he have heard something? There was such a shortage of manpower, it could be that the country was no longer able to afford executions. Already they could have formed two or three divisions from the number of men that had been killed for crimes against the state ...

'All right, don't kid yourselves!' bawled Stever. 'Germany can manage without—'

He broke off in some confusion as Stahlschmidt appeared and took up a position by his side.

'What are you shouting about? Are you holding conversations with the prisoners? Are any of these men talking?' He turned to watch them running past, and suddenly shot out

an arm and pointed at one. 'That man there! He was speaking!
I saw his lips move! Bring him to me, Sergeant!'

Obergefreiter Braun, standing guard with his rifle, waded
into the circle of running men and collared an Oberstleutnant
who had the white mark of the firing squad on his chest.
Stahlschmidt gave him a few sharp cuts across the back of the
neck with his riding crop and pushed him back again.

'Swine!' yelled Stever. 'Get a move on, keep your legs up,
keep your distance! What do you think this is? A game of
musical bumps?'

Stahlschmidt shook his head.

'Obergefreiter, you have simply no idea ... Just watch me,
and perhaps you'll learn something.'

He swaggered into the middle of the ring, cracked his riding
whip and opened and closed his mouth a few times, as if testing
the mechanism. At length a fierce strangulated shout filled the
air:

'Prisonaaaahs! Haaaalt! Form twos!'

The prisoners fell over themselves in their eagerness to obey
the order. Stahlschmidt flexed his knees a few times. It was
good to be a Stabsfeldwebel. He wouldn't be anything else, not
even if they offered him the rank of general. He had had every
grade of prisoner pass through his hands save a Stabsfeldwebel.
It seemed to him, therefore, by a logical process of deduction,
that Stabsfeldwebels were in some way exempt from the pun-
ishments that were meted out to more ordinary mortals. Even if
that matter of the two visitors on the forged pass was ever
brought back to the light of day ... but no, that was not possible. Bielert surely had more important matters to occupy his
mind?

Stahlschmidt opened his mouth and shouted again. The prisoners began to march forward in a rigid double line, their heads
turned to the left. They marched in this way for nearly ten
minutes, until one of their number fainted. They then went on
marching for another five minutes on exactly the same course,
backwards and forwards over the limp body.

'Obergefreiter,' said Stahlschmidt, casually, before he left,
'if that man hasn't recovered by the time the exercise period's
finished I shall expect you to do something about it.'

'Yes, sir.'

Stahlschmidt walked away, leaving his subordinate with an unconscious prisoner on his hands. The man in fact came to his senses a few minutes later and stood leaning against the wall vomiting blood. Stever looked at him angrily. Why couldn't he take his punishment like everyone else? Why did he have to crack up at the last minute? It seemed likely that for once Stahlschmidt had gone too far. The man was a Gestapo prisoner, and the Gestapo were sensitive over their prisoners. They didn't object to anyone having a bit of fun, but there would be hell to pay if one of their men died before he could be executed. Herr Bielert was most punctilious over such matters. Stever had heard it said that he had once arrested the entire staff of Lübeck Garrison prison for a similar mishap. And Stahlschmidt had already shit in his copybook once over the business of the forged pass.

Stever watched the prisoner vomiting for the fourth or fifth time and wondered if it might not be a good idea to pay a visit to Herr Bielert. Tell him a few of the facts about Stahlschmidt. After all, none of it was Stever's fault and it would be grossly unfair if any of the blame should be heaped upon his shoulders. He, after all, was nothing but an Obergefreiter, and Obergefreiters only carried out orders.

The following Sunday, Lt. Ohlsen heard the sounds of hammering in the courtyard, and two or three hours later Stever paid him a visit. He went straight to the window and began conscientiously to test each bar. He winked at Lt. Ohlsen.

'Just checking,' he said. 'Just in case you're thinking of sawing your way through them.'

'With what?' asked Ohlsen.

'Who knows?' said Stever, darkly. 'Prisoners get up to some very odd tricks.'

Lt. Ohlsen looked across at the bars on the windows.

'Has anyone ever actually succeeded in cutting his way out?'

'Not yet, but there's always got to be a first one, hasn't there? And I don't want that first one to be in MY block. They can do what they flaming well like in anyone else's, but not in mine ... Here.' He pulled out two cigarettes, lit them both and handed one to Ohlsen. 'Hold it down low, so no nosey parker looking through the door can't see it. I don't mind risking my life for any poor bleeder what's going to make the long journey, but I don't see any point in asking for trouble . . . know what I mean? And there would be, if they caught you at it. Not supposed to fraternize with the prisoners, we're not . . .'

Lt. Ohlsen lay down on his bed and smoked his contraband cigarette. Stever looked out of the window into the court-yard.

'Hear that racket going on out there? You know what they're doing? Had a look, have you? You can't see much from here, of course, but I daresay you can make a pretty good guess.'

'Mm-hm.' Lt. Ohlsen shook his head, wearily.

Stever grinned. He made a quick, decisive chopping gesture across the back of his neck.

'They're getting it ready. Party of sappers out there putting it up . . . Not just in your honour, of course. There's ten of 'em due for it altogether. All going off on the same day . . . They usually do it like that. Wait until there's a whole bunch, it saves money. They have to get the executioner down from Berlin, see. Him and his mates. They reckon it ain't worth bringing 'em down more than once a month.' Stever turned back to the window. 'They brought the coffins today, as well; nothing fancy, but not bad. Not at all bad. Nothing to worry about on THAT score . . . And the baskets. They brought them and all—'

'Baskets?' queried Ohlsen.

'Yeah . . . for the heads.'

There was a moment's silence, and then the Lieutenant gave a rather ghastly smile. His face was white and his lips seemed almost mauve.

'So they're putting it up, are they? They're putting it up at last . . .'

'Yeah, but that doesn't necessarily mean it'll be today they'll call for you,' said Stever, in rallying tones. 'I remember one time, they put the thing up and it stayed up for two bleeding months without nothing happening. That was on account of the SD not agreeing with what they said at the trial. Judges wanted to let the bloke off and the SD was out for blood. They got him in the end, of course. They always do ... It was a colonel, I remember. Peppery old sod. He was in this same cell as what you've got. Number nine ... We always keep this one for people like you.'

'Like me?'

'Well – you know.' Stever smiled apologetically. 'The ones what have had it in advance, like.'

'You mean you already know what the verdict's going to be when a prisoner first comes here? Even before he's had his trial?'

Stever glanced round the cell, looked over his shoulder, peered out of the window again and moved confidentially close to Lt. Ohlsen.

'I didn't ought to tell you, really. It's something I'm not officially supposed to know myself. But I don't reckon as you'll be with us very much longer, so—' He winked. 'Just keep it under your hat ... When a prisoner's delivered to us from the Gestapo, we get his papers as well. And down at the bottom, on the left-hand side, there's a little mark ... The judge has a duplicate set with the same little mark on it. And all the little marks mean something special, see? In your case, the little mark meant—' Again, he performed his execution mime. 'The Gestapo had already decided what they wanted, so we knew what was going to happen to you before ever you went for trial.'

'And suppose the court had decided differently?'

Stever shook his head.

'They hardly ever do. Not worth their while. Wouldn't get them anywhere.'

'No, I suppose it wouldn't,' agreed Ohlsen, bitterly.

'Mind you,' said Stever, 'we don't leave none of these papers lying around. Anything secret, it goes up in smoke the minute it's finished with. Even carbon paper. Even typewriter ribbons. They're all destroyed. And as far as I'm concerned, I don't know anything anyway. I tell you—' He nodded his head, sagely – 'if ever the time comes when this place falls into enemy hands – and I reckon it will, sooner or later – I got it all worked out, what I'm going to say. Me and the Vulture, we been over it together several times ... I'm only an Obergefreiter, I don't know nothing, I just did what I was told to do . . . Which, of course, is true,' said Stever, virtuously. 'And I defy anyone to say it isn't . . .'

He sat down on the bed beside the Lieutenant and jabbed him in the ribs.

'What's it matter which side you're on? So long as they pay you a good whack and you don't have to work too hard? I got a real cushy number here, and I reckon the enemy'll be pretty glad to keep me on when they take over – I mean, they won't have enough of their own men to keep the place going, they'll need people like me, stands to reason . . . And so long as they pay me, why should I care? So long as they pay me enough to go and get my oats whenever I feel like it . . .' He nodded and winked again. 'You want to get an eyeful of the bird I got at the moment! She not only knows a thing or two, she's got red hot knickers into the bargain . . . Go on all night if you let her. And do it just about any way you fancy – sit on you, give you a blow, you name it and she'll do it . . . talk about the Kama Sutra, it's got nothing on her!'

He licked his lips and glanced sideways to see if he was whetting the prisoner's appetite, but Lt. Ohlsen appeared not even to be listening. Stever stood up, scowling. He objected to wasting his efforts.

'All right,' he said, 'if you don't appreciate my conversation I'll take it elsewhere and leave you to talk to yourself.'

He walked to the door.

'You'll soon get browned off with your own company,' he said.

There was still no response. Stever left the cell as noisily as he could, slamming the door behind him and rattling his keys. He peered in through the spyhole, but Lt. Ohlsen was sitting in the same position and with the same expression as before. He seemed not even to have noticed Stever's exit.

On the following Monday morning, Major von Rotenhausen paid an official visit to read out their sentences to the various condemned men. He trembled nervously throughout, twisting one foot round the other and pinching his thighs together as if he needed desperately to relieve himself. At his elbows stood Stever and Greinert, PMs at the ready. Major von Rotenhau-

309

sen had a deep-seated dread of violent outbursts from the prisoners, and he was not a man who believed in putting on a brave front at the possible expense of his own safety.

Shortly before mid-day, a large fishy eye appeared at the spy hole of cell number nine and stared long and calculatingly at the occupant. It remained there for almost ten minutes, and then silently removed itself.

An hour later, Stever came on his rounds and stopped for a chat.

'The executioner's here,' he cheerfully informed Lt. Ohlsen. 'He's already had a look at you . . . Do you want to see his axes? He's brought three of them with him, they're in one of the cells up the corridor. Bloody great sharp things, make a cut-throat razor look like a kid's toy. He keeps them in special leather scabbards . . . The Vulture's already had them out and played with them. He's got a thing about knives and axes. Anything that cuts. He's dying to have a go at someone's neck . . .'

'The padre hasn't been round yet,' said Ohlsen. 'They can't do anything until he's been.'

'Don't worry, he'll be here. Not even the Prussians are that bad. They wouldn't send a man off without letting him say his prayers first.'

'So when will he come?' insisted Ohlsen.

'Soon. He always rings up first to check if he's needed, and then he arrives about two hours afterwards. I don't know whether he's rung yet or not. Probably not. I think he's out blessing some troops what are going off to the front. Something like that.' Stever laughed, reflectively. 'Funny, isn't it? Priests and chiropodists, they got more work than they can cope with just now. Before the war, nobody wanted to know. Now it seems people can't live without 'em.'

'Or die without them,' murmured Ohlsen.

That evening, the long, wailing cry of a human soul in torment echoed round the building. The prisoners woke up shuddering in their cells. The guards either cursed or crossed themselves, according to their temperament and beliefs. The cry rose and fell, dropped to a moan, then gathered forces again and became a slow shriek of mental agony. Seconds later, Stahlschmidt appeared on the scene. There came the sound of blows. The wailing ceased and an uneasy calm descended on the prison.

The priest arrived next morning at half-past ten. He was a small, bent man, with a receding chin and a mouth like a goat, mild blue eyes that swam in pools of excess liquid and a nose that had a constant trembling pearl at the end of it. He had forgotten his bible and had to use the one that belonged to the cell. But he brought some artificial flowers wrapped in pretty paper and a small figure of Jesus wearing a rather crumpled crown of thorns.

Outside the cell stood Stahlschmidt and Stever. Stahlschmidt had his eye glued to the spy-hole and was ghoulishly noting every detail of the scene. He kept up a low running commentary to Stever, ceded his position for a few jealous seconds, then brutally elbowed his subordinate out of the way and resumed his gloating watch.

'It's nearly over now . . . They're sitting on the bed, side by side, holding hands . . . Very touching. Very nice . . . Now the old bloke's starting to cry . . . there he goes! Blarting his bleeding eyeballs out . . .'

'What for?' said Stever, in surprise. 'It's not him they're chopping up.'

Stahlschmidt shrugged his shoulders, not sure of the answer.

'I reckon it's because he's a priest,' he said, at length. 'Man of God, see? He probably feels it's part of his duty to show a bit of emotion when he's preparing someone for the other life.'

Stever tipped up his helmet and scratched his head.

'Yeah . . . Yeah, I reckon you're right.'

They moved away from the cell. Stahlschmidt jerked a thumb back towards it.

'One thing's for sure,' he said. 'You and I won't ever be in that position. We're not going to have any bum priest fluffing and farting over us and telling us stories about God and the angels. We know how to keep our mouths shut and our heads on our shoulders.' He looked at Stever. 'Don't we?' he said, meaningly.

Stever gave a faint, imbecilic grin. The idea was still with him to contact the Gestapo and safeguard his own position. He glanced involuntarily toward Stahlschmidt's thick red neck, and he wondered if even one of the razor-sharp axes from Berlin would manage to cut through it at one blow.

'What are you staring at?' asked Stahlschmidt, suspiciously.

'Nothing,' babbled Stever. 'I was just – just looking at your – your neck . . .'

'My neck?' Instinctively, Stahlschmidt raised a hand to his throat. 'What about my neck?'

'It's very strong,' muttered Stever.

'Of course it bloody well is! It's the neck of a Stabsfeldwebel, isn't it? And the necks of Stabsfeldwebels, my dear Stever, do not easily part company from their bodies. Unlike the necks of other people, such as lieutenants and captains and Obergefreiters . . .'

Stever shuffled his feet on the stone floor.

'The axes they use are very sharp,' he muttered.

'So what?' asked Stahlschmidt, coldly. 'What's the matter with you today? Are you losing your nerve? Do you want me to send you to a head shrinker? Or are you drunk? Is that it?' He peered closely at Stever, who took a step backwards. 'Surely you've learnt by now that Stabsfeldwebels are never amongst those executed? Have you ever seen one here, in this prison? Of course you haven't! We're the backbone of society, that's what we are, and they wouldn't dare lift a finger against us . . . Have you ever thought how it would be, if we were to go on strike? Chaos! Complete chaos! Adolf, Hermann, Heinrich, they'd all collapse like a pack of bleeding cards.'

'I suppose you're right,' said Stever.

And he reflected that if he went to the Gestapo, Stahlschmidt, in his own prison, might be the first Stabsfeldwebel ever to face the firing squad.

'Bloody right I'm right!' roared Stahlschmidt. 'And you just remember it in the future!'

During the afternoon exercise period, Stever and Braun searched the cells of the condemned men, Stever taking one side of the corridor and Braun the other. They made one or two interesting discoveries.

In cell 21, Braun unearthed a slice of hard black bread hidden inside the mattress. In cell 34, Stever found two centimetres of cigarette butt pushed down a crack in the floor. In the cell next door was a pencil stub. And in cell number nine was the most interesting find of all . . .

They collected up all the treasures and tied them in a blue towel, taking them along to Stahlschmidt's office for his inspection. These few pathetic scraps of personal belongings were objects of intense emotional value to the condemned men, and he enjoyed gloating over them.

Lt. Ohlsen returned from the tortures of the exercise period and stopped in dismay on the threshold of his cell. Bare though the room was, Stever had succeeded in turning it upside down, and it was immediately obvious to its occupant that the place had been searched. Lt. Ohlsen flung himself at the bed and felt frenziedly under the mattress: nothing was there. He fell sobbing to the floor as the door opened and Stever crept silently in. He was holding a small yellow capsule between finger and thumb.

'Is this what you're after, by any chance?'

He stood, jeering, inside the door. Lt. Ohlsen scrambled to his feet and made a despairing lunge at the capsule, but Stever's truncheon crashed mercilessly down upon his head and shoulders, beating him half way across the cell and cornering him by the window.

'Stand to attention when there's an Obergefreiter present! You ought to know the rules by now!'

Lt. Ohlsen shakily pulled himself upright, wiping the back of his hand across his nose. Stever looked down at the capsule and shook his head.

'You're a deep one, you are. Where'd you get it from? How long have you had it? You can't have had it long or I'd have known about it.' He held it tantalizingly just out of reach. 'Going to swallow it just before they led you out to the scaffold, were you? All the trouble they take to get up a nice funeral for you, all the money they spend on you, and this is the way you try to repay them! Ought to be ashamed of yourself, you did . . . Mind you,' said Stever, sagely, 'I can't say I'm all that surprised. I sort of guessed you were up to something. You were taking it all too calm . . . You got to remember I've had a lot of experience in these matters. I seen more men die than you've had hot dinners ... Some people,' said Stever, 'think I'm slow. And that's where they make their mistake, because I know everything what goes on in this prison, and I've even got eyes in the back of my bum ... That way, I save myself a packet of trouble. I know all the rules by heart, and I stick to them. Anyone tells me to do something that sounds a bit off, and I get 'em to put it down in writing. That way, see, they can't never get me for anything. Someone comes up and says, "Stever, you've committed a murder, you've done something wrong," I just show 'em the order, written down in black and white. And I'm only an Obergefreiter, I only do what I'm told ...'

He held the capsule in the palm of his hand and looked at it curiously.

'How do these things work, then? Kill you straight out, do they?' He laughed. 'I think I'll give it to Stahlschmidt's cat. It tried to scratch me the other day and I told it at the time I was going to wring its bleeding neck as soon as I got the chance ... This'll do just as well!'

Lt. Ohlsen stood to attention. His lower lip was trembling and his vision was blurred by the tears that coursed down his cheeks and splashed to the floor. That capsule had been the ace up his sleeve, his precious trump card, his one salvation. The knowledge that he had it in his power to decide when and where he should die, by his own hand and no one else's, had sustained him during the long weeks of imprisonment. And how he cursed himself bitterly for a fool not to have taken it the minute the trial was over. Who but a pathological optimist would have hung on so long, despairing and yet hoping for a last-minute reprieve that would never come?

He looked across at Stever and held out an appealing hand.

'Give it to me, Stever. For God's sake, give it to me!'

'I'm sorry,' said Stever. 'I just can't do it. Against the rules, you see. Besides, the Gestapo's out for blood and if they don't get yours the chances are they'll want mine instead.' He shook his head. 'You wouldn't ask that of me, would you?' he said, reasonably. 'We're both bound by the same laws, you know ...

But look here, I've got something else might interest you. I couldn't give it you before, Stahlschmidt never lets condemned men have letters in the case the ink's poisoned. It did happen once – not here, in Munich. Quite a song and dance, there was, and now Stahlschmidt always holds on to any letters that come. But I managed to smuggle this one out for you. Against the rules, of course. I was taking a big risk. You ought to be very grateful . . . I thought it might be from that little guy with the scar. The one that come to see you that time . . .'

Lt. Ohlsen wiped his eyes on his sleeve and listlessly took the letter. Stever watched him with narrowed eyes.

'Just read it,' he said. 'Don't try eating it.'

The Lieutenant ran his eyes quickly over the few lines of writing. They were from the Old Man, but nothing could interest him, nothing could comfort him, now that his capsule was gone.

Stever held out an impatient hand, snatched the letter back and began himself to read it.

'Who's this bloke Alfred he's on about? It's that character with the scar, ain't it?' He looked across at Ohlsen, who nodded. 'I don't know what it is,' said Stever, 'but I still got the feeling he holds a sort of grudge against me. I don't see why he should. After all, I'm only an Obergefreiter, it's not my fault if people got to die . . .'

He brooded uncomfortably a few moments, then his face slowly cleared.

'I tell you what. You could do me a good turn, if you felt like it. After all, I done you a good turn bringing you this letter . . . All you've got to do is write a few words about me on the back of it. Obergefreiter Stever is a good soldier what always carries out his orders . . . He has treated me well . . . Something like that. How about it? Eh? With a PS saying about how I'm a friend to all the prisoners . . . And then put your name and rank and the date and all, that'll make it official, like.'

Stever pulled out a pencil and offered it to the Lieutenant. Ohlsen raised an eyebrow.

'Prove it,' he said. 'Prove you are a friend to a prisoner and I'll do it for you.'

'Prove it?' Stever laughed. 'You've got a nerve!'

'You don't think you've got an even larger one?' mildly suggested Ohlsen.

Stever bit his lip. He looked down at the letter and read again the dreaded name of the type with the scar.

'What do you want?' he asked, sullenly.

'Give me back the capsule. That's all I ask.'

'You must be raving! I'd be for the high jump myself if they found you'd gone and killed yourself before they could get their hands on you.'

Lt. Ohlsen shrugged. He was suddenly past caring.

'It's up to you. I've got to die anyway, so I'm not that interested. I thought I was, but I'm not. Now that it's actually come to the point, I'm not . . . But if I were you, Stever, if you value your life at all. I should think very seriously about getting a steel corset made for yourself . . . You can't escape from the Legionnaire, you know. He always catches up with people sooner or later.'

Stever gnawed anxiously at his bottom lip.

'I'd like to help you, I really would. I'd do anything to get you out of this fix . . . only I can't give you the capsule, it's more than my life's worth . . .'

'Please yourself,' said Ohlsen, turning away and not bothering to stand to attention. 'I couldn't give a damn either way.'

They came for him just after the evening meal. They took him out to the courtyard through an underground passage. The priest led the way, intoning a mournful prayer. The executions were to take place in a small, enclosed courtyard that was safe from the prying eyes of unauthorized persons. The scaffold was set up, and on the platform were the executioner and his two assistants, dressed in frock coats, top hats and white gloves.

The condemned men were to be executed in pairs, and Lt. Ohlsen's partner in death was already waiting. When they were both present, the prison Governor checked their identities and the first assistant stepped forward and cut off the epaulettes, depriving them of their rank and finally dishonouring them.

Lt. Ohlsen stood watching as his partner slowly climbed the ladder. The priest began to pray for the salvation of his soul. The two assistants helped the man to position himself and tied him down. The executioner raised his axe. The crescent-shaped blade flashed bright in the sinking rays of the sun. The executioner opened his mouth and shouted out his justification of the deed he was about to perform.

'For the Führer, the Reich and the German people!'

The axe fell. It met the resistant flesh with a faint thump and sliced straight through it. It was a clean blow. Strong and well placed by a man who was an expert. The head rolled neatly into the waiting basket and two jets of blood spurted from the surprised neck. The body twitched and contorted. With quick, deft movements the assistants tipped it off the platform and into the waiting coffin. The head was snatched up and set between the legs of the corpse.

The audience relaxed. Oberkriegsgerichtstrat Dr. Jeckstadt, President of the court which had passed sentence, slowly lit a cigarette and turned to Dr. Beckmann.

'Say what you like about execution,' he remarked, 'but you can't deny that it's quick, efficient and simple.'

'When it goes according to plan,' muttered a Rittmeister, who was standing behind Jeckstadt and had overheard him.

'I must confess,' said Dr. Beckmann, 'that I find it an unpleasant spectacle. I never seem able to stop myself wondering how it must feel to be up there, waiting for the axe to fall . . . a curious sensation—'

'My dear fellow,' said Jeckstadt, comfortably, 'why torture yourself with fruitless speculation? These people have betrayed their country and they deserve their just punishment. But you and I—' He smiled, as at an absurd idea – 'you and I are never likely to find ourselves in such a situation! One thing is quite certain, my dear Doctor; if it weren't for us legal fellows, the country would soon be in chaos. We are, if I may make so bold, virtually indispensable.'

'Of course, you're quite right,' agreed Beckmann, turning back to watch the second show of the evening. 'No country can survive without its legal system.'

Lt. Ohlsen climbed slowly and steadily up the ladder. The assistants positioned him. His mind was a blank. Almost a blank . . . He remembered that in the seconds before dying a man's whole life is supposed to pass before his eyes, and he wondered almost fretfully why his own life was not even now unfolding before him, spreading out its memories for his last-minute contemplation.

He began consciously to force his mind back into the past, back into his own previous private memories, his own personal history, but before any very vivid pictures could come to him the axe crashed down and his life was over.

Down in the depths of Porta's stomach, fourteen pints of beer, nine vodkas and seven absinthes were fighting for possession, while Porta himself staggered across the room towards the piano. He walked bow legged because he was too drunk to control his muscles. He rolled from side to side, belching and clutching at tables and chairs to support himself. Now and again, during his passage across the room, he swept bottles and glasses to the floor. Three times he himself fell to the floor and had to be picked up again.

At last he reached his goal, but the effort had proved too much for the disputatious contents of his stomach. Sprawling across the piano, Porta opened his mouth and let everything pour out.

The pianist fell backwards off his stool.

'Filthy sodding shit!' he cried. 'Look what you've done to my flaming piano!'

By way of reply, Porta merely shot out an involuntary hand and swept a full glass of beer over the keyboard. He rolled round to the front of the piano and collapsed heavily on to the stool. With a frown of concentration on his face and his fingers large as pork sausages, heavy as lead weights, uncertain of their direction as straws in a gale, he began drunkenly to play the semblance of a well-known tune.

Bernard the Boozer jumped upon a table and thumped at the ceiling with two bottles of champagne. The room rang with the sound of drunken voices in something roughly approaching unison:

'Vor der Kaserne, vor dem grossen Tor,
 stand eine Latern und steht sie noch davor
 so woll'n wir uns da wiedersehn
 bei der Laterne woll'n wir stehn
 wie einst, Lili Marleen.'

Only Tiny did not join in. He had a girl on his knee and was steadily undressing her, with the same careless determination with which one might pluck a chicken. The girl was alternately kicking and screaming, not sure whether to enjoy herself or to be outraged.

319

The pianist, unable any longer to stand the sight of his piano covered in beer and vomit, made a determined effort to oust Porta from the stool. Porta stopped playing, wound his arms lovingly about the man's neck and hung on. Seconds later, the unfortunate pianist found himself flying headfirst across the room in the direction of the kitchen. He fetched up against the wall, at the feet of Heide and an almost comatose Barcelona.

At the same time as these festivities were taking place, a procession of people trod solemnly along a passage in the prison of Fuhlsbüttel. There were six SD soldiers, a priest, a doctor, several court officials and an old lady. They walked haltingly, almost reluctantly, towards a green baize door at the end of the passage. It seemed that they were anxious to postpone the moment when they would have to turn the handle and enter. But the moment inevitably came, and the procession moved slowly through the door and into the room beyond.

Quarter of an hour later, the door re-opened and the procession re-appeared. They were walking faster now. Six SD soldiers, the priest, the doctor and the several court officials. Only the old lady was no longer with them.

CHAPTER NINE

A Birthday Party

THE noise that poured out from the 'Three Hares' on the Davidstrasse could be heard in hideous clarity several streets away, even as far as the infirmary on Bernhard Nocht Strasse, where envious patients tossed and turned and cursed. It was the noise of sheer, exhilarating, incapable drunkenness and it bellied forth into the night in a continuous crescendo of sound.

The owner of the 'Three Hares', popularly known as Bernard the Boozer, was celebrating his birthday in a private room at the back of the bistrot. Only the most favoured of the establishment's regulars had been allowed in.

Tiny was one of the first to arrive, early in the afternoon. He had found the Boozer enthroned on a small step ladder, directing the operations for the evening's entertainment. Paper garlands and Chinese lanterns were being strung across the room, crates of beer and champagne stacked in the corners.

'Someone told me it was your birthday,' began Tiny.

Bernard nodded.

'Someone was right.'

'O.K.,' said Tiny. 'In that case I'd like to wish you many happy returns. Just wanted to get my facts right first.'

'Yeah?'

Bernard looked at him and smiled knowingly, then swung round on his ladder and shouted at a youth who was staggering beneath a crate of beer.

'Not out there, you fool! Over there in the corner!'

Tiny's eye hungrily followed the crate on its journey across the room, then switched back casually to the Boozer.

'You – ah – having a bit of a do, are you?'

'That's it.' Bernard blew his nose between his fingers, directly over a large pan of meat. He looked down at it, indifferently. 'It's all right, it's only a stew, it can do with a bit more seasoning. In any case, everything tastes pretty much the same once it gets into that lot . . . One of the girls emptied the coffee grounds into it last week – nobody said a thing. All mixes in together, you can't taste the difference.'

'No,' said Tiny. 'I guess not.' He gazed in wonderment at the rows of bottles ranged behind the bar. 'Who's going to get through all that lot, then?'

Bernard looked at him a moment, then turned and spat through the open window.

'My mates,' he said, simply.

Tiny grunted, not sure whether to lay immediate and automatic claim to being amongst the Boozer's most intimate circle of acquaintances or whether to pursue some other tactic.

'We're going away again soon,' he ventured, wiping the back of his hand across his panting mouth.

'Yeah. That's the way it goes.'

The Boozer nodded his head without sympathy. Tiny persevered.

'We're being sent back to the front. The battalion's

almost up to full strength again. We've got a whole lot of new tanks and all . . . only keep that under your hat, it's supposed to be top secret. It's all right telling a pal like you, I can trust a pal like you to keep his trap shut, but don't go gabbing it around, like.'

'Shouldn't dream of it,' said Bernard. 'Don't know anyone who's interested.'

He pulled himself upright, stepped on to the top rung of the ladder and casually attached a paper chain to the portion of the ceiling immediately above his head. The ladder remained firm, but the Boozer wobbled perilously. He had been drinking beer since long before breakfast.

'Watch it,' said Tiny, stretching out an enormous calloused hand. 'Don't want to go breaking your neck on your birthday, do you?' He settled Bernard back on his perch and gave him an ingratiating smile. 'How many years does this make, then?'

'Forty-two . . . and you can get a couple of bottles of beer over here and drink my health if you like.'

Tiny's arm instantly stretched out to the nearest row of bottles and his vast hand closed over two of them. He passed one over to the Boozer and raised the other to his mouth, closing his teeth over the cap and starting to prise it off.

'Hang on a minute,' said Bernard. He held out a hand and looked Tiny squarely in the eye. 'Where's my present? You can't come here drinking my booze and saying happy birthday without bringing me a present.'

Tiny lowered the bottle.

'You're quite right,' he agreed, cordially. 'Got it right here with me, as a matter of fact. Good thing you mentioned it, I got a memory like a sieve.'

He sunk a hand into the depths of a trouser pocket and emerged with a minute packet done up in crude pink paper. He held it out to Bernard, who examined it with interest.

'What is it?'

'You'll never guess,' said Tiny, wrenching open his bottle. 'Not in a million years . . . It's just what you've always wanted.'

Bernard tore open the paper to disclose a cheap bottle opener. He hurled it across the room with an oath.

322

'That's the tenth bloody bottle opener I've received today! Don't you load of imbeciles have any imagination?'

'It's the thought that counts,' said Tiny. He tipped back his head and poured half the bottle of beer straight down his throat. 'Didn't no one ever tell you that?'

'Sod the thought!' growled Bernard. 'Who wants five hundred bleeding bottle openers?'

'Ah, well,' said Tiny, wisely. 'It's always the same on birthdays, ain't it? You don't never get what you really want.'

Tiny stayed on after drinking Bernard's health. He stayed on to help with the stage managing and to drink his host's health a few more times in a goodly variety of beer and spirits. And when he had done all that, the first of the guests began to arrive and he stayed to look after them and make them welcome. And then the guests drank Bernard's health, and Tiny joined in, and then more people came and more toasts were drunk, and even before the celebration had officially begun Tiny had his head out of the window and his fingers down his throat, making way for the next round of drinks.

Porta arrived mid-way through the evening. It was evident that he had stopped somewhere en route. He forged through the crowd and hit Bernard lustily on the back.

'Many happy returns! Many many happy returns! Many many – did you get my present, by the way?'

Bernard blinked, at once suspicious.

'What present would that be?'

'Well, it was a bottle opener in the shape of a woman – Tiny was going to bring it—'

'Yeah, I received that piece of crap,' said Bernard, contemptuously.

'That's O.K., then. It was from Tiny and me both. Joint present. We chose it together. Just what old Bernie the Boozer could do with, we said. Save his teeth. Save his false teeth. We thought you'd go for that. We thought you'd—'

'Ah, give your arse a chance!' snarled his host, pushing him to one side.

At some stage in the evening, before we became paralytic, we sat down to dinner. There was much pushing and jostling and general vituperation, one or two fights broke out and one or two chairs were broken, but finally everyone was seated more or less to his satisfaction. Bernard called on the two serving girls, who were dressed – overdressed, according to some people present – in black briefs and tiny aprons the size of postage stamps.

'Hey, Helga!' Porta called out to one of them as she came towards him with a plate. 'Tiny tells me you gone and shave yourself like a French tart! That right? Can I have a feel?'

Helga slammed a plate of cabbage in front of him and stalked away without a word, her buttocks moving haughtily from side to side in their tight black pants. Porta whinnied like a horse and slapped a fist straight into his dish of cabbage.

At the end of the meal we fêted Bernard with a birthday boozing song. It had nothing whatever to do with birthdays, being almost exclusively preoccupied with sexual contortions and the perversion of a language, but Bernard accepted it as a fitting tribute to a man celebrating his 42nd year on earth.

We drank so much there was not one amongst us who had not yet vomited. With an inebriated sense of our own powers, we snatched up our host, tossed him into the air and caught him as he came down. The third time we all collapsed heavily to the floor, with Bernard buried beneath us. Porta staggered on to the table and stamped for silence. Heide supported him by banging two bottles together. The bottles promptly broke and a shower of glass rained down upon the group on the floor.

'Shut your bleeding cakeholes!' shouted Heide. 'Joseph Porta wants to speak!'

At last we sorted ourselves out again and a sort of silence fell upon us, broken only by belches and the breaking of wind, by the sound of a man retching or by the pouring of beer.

'Bernard the Boozer,' began Porta, in stern, serious tones, 'Bernie the Boozer, old pal Bernie, you're forty-two today and we all know you're the biggest shit that ever walked this flaming earth, but we love you for it all the same!' Porta threw out his arms in an expansive gesture and almost fell off the table. 'We're all shits together!' he cried, in tones of ringing exultation. 'That's why we're here tonight, drinking the health of the biggest shit of the lot! And now we'll have another song . . . one, two, three!'

He beat time with his feet on the table. One foot he raised

too high and brought down too hard. It missed the table altogether and crashed down in to Heide's lap. They disappeared together in a cursing tangle over the side.

At the far end of the table, Tiny had taken possession of Helga and was tugging manically at her black pants. Helga was kicking and biting for all she was worth. One or two people were placing bets on the probable winner.

Heide stayed under the table, leaning drunkenly against someone's legs and talking to himself. He talked about war and being a soldier. It was all very tedious and it was not surprising that he soon fell into a stupor.

Barcelona, finding himself next to Bernard the Boozer, began compulsively to tell him about Spain. Barcelona always told anyone who would listen, or at least keep a decent silence, about his experiences in Spain. He demonstrated bull fighting and a battle with tanks somewhere near Alicante, and the two activities became somehow inextricably merged until Barcelona was charging up and down the room with his head lowered in imitation of a bull and an imaginary sub machine gun firing straight into the floor.

'What the hell's that meant to be?' demanded Porta, crawling out from under the table and blinking as Barcelona flashed past.

Barcelona screeched to a halt, regarded Porta with drunken dignity and sat down.

'It was at Alicante I scored one of my greatest military successes,' he said, very coldly.

He picked up a spare glass of beer and poured it down his chest, then wiped his mouth with an air of apparent satisfaction.

'Sod your successes,' said Porta. 'What about that Spanish whore you screwed? Tell us about her.'

Barcelona hiccuped so violently in remembrance that had the Old Man not kept a firm grip on his collar he would have fallen to the floor.

'Drunk as a lord,' said Porta, in disgust.

Barcelona leaned towards him, with the Old Man still hanging on to the back of his neck.

'Obergefreiter Joseph Porta,' he said, slurring everything

into a single word of elephantine proportions, 'for the one hundred and twentieth time I'm warning you: address me correctly when you speak to me. I am a Feldwebel, the backbone of the German Army.'

'Backbone, my arse!' said Porta, scornfully. 'An old soak like you?'

He rolled across to the bar, collapsed against it, clawed up the nearest bottle and wrenched off the top. It went off like a gun, it was champagne, and half the guests instantly dived beneath the table. Porta raised the bottle to his lips and drank in great gulps.

'I am a lover of the Arts!' screamed Barcelona, into the hubbub.

Porta turned back to look at him a moment.

'Well, get you!' he said. 'Feldwebel, sir,' he added, sarcastically.

'Not only me,' continued Barcelona, 'but my very dear friend Bernard, as well. He also is a lover of the Arts.' And he leaned across and planted a heavy wet kiss on the Boozer's forehead as a mark of their great friendship. The Boozer smiled, foolishly. As he swayed back to his original position Barcelona crashed into the Old Man and they seesawed perilously for a while on the edge of the bench. 'Who,' shouted Barcelona, recovering his balance, 'who in this drunken band of cretins and sex maniacs has ever been into a museum and tasted the beauties of Art? Who,' he went on, growing rather muddled, 'has ever drunk at the tree of knowledge? Which of you lousy philistine bunch has ever heard of Thorvaldsen? Eh? Which of you has ever heard of him? You probably think he's a pimp on the Reeperbahn . . . well, he isn't.'

Barcelona wagged a finger in the air and paused to look at it. That pause was the start of his undoing. It seemed to him that in some miraculous way he was wagging a dozen fingers all at once. Which was remarkable, when he was ready to swear that he only had five on either hand. And two hands made ten, and that was including thumbs . . . He watched for a while in fascination. He began speaking hypnotically of artists and heroes, passed on to a roof-raising speech about liberty, shouted angrily at us that we were all brothers and that he loved us, and ended up in the inevitable impasse of general obscenity and abuse, without ever realizing how he had arrived there.

He broke off in the midst of a string of curses and stared in amazement as the world rose up before his eyes and began slowly to close in upon him. He blinked and shook his head, and the world receded.

Barcelona was moved to thump vigorously on his chest, indicating his row of multi-coloured ribbons and decorations and declaring in passionate tones that none of them meant a damn thing to him and that he would be only too glad to get rid of them. He offered them all round as free gifts, attempted to claw them off his tunic and scatter them amongst us, but the effort was too much. He fell forward, headfirst on to the table, and lay with his head in a pool of beer singing a somewhat curious song about bird droppings.

After a while, someone sitting opposite, taking a sudden dislike either to the singer or the song, reached across and pushed him backwards on to the floor. Barcelona's last words before he gave way to temporary oblivion were a fanatical, 'Viva España!'

For a moment, Bernard the Boozer sat contemplating the inert figure of his art-loving friend. The sight seemed to move him very deeply. With the aid of Porta and the Legionnaire, he crawled walrus-like on to the table and prepared to make a speech, and there he stood, swaying in pendulum fashion from side to side, with the Legionnaire hanging on to both ankles and Porta waiting to catch him should he fall.

'My friends!' He held out both arms to embrace us. The electric light bulb went crashing to the floor. A paper chain came adrift and festooned itself round Bernard's neck. 'My friends, I trust you've all got enough to drink and there's nobody going thirsty? Because I can tell you, here and now, that there's enough liquor in my cellar—' At this point he swayed backwards, into the waiting arms of Porta, and there was a pause while he was set back on an even keel. 'There's enough booze in my cellar to keep the whole German Navy afloat ... and you're welcome to it! You're my friends and you're welcome to it! Drink it all! Drink it until it's coming out of your eyes and your ears and your arseholes ... My friends!'

And now he swayed forward, and the Legionnaire held on to his ankles while Porta ran round to the front and caught him before he reached the table. He tilted him back again, towards the Legionnaire. 'My friends, I hope you think of this little place of mine as being a home from home ... a real home from home, where you can piss and shit and fornicate just like you would by your own fireside ... Being a publican, it's not just a job, it's a vocation ... you know that? 'S a real vocation ... Where do you lads go when you're browned off and you want cheering up? Back to barracks? Back to the wife and kids? Like hell!' With a joyous gesture, Bernard swooped round through an arc that brought him dangerously close to scraping his nose on the table. By some miracle the force of his momentum was strong enough to carry him onwards, until he had again reached the perpendicular and the Legionnaire was able to reach up a hand and prevent his going off on another turn. 'Like hell!' roared Bernard, undaunted. 'You don't go anywhere near 'em ... this is where you come! Round to good old Bernie's place! Round to the boozer! Bernie the Boozer, that's what you call me ... and not for nothing, lads! I'm not called that for nothing! I been in the business a good long time and I know what it's all about, and when you lads come here in search of a bit of comfort I make bloody sure you get it! Not one of my boys ever goes away from here without a gutful!'

'That's right,' affirmed some wag from the far end of the table. 'A full gut and an empty pocket!'

Bernard smiled benevolently, not catching the implications of this remark.

'In my establishment,' he declared, 'the common soldier is king. Privates, corporals, sergeants ... they're all welcome! There's only one class I won't abide, and that's officers. Officers, my friends, are the most anti-social, arse-licking, yellow-bellied—'

The rest of his feelings on officers were lost in a general storm of cheers and catcalls. Bernard raised both arms above his head, clenching his fists and prancing about the table like a triumphant boxer. The Legionnaire and Porta hovered anxiously at his side.

'Gentlemen!' roared Bernard, his voice rising above the

swelling hubbub, 'we belong to Hamburg! Hamburg is our city! Hamburg is the last bastion of Europe!'

The cheers rang out again from all and sundry. Most of us had no affection whatsoever for Hamburg, but that did nothing to dampen our enthusiasm. We yelled and stamped and threw our arms round one another in a fervour of love and loyalty. Much encouraged, Bernard stamped energetically upon someone's fingers and tramped down to the far end of the table, treading in plates and overturning glasses as he did so.

'Sylvia!' He lurched sideways, extended a hand and grabbed one of the passing serving girls. 'Where are you going, wench? What do you think you're doing? You're on duty as long as the booze lasts . . . Bring on some more beer and let's have a ball!'

Loud whistles filled the air. Feet stamped, hands clapped. Men opened their mouths and shouted wordlessly, for the pure delight of making a loud noise. Some of those who had temporarily withdrawn from the scene recovered their senses, vomited and returned to the fray. Bernard stumbled back down the table, waving his hands frantically towards the piano.

'Let's have a song! Ready for the song of Hamburg, lads! All together, now . . .'

The choir of voices filled the room. Harsh, unmelodious, out of time, out of tune, we bawled together Bernard's song of Hamburg:

'Das Herz von Sankt Pauli
das ist meine Heimat,
in Hamburg, da in ich zu Haus.'*

The song was brought to a full stop by Steiner, who staggered back from the washroom to announce that the first dead-drunk, out-like-a-light of the evening, was to be found on the floor. A roof-raising cheer went up and the entire party at once crushed its way into the washroom to inspect the victim. It was a Feldwebel. He was out cold and no amount of rough handling would bring him back again. With wild cries of jubilation the six fittest men transported him outside and flung him into the

* The heart of St Paul, that is my home . . . in Hamburg, there I am at home.

gutter. Porta laughed so long and so loud that he dislocated his jaw, but Tiny soon put it back in place for him with a well-timed upper cut.

During the next hour, another seven of the guests ended up in the gutter. Bernard the Boozer's birthday party died slowly out in a stale sea of overturned beer and a hovering pall of smoke. The floor was covered in débris and drunken bodies. The boozer himself lay upended in a packing case.

The eight of us from the 27th, strung out arm in arm across the width of the pavement and half way across the road, supported each other through the night on our way back to barracks.

'I'm thirsty!' howled Porta; and the narrow, crowded buildings of the Herberstrasse flung the words back at him, echoing and re-echoing.

As we swayed past an underground station we saw an old man fighting with a brush and a bucket of paste to stick up a notice, and we naturally stopped to help him. For some reason he took fright and went hobbling off into the dim dawn light, leaving us to cope rather ineptly with the poster.

'Whozzitsay?' demanded Porta.

Steiner held it up and managed to read out the first word – NOTICE – before Barcelona pulled it away from him and dunked it in the paste pot.

'Who the hell—' Porta lost his balance, fell to the ground and foolishly attempted to pull himself up by my ankles. We collapsed together. 'Who the hell sticks these damn things up at this time of night?'

It took us the best part of fifteen minutes to get that poster posted. We overturned the paste pot, we lost the brush, we tore the thing in half, we stuck it over ourselves and each other, and we finally got it back to front on to the wall and wondered why we couldn't read it. It wasn't until the Legionnaire, leaning against the rest of us for support, solemnly peeled the thing off and turned it round that the mystery was solved.

'Whozzitsay?' Porta fretfully demanded for the second time. He was on the ground again and couldn't see.

Steiner and Barcelona stood with their heads together, taking each other's weight and attempting to bring the lettering into focus. The poster was upside down, now. It looked like Russian to me. Steiner muttered the words aloud, and Barcelona politely corrected him as he stumbled over the more difficult syllables. Steiner kept saying 'Thank you' and 'So sorry', and Barcelona kept on saying, 'Forgive me if I put you right, won't you?' and it was really quite a charming scene except that the rest of us found it almost impossible to stand still and wait, one or other of us constantly falling down and having to be picked up again.

'Friends!' shouted Barcelona, at last. He turned to us with a finger on his lips and his eyes open wide. 'Don't panic! Keep calm! It's a message from the Gestapo!'

Steiner, left suddenly without support, pitched forward towards the poster, bumped into the wall and sunk slowly down it on his way to the ground.

'I'm so thirsty,' he moaned.

'WhozzitSAY?' demanded Porta, querulously, for the third time.

Barcelona put out a hand to steady himself.

'It's someone who's to be hanged.'

He brought the words out with difficulty. His eyes were round and owlish. His mouth was slack.

Porta, apparently satisfied, turned and vomited down the steps of the underground. The Old Man sat down with his back against a lamp post. He made an attempt to speak, waited a moment, then tried again. The words came out one by one in a slow motion blur.

'Who . . . is . . . to be . . . hanged?'

Barcelona put his head right up against the poster.

'Traitor to the Führer . . . to the German people . . . and to her country . . . will be executed today at 17.15 . . . Emilie Dreyer . . .'

We picked up Steiner and Porta and continued on our way, arm in arm on a zig-zag course towards the Palace of Justice. Barcelona and the Legionnaire were roaring and hiccuping:

'Dragoner sind halb Mensch, halb Vieh.

Auf Pferd gesetzte Infanterie.'

'That woman – that woman they're going to hang–' I looked round for help in finishing the sentence, but no one was in a fit enough state. 'That woman,' I said, again. 'Did we – have we – was she the one we—'

There was a silence.

'Could be,' said the Legionnaire.

'So many people die,' said the Old Man, wisely. 'They go to war. They die. You can't remember them all.'

'We're going to war soon,' said Heide. 'The battalion's been alerted.'

'Hurray!' cried Tiny. 'I'm a hero!'

We turned into the barracks. Porta suddenly sank down on all fours, on to the beautiful velvet lawn outside staff headquarters. With some difficulty he pulled himself up into a sitting position. The rest of us stood swaying in a row above him.

'Let's sing a song for all them lazy sleeping shits,' he proposed. 'Let's have a little sing song ... Colonel Hinka's got a whore in his bed.' He attempted a sly wink, but one eye refused to close without the other. 'I know his whore, she's a filthy clap-ridden slut that won't even pass the time of day with an Obergefreiter ... Let's give 'em a sing song and wake 'em up ...'

His voice rang out across the sleeping barracks; rude and powerful like the roaring of a bull in agony. The rest of us joined in.

'Im schwarzen Keller zu Askalon,
da kneipt ein Mann drei Tag,
bis dass er wie ein Besenstiel
am Marmortische lag ...'*

* In Askalon's dark cellar a man drank for three days until he became as stiff as a marble broomstick

'Hell's bells and buckets of blood!' swore the Legionnaire, tossing his equipment disdainfully into a corner. 'What a sodding stupid job for a man of my age to be doing!'

He was an instructor in the art of single combat, and he had the task of training all the recruits that came regularly to us from prisons, barracks and camps.

Tiny shrugged his shoulders and tore off a mouthful of ham from the tin he had stolen from 8th Company stores.

'Why do it if you don't like it?' he mumbled.

The little Legionnaire hunched his shoulders, lit one of his perpetual cigarettes and filtered the smoke slowly and reflectively through his nostrils. He leaned across the table and thoughtfully applied the glowing tip of the cigarette to the backside of a dying bee, watching its reactions. The bee promptly expired and the Legionnaire sighed.

'Well, well,' he said, straightening up. He looked at Tiny. 'Why, might I ask, did you become a soldier?'

'Easy,' rejoined Tiny, spitting food in all directions. 'Didn't have no choice, did I? It was either the bleeding Army or starve on the bleeding streets . . . so I joined the Army.' He gnawed off another lump of ham. 'I had a bash at the cavalry first, only they said I was too big – too big for the horses, like – so they sent me off to the infantry . . . and that was sodding awful, that was,' said Tiny, reminiscently. 'Nothing but bloody marching day after bloody day . . . and those bloody officers!' He spat, remembered too late that he was eating, and crawled about the floor in search of stray pieces of ham. 'Thought they could treat you like dirt, just because you was a charity kid . . . lived on public assistance, like, before I joined up.'

The Legionnaire nodded.

'Fair enough. In that case, I agree that you had no choice. It was a case of one evil as compared to another, and for my money that doesn't constitute a choice.'

'Bleeding right it doesn't. Still—' Tiny wiped the back of his hand across his mouth – that's the way it goes, ain't it? How about you?'

'Me?' The Legionnaire smiled, grimly. 'I didn't have any choice, either. I was never on public assistance and I was never in any real trouble with the police – never in a remand home,

333

nothing like that. All I knew was being out of work and being hungry . . . my belly used to rumble for days on end. I used to chew paper when I could get hold of it. Even that wasn't so easy to come by, but it did keep the pains at bay . . . So in 1932 I said goodbye to the shit of Germany and headed for the sun of France – only when I got to Paris it was just as grey and wet and sodding miserable as Berlin.'

'So what d'you do?' asked Tiny, chewing busily on his ham. The Legionnaire gave him a mischievous wink.

'Got myself picked up by a prostitute at a bus stop . . . I was very young in those days. Had a sort of wistful appeal for women – especially in bed.' He grinned. 'She taught me a thing or two, that old cow . . . including French. That was quite helpful, as it turned out.'

'What made you join the sodding Foreign Legion?' said Tiny. 'I never did understand that.'

'I told you – no choice. The cops came round inquiring after my sugar mummy, and I decided it was time to piss off. It was either the cop shop and the likelihood of a spell in nick or burning my boats in the Legion. So I joined the Legion.' He shrugged. 'It could have been worse. There always is something worse . . .'

He walked across to the window and stood looking out a moment.

'Hey, you!' He picked up a boot and hurled it at a passing recruit as the quickest way of gaining his attention. 'I've got some equipment needs cleaning. Pronto. And make sure you do a good job on it if you want to keep your head on your shoulders!'

The recruit, a man in his early sixties, and broken and bent even beyond his years, turned and regarded the Legionnaire with rheumy eyes. The Legionnaire jerked his head and the old man shuffled obediently towards him. For the moment he was destined to polish someone else's equipment until it shone like silver. For the future his fate was more glorious, though possibly just as futile: he was to die a so-called hero on the banks of the Dnieper, to the north of Kiev.

The Legionnaire closed the window and stubbed out his cigarette.

'There's always something worse . . .' he murmured.

334

CHAPTER TEN

Departure for the Front

THE following day, a most regrettable incident occurred on the rifle range: Feldwebel Brandt was shot dead. Four times, straight through the forehead. The only comfort was, he could have known nothing about it. Death would have been instantaneous. Nevertheless, we were all very properly shocked. The officer in charge was at once arrested and questioned non-stop for several hours, but they released him in the end.

Tiny and Porta volunteered for the grisly task of removing the body. They went out together and loaded it on to the back of a truck.

'How come it's so bleeding heavy?' grumbled Tiny. 'You'd think he'd have lost a bit of weight, wouldn't you, giving up his soul the way's just gone and done?'

'Didn't have no soul,' grunted Porta.

They climbed into the truck and pulled out a pack of cards, sitting one on either side of the late Feldwebel Brandt and using his corpse as a table. Porta put his hand into his back pocket and yanked out a bottle of schnaps. He offered it to Tiny.

'Ta.' Tiny took it and swallowed deeply. He wiped the back of his hand across his mouth, snorted and spat. 'We fired at the same moment, Julius and me. Exactly the same moment . . . I wouldn't like to say which of us got the bastard first.'

Porta held out his hand for the schnaps and laughed as he recalled the scene.

'Did you see how all the rest of the shits turned green? When it happened, they all looked sick to their bleeding stomachs . . . They knew we'd done it on purpose, all right, only they can't

335

prove nothing . . . What's the betting we get stood free drinks all night as a result?'

'Here's hoping,' said Tiny, and he spat again on to the card table. 'You reckon the bugger's in hell by this time?'

'Where else? Him up there wouldn't want the sod.'

'No . . .' Tiny snatched back the bottle and stared thoughtfully at it a while. 'Wonder if He'll want us when our time comes? . . . Eh? What d'you reckon?'

'I don't reckon nothing.' Porta shuffled the cards and rapidly dealt out two hands. 'Got more important things to think about. Pick your cards up and get on with it.'

'Yeah, all right.' Tiny set down the bottle, obediently scraped his cards off the Feldwebel's broad back and took a cursory glance at them. 'His brains was splattered all over the place . . . Did you see 'em there? When we picked him up? All over the place, they was.'

'So?'

'So nothing.' Tiny hunched a shoulder. 'I just wondered if you'd seen 'em, that's all . . .' Another thought suddenly came to him and he closed up his hand and beamed across at Porta. 'I reckon I'll go and visit his missus, that's what I'll do. Cheer her up, like. Tell her he was just a lousy mean bastard anyway, so she hasn't lost nothing by it . . . specially not if I get into bed with her. She won't know what's hit her. She won't know her bleeding luck . . . After all,' he said, reasonably, 'it's only what's fair . . . I bump off her old man, it's only right I go and screw her. You could almost say I owe it to her.'

'You do,' agreed Porta, solemnly. 'That's a very lovely idea. I like it. It takes a big-hearted bloke like you to think of it . . . Matter of fact, I'm not at all sure the whole Company doesn't owe it to her . . .'

Together they finished off the schnaps and threw the bottle overboard. Porta laid out his hand with a flourish across the Feldwebel's backside.

'Full house,' he said, simply.

It was late when they arrived back at the barracks, so they parked the truck and left the body in the back. It was there for almost a week before anyone remarked upon it.

A couple of days later, shortly after the Regiment had received orders to prepare for departure, a small detachment of new troops was marched across the courtyard. A group of us were standing by the windows, watching them, and quite suddenly the Old Man turned and shouted to the Legionnaire.

'Hey, Alfred! Come and have a look at this!'

The Legionnaire pushed his way to the front of the group and stared in the direction of the Old Man's pointing finger.

'Well, by all that's wonderful!' He laughed and punched the Old Man joyously in the ribs. 'If it isn't our old friend the Stabsfeldwebel! Let's say hallo to him.'

They opened the window and hung out, waving and shouting. Stabsfeldwebel Stahlschmidt looked up. He evidently recognized them at once, because even from that distance I could see him turn pale. The man marching at his side was Obergefreiter Stever. He took one quick look and turned away again with eyes full of dread. He was a man who has lived to see his nightmares come true.

Porta stuck his head out of the window, between the Legionnaire and the Old Man, and gave a shout of derisive welcome.

'You just made it! We're pulling out of here soon . . . another couple of days and you might have missed the train!'

The column marched on. In the centre was a man with a trumpet. On the green collar of his tunic could still be made out the marks of the black SS badge which had been ripped off. He looked up as he passed the window, and his eyes rested with brief hope on Porta and then turned downwards again.

'Who's that?' I said. 'A friend of yours?'

Porta smiled.

'Just a business acquaintance,' he murmured.

Hauptfeldwebel Edel treated the newcomers to his usual warm welcome with a speech full of threats, full of abuse and hatred and withering scorn.

'Anyone will tell you,' he roared, 'that to them as I like I'm as mild as a bleeding lamb and as sweet as sugar . . . Unfortunately, there aren't that many people I like . . .'

The new troops were left in no doubt as to his feeling towards them. He put them on ablutions for the rest of the week, with a warning that if the lavatory pans were not polished to a high gloss at least twice a day he would see to it personally that someone suffered for it.

Colonel Hinka strolled up as Edel came to the end of his introductory speech. He smiled benevolently all round, and for a moment the hearts of the new men lightened.

Edel swung round, clicked his heels together and smartly saluted.

'Sir!' Hauptfeldwebel Edel, sir, 5th Company, with twenty new recruits.'

Hinka cast his eye over them and laughed softly to himself. There seemed, on the face of it, no very good reason for him to laugh, and the twenty new recruits found their hearts automatically sinking again. Colonel Hinka raised his head and looked across at the members of the 5th Company who were hanging from the windows enjoying the scene. He smiled.

'Thank you, Hauptfeldwebel. Get them warmed up a bit, will you? Make them feel at home ... I think we'll put—' He looked again at the windows, and his smile broadened – 'I think we'll put Kalb in charge of them.'

'Yes, sir.'

Edel turned in search of the Legionnaire, but he had already left the room and was at the door. He walked across to the Colonel and they exchanged salutes.

'Twenty new recruits ... we'll need to make them feel at home, get them used to our ways and so on ... haven't got much time, but do the best you can ... think you'll be able to manage it?'

The Legionnaire ran his eyes calculatingly over the twenty anxiety-ridden men.

'No doubt about it, sir.'

'Good man. Let us just introduce ourselves and then I'll leave them in your hands.'

Slowly, graciously, the Colonel moved through the ranks of the new troops. He was followed officiously by the Hauptfeldwebel, smoothly and silently by the Legionnaire. Hinka paused before Stahlschmidt.

'Your name?'

'Stalschmidt, sir. Stabsfeldwebel—'

Hinka glanced through the papers he was holding.

'You're from the garrison prison? Never been to the front before . . .'

'No, sir, I couldn't, I—'

The Colonel held up a hand and silenced him.

'Don't bother yourself with excuses, they're no longer necessary. It won't be so very many hours now before you see some fighting. I'm afraid your palmy days are over, the time has come for you to make a real contribution to the war effort. We shall see how you take to it.' He looked back at the papers and frowned. 'So . . . The reason you were sent to us was that you were found guilty of ill-treating the prisoners in your charge?'

'They've got it all wrong, sir.' Stahlschmidt spoke in a hoarse undertone, very much aware of the little Legionnaire lurking like a beast of prey in the background. 'It's all a mistake, sir, I never did anything like that, I wouldn't, I wouldn't be capable of it—'

'That's all right, Stabsfeldwebel. You don't have to explain. Everyone who is ever sent to us claims to be here by mistake. It's quite the accepted thing, I assure you.'

The Colonel passed on. Edel passed on. The Legionnaire stood a moment, staring up coldly at Stahlschmidt. At last, rubbing a finger thoughtfully up and down the scar on his face, he gave a slow smile and walked on without a word.

Hinka had now paused in front of Stever.

'Another from the prison? They must have been having quite a purge down there.'

Stever gave a sickly smile.

'It was all very unfortunate, sir . . .'

'I'm sure it was.'

The Colonel nodded and passed on. Edel passed on. The Legionnaire paused.

'Go and find Obergefreiter Porta. Tell him I sent you. He'll know what to do with you. I've already had a word with him. He knows all about you.'

Stever was too terrified to move. He stood staring at the Legionnaire, mesmerized by the long, livid scar, by the deep-set eyes, by the firm, hard mouth.

'Well?' The Legionnaire raised an eyebrow. 'I gave you an order. I suggest you carry it out.'

He moved on in the Colonel's wake, not troubling to look back and check that Stever left the ranks.

Hinka had stopped now before the ex-SS driver. He gestured towards the trumpet.

'You play that thing, do you?'

'Yes, sir. I used to be a bugler in a cavalry regiment, sir. SS Florian Geyer.'

'Did you, indeed? And what brings you to the front line with us?'

Kleber swallowed painfully and dropped his eyes.

'Theft, sir . . . and dealings on the black market.'

'What did you steal?'

Kleber grew hot and flushed.

'Er – potatoes, sir. Potatoes and sugar.'

'Potatoes and sugar . . . Rather stupid of you, wasn't it?'

'Yes, sir.'

'Hm. Well – it'll do you good to see some fighting. Take your mind off food, perhaps.'

One by one the newcomers were scrutinized. Each of them eyed the Colonel with awe, Edel with apprehension, and the Legionnaire with something approaching naked terror. At last the Colonel saluted and turned away, followed by Hauptfeldwebel Edel, and they were left alone with the Legionnaire.

He at once tipped his kepi over his left eye (in his imagination, it was still the white kepi of the Foreign Legion) and stuck an illicit cigarette in his mouth. He lit it and spoke without taking it from his lips.

'Listen to me, you load of lousy bastards. You're new here and you don't know the ropes, but there's one person I advise you not to cross – and that's me. I've served with the French Foreign Legion. I've done three years with a special battalion, at Torgau. And now I'm here, and so are you, and all I can say is God help the lot of you!'

The Old Man watched from the window as the Legionnaire marched his little band of unfortunates away in the direction of the furthest and most secluded exercise yard, where he could do with them as he wished. The Old Man grunted.

'Well, that'll keep him happy for a bit . . . This is something in the nature of a personal revenge, as far as he's concerned. The Legionnaire doesn't forgive in a hurry . . .'

He worked hard with his new recruits. For over three hours he kept them at it, running barefoot up and down the hard stone of the courtyard, out into the mud, crawling on their hands and knees, half drowning in the thick, glutinous earth, jumping over the ditch, back into the mud all those who failed to make it, mud up to their ears, mud in their eyes, mud in their mouths. And the Legionnaire working as hard as any of them, encouraging them with oaths in French and German, sweating as he ran up and down behind them, the eternal cigarette drooping from the corner of his mouth.

'Don't think I've got anything against you!' he yelled at them. 'Far from it, I'm only doing my duty, I'm only thinking of your own good . . . a few weeks with me and you'll be able to stand up to any amount of this sort of thing! Down on your knees, that man over there . . . down, I said, DOWN! Never mind the blasted mud! Swallow the stuff, eat the stuff, what's it matter? Get through it first and worry about breathing afterwards!'

Colonel Hinka was standing nearby, leaning wearily against a Tiger and watching as the Legionnaire put his men through their paces. Alfred Kalb had come through a harsh school – starvation, the Legion, Torgau, the 27th Tank Regiment – he had fought the war on many fronts and he had survived. A man had to be tough to survive. The Colonel laughed and shook his head. He did not envy the sweating, struggling men in the Legionnaire's capable hands.

'Right, let's get running again!'

The Legionnaire seated himself on an upturned packing case. He set them running up and down the courtyard, into the mud, back up the courtyard, back into the mud. His voice grew hoarse with shouting and he brought out his whistle and taught them how to respond to it.

'One blow – that means you run. Two blows – down on the ground on your bellies. Three blows – jumping with your feet together. Right? Right. Let's give it a try.'

They gave it a try for another hour. The men began to wilt, but the whistle was as fresh as ever.

'O.K., that'll do.' The Legionnaire looked them over with a critical eye. 'God knows how you'll make out at the front, in that condition. You won't last five minutes ... Look, I'll tell you what I'll do. For your own good, mind. I shouldn't really waste the time on you, but it breaks my heart to see you like this ... So for your own good and to toughen you up, we'll have a final hour's marching ...'

The twenty new men were dispersed amongst various barrack rooms round the camp. Stahlschmidt was moved in with us. We gave him a cupboard and he began putting his belongings away. He was silent and sullen and his face was awash in a permanent sea of sweat. He was stretched out on his bed when the Legionnaire came in. The Legionnaire walked straight across to him.

'There's something I want to say to you, Stahlschmidt. That show I just put on out there, that was entirely for your benefit. And there'll be more to come ... The rest of them, I don't know and don't care about. It's you I'm interested in. It's providence has brought you here to us, and I aim to take every advantage of it.'

Stahlschmidt sat up, still sweating. He gnawed at his lower lip.

'Listen, Kalb, I know you've got it in for me because of what happened to your lieutenant, but it wasn't my fault they executed him, for God's sake!'

'It was your fault he'd been kicked around and ill treated and half killed before they even got him up there!' The Legionnaire pushed Stahlschmidt back against the wall, one hand gripping his throat. 'Unfortunately we haven't yet been able to lay hands on the bastard that runs the show. He was clever enough to get you sent here, out of harm's way, while he still sits smug on his backside twiddling his thumbs in his office ... I refer to Bielert, in case you hadn't realized. His turn will come, don't you worry, but right at this moment it's your turn, and I'm going to make the best of a bad job and work out my feelings on you ... If you don't die at my hands, Stahlschmidt, it'll be the Russians that get you. Either way you're going to be put through the

342

hoop until you're screaming for mercy ... and there isn't any mercy at the front, Stahlschmidt.'

He suddenly crashed the Stabsfeldwebel's head hard against the wall.

'Stand up when you speak to me! That's one of the first things you've got to learn!'

Stahlschmidt stood up. The Legionnaire stepped back a pace, looking at him through narrowed eyes, then grunted and walked off to his own bunk. As soon as he was safely out of the way, Stahlschmidt raised a foot and gave a mighty kick of defiance at a nearby pair of boots, then collapsed once again on to his bed. Unfortunately, the boots he had chosen to kick belonged to Tiny, who was sitting up cross-legged on a bunk stuffing a sausage into his mouth.

As Stahlschmidt's head met the pillow, Tiny was upon him. With a loud shout of wrath, he grabbed Stahlschmidt by the shoulder, pulled him round to face him and sent a fist crashing into his jaw. A volley of blows was heard, a series of thuds and a scream of protest from Stahlschmidt, who presently rolled off the bed and lay twisting and groaning on the ground at Tiny's feet. Tiny rolled him over on to his stomach, jumped up and down a few times on his back, then kicked him disdainfully into a heap under the bed. He clambered back into his own bunk and picked up a couple of bottles of beer, which he opened with his teeth and from both of which he began to drink at the same time – a feat of which no one but Tiny was capable. He tossed the empty bottles contemptuously upon the moaning Stahlschmidt, who was painfully pulling himself to his feet. Stahlschmidt promptly collapsed again.

A new era had begun for the Stabsfeldwebel: an era of hard work and danger, when it was he who received all the blows.

Late in the night, full of beer and goodwill towards each other, Porta and Rudolph Kleber walked together up the steep, winding path of Landungsbrücke towards the School of Navigation behind the Military Hospital. At the top of the hill was a bench. They sat down side by side and were silent a while, listening to the muted night sounds of the city.

'Well, all right, if you play as well as you say you do,' remarked Porta, at last, 'you'll be O.K. But I'm warning you, old

Hinka's the very devil to please. You got to be really spot on – know what I mean?'

'Let me show you. Just let me show you!'

Kleber reverently brought out his silver trumpet from its case. He licked his lips a few times, took the instrument up to his mouth and regarded Porta sideways, from the corner of his eyes.

'I was with one of the very best regiments,' he said. 'Real pukka, it was. I played at Nuremberg for the grand parade. I played at one of Adolf's banquets. I played—'

'Sod the boasting, get on with the performance!' snarled Porta.

Kleber stood up. He took a deep breath and raised the trumpet to his lips.

A cavalry fanfare rang out over the dark town.

Porta sat picking his nose, determinedly unimpressed.

Kleber followed up with an infantry fanfare. He turned to Porta and spoke impatiently.

'Well, all right, what do you want? What do YOU suggest I play?'

Porta stifled a yawn.

'Search me . . . Depends what you know, doesn't it?'

'I could play you a blues.'

'Couldn't have that,' said Porta. 'Unpatriotic. The blues is a Yank thing. We'd go straight to the nick if anyone heard you.'

Kleber drew back his lips in a challenging sneer.

'That trouble you?'

'Certainly not,' said Porta. 'But don't crucify it, that's all I ask. I'm always meeting people say they can play the blues and haven't got the least idea.'

'Just listen to me,' said Kleber. 'Just shut up and listen.'

The silvery-brass bray of the trumpet blared deep into the night. Kleber knew well the risk he was running, but he was at heart a musician and the moment was all that mattered. He arched his back, pointing the trumpet up at the sky, up at the stars, and the sound rose wailing into the darkness. Some clouds sailed apart and revealed the moon, and the moon was reflected in the silver trumpet.

Porta nodded.

'That's not bad,' he said. 'You can give us some more of that.'

The sound burst exultantly upon the sleeping town. It could not help but call attention to itself. It was not long before a police constable appeared, puffing as he toiled up the hill. Kleber advanced reproachfully upon him, frowning, daring him to interrupt. The policeman stood a while, catching his breath. He held his head on one side, listening to the music.

'Memphis Blues,' he said. He walked over to Porta. 'Memphis Blues . . . well, it's a long time since I heard that.'

He took off his helmet, wiped a sweating bald head with his handkerchief and sat down on the bench.

Two girls came wandering up the hill, lured there by the magic of Kleber's trumpet. Kleber was playing as if his very life were at stake. His audience sat in silence.

Kleber cocked an eyebrow at Porta.

'Well?'

'It's all right,' said Porta. 'How about this one?'

He whistled a few bars.

'Ah, yes!' said the policeman. 'Deep River . . . I know that one.'

'Hang on,' said Kleber. 'Don't rush me.'

He was the artist now. He had them in his power and he knew it. He made them wait.

And the old blues melody caught them all and held them, and they heard the compulsive rhythm of the slaves, the beat of a million marching feet, the pounding of horses' hooves across the hard ground, the throbbing advance of tanks and motorized vehicles on their way to meet the enemy . . .

Kleber stopped playing. He was out of breath. He turned again to Porta.

'Now what do you think?'

Porta looked at him.

'Heard worse,' he admitted. 'I have heard worse.'

'I should think you have!' said the policeman, indignantly. 'What more do you want?'

Porta looked at him.

'You don't understand,' he said. 'This lad wants to play

officially, like. For the Company . . . You got to have the touch of the gods to do that . . . Not like playing with a band. Anyone can do that. You play for us, out at the front—' He looked hard at Kleber – 'you're sending men off to their death, aren't you? Last thing some of 'em will ever hear, that old tin trumpet of yours . . . know what I mean, do you?'

There was a silence. Porta had touched upon a world to which the rest of them had never belonged. A world where death was the only familiar, dependable fact, and where grown men became as babies as they struggled out of this life and into another.

'Yeah, I see what you mean,' said Kleber. 'I never thought of it that way before.'

'It's not like playing for a grand parade,' said Porta.

'No, I reckon you're right . . .'

'It's not like playing at one of Adolf's lousy banquets.'

Kleber pursed his lips.

'How about this one?' he suggested, suddenly brightening. 'The Death of a Musician . . . Viva la Muerte . . .'

The trumpet's sweet-strident voice rose sobbing into the still night air. It rose and it fell, weeping, sighing, trembling, as it told of the musician who played himself to death. Kleber bent down to the earth beneath his feet and bent back to the sky above him. The air was full of sorrow.

Viva la muerte. Viva la muerte . . .

'All right,' said Porta. 'I'll see to it. You can play for the Company, I reckon you'll do.'

They went off together, without a word to the police constable or the two girls.

Eight days later, the Regiment received its marching orders and at once there were the usual scenes of feverish activity in the barracks. For ourselves, we still had not been sent a replacement for Lt. Ohlsen. Colonel Hinka was going to take over temporarily, until we reached the front. By then, they would surely have sent us someone else? But for the meantime we were quite content to have the Colonel. He was preferable to a stranger, he had commanded the 5th Company in the days before his promotion and he was known to all of us old hands.

Before we left, our new musician showed us what he could do. He played the fanfare of farewell, while we all stood listening.

'Adieu, vieille caserne,
Adieu, chambrées puantes . . .'*

We were off again. Back to the front. It caught you unprepared every time. We had known how it must be, we had known it for sure these last few days, but still it caught you unprepared, and Kleber's plaintive trumpet calls brought lumps to many hardened throats.

Slowly the train pulled out of the station. Out of Hamburg, out of Germany, on our way back to the front. On our way to Monte Cassino. We didn't know it then, of course, Colonel Hinka hadn't yet opened his sealed orders. But that was where we were going. To Monte Cassino . . .

* Farewell to the barracks, farewell to the stinking barrack-rooms

REIGN OF HELL by SVEN HASSEL

Burning, looting, raping, murdering, Hitler's Penal Regiments advanced on the centre of Warsaw leaving in their wake a bloody trail of death and destruction. They killed indiscriminately. Pole or German; young or old; man, woman, child – anyone who crossed their path was eliminated. For Himmler had sworn that Warsaw would be razed to the ground – if it took every member of the German army to do it! And against the Führer's expendable battalions, for whom life had no meaning, the battle for Warsaw became an inferno – an endless REIGN OF HELL . . .

0 552 09178 2   £1.75

SS GENERAL by SVEN HASSEL

The 27th Panzers in Hitler's Penal Regiment had fought through the winter in the hell-hole that was Stalingrad. Now there were few survivors from the last massive Russian attack. Weary and nauseated by the horrors they'd seen on the Russian front, they crawled into a bunker near the banks of the Volga. Hunger, they had discovered, was more demoralizing than fear or defeat. Then the brutal SS GENERAL arrived . . .

0 552 11317 4   £1.25

MARCH BATTALION by SVEN HASSEL

Into the screaming inferno of the Russian Front were thrown the Tank Battalions of Hitler's Penal Regiments – men whose lives were considered expendable by the German high command.

And because they were treated as animals, they learned to live like animals – to steal and cheat and whore in the manner of beasts – to fight, not only the enemy but each other – to die brutally and bloodily . . .

These were the men sacrificed in the Führer's Russian Offensive . . The men of the MARCH BATTALION.

0 552 11411 1   £1.50

THE WILD GEESE by DANIEL CARNEY

The dramatic, action-packed story of a band of fifty steel-hard mercenaries whose contract takes them into a dangerous Central African state to snatch a deposed black president from the clutches of his country's new ruler . . .

'The story is fast, gripping and exciting. It reflects faithfully the spirit of men who fight for money or adventure.'

Colonel Mike Hoare, Ex-Mercenary Leader

'Extraordinary build-up of tension makes this tale of a mercenary rescue mission one of the rare stay-up-all-night-to-finish kind.'

Glasgow Herald

0 552 10869 3   £1.50

HOLOCAUST by GERALD GREEN

Two families – the Dorfs and the family Weiss – one swept up in a frenzy of murderous rage, the other, anguished victims . . . victims of the most monstrous crime the world has ever witnessed, victims of the HOLOCAUST.

Erik Dorf . . .
His Diary reveals a charming, brilliant young German lawyer; the SS officer so consumed with love for his country and Führer – and so aflame with ambition – that he can justify plans for the mass murder of Jews.

Rudi Weiss . . .
His story exposes a spectacularly fearless young Jew; a man so tough, so brave, he rushes into love and defies death in a world ablaze with passion and hatred.

Two men, two families, all tossed into a maelstrom of terror, where simply to survive was to succeed. HOLOCAUST is a story of heroism and survival . . . a story beyond tears of a time without compassion.

0 552 10889 8   £1.25

633 SQUADRON by FREDERICK E. SMITH

This was the mission on which the success of Operation Overlord – the invasion of Europe – depended. The chosen squadron was No. 633 whose pilots flew with skill and daring.
  Their target was a fjord in Norway, where the Germans were known to be developing something so secret, that not even the crews of the Mosquitoes which were to fly on the mission could be told about it. They knew it was a dangerous mission, but they could not know just how dangerous it would turn out to be.

0 552 08169 8   £1.25

THE SCOURGE OF THE SWASTIKA
by LORD RUSSELL OF LIVERPOOL

'His book is far from being an indictment, nor has he simply catalogued all the worst atrocities. The summary is fair and usually unadorned.'
The Times

'This book contains a true story, fairly told. He indulges in no lurid appeal and abstains largely from comment of any kind.'
Times Literary Supplement

'A cold, factual and unchallengeable book.' *New Statesman*

'It is a book which should be read by everybody.'
Yorkshire Evening Post

0 552 10300 4   £1.50

BLITZFREEZE by SVEN HASSEL

The Führer's commands were simple – forward to Moscow! And so the mighty Panzer regiments thundered into action – killing, raping, burning their way across the great wastes of Russia . . .

But this was to be the bloodiest of all Hitler's wars – a war where Russian infantrymen threw themselves before the on-coming tanks, where women fought as savagely as men, where German guns killed Germans and Russians alike, mangling them indiscriminately into tattered hunks of meat . . .

And finally Porta, Tiny, Barcelona, all of them – caring nothing for who should win the war – thinking only of their own survival – began the long retreat – back through the corpse-littered plains where blood and bodies were already frozen beneath the winter ice . . .

0 552 09761 6   £1.25

A SELECTED LIST OF
WAR BOOKS
PUBLISHED BY CORGI

WHILE EVERY EFFORT IS MADE TO KEEP PRICES LOW, IT IS SOMETIMES
NECESSARY TO INCREASE PRICES AT SHORT NOTICE. CORGI BOOKS RESERVE THE
RIGHT TO SHOW AND CHARGE NEW RETAIL PRICES ON COVERS WHICH MAY
DIFFER FROM THOSE ADVERTISED IN THE TEXT OR ELSEWHERE.

THE PRICES SHOWN BELOW WERE CORRECT AT THE TIME OF GOING TO PRESS

☐	10869 3	THE WILD GEESE	*Daniel Carney* £1.50
☐	10889 8	HOLOCAUST	*Gerald Green* £1.25
☐	11168 6	COURT MARTIAL	*Sven Hassel* £1.50
☐	10400 0	THE BLOODY ROAD TO DEATH	*Sven Hassel* £1.50
☐	09761 6	BLITZFREEZE	*Sven Hassel* £1.25
☐	09178 2	REIGN OF HELL	*Sven Hassel* £1.75
☐	11317 4	SS GENERAL	*Sven Hassel* £1.25
☐	08779 3	ASSIGNMENT GESTAPO	*Sven Hassel* £1.75
☐	11414 6	LIQUIDATE PARIS	*Sven Hassel* £1.50
☐	11411 1	MARCH BATTALION	*Sven Hassel* £1.50
☐	11412 X	MONTE CASSINO	*Sven Hassel* £1.50
☐	11377 8	COMRADES OF WAR	*Sven Hassel* £1.50
☐	11259 3	WHEELS OF TERROR	*Sven Hassel* £1.50
☐	11417 0	LEGION OF THE DAMNED	*Sven Hassel* £1.50
☐	10343 8	CROSS OF IRON	*Willi Heinrich* 75p
☐	08371 2	THE DIRTY DOZEN	*E. M. Nathanson* £1.95
☐	10954 1	THE FIVE FINGERS	*Gayle Rivers & James Hedson* £1.50
☐	10300 4	THE SCOURGE OF THE SWASTIKA	*Lord Russell of Liverpool* £1.50
☐	10301 2	THE KNIGHTS OF BUSHIDO	*Lord Russell of Liverpool* £1.25
☐	11075 2	633 SQUADRON: OPERATION VALKYRIE	*Frederick E. Smith* £1.50
☐	10741 7	633 SQUADRON: OPERATION CRUCIBLE	*Frederick E. Smith* 80p
☐	10155 9	633 SQUADRON: OPERATION RHINE MAIDEN	*Frederick E. Smith* £1.95
☐	08169 8	633 SQUADRON	*Frederick E. Smith* £1.25

*All these books are available at your bookshop or newsagent, or can be ordered direct from the publisher
Just tick the titles you want and fill in the form below.*

CORGI BOOKS, Cash Sales Department, P.O. Box 11, Falmouth, Cornwall.

Please send cheque or postal order, no currency.

Please allow cost of book(s) plus the following for postage and packing.

U.K. CUSTOMERS. 40p for the first book, 18p for the second book and 13p for each additional
book ordered, to a maximum charge of £1.49.

B.F.P.O. & EIRE. Please allow 40p for the first book, 18p for the second book plus 13p per copy for
the next three books, thereafter 7p per book.

OVERSEAS CUSTOMERS. Please allow 60p for the first book plus 18p per copy for each
additional book.

NAME (block letters) ....

ADDRESS ....

....